# Manitou Murder

To: Jeannie's
Hope you've liked
these books.

C. C. Canby
(Sid Jackson)
A.K.A:

Oct 9, 2020

Reviews of C. C. Canby's first Murder Mystery:

# Masks of Murder

"C. C. Canby has written an exciting police procedural in the tradition of Christine McGuire and Paul Bishop"— Harriet Klausner, reviewer for Blether:the book Review Site. (Masks of Murder received the Blether Gold Award with a rating of 10:"A truly exceptional read, the finest example of a genre, a book with which the reviewer can find no fault, and which will usually have universal appeal.")

". . . exciting action in the style of James Patterson, but with a subtle noir touch that would keep the reader intrigued and thrilled" —Narayan Radharkrishnan, for newmysteryreader.com.

"In a word WOW!Canby provides interesting characters, sharp dialogue and plenty of thrills. This first novel succeeds in whetting the appetite for more."– Pat Frovarp, owner/proprietor of Once Upon a Crime book store, Minneapolis, MN

"Much like the cover illustration, which depicts an actor putting on a mask, the mask covering the killer's face is gradually removed. In so doing, this novel becomes less a murder mystery and more a literary style work in that the action is slow moving and character development is used to advance the work. By novel's end, one man's inner delusions are revealed, as are the permanent repercussions of his actions."—Kevin Tipple, for Blueirisjournal.com

". . . there is more here than a simple whodunit. Abrupt and unexpected death doesn't give the deceased any opportunity to tidy up loose ends . . . The book is short, concise and well written in a straightforward manner that takes us step by step to a surprising conclusion."—Carl Brookins, author, for Mystery Scene, holiday issue, Number 82, 2003.

"C. C. Canby's excellent first novel, Masks of Murder, is filled with creepy, yet appealing characters and a unique and compelling plot. Once started, I was obliged to finish it even if it meant staying up into the wee hours."—Bruce Southworth, mystery reviewer for the Minneapolis Star and Tribune.

# Manitou
# Murder

By

C. C. Canby

**j-Press Publishing**
**4796 126th St. N.**
**White Bear Lake, MN 55110**
**jpresspublishing.com**
**1-888-407-1723**

# Manitou Murder

Published by j-Press Publishing
4796 126th St. N.
White Bear Lake, MN 55110
Phone/Fax: 651-429-1819

Visit the j-Press website at http://www.jpresspublishing.com

Printed in the United States of America.
First printing
10 9 8 7 6 5 4 3 2 1

Library of Congress Cataloging-in-Publication Data

Canby, C. C., 1937-
Manitou murder / by C.C. Canby.
p. cm.
ISBN 978-1-930922-07-5 (alk. paper)
1. Family--Crimes against--Fiction. 2. Murder--Investigation--Fiction. 3. Kidnapping--Fiction. 4. Minnesota--Fiction. I. Title.
PS3603.A535M36 2008
813'.6--dc22
2008017199

**Order copies of this book at www.jpresspublishing.com or through Amazon.com or Barnes&Noble.com**

For Sue

"The heart has its reasons, which the reason knows not of"—Blaise Pascal, "Thoughts."

# Manitou
# Murder

*by*
*C.C. Canby*

# Chapter One

Some say the dead tell no tales but Sabriga Quill had been talking to people on the other side as long as she could remember. Only moments ago, visions from the dark world had flashed in and out of her consciousness like quick cuts in a movie. The visions had ceased now but Sabriga thought they would probably return. Sometimes they did, sometimes not. Sabriga had long ago concluded that she was merely an instrument for the powers beyond, powers of a shadow-universe that even a seasoned psychic like her self stood before in awestruck silence, humbled with the knowledge she had no real understanding of the forces she channeled, nor of their purposes, nor of the reasons for her having been chosen as their messenger.

She wiped her slim blue-veined hands with a dish-towel, placed the frying pan she'd been drying in the kitchen cupboard and walked into her dimly lighted living room. She lowered her thin-framed body into an overstuffed chair, her angular features in silhouette against the diffused light filtering through the white, laced sheer curtains of the east window. It was completely silent in the darkened room, furnished with 1800s antiques. This was the period from which she'd come, she believed, to take up her next life in the 21st century. She closed her soft dark-brown eyes and tried to relax.

She felt the tingling and stiffened. They were coming back. The images flooded in. There was a lot of red, a lot of sound, too, primarily human voices, yelling, beseeching, a baby crying. And there were party horns, like those blown on New Year's Eve, blatting; and music, a band playing in the background. There were thuds, too, like something heavy and blunt pounding on something soft. Visually, there was an explosion, a momentary flash of fire, a pale face petrified in fear, the mouth open, the eyes wide, the nostrils flared, the head flung backward as if jerking away from something horrible. And there were sinister, ghostly human figures, tramping deliberately, relentlessly through the dim, shadow-casting light, wearing billed caps, long thick strands of hair flying out the sides.

Sabriga doubled over. The scenes were as ghastly as any she'd ever seen. Despite the horror, she tried to extract more detail. No matter her anguish, she rehearsed the memories over and over. She had to retain as many as possible, she told herself. Whether they told of something that had happened or was about to happen she didn't know; she'd experienced both.

The pain subsided. She breathed easier. Her heartbeat slowed. She straightened and sat for a few minutes more, waiting. No more images occurred.

Sabriga continued sitting, remembering. She thought she might have seen one of the human figures somewhere. Then she recalled: one of the men in the grocery store, that very morning, he'd looked like that. She felt goose pimples across her arms. Almost certainly the horrible event she was experiencing hadn't happened yet!

With little effort—for despite her frail appearance she was fit—Sabriga arose from the chair, walked quickly across the room to a large wooden desk upon which sat two tall, unlit candles, a box of tissues, a phone, and a pen. She sat down in the large, leather swivel desk chair and from a side drawer pulled out a small box of matches. She struck one of the matches, allowed the flare to settle into a steady flame and lit both candles. She began to feel some measure of comfort in the flickering light. She sat there for a moment, composing, remembering again what she'd just experienced.

Now, from another side drawer, she drew out a small phone book. Leafing through the pages, her finger lit on a number. She raised the phone and started to press the buttons. Then she paused and shook her head, thinking better of what she was about to do.

She replaced the phone in its cradle and reached for the pen. Wiping thin perspiration from her forehead with a tissue, she drew out a sheet of paper from the middle drawer and began to write. When, within the hour she had finished, she folded the paper neatly and put it in an envelope already stamped with her name: Mrs. Sabriga Quill, 8646 Tammany Lane, Trane, Minnesota, 55604. She wrote out the Cook County sheriff's address carefully, slowly, again reconsidering what she was doing. Maybe she should make that call. But no, she probably couldn't get through to the sheriff anyway, and she knew they thought she was crazy. She shook her head; it was the best she could do. She sealed the envelope, rose from the chair, slipped a cotton robe around her shoulders and walked down her driveway and out to the street through the chilly, late October air, put the letter in her mailbox and raised the flag.

*** 

On the 26th of October 2006, about seven hours later the same day Sabriga had her visions, approximately three hundred miles south of Sabriga's house, Silas Halladay sat in a booth looking out the front window of a small café situated in the middle of downtown White Bear Lake, Minnesota. The city was named after the lake that it abutted. Silas had seen the lake for the first time that morning, fairly large, its bulk stretching mainly westward and eastward. It surrounded Manitou Island, which was really not an island, technically, but a large promontory, separated from the mainland by only a thin, short stretch of water over which a wooden bridge provided access to the island's inhabitants. The island was privately owned. A sign at the front of the bridge warned that trespassers would be prosecuted.

After arriving in White Bear Lake, Silas and Curtis Nelson, son of the owner of Nelson's auto dealership in Trane, Minnesota, had driven along the Lake's south shore, and the kid had pointed out the house they were going to hit that night. It sat on the south shore of Manitou Island across the lake from where they were parked. Silas studied it carefully through the binoculars Nelson gave him. Then they drove on around the lake to the city of White Bear proper and Nelson had dropped him off, saying that he'd be back soon.

That was over an hour ago and Silas was already on his fifth cup of coffee. Curtis had said, as he left, that he had to meet someone. He'd said that this person couldn't know about Silas, that he and this person had to "wrap up some details."

Silas wondered why Nelson insisted on keeping his participation a secret. He answered himself: probably the "person", whoever he or she was, was covering his or her tracks. Silas figured some kind of conspiracy was afoot between these two. But it didn't matter. He was sure their conspiracy, whatever it was, didn't involve him. He was only an operative, and, besides, he was quite content to keep his own identity a secret.

He looked up as a car passed by the café window but it was not the one he was expecting. After the car passed, a black man, strolling into the small park across the street, caught Silas' attention. Silas continued watching idly as the man sat down heavily on one of the metal benches near a public fountain, leaned over and opened the duffel bag he'd unshouldered, searching through it. Pulling a plastic container from the bag's interior, the man withdrew some food and began to eat, poking the morsels into his mouth with his fingers, sucking them clean and wiping his hands on the front of his thick , wool army coat.

Halladay—tall, gaunt, unkempt, with stringy, long, dirty-blonde hair falling to his shoulders—looked away and took a yellow sheet of paper from his army fatigue-jacket pocket and spread it on the table before him, a diagram of the interior of the house on Manitou Island, the one they'd scouted out earlier. The diagram was roughly sketched in ink, and the paper was rumpled and creased and he had to smooth it out once again to read it. His elongated thin fingers were rough. His fingernails were dirty blackened crescents from the grease of automobiles and there were black smears on his jeans. Reading the diagram now was just to pass the time, for he had memorized every detail since Nelson had given it to him a month or so ago.

He glanced at his watch. Curtis was taking way too much time. Halladay assessed his and the kid's relationship once more. He'd heard of Curtis Nelson when he first went to work at the auto dealership, had seen him around the place now and then but had sized him up as a college kid with rich parents, of no consequence to him. They'd never spoken to one another. Then, one day, strangely enough, Curtis had shown up at the dealership and called Silas aside and offered to buy his lunch. Silas took it almost as a joke. But that's when the kid had delicately, cautiously, put the deal before him, asking him to be a part of it, pushing a fat envelope across the table.

Halladay was wary of Nelson's offer. Ordinarily he wouldn't have had anything to do with him. He'd already labeled the kid as bad news. But the envelope contained several thousand dollars and there was supposed to be a lot more where they came from. He'd signed on. From that time on they'd met intermittently in discreet places and Curtis had filled him in gradually with the details of the plan, always, it seemed, checking Silas' response, as though Silas was some kind of consigliere.

Silas drained the remainder of his coffee and set the cup back on the table. The little cafe was mostly empty of customers. The check lay where the waitress had placed it—had been lying there for over an hour and she was plainly growing annoyed. She kept glancing at him.

Halladay had what could only be described as "smoldering" eyes. He sensed the waitress's aversion and even, he thought, a little fear. This was nothing new for him. He was often stared at, the last time by a little old lady in a grocery store that very morning, just before he and Nelson started for the Twin Cities. Ordinarily, when he returned somebody's stare, the other person quickly averted his gaze and engaged busily in something else. Not the old lady, though. She'd even made *him* nervous. But the waitress' attention and plain agitation now only amused him. He remained sitting where he was.

Thinking about it, why Curtis had singled him out among the other mechanics was a mystery. Maybe the kid had judged Silas as down on his luck, as a hard case, receptive to a deal—perhaps as a man from "the other side," so to speak, who could handle the kind of job he had outlined. Or perhaps it was only that

Halladay was a new employee, the others too well known. Maybe, simply, like Halladay himself, Curtis just wanted help, as he'd hinted, in gaining his freedom — in Curtis' case, freedom from his father's desires to make him a part of the business. Taking over the business, he'd wailed, was the last thing he wanted to do with his life.

Freedom! The thought turned Halladay's attention back to his half brother, Jeffrey, back to the row they'd had over a month ago when he'd informed Jeffrey that he was thinking about moving out. The encounter had left him shaken, but nothing had come of it other than to convince Silas further that he had to get away. He'd decided he had to get out of that house, take a job, get a little money on his own, without Jeffrey's say-so, do some drinking and find a woman. He'd had enough of Jeffrey!

A few days after their argument, when Jeffrey left with the old station wagon to go on one of his errands, Silas seized his opportunity and walked rapidly down the lane that was barely a road, to the main high way— a walk of about three miles—and hitched a ride to Grand Marais. He could only hope he wouldn't meet Jeffrey coming back along the road. Once he got to Grand Marais, to keep Jeffrey from finding him, he decided to hitch a ride farther north to Trane, a town about forty miles up Highway 61. He figured he would be safe there till he could get enough money to get back to "civilization." In Trane he took a room in the town's motel and a few days later got lucky and landed the mechanic's job at Nelson's Auto. That was where he'd first become vaguely aware of Curtis Nelson.

And now, here he was, sitting, waiting for the kid, listening to the clink of cups and saucers and plates, to the shouted exchanges between the cooks and waitresses, the drone of the few customer's voices, smelling the odor of frying meat and French fries, and going over the diagram for the hundredth time.

He looked out the window. The black man still sat there. Silas's irritation at Nelson was growing. Where was that kid, anyway?

A young woman came through the restaurant door, diverting Silas's thoughts, a blond, followed by two others, one younger, looking as if she was of Chinese extraction, dark tresses falling about her bare shoulders as she removed her jacket, the third one, older, with auburn hair.

The strong odor of perfume filled the air as the door closed behind them. They sat at a table not far away, within Halladay's line of sight, chattering and laughing. The blond was wearing one of those blouses that puckered around her breasts and the other, Asian-looking woman, showed a very nice cleavage. The older woman wore an unflattering dress, but she was attractive, maybe in her late forties. Halladay watched them lasciviously, unperturbed by their uneasy glances at him. He imagined what it would be like to have either one of them, or all three (why not?), in bed. Such a thing might be possible after tomorrow.

Yesterday, borrowing a car from the car dealership, before he'd linked up with Nelson to make the drive south, he went back to the house in the forest to pick up some clothing, despite his trepidation. He had to face Jeffrey sometime, anyway. Sure enough, there was another row, another argument, and the brothers nearly came to blows once again.

"You're jeopardizing the whole plan," Jeffrey had said.

Well, that was Jeffrey, using a big word like 'jeopardizing,' and having a 'plan.' Sometimes Silas had to pause to decipher what the hell Jeffrey was saying. It was just one of the things about Jeffrey that irritated the crap out of him. He often wondered how Jeffrey could be so different, being his half brother and all. He could only blame their differences on Jeffrey's father, whom he'd never seen, and on his hi-falutin education.

Silas shook his head, compressed his lips into a hard thin line. They'd been together for over a year now, in that god-forsaken cramped little house in that god-forsaken empty forest in northern Minnesota. In such close quarters, almost immediately they'd begun to get on each other's nerves. To avoid outright conflict, each tried not to show his irritation by sticking to the strict division of labor they'd established— Jeffrey getting breakfast because he was the early riser, Silas helping to keep the house clean, though Jeffrey had begun to complain that he was still always having to pick up after him. It just wasn't working. Their irritation kept growing. There would be a fight.

It had always been like this ever since Silas could remember. Those memories hurt. You were supposed to love your brother, he thought, even your half brother. And he did, in a strange way, looked up to him. Jeffrey had always been his protector, even after Silas had gotten into trouble and was convicted of raping that woman. Twelve years in prison! And the little bitch had invited it! But when he got out, it was Jeffrey and Christa, not his parents, who had allowed him to live with them while he was trying to make his way "back into society," as the judge had put it. He gave Jeffrey credit for that.

Jeffrey had changed since he'd gone into the army and since Silas had gone to prison. Silas saw it immediately when he came to live with them after getting out. There was a deep bitterness in Jeffrey's eyes. He'd grown quiet but Silas sensed the inner rage. Despite the change, they'd gotten along pretty well at first. Then, just as always, the uneasiness between the two brothers had resurrected itself. With no money he'd had no choice but to stay, though. And he'd heard Jeffrey's wife, Christa, complaining about him.

His frown returned at the thought of Christa. The blood-drained image of his brother's wife's face rose in his consciousness. He forced it back down. If Jeffrey ever found out, God help him! Jeffrey was no one to fool around with. Jeffrey would hunt him down and kill him if Silas couldn't kill him first, no doubt about it. The way things were going, especially with his leaving against Jeffrey's wishes, he might have to kill him anyway. His thoughts flitted frightfully in that direction.

Until Curtis had taken him to lunch that day, it was a bad situation, appearing to have no remedy. Halladay cursed beneath his breath at the thought of having to depend on this stupid kid whom he had grown to loath. He turned to the waitress to see if she'd heard but she was going on obliviously about her work. The women at the near table were still chattering and laughing. An old man who'd sat down at another table near him was dribbling soup in his long beard. Halladay glanced out the window. The black man was still sitting, eating, staring off into space.

Silas recognized Curtis' car as it passed by the restaurant. The car slowed momentarily as the kid spied him through the window, nodding recognition. Curtis drove on down the street, probably to find a parking space. Silas took in a deep breath. After this day, tomorrow, he—Silas Halladay, the hard case, the little brother who wasn't ever expected to amount to anything—would be rich. His relationship with Jeffrey and his parents really wouldn't matter to him one way or another, then. Tomorrow he'd be free.

Curtis Nelson walked by the café window and entered, located Halladay, and scooted into the booth across from him, giving him a thumbs-up sign. Halladay watched Nelson drolly as he ordered a cup of coffee and a hamburger. Silas refused again when the waitress asked him if he'd like another refill. He slipped the yellow sheet of paper in his coat pocket, smiling inwardly. He would work with Curtis for now. Curtis Nelson, the dumb, naive college kid; like a lamb about to be slaughtered, he thought.

***

By 2:45 P.M., Ezra Grinnell had picked his lunch from the garbage bins and stuffed it in a plastic bag—some half-eaten fruit, a half-full box of French fries, some moldy bread, and a not-quite-empty plastic jar of strawberry jelly. It would be enough to tide him over until he hopped a freighter later that night, continuing south away from the coming northern winter. He'd slept late.

Ezra made his way out of the alley to a small park, found an aeruginous colored bench beside a fountain, lowered his duffel bag to the ground, and sat, resting his back. At this late date in October the fountain had been turned off. He sighed, closed his eyes and listened to the sounds of traffic. By habit he rested his hand upon the duffel bag. He'd gotten it from a military surplus store. It was a blue, Air Force bag and it contained all his worldly possessions: another heavy overcoat, a sleeping bag, two blankets and two sweaters, a couple of cans of soup that he kept as backup, and a few packs of cigarettes, as well as the food he'd gathered that morning. A smaller box inside carried his toiletries, as well.

Ezra's skin was black as jet. He wore a ragged goatee that was just a little grizzled. A dirty, wrinkled baseball cap sat on the back of his head, the bill pointing slightly upward. His hair jutted out around the sides in wisps.

Ezra opened his eyes and looked around. This was

a nice town, clean, crisp lines. Up north in Canada, from where he'd come, sneaking across the border in a wooded area then hitching a ride on a southbound freighter, the leaves had mostly fallen, leaving the towns along the railroad looking bare and unclothed. Here, in east central Minnesota, in late October, the leaves of the maples and birches were still showing some brilliant color, though the leaves of the oaks were now almost all brown and drifting lazily downward. The air had taken on less of a chill than what he'd felt yesterday, but it was still cool. A temperature gage on the bank-sign not too far from where he sat, showed forty-two degrees.

Ezra reached into his duffel bag and pulled out the plastic container of food. He ate the food assiduously, a man who appeared to have shed the tyranny of time, relishing the morsels, ignoring for the most part the curious looks of the few passersby. He knew what they thought: a bum, a black man, in a white town. And they were right. He hadn't always been a bum. But that was a story that he preferred to leave dormant, though the task was proving to be more and more difficult as time passed.

Ezra finished his meal, carefully put the remainder back in the plastic bag and stuffed it inside his duffel. He heard voices behind him. Two men had come out of the cafe across the street. The taller slim one drew his attention. From the way he held himself and the way he walked, Ezra could tell that the man was a dude not to be fooled with; probably an ex-con. Ezra tabbed the shorter one as a preppy type, of no interest. He wondered what they were doing together, two men so different.

Ezra watched the two of them talk a bit then turn and walk toward the end of the block. A yellow sheet of paper fell from the taller man's jacket pocket and settled into the gutter. The man hadn't noticed. Ezra continued to watch them as they walked on, got into a car and drove off.

Checking to see whom else might be around and seeing no one, Ezra arose from the bench, sauntered over and picked up the piece of paper and stuffed it in his pant's pocket. After he'd returned to the park bench and sat back down, he pulled the paper from his pocket and rotated it so he could read the letters.

It looked to him like a floor plan of a house, roughly sketched, in ink. The plan showed three levels. It also showed a circular driveway, and the front of the house was labeled with an arrow pointing toward the door. There was print beside it saying, "Key here, in pot," and there was a long rectangle off to the right, labeled "garage." On the part of the map showing the third story there were bedrooms, and, again, arrows leading to and from the rooms and down hallways.

What caught Ezra's eye, though, were the words "money here," inscribed once on the basement portion of the map and once again on the second-story portion. "Jewelry here" was also inscribed on one of the bedrooms of the third story, the room labeled with two names. On a part of the yellow paper that was stained, Ezra could make out the faint numbers of a street address and the blurred name "Lunzer." And tucked in a corner, the most interesting item of all, was another set of numbers, and beneath them was written "security code."

Ezra tried to fathom this diagram he held in his hands and, mostly, what it could possibly mean for him. A vision was emerging, of a large house, full of money and jewelry. And here, in his hands, he held easy access to this house, and possibly a new future. He just sat there, looking at the diagram, going over it and over it, and he thought of that day a couple of years ago when he'd been shown the door at the company he'd worked at for over thirty years, cast out on the street and forced to live like a common vagabond because "they" had moved his job to someplace overseas to be done by someone at a fraction of his pay. And he thought of the shame he felt at being nearly sixty years old and not being able to put food on the table, of having to look into his wife's accusing eyes in the evenings when she returned from her job at the hospital, the job of removing the food trays, cleaning the bedpans and mopping the rooms. A single tear rolled down his cheek.

Ezra looked back at the sound of a car door slamming. A police squad car had stopped at the curb behind him. A uniformed officer got out and ambled toward him. Ezra quickly wiped away the tear and placed the yellow paper in his coat pocket and waited, assuming as kindly and innocent expression as possible for a middle-aged, itinerant black man in a white town.

***

When Sergeant Detective Richard Lanslow got home at about 6:00PM Laura was not there and he had to apologize to Agnes, their babysitter. Agnes hadn't said anything but he could tell she was pissed. Now he'd have to take care of Melanie, which he didn't mind but which he was not good at. Luckily, he'd stopped at a toy store on his way home and bought a new, gaily-painted toy and a chocolate cookie with colored icing. She could happily eat the cookie while she punched the buttons on the toy and different animals would pop up and diverse sounds would come out, identifying the different animals pictured on the buttons. It would keep her busy for a while, he hoped, at least till Laura got home. He could hear Melanie in her room, now, chattering. He removed his worn-at-the-elbows, green corduroy sport coat and hung it in the foyer closet, unbuckled his belt and slid the holstered gun off and placed it in a dresser drawer in the bedroom. He returned to the kitchen and shuffled through the mail, placing it back upon the kitchen counter where Laura could go through it. She had left no message on the phone.

Lanslow usually bore an easy smile on his face. It was a good face, square and symmetrical, ruggedly handsome. But the lines in that fine face were now compressed into a frown. He was worried over Laura being late, yet he was aggravated at the same time. It seemed to him she'd been late several times now. It was not like her.

He combed back his thick brown hair with his fingers and reluctantly considered preparing dinner. Cooking was another thing he'd never been any good at. Wearily, he searched in the refrigerator freezer for something he could put in the microwave, found a package of spaghetti and meatballs and pulled it out. Melanie loved spaghetti. Laura didn't, but he felt spiteful.

He removed the dish from the container and placed it in the microwave oven then remembered he had forgotten to put a slit in the plastic covering as per the instructions. Irritably, he retrieved the package, plucked a paring knife from the drawer, cut through the plastic, replaced the package, and reset the oven's timer. Melanie still chattered. The sounds of elephants and lions and roosters and pigs emanated from down the hallway. He hoped she hadn't made a mess with the cookie but didn't care much if she had.

He settled down in an easy chair in the living room, next to the sheer curtains that covered the patio doors overlooking the parking lot to their apartment. They lived on the second story of the apartment complex. It was their first home. When Melanie was born a year and a half ago they'd intended to move but had remained in their present location, mostly out of inertia.

Five minutes passed. Absentmindedly he picked up the remote and turned on the TV to hear the president assuring his selected, sympathetic audience that the war in Iraq was seeing progress, that more time was needed to create a democratic, independent, peaceful ally in the Middle East. The oil, he thought, ruefully," The Prize," as he'd heard it called; that was what the war was all about. Billions of dollars spent on the Iraqis while he had to fight crime in the streets here at home committed by people who couldn't get by without stealing or selling drugs.

It had been a long day despite the relatively routine cases he and his partner, Leonard Wilenski, were working on, and he was tired.

Hearing the timer go off on the microwave, he shut off the TV and went into the kitchen. He glanced at his watch. Where the hell was she, anyway?

Thinking Laura might not get home for some time yet, he placed the package in the conventional oven and set it to low heat. He searched through a cabinet and found half of a loaf of hard Italian bread. He set it on the table in the dining nook along with a tub of butter and began to get the plates and glasses and silverware.

As he was about to finish, through the kitchen window, he saw Laura's car pull into their spot in the lighted parking lot. He went to the patio door and watched as she exited the car and walked across the pavement. Even through his anger, he could appreciate the sway of her hips, her always-purposeful stride.

"Why so late?" he said, immediately, when she came in, unable quite to contain the edge in his voice as he glanced at the clock. It was past 7:00 PM, nearly three hours beyond her usual time to get home.

Still in her coat and gloves, Laura picked up the

day's mail on the kitchen counter and began to scan the pieces quickly. "We had parent conferences," she said, offhandedly. "A couple of parents showed up at the last minute. I thought I told you about the conferences this morning. Where's Melanie?"

"She's playing in her room—but I don't think you told me you'd be home so late, maybe you did."

"Have you fed her?"

"She's had a cookie. I thought we'd eat together, so we've been waiting. Agnes was a little upset that she had to stay."

Laura shrugged. "Agnes is always upset at something. Melanie shouldn't be eating cookies before mealtime."

"I didn't know you'd be late and Agnes said you hadn't told her, either."

"She agreed to stay as long as she had to when we hired her."

"She'd had plans. We're supposed to tell her when we're going to be late."

"Well, I guess I forgot. I'll apologize when I see her tomorrow."

"It'll have to be a good one. She was pretty upset."

Laura looked up at her husband curtly for a moment as though she was going to say something further, then just shook her head slightly, pulled off her gloves and began to go through the mail again, sorting the junk from the letters, the catalogs from the rest. Lanslow watched her. He could not help but notice her long supple fingers, the fresh dewy look of his wife's face, the pouting under lip that just begged for a kiss. His anger dissipated.

"You hungry?" she asked. "I don't feel like cooking. Let's order in." She disposed of the junk mail and placed the rest in a stack.

"I fixed some spaghetti and meatballs," said Lanslow. "It's warming in the oven."

"Oh, you're a dear," said Laura, surprisingly, and pecked him lightly on the cheek.

"Is that all I get?" he asked, "Just a peck?"

"I'm tired, Hon," she said, "I need to say hi to Melanie. Maybe later, okay?"

But later, after dinner, when Melanie had finally been put to bed and he had finished his shower and come into the bedroom, hoping Laura would still be awake, she was lying on her stomach, eyes closed.

He crawled beneath the covers, disappointed, troubled, and couldn't get to sleep. They hadn't had sex for nearly two weeks. As he thought about the evening, Laura had seemed distant, preoccupied. Instead of her usual perky self she seemed almost morose, long faced. He'd asked if anything was wrong, but she wouldn't talk, wouldn't let him hold her, had insisted there was nothing amiss.

Staring into the darkness, try as he might, he could not think of anything that had happened out of the ordinary. Laura was working longer hours at school lately, for one thing. Maybe that was it. His long irregular work hours, too, had always been a sore spot in their marriage, even during their engagement. Her longer hours now served only to worsen the problem. But Laura no longer said much about his being gone so often. It was as if she no longer cared, as if she had become oblivious to it, resigned — which was even more troubling. He was well aware of the frailty of marriage among law officers.

His last thoughts before he finally went to sleep were that Laura had changed, somehow, and he wondered if he was seeing the first faint cracks in his own marital status.

## Chapter Two

The boat was nothing fancy, just a rented Lund Jon boat with two seats across the middle and one in the bow and an outboard Mercury motor. The night was getting colder, down to forty degrees, which felt colder especially on the lake with the wind. The man at the stern kept the motor throttled low all the way across the lake so that it emitted only a low, gurgling throb. A second man sat in the seat at the bow. When they neared the dock, the man at the rear cut the motor off completely, and all that could be heard was the soft lapping of the water against the shoreline.

It was hard to see but the half moon shining on the lake's surface had allowed them just enough light to find the place they were looking for. The vessel glided smoothly alongside the dock and the man at the front stood up and stepped out, looking around nervously, shivering in the breeze. He tied the bow of the boat with a rope, securely, then he reached down into the boat and grasped a canvas bag which he hoisted, nestling it in the crook of his arm, waiting.

"Maybe we should point the boat back the way we come, just in case," the man still in the boat said, in a low voice.

The other man dropped the bag to the dock and its contents clanked inside it. The man untied the bow rope and the man in the boat pushed it off from the dock. The man on the dock pulled on the rope, turning the boat around, its prow now pointing back across the lake in the direction from whence they'd come, then he began securing the boat to the dock once again.

"Be sure and keep the knots loose," the man who had remained seated said, and then he stepped out of the boat, too. "Got everything?" he asked, looking at the bag.

"Got it."

Cautiously, the two dark figures made their way up the stone steps to the back yard and toward a large house, sitting atop the knoll. Behind them, the lake's glassy waters were tinted whitish-grey in the moonlight and the shoreline on the other side was a black silhouette. Somewhere far off, a dog barked.

"You said there were no dogs?" asked the man behind.

"That's what I was told," said the man in front. "What's the time?"

The second man swung the bag to his left shoulder, took a penlight from his pocket, cupping his hand over it carefully to shield the light, and looked at the dial of his watch. "We're doing fine," he said. "Almost three."

He flipped the light off and put it back in his pocket. "You sure there ain't any dogs?"

"God damn it!" said the other man in a nervous low breath. "You're always worrying. Don't worry about no dogs." He stopped abruptly, putting his arm out. "Hold it! Quiet!" he whispered. He dropped to one knee. "There's someone up there."

The second man squatted quickly behind the first then rose slightly to peer ahead over his partner's shoulder. He couldn't see anything immediately then he caught the dark outline of someone moving toward the house about thirty or forty yards in front of them, approaching from their left.

"What the hell ...?"

"Quiet!" whispered the first man.

The figure had now disappeared.

"What do we do? You think he saw us?" asked the second man.

"Na, he wouldn't be just walking on like that. Wait a minute, just let me think."

"Maybe it's a guard. Maybe we ought a get the hell out of here."

"Just wait a minute, damn it! There ain't supposed to be no guards."

They waited.

"I can't see anything up there," said the first man.

"Let's get a little closer."

"I think we oughta call it off. We didn't plan on this," said the second man.

"Nothing's gone down, yet. It won't hurt to take a look. Not much else they can do 'cept tell us to get off their property. We got a lot to lose here."

"That's for damned sure," said the second man. "A lot to lose—more than money."

"We might be able to pull this off yet, though. I'm going up to take a look. You can stay here."

"Oh, what the hell. I'll follow you. Let's go."

*\*\**

Ezra Grinnell pulled the collar of his coat tighter about his neck. He'd become chilled while hiding in the trees and underbrush, waiting for his opportunity. From where he lay, watching, he could see the house plainly and it looked like the people who lived there were having a party or some kind of celebration. Cars were coming and going. He could see silhouettes moving back and forth across the windows of the mansion, and could hear music echoing faintly from within. He'd made sure to find a hiding place far enough away so he wouldn't be easily discovered. There was no doubt in his mind that he'd hit the jackpot. The house was huge, as were most of the others. Rich people lived here. It was a risky business, but he was desperate.

Hours passed. Ezra began to think he might have to call off his plan. But what he'd seen on the diagram was too enticing, and he had found a place where he could sleep, anyway. More hours passed and he fell asleep again, but a sound, like a shot from a gun, though muted, awakened him. He rolled into a position to look at the house. All he could see were occasional silhouettes hurrying around. Another half hour passed and he saw the lights go out, and the last vehicle, as far as he could tell, was leaving.

He continued to wait. He checked his watch and now, at a few minutes before 3:00 A.M., the house had remained dark for sometime and everyone seemed to have left, the occupants gone to bed. It seemed like he might be able to pull off the burglary at last. He made his way out of the trees, leaving his duffel bag and sleeping bag behind, and walked along the beach until he reached the house. He didn't intend to burglarize the upstairs, just the basement where he thought he could enter and leave quietly.

Ezra didn't realize he'd been spotted. He stopped, thinking he'd heard a sound. Half a minute passed, then another. He heard nothing more. He moved forward again, stopping to listen once again as he tried to peer through the darkness. Satisfied, he rounded the corner of the house and made his way to the front. He stopped again, listening, watching. He was tingling inside, thinking this might have been his lucky day at last, a way out of the mess his life had turned into.

Just in front of him, in the half moonlight, he could barely make out two large pots beside the entryway, holding small evergreen shrubs. The map had shown two round circles and had pointed to the one with the key but he couldn't remember which. He thought about taking the diagram from his coat pocket and trying to see which of the pots held the key but dismissed it as impossible in the semidarkness. Well, it had to be one of them. Shrugging, he moved to the first potted evergreen, stooped and dug around in the potting soil. There was nothing there. He moved to the other pot and ground the dirt through his fingers, but, again, he found nothing. He stood up, puzzled. There was no way he was going to try to break in. Just too dangerous.

He thought he heard another sound. Turning, he saw a dark figure looming out of the darkness, swinging a club. Reflexively he raised his forearm and took the blow, hearing the bone crack, feeling the sting of pain. He started falling backward and the figure was on him again, the club coming down, smashing onto the side of his head, stunning him, and he lost control of his legs, falling to the ground. He tried to roll away from the next blow he knew would come, but it crashed on his shoulder and then he was being hit repeatedly and there were two of them, pounding and pounding. He blacked out, came to, almost blacked out again, and then he just lay still, unmoving and barely conscious. The reign of blows had stopped.

"God damn it, what did you have to go and do that for?" Ezra heard a heaving voice say.

"We got a job to do," said another voice. "We can make a lot of money on this. Forget about him."

"Who is he? What the hell do you think he was doing here?" said the first voice.

"What the fuck do you think, man, the same thing as us; What was he doing in those pots, anyway?" The man was wheezing, sucking in deep drafts of air.

"Maybe looking for a key," said the second man.

"You think he found it?"

"Don't think so."

Ezra was only faintly aware of the two of them standing over him. The pain in his arm nearly made him cry out but he managed to lie as still as possible, keeping his eyes almost closed. He felt rough hands patting him down and grabbing at his his own hands, prying them open. Still, he kept absolutely still.

"I don't think he has no keys," said the second

voice.

"Keep that light down! We made enough noise to wake the dead," Ezra heard the first voice say.

"They're still asleep, looks like," said the second voice.

"God damn! Come on. We got to move it. Let's go. We don't need the fucking keys, anyway."

"What do we do with him?" said the second voice. "He's seen us."

"Naw, he hasn't seen us. Is he dead?"

"Looks like it."

"No problem then. He can't identify us, anyway. We got to move it. We can still do this."

Ezra heard the men going away. He still couldn't move, there was throbbing pain in his arm, blood in his mouth, sliding across his lips. After a few moments, his head began to clear. He tried to move again.

They're doing the same thing I was gonna do, he thought. This was sure as hell no railroad fight with drunken hobos. They were trying to kill him.

Ezra managed to roll on his back and look at the night sky, brightening now somewhat, a few stars visible. He couldn't move, felt helpless. He was hurt bad, he knew. For a moment, he contemplated his death and he began to cry. He heard himself say her name: "Alice." He wondered what she was doing now and if she would ever know of his death and whether she would forgive him for leaving, or even care. His eyes grew heavy and he fought unconsciousness. They'll be back, he thought. They'll be back, and this time they'll try to finish the job. He wanted only to sleep, but even as he drifted off he thought about the opportunity he'd missed. He wondered what had happened to the key that was supposed to be in the pot.

When he opened his eyes again, he had no idea of how long he'd been out. He felt a little better, a little stronger, his will was returning. He looked at the house. There was a light on in one of the upstairs rooms. He tried rolling over, made it, and struggled to his knees, then to his feet, his arm hanging limply. Dazed and unsteady, he tried to remember in which direction he had left his duffel bag. Remembering now, he staggered back the way he'd come, and fell, grunting in pain. He regained his footing again, swaying toward the small copse of trees near the beach where he had waited throughout the night. He reached the sandy beach and was within twenty yards of the trees when he heard sounds behind him and knew the men were coming back.

"Get him! Get him!" he heard one of them saying.

Fear gave him strength and he began to lope away one-leggedly in a desperate attempt to save his life.

***

At 5:45 A.M. on Friday morning it was still dark when Derek Lunzer pulled onto the curving road leading to his parent's home, the motor of his silver colored Jaguar XK8 convertible making a deep, low rumble. As he crossed the short bridge connecting Manitou Island with the mainland, the car's lights caught the figure of a man running off the road and toward the lake just to Derek's left, casting a furtive look backward as he disappeared.

"What in hell?" Derek shook his head, slowing the car a bit. He speeded up, then, as the man disappeared from sight. "Wonder what the hell that was all about?" he said aloud to himself.

He continued to his home, negotiating the twists and turns of the road deliberately, carefully. He was drunk and maneuvering the car was a difficult chore. But he managed to pull to the front of the garage and touched the remote control. The door to the extreme right of the multi-car building slid open. He turned the car's lights on bright and pulled inside, bringing it to a lurching halt. He sat for a moment, staring at the back wall, remembering the running man. He looked at his watch, its face visible in the dash lights, and wondered what the man he'd seen was doing on the island at 5:45

A.M. He bent over the steering wheel, letting his forehead drop against it repeatedly, as if this would help clear the alcohol from his brain. He raised his head, stared once more at the back wall of the garage, then turned off the motor and lights and opened the car door.

"Damn!" he said, as he banged his knee on the steering column, nearly tumbling from the car. "I'm drunk. Drank too much. Shouldn't have, 'speshally not tonight. Stupid bastard!"

He slammed the car door shut, pressed the remote control to the main door, then exited out the garage's side door. He staggered down the walkway toward the house, trying to gain control of his body.

"Stupid bastard," he said, again. "Stupid Vickie! Shouldn't have listened to her."

At this late date in October at 5:50 A.M. there was only the faintest light in the East. The house was dark except for a single light from one of the bedrooms, the "baby's room," as they called it, where his baby niece slept when his sister, Jaqueline, visited. He stopped mid stride and stared at the window. The light was too bright for a night light. It shouldn't have been on.

"What the hell ...?" He shook his head then continued walking, swaying and stumbling as the alcohol still clouded his brain. He'd hardly been able to drive all the way from Vickie's house and now he realized his luck at not being pulled over by a cop.

When he got to the door, he tried several times to insert the key in the lock before he finally had to help steady his right hand with his left to try and hit the hole. As he turned the key, he realized the door had been unlocked all the while.

"What the hell?" he muttered, again.

He hesitated, then pushed the door open farther and entered the foyer. He fumbled for the light switch, flipped it, but nothing happened. He felt in the darkness for the security pad but couldn't find it. The time in which it should have gone off elapsed but he didn't hear anything. Now he could feel his heart pounding.

In the darkness, he felt his way down the familiar hallway toward the stairs. Four strides down the hall, he tripped over something, falling forward, banging his elbow on the floor, and twisting his left leg.

"Damn!" he said, lying there, assessing his pain and injury. He flexed his leg. Nothing broken. He got to his feet and made his way toward the living room in the darkness, his hands stretched out ahead of him, hearing crunching sounds beneath the soles of his shoes. He reached the wall and flipped another light switch. This time the light, in the living room, went on.

He looked around at the scene. Colored streamers

hung from the ceiling, and balloons perched lightly on the floor and the furniture. Several masks lay here and there. There was the stench of liquor and cigarette smoke in the air.

Derek looked backward down the hall to the foyer from where he'd come. The flower stand, over which he had tripped, lay on its side; the silk flowers from the vase were strewn across the carpet. On down the hall, a chair that he had somehow missed in the darkness, lay on its side. The wall-phone receiver to his left dangled at the end of its cord. Shards of glass from the broken hall-light lay strewn across the plush carpet.

He heard a sound beside him and wheeled. Beyond, on the floor near the doorway to the kitchen, sat the calico cat, Morgana, eyeing Derek with off-handed familiarity.

"Come here, Morgana," Derek said, kneeling, extending his hand. "Here kitty, kitty. Come on over here. Come on."

The cat made no movement, staring at Derek.

"Fucking cat! I hate you, fucking cat!"

Derek rose and put the telephone to his ear. There was no sound. He hung the phone in its receptacle, then lifted it again and listened. This time he got a dial tone. Should he call 911? He didn't know what had happened and he needed to know more. Replacing the phone, he walked up the base of the stairway and flipped the light switch. He looked upward for a moment toward the landing, but didn't see anything. Cautiously, step-by-step, he walked up to the second floor landing, then to the third. He looked down the hall but it was empty. At the door to his parent's bedroom, he knocked lightly. There was no answer. The door was slightly ajar. He knocked again. Again there was no answer. He pushed the door open tentatively and peered inside.

The light from the hallway fell across the bedroom floor exposing a large bare leg extending from the left side of his parent's bed, a hairy leg, the sole of a bare foot, toes pointing upward. He tried to clear his head, focus, and interpret what he was seeing.

"George? Sophia?"

Derek flipped on the bedroom light. At the side of the bed, George Lunzer lay partially wrapped in a bed sheet and blanket. Derek's stepmother, Sophia, lay on her stomach on the other side of the bed, the sheet and blanket covering only the lower portion of her body. She was still in her nightgown, her face turned toward the wall. Derek could see a wide, splotch of red color on the back of the gown and around Sophia's body on the bed.

The room's contents were scrambled. The night-stand lay on their sides and the contents of the dresser drawers were strewn about. Derek could now see his father clearly, lying on his back, on the carpet, clad only in boxer shorts, a vast red stain covering his hairy chest, streaks of red running up and down his arms. The arms were flailed backwards above his head like someone shouting for joy. The carpet beside the right of his body was darkly stained, soaked and spattered with what Derek now knew was blood. George Lunzer looked like he had just fallen from the bed, his left leg still lying upon the bed's edge.

Derek backed away, his hand to his mouth, his breath coming hard, in gasps. He heard a baby cry. He backed out of his parent's bedroom, turned and strode quickly to the room where he'd seen the light. He went over to the crib and there, covered lightly in a pink blanket, was his baby niece, Erica. She rolled over and looked up at him.

Derek's vision blurred, his eyes refused to focus. He staggered back to the room where his sister usually stayed when she remained overnight and opened the door. The room was empty, the bed unmade, covers lying tossed to the side. He lurched back to his parent's bedroom. He crossed to the bed, staring down at his stepmother, reaching down to feel her forehead. She made no sound, made no movement, eyelids half open, dead eyes, seemingly looking inward just before death.

He pulled the sheet up over her shoulders and around her neck. He walked to the foot of the bed and around it to stare down at his father. His father's eyes, too, stared vacantly upward, his face warped as if in surprise and terror, and the eyes seemed to be looking directly at him.

Derek drew back in horror. He stepped backward and stumbled against a chair. He fell to his knees and began sobbing and moaning.

Morgana sat in the doorway of the bedroom and watched impassively.

## Chapter Three

The eastern sky glowed pink and lavender as Detective Richard Lanslow pulled up to the bridge crossing to Manitou Island. A uniformed officer stood on guard. Lanslow nodded in greeting and was greeted back. The officer waved him through and the detective drove on around the winding tree-lined road leading to the Lunzer home. The dispatcher's words came to him again: A double homicide on Manitou Island; that would mean one of the more prominent families of the community. Only the bridge allowed access to the island. Although homes on the island were worth millions, there was no guardhouse at the bridge, either.

Lanslow rubbed the stubble on his cheeks and ran his tongue over his teeth; both actions would have to substitute for shaving and brushing, as usual. Laura had only groaned and rolled over in bed when the phone rang. He had practically jumped into a pair of khakis, sliding the holster of his gun around his belt, pulled a polo shirt over his head and shoulders, gulped orange juice straight from the carton, slipped on his green corduroy coat, checked his daughter Melanie to see if she was still asleep, and left as quietly as possible.

Several police first responders were already at the Lunzer's estate, their squad cars parked at odd angles to one another, the strobe lights brilliant in the early morning light. Crime scene tape had been stretched around the whole estate. A crowd of uniformed officers, including reservists, was already on the grounds. Detective Leonard Wilenski, his new rookie detective partner, was standing a short distance outside the entryway, talking to another officer. Wilenski must have raced to the scene early, had already taken charge and obviously had been busy.

Lanslow exited his car and walked toward them.

"Well, well, Sergeant," said Wilenski, in greeting. "I think we have a real one on our hands this time, huh?"

"Looks to me like you're pleased as punch about it, too, Leonard. You get to be a real detective for once, eh?"

Leonard just smiled. He was as tall as Lanslow but more willowy. "Wait'll you see this," he said, inclining his head toward the Lunzer house.

Lanslow fell in beside Wilenski as he headed toward the front door. "What do we have?" he asked.

"Two bodies, a man and a woman, both in their late sixties, shot in bed. According to the son, Derek, the victims are George and Sophia Lunzer, his father and stepmother. They own the estate. The house has been ransacked, top to bottom. The son says he thinks his sister, Jacqueline, must have stayed overnight. Her baby is here but she's missing."

"The Lunzer's daughter's missing? How old is she?"

"Twenty-three, according to the Lunzer kid."

"Where's the baby now?"

"She's being taken care of by Officer Krube. We're getting the names of relatives."

"What about the daughter's—you said her name was Jacqueline?"

"Yeah, Jacqueline Bideau."

"What about her husband? Has he been notified?"

"Her husband is a Frenchman. He's in France. Derek Lunzer says they're separated. I haven't tried to get hold of him yet."

"The daughter is staying here with her parents?"

"No. She has her own place, Vadnais Heights."

"You got that covered?"

"Sent it through dispatch. We should have men over there by now. We found her car parked in one of the garage stalls here."

"Okay. The son reported this? He lives here?"

"Yeah. Derek Lunzer called nine-one-one. He came home this morning from an all-night party, around six, and found them. He's the one who reported his sister missing, too."

"You have the whole island under control then?"

"Sure thing. No one gets on or off. We've got people checking the neighbors, and we'll get a search party looking across the island."

"Chief's been notified?" asked Lanslow.

"Yeah, I got hold of him right after you were contacted. He said he's on his way back. The CSI unit and ME are on their way, too—Doc Hagen, I think."

"Just the parents and the daughter and baby were in the house, none of the help?"

"No one, according to the son. He said something about a maid being dismissed. I'll follow up on that."

"Okay, Len" said Lanslow. "Good work."

Leonard was black but his complexion was light enough that Lanslow would have sworn he saw him blush. Wilenski reminded Lanslow of a male model he'd once seen in a clothing catalog. He had the looks, one of those types that got as close to the European image as possible yet satisfied the management's requirement for "ethnic diversity." He was wearing a brown suede jacket over a pair of jeans. Every time he saw Wilenski, Lanslow wondered how he'd gotten his Polish-Jewish name and always meant to ask and then always forgot. Leonard was proving himself as a rookie detective, a damn good one at that.

They nodded to the uniformed officer at the door,

who nodded in return and stepped aside as they entered. Lanslow stood in the entryway for a moment, surveying the scene, the overturned stand and chair, the vase and flowers on the floor, the shards of glass. They walked carefully on into the living room and Lanslow noted the masks lying about and colored cardboard horns and confetti and balloons and multicolored streamers hanging from the ceiling. He looked at Wilenski inquiringly.

"The son says it was a Halloween party," Wilenski said.

"Hell of a party. We need lots of our own photos here," said Lanslow. "Where is he?"

"Sergeant Polfus is with him right now. He's in the living room, hung over."

"Hung over?"

"Yeah. Like I said, he was at an all-night party, over in Edina. We're checking that out."

"Polfus took the call?"

"Yeah, him and Krube."

"Bodies?"

"Upstairs," said Wilenski, nodding toward the stairway. "No one else has been up there 'cept me and Polfus and Krube — and the Lunzer kid. Krube's still up there, in the baby's room."

"Alright, let's take a look."

"By the way," said Wilenski, "the press is on their way, what do you want to do?"

"Ha! For once we got'em locked out. Keep them off the island as long as we can. They'll be here in boats and planes soon enough anyway."

They started up the stairway.

\*\*\*

"Jesus!" said Lanslow.

His gaze riveted on the two bodies, then swept the room. He noted the drawers that had been pulled out, their contents dumped on the floor. A reading lamp beside the bed looked as if it had been swiped off the table, the lampshade lying against the wall, the bulb smashed. The clothes closet had been practically stripped, the clothing thrown on the floor, shoeboxes emptied.

"Are all the rooms like this?"

"Yeah, top to bottom," Wilenski said.

After surveying the room for a few moments longer, Lanslow walked carefully over to the corpse of George Lunzer and stared down at it. He turned to Wilenski.

"Chest wound, looks like a shotgun, close range. I suppose there were hundreds of guests?"

"Don't know that yet, Rich, but I think it was less

than that."

"Oh, that's good! Less than hundreds!"

"Yes sir," said Wilenski, oblivious to the sarcasm.

"The missing woman will be the first priority here, Len," said Lanslow. "We need to get the word out to the media and other jurisdictions—a picture of the woman."

"Right, we're on it. We've called extra people in."

Lanslow walked around the bed to get a closer look at Sophia Lunzer.

"Shot in the back?"

"Yeah, same kind of wound, probably the same weapon," said Wilenski.

"There should be blood, pellet holes in the sheet. Someone has pulled the sheet over the wound?"

"Yeah. Derek Lunzer said he covered his stepmother up."

Lanslow pulled on a pair of latex gloves he'd taken from a paper sack in his pocket. He removed the sheet from Sophia Lunzer's neck and shoulders. "Looks like Mr. Lunzer was shot first," he said, absently, staring at the ugly wound in the woman's back. "Mrs. Lunzer probably never knew what happened."

Wilenski nodded. "Yeah. Mr. Lunzer might have been on his way up out of the bed when he took it, then fell on the floor there."

"Uh huh. Could be." Lanslow circled back around the foot of the bed to the other side and peered down again at George Lunzer. "Poor bastard," he said, "probably had just enough time to see the gun pointed at him."

"Must've known it was coming," said Wilenski.

Lanslow turned to leave the but spied something at the foot of the bed. "Hello? What do we have here?" he said, bending down to look at the rug more closely. There was a black smear that looked like grease or mud.

Wilenski moved to Lanslow's side and peered down more closely. "A shoe print?" he asked.

"A partial," said Lanslow, down on his knees. "Tread looks like a hiking shoe, or a boot of some kind. Let's get real careful in here."

"Yeah, we'll get pictures."

"CSI'll take the carpet, but we need our own pictures too," said Lanslow, straightening. "Be sure and check it out against the Lunzer kid. Where's the baby?"

"Down the hall, that way."

They walked down the hall and Wilenski opened the door to one of the rooms. Officer Deborah Krube looked up from her cross-legged sitting position on the floor. The baby, looking to be about seven to eight months old, was exploring a pile of toys. Lanslow thought of his own daughter Melanie, at home. She would be up and Laura would be getting her breakfast and she'd probably be watching Sesame Street. Until Agnes, their babysitter, arrived, Laura would be doing her best to get ready for school. He was going to miss another weekend with his wife and daughter, no doubt.

"Nice police work, Krube," he said to the female officer.

"Thanks, Sergeant. Polfus is going to pay for this. Just because I'm a woman!"

"In the line of duty," began Wilenski.

"Cut the crap, Wilenski," Krube said. The baby crawled to her and up into her arms. "Actually, I've already fallen in love with her."

"I can see why," said Lanslow.

Lanslow and Wilenski exited the baby's room and went to the guest room where Derek Lunzer had told Wilenski his sister usually slept when she stayed the night. In the walk-around they found nothing of any portent. The covers on the bed had been thrown back. Lanslow imagined her hearing the gunshots, dashing out of bed. What happened after that was anyone's guess.

Lanslow's radio crackled and a voice announced the arrival of the medical examiner and the crime scene investigation unit from Ramsey County.

"All right," said Lanslow. "Doc Hagen and his crew are here. Let's get out of the way and let him and the techies do their work. I want to talk to the son."

"While you're doing that," Wilenski said, "I'll check on how they're doing over in Vadnais Heights."

***

Derek Lunzer sat hunched in a large easy chair in the spacious living room. The young man had his head in his hands, nodding one way or another to Sergeant Polfus' comments and questions. Lanslow watched unseen for a moment before he entered the room. Lunzer seemed dazed, as would be expected. His answers were mumbled and Polfus would have to ask him to repeat what he'd said. It appeared to Lanslow that the kid wasn't being too cooperative, but, after all, he'd just found his parents dead and could be in shock — as well as suffering still from the all-night party hangover. Lanslow reserved his judgment. He walked on into the room.

"Mr. Lunzer?

Derek looked up. "Yeah?"

"Derek, I'm Detective Sergeant Lanslow, White Bear Police." Lanslow extended his hand. Derek rose from his seat, grasping Lanslow's hand limply. Lanslow could see Derek sizing him up, taking his measure. The young man was as tall as Lanslow, slim build. He looked haggard, eyes red-rimmed.

"Please, keep your seat, Derek," Lanslow said, motioning toward the chair from which Lunzer had just risen.

Derek sat back down. He had to keep wiping back an unruly shock of dark brown hair that spilled over his forehead.

"I know this must be a terrible time for you, Derek, but I'd like to ask you some questions if I might."

"Why now?" Lunzer asked. "I'd rather not. I've already told Officer Wilenski as much as I can—and Sergeant Polfus, here."

"Mr. Lunzer, I am sorry but it's important to get as much information as we can as soon as we can. If we're to find your sister and get some idea of who might have killed your parents, then we have to act quickly. I'd just like to verify some things."

Derek waved his hand listlessly. "Go ahead, then," he said.

"Detective Wilenski tells me you were returning from a party when you found your parents?"

"Yeah."

"Where was this party?"

"My girl friend's house, in Edina. I've already given

Detective Wilenski the address. And the names, as many as I can remember."

Lanslow nodded. "Okay. About your sister—Jacqueline?"

"Jackie wasn't here when I left yesterday morning. She must have come later, for the party. That's all I know."

"Your sister lives in Vadnais Heights, doesn't she?"

"She has a town-home, over there. I gave her address to the other detective."

"Okay, good; exactly what time did you say you left for the party in Edina, Mr. Lunzer?"

Derek looked up and stared quizzically at Lanslow for a moment, then said, "Well, detective, I didn't say, *exactly*, but it was yesterday morning, around eleven. Why are you questioning me about this?"

"You went directly to the party at that time?"

"Yeah, around then. I drove to my girl friend Vickie's parent's house, got there around noon or so. I got home about an hour ago."

"What would be Vickie's last name?"

"Holland. You want her address? I already told Officer Wilenski."

"Alright. You say the party went from noon yester-day till when?"

"Like I said, I got to Vickie's about noon or so, left

around five this morning. It was about over by then."

"Must've been a heck of a party," said Lanslow. "Were the parents home?"

"No, they're away, somewhere. It was Vickie's birthday," Derek said. He brushed something from the sleeve of the black pullover turtleneck shirt he wore, tucked loosely into a pair of brown corduroy trousers.

"Have you been able to check to see if there's anything missing, Mr. Lunzer?"

Again the quizzical look. "Are you kidding? They've torn the place apart! George and Sophia's room is a complete mess. I haven't looked much downstairs, but, hey, my parents were having a party. Things are pretty messed up all over, anyway. It's hard to tell."

"What's downstairs, sir, the basement?"

"Yeah; another lower level. A walk out."

"Okay. If you don't mind, Mr. Lunzer, we'd like you to list down everything that is missing, as soon as you can — anything, everything you can remember. And, of course, we'll need you to make a formal statement."

"Sure," said Lunzer, shrugging. "I'm not sure I can identify much, though."

"Just make your best guess, sir, if you would. Anything you can think of. Officer Polfus, here, will assist you, okay? Here's my card if you need to contact me."

"Sure," said Lunzer, taking the card without a glance at it and stuffing it in his pant's pocket.

At that moment Wilenski came in the room from outside and motioned for Lanslow to come over.

"What's up?" Lanslow asked.

"Our guys found another body down by the lake. Not the woman. A black man."

\*\*\*

Lanslow and Wilenski stood with Patrol Officer Sergeant Carl Rogers, the watch commander, and stared at the body, floating spread-eagled a short distance from the shore. Small waves gently pushed and tugged at the corpse. Only the back and shoulders showed plainly at that distance even though the water of the lake was clear. The morning was sparkling clean and under any other circumstance would have been perfect for a stroll by the waterside. Lanslow would have loved to be doing that, with Laura and Melanie. But that dark body in the water spoiled it all. Lanslow just stood there, watching the body rise and fall gently in the waves.

He turned to look back toward the house. A line of three different sets of shoeprints led from the house to the beach. All around the area, near the water, were more shoeprints, deeply gouged in the sand, pointing in all directions. Another line of two sets of shoe prints led back toward the lake and the boat dock.

A crime scene technician, sent by Doc Hagen, the Ramsey County medical examiner, was already taking pictures.

"That looks like the guy I saw yesterday," Rogers said to Lanslow.

"You saw him? Where?"

"Downtown, in the park across from the bookstore and cafe. Got a report he was littering. I talked to him a little. He was eating. Seemed harmless. Said he was just passing through, traveling south."

"That's in your report?" Lanslow said and Rogers nodded.

"Who reported him?"

"The café owner, across the street from the park. Claimed he was littering."

The technician straightened and turned to Lanslow. "Finished here, Sergeant," he said.

"We're getting pictures of these?" Lanslow asked, pointing to the tracks leading toward the boat dock.

"We're on it, Sergeant. Ted's gone to get the plaster now to get molds of the tracks if we can get them. Doc will be down pretty quick to take a look, too. I just talked to him. We found this cap just over there." He handed a plastic evidence bag, enclosing a baseball style cap, to Lanslow. "There was a struggle here, looks like. Could've been knocked off his head. There's an old Air Force duffel bag and a sleeping bag in the trees there, too, tracks leading in and out toward the Lunzer house, looks like."

Lanslow took the plastic bag and held it to the light briefly, then handed it back. "Might've been his," he said, "or it could be someone else's. Was he wearing this hat when you talked to him?" he asked Officer Rogers.

"Looks like the same one," said Rogers, "far as I can remember."

"Okay. You say there are bags in the trees? Let's take a look up there."

They walked up the beach toward the trees, making sure their own tracks were separated from those leading from the area. About ten or twenty feet into the trees they found the duffel bag lying at the head of a sleeping bag that had been placed next to a fallen log.

"Sure looks like someone slept here," said Wilenski.

"Pretty much," said Rogers.

Lanslow appraised the area briefly. "Someone slept here, all right," he said. "But we'll let Doc Hagen and his crew take a closer look." He turned back to the scene on the beach. "What do you make of all this,

Len?" Lanslow asked, exiting the area and walking back toward the floater.

"Damned if I know," said the detective. "A lot of action went on there." He pointed to the shoeprints. "This guy may have been in on the job. Could be some of the perps decided to increase their share of the loot."

"Possibly," said Lanslow, "possibly."

"Look at those tracks, Sergeant," Leonard said. They were back at the water's edge, now. "There are three different sets of shoe prints coming from the house there. Can't be sure but it looks like the vic was running, the others following. There are only two sets of tracks leading back, over there, toward the boat dock. And it looks like whoever slept in the trees there was walking toward the house."

"We need to get a K-9 unit here, Len. We might be able to find something by following those tracks, not only around here but from those trees."

Wilenski pulled out his cell phone, punched some keys and walked away a short distance.

"Got any idea what killed him?" Lanslow asked the technician.

"Hard to tell from here. He's got a lot of blood still in the hair. The water has probably washed most of it away, though. He may have been knocked in the head and drowned. We're just waiting for Doc to get here."

"No other wounds?"

"Haven't checked that, yet. Doc Hagen will take a closer look. Here he comes, now."

Lanslow turned and watched Hagen approach, along with another technician. Hagen wore a mustache that always reminded Lanslow of a walrus, and his short, rotund physique didn't diminish the image. He was plodding, trying to get traction in the sand. Hagen's appearance brought to mind a scene of another murder, almost exactly two years ago, when Lanslow's partner and mentor, Sergeant Zeke Mallard, had been found murdered in his own garage. Since that time, the department had had only one other case where Doc Hagen was called in; but he remembered Lanslow.

"For God's sake, Detective!" Hagen said. "You had to scrape up another body? You didn't think we had enough already? How many more you got 'round here?" He stared at the dead man in the water, his practiced eye noting the details others might miss.

"We're still searching the island, Doc. You never know."

"Remind me to carry some rubber boots from now on, Lanslow," Hagen said, as he walked to the edge of the lake and looked down at the body, knowing he was going to have to walk into the water.

Ted, the technician, was taking close up pictures of

the shoeprints and the other technician was spraying a shellac stabilizer in other prints in preparation for the dental stone molds that would be taken.

"Sorry we don't have a pair for you, Doc."

Hagen just sighed and removed his shoes and socks, rolled up his pants as best he could around his stubby legs and waded carefully into the water. He tried to keep the pants dry but a wave from the lake splashed upward and soaked one of the legs. A whispered expletive escaped his lips and, realizing the uselessness of trying to stay dry and the need for both hands, he simply dropped the legs of his trousers in the water. He bent over to take a closer look. After he had examined the dead man's head for several moments, parting the hair in several places gently, he said to no one in particular, "Multiple blows. Blunt force."

The doctor stepped out of the lake, sat down on the beach, dried his feet of water and sand with the tops of his socks and put on his shoes. He labored to his feet and nodded to the two technicians. "All right, you can get him out now. Pick him up and put him out here so we can get a closer look."

The technicians, who had anticipated their task, stepped into the water, barefooted, one on either side, each one's face registering as much distaste of the cold water as Hagen's had. The dead man was heavy, and his clothing was soaked, making him even heavier.

"Careful, now. We don't want any secondary marks on him. Lay him on his back," said Hagen. He looked quickly at one of the technicians, as if remembering something. "You got pictures of all this?" he asked, sweeping the contours of the beach.

"Yeah, Doc. We took the pictures and we're recording," said the one, grunting as he and the other man laid the body down on its back on a low gurney. The dead man's eyes and mouth were closed.

Hagen knelt by the body and took the man's temperature then pulled a penlight from his pocket, pushed open the man's eyelids and peered into his eyes. He poked the cheeks lightly, then the ankles. He shook his head. "Being in the water like this will complicate things," he said, as if to himself.

"Did the blow to the head kill him, Doc?" Lanslow asked.

"Well, the wound is bad enough he might have been killed from that. On the other hand, he may have drowned. Water in the lungs will mean he probably drowned. If not, then he probably died as a result of the blow or blows to the head. Looks like he's been in a hell of a fight." He began to search the dead man's clothing. He reached into the man's coat pocket.

"Uh huh, we have something here." He carefully

pulled out a folded sheet of yellow paper, totally soaked, holding it gingerly between his latex gloved fingers. A camera flashed, and only a little farther back, another technician held a video camera, recording every moment.

Hagen examined the yellow paper cursorily. "We'll have to take this to the lab," he said. "I don't want to destroy any evidence on this, if there is any." He produced an evidence bag and put the paper in it carefully.

Wilenski had rejoined them. "Anyone find any loot on this man or around here close?" he asked Commander Rogers.

"No, sir," Rogers said. "This is just how we found him."

"Is that blood?" Wilenski asked, pointing to a smear showing on the yellow sheet of paper inside the bag.

"Maybe," said Hagen, "doesn't look like blood to me right now; too thick. We'll check it in the lab."

Lanslow stared down at the body. The man's overcoat was of heavy cloth and was dirty and soiled. He had an untrimmed goatee, flecked with gray, and his hair was unkempt, with kinky long strips, now matted together from the water.

"This man was a transient," said Lanslow, remembering what Officer Rogers had said and eyeing the very black skin, the scuffed, worn, high-top shoes, the ragged and torn clothing. "Probably a hobo."

"What the hell is a hobo doing on Manitou Island?" said Wilenski.

"Good question, Detective," said Lanslow, "a very good question. Whatever he was doing, it was his last."

## Chapter Four

Jacqueline Bideau was lying on her back. She'd been lying like this for only a few moments, having been carried over some man's shoulder, down a flight of steps, and dumped unceremoniously in a bed. He had proceeded to hold her down with a knee pressed to her chest while he tied her to the bed frame. The pain of his weight was almost unbearable. The strip of cloth that had been across her mouth was still there but the blindfold was removed. The man had quickly turned and left before she'd had a chance to recover. As he went back up the stairs he turned the light off.

In the ensuing darkness, she at first could make out nothing except what was apparently a digital clock above her, to her right, its numbers glowing red. The numbers read 9:27. Just to the right of the clock she could make out a thin, square outline of light that looked like a covered window. She'd been awake all during the time of the trip to this house so she was sure it was still morning. She heard a popping and crackling noise and turned her head to the left to see small dancing lights in the darkness and realized it must be a fire inside a wood burning stove with a small window on the door. She felt a blanket covering her from the waist down. She tried to move and felt pain, especially around her head and neck and chest. Her arms were stretched backward and outward at angles above her body, cords around her wrists. She tested her speech, sounding guttural. She tried to move her legs but they had been bound one to either side of the bed, in spread-eagle fashion.

The flickering light from the stove illuminated the room somewhat. Squinting, she began gradually to make out forms: a chair, perhaps, a table, maybe. She was cold despite the fire in the stove and could smell what she thought was the musty odor of earth and mud and old cement blocks. She thought she might be in a basement.

Panic seized her. She felt as if she were smothering, unable to get her breath. She pulled at her bonds. She sucked for air through the gag and tried to call out. She heaved and panted until she lay in a sweat. She became exhausted. She lay quiet for a moment then tried to calm down and think and she began to breathe a little easier. The sweat from her exertions began to cool her skin and she became chilled.

From above and to her left she heard a sharp bang, as if a door had opened and slammed shut, and there was the sound of footsteps across the floor. Panic gripped her once more, but she fought it and lay still, listening intently. She heard the sound of speech rising and falling, as if in heated conversation. She recognized one of the louder voices as that of one of the men in the automobile that had brought her here. The other voice was unfamiliar. Then there was silence.

Her thoughts raced backward to the first sound—of an explosion it seemed—that had jerked her erect in the bed in her parent's house and sent her rushing to the bedroom door, peering out, down toward her parent's bedroom to her right. The light from her parent's bedroom was on, streaming through the open door, illuminating the hallway. She remembered a second explosion a split second later and seeing a flash coming from the open door. In an instant she'd known that someone had broken in, that they were in her parents room, that she had to get to her baby, and she'd rushed toward the baby's room just down the hall to her left and that was when someone, a man, grabbed her from behind, arms wrapped around her, his weight crushing her to the floor. She could remember him cursing, and cuffing her about the head, his knee pressing into her back, strong hands around her neck, squeezing.

After that, she could only remember finding herself bound, gagged and blindfolded, lying on the hall floor and hearing loud voices, at least two, shouting to one another, and it seemed that she lay there for a good half-hour or more and then was lifted by someone at her shoulders and by someone else at her feet and being carried down the stairs and out the front door, being dumped in the back of a vehicle and then being covered, with something like a canvas tarp and a sleeping bag, and the vehicle's doors slamming shut and the jostling and bumping and—seemingly for hours—the sound of the vehicle's tires slapping on rough and curving pavement that jolted her and rocked her from side to side. There was something hard that kept jabbing her in the back as the vehicle lurched from side to side.

She'd lain there in the back of that vehicle in pain and terror, listening to her captors' voices, not quite able to hear clearly everything they were saying. What she did hear were voices of protest and then the one man saying something to the other about a killing, of a woman, followed by the man's cackle. The conversation sent chills of fear through her. She felt nauseated and thought she was going to throw up, thinking she was going to be killed, thinking that her parents had perhaps already been murdered and that maybe she had failed to protect her baby, thinking then, immediately, that no one would be cruel enough to murder or harm a sleeping baby, that her little Erica would still be alive and would be okay when her brother got home from Vickie's party.

The vehicle had stopped a couple of times, as far as

she could remember, and during one of the stops she'd heard men's voices in conversation and what she thought was the double thump of the auto's doors and a gas pump nozzle being inserted in the gas tank receptacle. They'd left the motor running and loud music playing. She'd tried to scream and kick free of the covering but the exertion overwhelmed her. The men reentered the vehicle and it had begun moving again and the sound from the tires changed to a sound like the crunching of gravel and she could occasionally hear rocks striking the vehicle's underside. Again, it sounded to her as though the two men were arguing.

After a time, the automobile had stopped again and she heard the two men get out and the doors slam shut, and loud voices again that faded in the distance. She'd lain there for a considerable length of time until she thought she could stand it no longer, till she thought she would go mad, and then a door opened and she heard someone get in on the driver's side but no one got in on the passenger side, and the vehicle began to move again and had traveled only a short distance when it stopped again and, she believed—because it had backed and pulled forward several times—turned around, and she thought she must have fainted for she didn't remember anything else after that.

Now, trussed to this bed, in this dank and dark

basement, she didn't know whether her baby was safe, nor what exactly had happened to her parents, though she feared the worst for them, nor what was going to happen to her, though, again, she feared the worst. All she could do was moan and sob and stretch and despite the pain pull as hard as she could against her bonds. In a little while, exhausted again, she lay still and watched the flickering firelight growing smaller and at last she closed her eyes and a semi-sleep came mercifully.

When she woke once more it was to the sound of voices and movement above. She heard a door opening somewhere above her and a dim, naked light bulb came on near the foot of the stairs. Quaking in fear, she struggled to remain still, to keep the scream in her throat. The man came down the stairs and stood at the bottom. She could see nothing of the face in the dim light or anything else except the silhouette of his body and head in the backlight. He appeared to have blonde hair. He remained there for a few moments then he turned and went back up the stairs, turning off the light and closing the door and darkness fell around her again, .

Jacqueline lay trembling, her mind racing, keen to every sound above, staring into the gloom. The light from the fire had gone out. Sounds of voices came to her once more.

" ... stupid damn thing to do," she heard someone say.

The voices faded. Then she heard a familiar voice.

" ... tired of it all. I'm fed up with ... " and once again the voice faded.

There were sounds, like scuffling, then "You can't ... "

"Can't what? Can't what, you ... "

She heard these words distinctly, then more scuffling and feet thumping on the floor above.

"Hey! Hey!" she heard someone yell, and then more scuffling sounds, sounds of objects crashing to the floor, then silence.

After some time, she heard footsteps cross the floor and the door at the head of the stairs opening and she saw a different pair of legs descending. She watched as the person came down, this time all the way. She was quaking as the person neared the bottom stair. The man stood there for a moment in silhouette, seeming to be observing her; then he approached. When she saw him at closer range she tried to scream but the cloth in her mouth allowed only a low muffled moan to escape around it.

\*\*\*

When they got back to the station, Wilenski left the room to get some coffee and Lanslow removed his jacket and draped it on the back of his chair. He sat down and leaned back, put his feet up on the desk, laced his fingers behind his head and stared out the darkened window.

The Investigative Section Office out of which the detectives worked was relatively small, with three desks arranged along the walls of a room of about twelve by twenty feet. The third desk was empty and bare since Lieutenant Johnson, former head of the Investigation Office, had left to work in another city. Lanslow had been placed in charge when Johnson left. The detective's work areas were typical: in- and out-boxes, hold-boxes, computers, manuals, books, phones, family pictures, wall calendars, etc.

Lanslow reviewed what had been a long day: he felt they had done all they could for now but there was still work to be done. The Lunzer mansion had been secured; they would search the entire house once more tomorrow, though, and it would perhaps take the technicians days to process the crime scene further; The bodies of the Lunzers and the as-yet-unidentified black man had been transported to the morgue, accompanied by Wilenski, where autopsies would be performed later, and one of them, himself or Len, or perhaps both, would probably attend when they got the call from the medical examiner's office. This was a part of their duty that Lanslow found most odious, no matter its necessity.

Dr. Hagen had promised to get them his preliminary report "as soon as I can." The crime scene technician's preliminary reports had been filed, as well as those of the first responders and of the interviews of neighbors, conducted by patrol. Derek Lunzer had been interrogated further at the station, his statement taken, and he was allowed to leave. As far as they could tell, his story checked out. Derek would take his little niece and stay with an aunt and uncle who lived in the community of North Oaks, just west of White Bear Lake.

Lanslow's thoughts turned to the missing daughter. The search of the island for the woman hadn't turned up anything. A search of the Bideau's home in Vadnais Heights hadn't yielded anything unusual, either. As far as they could tell she had not taken any of her hairbrushes or clothes or toothbrushes or other personal effects. They'd found her purse, empty of money and credit cards, at the Lunzer home. Her car was in one of the parking stalls of the Lunzer's garage. There was nothing to make them suspect she had left or packed for a longer trip. She was simply missing. They would drag the lake tomorrow and send down divers, although

Lanslow suspected it would be for naught. It was a big lake, with some spots very deep, so they might never find a body even if it was there; but Lanslow believed everything pointed to abduction.

Interviews of the neighbors had picked up some gossip: Sophia Lunzer was known to have a roving eye for good-looking young men. And George Lunzer was no saint in that respect, either, reportedly having an eye for the women. But their marriage seemed stable for all of that, perhaps by some mutual understanding: it had lasted now for twenty four years. Sophia was George's second wife, the mother of Jacqueline Bideau. His first wife, Alexandra, the mother of Derek, had died in an automobile accident. Lanslow's thought upon hearing these reports was that the gossip of extramarital interests, if it was true, only further complicated their search for suspects.

Wilenski came back into the room with two Styrofoam cups of coffee and set one of them down on Lanslow's desk then went to his own desk across the room. He too hung his jacket over the back of his chair. It was nearing 6:00 P.M. The two detectives were ready to begin writing their own reports, sifting through the other preliminary reports, and putting the rest of the case file together.

Lanslow glanced at his watch, realizing he was

going to be very late. He called Laura from his desk phone. The babysitter answered.

"Agnes? Laura's not home yet?"

"No, Mr. Lanslow. She called a while ago. Said she'd be late."

"What was the reason?"

"She said there was a meeting, something like that."

Lanslow swore under his breath. "Okay, Agnes. Can you let her know I'm going to have to be late? Is that going to be okay with you?"

There was an embarrassingly long pause on the other end of the line. Finally Agnes said, "Mr. Lanslow, I agreed to stay late if I could know ahead of time. I just need to know ahead of time. My husband  ... "

"Yes, Agnes, I know. I'm sorry. I'll talk to Laura. How's Melanie?"

"Melanie's fine. She's playing."

"All right, Agnes. You can stay, then?"

"Yes, of course," Agnes said, her resignation apparent even over the phone. "When will you be home?"

"I'm not sure, Agnes. You've heard about the murders?"

"Yes. Such a terrible thing!"

"I'll get there as soon as I can, Agnes. Laura should be home anytime."

"All right. I hope so." She hung up.

Leonard Wilenski was looking at Lanslow. "Problems?" he said.

"Na, just a little misunderstanding. Babysitters, you know."

"Sorry," said Len. "I don't."

"Why aren't you married yet, Len; A good looking guy like you?"

"I'm having too much fun right now, Sarge, too much fun."

"Yeah, well, keep having fun as long as you can. Marriage does change things, that's for damned sure."

"That's what I hear," Wilenski said.

***

Lanslow's phone was ringing. It was Doc Hagen.

"I thought you'd want to know this ASAP," he said. "It'll be in our final lab report but it's important enough that you should know it now."

"What do you have, Doc?"

"That piece of paper on the black man? We took a look at it. It's an ink drawing of the interior of the Lunzer's home. The lines are blurred from the water but under magnification we can make them out. The Lunzer's address is at the bottom. Now, get this, there are notes showing the placement of jewelry and money in various locations. The diagram shows where a key is hidden in a pot, just in front of the doorway—a potted plant of some kind, probably one of those evergreens at the front door. The security system's code was also shown as well. There's dirt underneath his fingernails that matches the dirt in the pots. It sure looks like the man was in on a burglary, certainly, maybe the murders, too. Oh, and the red smear was nothing but strawberry jelly"

"Anything else ... prints?"

"We have to check on that. The water has probably destroyed them if there were any. Oh, by the way, we don't have the proper test results back yet but I'd estimate, from what we do know, that the Lunzers probably died at sometime between 1:00PM and 2:00PM."

"Okay, Doc. Thanks for the heads-up. That certainly helps."

"No problem. Like I said, it'll all be in our lab report, a lot more detail, but you have the gist of it."

After he'd taken Hagen's message, Lanslow swung his feet from the desk to the floor and sat up straight. He related the gist of Hagen's message to his partner. "So, Detective Wilenski, what's your take on the case now?"

"Well," Wilenski said, plucking two packets of sugar and a packet of powdered cream from his desk drawer and stirring their contents into the steaming black liquid, "Hagen's report sure changes things. The black dude was obviously out to burglarize or rob the Lunzers. He had the diagram. He knew where the key to the door was. I saw those pots, and someone or some thing had been digging in them. There was no sign of a break-in. So he probably got the key and used it to get in."

"It seems he wasn't working alone," Lanslow said. "That shoe print inside wasn't his. Seems strange there were no other shoe prints inside the house," he added, reflectively."

"And there were two different shoe prints on the beach where he was killed," Wilenski said. "We got at least four people involved in a burglary and a murder. Doc said the Lunzers' time of death was around one or two? One of the guests reported he was last to leave the party around 11:30. Derek Lunzer found the bodies this morning at 6:00. The perps had plenty of time, probably four or more hours."

Lanslow took a quick swallow of coffee. He was merely listening and nodding from time to time, allowing Wilenski to fill in the story.

"My guess is," Wilenski continued, "that these guys went in there, after the party, during the early morning hours, to get money and valuables—the Lunzers stood in their way and they killed them. The woman wasn't supposed to be there but they decided to take her. There must have been a falling out or something to get the black man killed later, on the beach. The others then made their getaway back across the lake."

"Uh huh." Lanslow was looking at his notebook that he had removed from his coat pocket. "Only one problem: There's no sign of the woman being taken to the dock, or to the beach. The dog followed her scent between the house and her car in the garage, no where else."

"Maybe they were carrying her," said Wilenski.

"The guys on the beach?"

"Yeah, or the other guy, the guy whose boot print we found in the house."

"You saw the tracks. There was quite a chase and a struggle on that beach. The two on the beach who killed the black guy probably wouldn't be carrying the woman and murdering him at the same time."

Wilenski hesitated. "Well, like I said ... maybe the guy who made the track inside the house carried her out to the boat. If he did, there'd be no trace of her that way, either."

"There was no trace of the third guy going to the boat," Lanslow said. "He would have left a scent if he'd gone to the boat. All the dog got was a trace of him from the house to the driveway, or vice versa."

They both went silent. Finally Wilenski said: "Then what's the connection between that shoeprint inside the house and the ones on the beach?"

"That, my friend, is the million dollar question."

"You got to wonder why the perps would use a boat to begin with," Wilenski said. "But they did, that's a fact. I guess it'd be one way to get on the island without having to go through the gate and risk being seen, especially in the early morning hours. Still ..."

He had reached a momentary standstill.

"And here's something else," Lanslow said, after a moment. "Rogers said he got a report yesterday afternoon of someone littering, in the park, across from the café and bookstore downtown. Rogers ID'd the black guy this morning as the same person. He said he didn't see him there with anyone else. The guy's almost surely a transient."

"You're saying he was working alone?" said Wilenski. "How'd he get that map of the house?"

"I don't know, but if he was with them, why'd they kill him?"

"Like I said, maybe they decided they wanted a bigger share of the loot."

Lanslow shook his head. "That's possible. But the black guy just doesn't fit in. I know he had the diagram.

I don't know how he got it. But whatever way he got it, I think he just fell into something over his head and got whacked."

"There was no break in. They knew where the key was," Wilenski said. "I saw those pots the Doc mentioned. Something had been digging in them. At the time I just thought it was some animal. But now we know that the black guy had the diagram showing where the key was supposed to be. He or someone else dug it out and used it to get in that house."

Lanslow just shook his head again, puzzlement written across his face. "Doesn't make any sense," he said. "How in hell would he get hold of that kind of information? There would be only a few people who could furnish him with that info."

Wilenski took another drink of coffee, grimaced, opened his desk drawer, retrieved another packet of sugar and emptied it into the container. "Had to be an inside job," he said.

"And that narrows it down to the Lunzer's kids" said Lanslow. "Or maybe some of the help. Derek Lunzer has an alibi, and the woman's been abducted. That would seem to let them both off the hook. Unless ... "

"Uh huh, unless one or the other of them had the job done for them." Wilenski took another drink of coffee, swished it around in his mouth, seemed satisfied and sat it down. "Wonder how much the Lunzers are worth?"

"A lot, no doubt," said Lanslow. "The kids could have hired the perps to kill their parents, ransack the house to make it look like a burglary. They'd know about the party, use it to confuse things even more. And then they'd inherit their parent's fortune."

"But then there's the abduction. That would have to be a ruse if they're both in on it," said Wilenski. "You really think the daughter might be in on it?"

"No, actually I don't, primarily because the baby was left behind. Pretty hard to believe she'd do that. The fact the baby's still there points more to abduction."

"On the other hand, they could have been planning that Derek would return soon enough that the baby wouldn't be in any danger," said Wilenski.

"That's so." Lanslow sipped absently at the fast-cooling coffee and slouched back in his chair again. "Just doesn't hit me right, though."

"Maybe we got a ransom situation here, then," said Wilenski. "They take the woman and ask the kid for more money."

Lanslow considered this for a moment. "That would suppose whoever the kid hired to do it would be doublecrossing him. If they were going to do a ransom, why take the sister and not the baby—or maybe both? Anyway, Ms. Bideau wasn't supposed to be there, if we're to believe Lunzer."

"That's a big if," said Wilenski. "Just because the woman wasn't supposed to be there wouldn't mean they didn't take her." He paused, his mind switching to another track. "Or just maybe the perps wanted something different than a ransom," he said.

"Like ...?"

Len pulled a photograph from a large manila envelope and handed it to Lanslow. Lanslow set his notebook on his desktop and took the picture and studied it. The photo of Jacqueline Bideau had already been sent out to all units and other jurisdictions across Minnesota and the rest of the U.S., as well as to all of the media.

The picture showed a sophisticated looking young woman, her auburn hair swept backward from her forehead behind her ears. She wore a small confident smile on her lips, reminding Lanslow of the Mona Lisa. Her cheekbones were high, her eyes were blue, her nose straight, all in perfect symmetry. She wore a black leather jacket over a black turtleneck sweater. A long pendant on a golden chain showed through the half opened jacket. The photo caught her from the waist up, standing in front of French doors.

Lanslow took his time. "Yeah, she's pretty, all right," he said.

"Pretty? Is that all you can say? She's drop-dead gorgeous and you know it."

"All right, so she's gorgeous. Maybe you have a point there."

"You bet," said Wilenski, "you bet."

"She's also separated," Lanslow said, looking at his notes again, "with a young baby—and her husband is in France. Jeez! What a world."

Wilenski leafed through his notebook. "Her husband's first name is Louis, Louis Bideau. The Lunzer kid said she'd met him in France when she studied over there. They lived here for a time then he split. Seems Miss Bideau is not only beautiful but she's smart, too; she's finishing her Ph.D. in religious studies at the American University of Paris."

"Still not out of the question her husband might have had something to do with her abduction and the murders, though," said Lanslow, jotting notes. "He has a motive. Maybe he wants custody of the daughter and maybe there are monetary arrangements we don't know about. We'll check him out—and we can't rule the daughter out just yet, either. But I'm beginning to suspect her less and less. Who benefits most from the parents death? The kids. Now, the sister is abducted and that may leave the whole thing to Derek."

Wilenski nodded, stroking his chin. "Okay, here's what I think we got," he said, trying out his theory once again. "Let's say the kid sets this all up. He hires some thugs to kill the parents. He furnishes these guys with the diagram. The deal is, the burglars get whatever they can and maybe some cash as well. The burglary is part of the deal and meant to mislead us. Lunzer even sets the deal up to take place when the parents are having a party just to confuse the matter more. He arranges what he thinks is an airtight alibi. Now, the perps burglarize the home, kill the parents, but find the woman. She wasn't supposed to be there. Maybe the perps have a falling out, probably over the loot, or the woman. They kill the black dude, take the woman and make their escape back across the lake."

"You got the black man still in on it with the rest of them?"

"Yeah. He had the diagram. I can't get over that."

"Neither can I," said Lanslow. "He had it, for sure. What bothers me, though, is that the dog traced the black guy's scent back into that brush. What do you make of that? It looked like he'd been sleeping there, or camping, too."

Wilenski sat back in his chair and stretched. "Yeah. You're right. The guy was a hobo, no doubt," he said.

"Most of that food in the bag was damned near spoiled. He obviously got it from a garbage can or something. And he camped out on the Lunzer estate."

"A bum? Wandering through Manitou Island? With a map of the Lunzer estate?"

"It's unusual he'd wind up on the island, but that's how it shakes out to me. He had the map, that's a fact. That's why he was there. Maybe the dude was casing the joint, acting as their lookout; you know, one if by land, two if by sea, and all that."

Lanslow laughed out loud. "Wilenski, you're some detective, you know?"

Wilenski laughed, too. "I do my best, Sarge."

"And you still think they escaped with the woman across the lake? Remember, there's no sign of that. These perps followed the black guy from the house to the beach, killed him there, for whatever reason, and then went directly to the dock, according to the K9 people."

"Well," said Wilenski, "They did kill him, that's for sure. And they did go directly to that dock."

"And we've got this third guy," said Lanslow, "the guy who left the shoe print on the rug."

"He might have been the one who carried the woman to the boat," Wilenski ventured.

Lanslow took another swig of the cold coffee, finishing it off, peering at his partner over the rim of the cup. He tossed the cup in his wastebasket. "But the dog didn't follow the third guy's track to the boat," he reminded his partner mildly. "He followed it outside to the driveway. And that's the only trail for that print that the dog picked up."

"We're putting an awful lot of weight on that partial print," Wilenski said. "It may have no connection to the case at all."

"Uh huh. You may be right. But I think it does. It's the only print that couldn't be identified and it was in a perfect place to use a gun to kill the Lunzers, just as they were, in fact, killed."

"The shotgun's a funny weapon to be used in carrying off a burglary," said Wilenski, almost as an afterthought.

Lanslow nodded. "Just another weird aspect of this case," he said.

"You think murder was the main motive, then, not burglary?" asked Wilenski.

"Yeah, I do, as well as burglary. Here's another thing: why do you think they killed the black dude with a club, or whatever, rather than a shotgun?"

"Maybe whoever did it was afraid the shot might be heard. Or maybe it was the third guy who had the shotgun and that was the only way they could kill him."

Lanslow frowned. "Damn! That third guy keeps showing up, but I can't figure out how he's mixed up in it. And I'm still thinking the black man wasn't part of the deal—at least with the others," he said. "I think he stumbled into it. I'd bet that the murder was the main motive. The Lunzer kid inherits the money. It's like you said: he gets some people to do the job; he furnishes the map, or at least lets them know where the key is. Somehow, the black guy gets the diagram, shows up at the wrong time. They murder him, find the woman, abduct her and abscond with the money and jewelry."

"By boat?" asked Wilenski.

Lanslow's brain was whirring now. "No, probably by automobile. The guy's tracks were followed to the driveway."

"Meaning he was the one who abducted the woman? By automobile?"

"How else can you explain it?"

"They were working with both a car and a boat?"

"That's the way it looks to me," said Lanslow."

"What do you think happened to the boat?"

Lanslow shook his head. "Hell if I know. It's like everything else in this case. Just goddamned crazy. I find it hard to believe the third guy, the one who left the track in the house, was working alone," he said, as an afterthought. "They had to be working together. It's highly unlikely that a bunch of strangers just showed up on the same night to murder the Lunzers and burglarize their house."

He was silent for a moment. He stared off into space, his fingers drumming on his desk. Wilenski was looking hard at his notes.

"Did Lunzer tell you about the man he saw running off the island when he was coming home?"

Lanslow looked at Wilenski sharply. "No, he didn't. When did he say that? What about him?"

"Sorry," said Len. "I thought he'd told you. Anyway, Lunzer said he caught sight of this man in his headlights running off to the side of the bridge to the island when he was returning home this morning. Couldn't remember anything about him, 'cept he thinks he was short and stocky and had black hair. Couldn't give me anything more."

"Well, hell, that sure helps!" Lanslow picked up a pencil and flipped it across his desktop against the wall.

"Maybe he's the one who left that track inside," said Wilenski, carefully, aware of Lanslow's exasperation.

Lanslow shrugged. "We'll check it out," he said. "Someone else might have seen him, too." He got up from his chair. He began to do some stretches and squats, Wilenski watching him intently. Pretty soon

Wilenski got up and started doing stretches and squats.

"What the hell are you doing?" Lanslow asked, stopping in mid motion.

"Just trying to see if it helps."

"Well, does it?"

"Nope." He went back to his chair.

Lanslow sat back down, too, a small smile on his lips. "All right, let's go over it again," he said. "The track at the foot of the bed in the bedroom was probably the murderer's. It was different from those on the beach. We have three sets of tracks on the beach. One of the guys who made them is dead, the other two went to the dock and apparently left the scene by boat across the lake. There was no sign of the first guy's track leading to the dock. He must have been working alone or left behind by the others or was there earlier. He must have been the one to get the key and that's why it's gone. My guess is he's the one who murdered the Lunzers, abducted the woman and left the island with her by automobile."

"You think he was working alone?"

"No, but the other perp, or perps, whoever he or they were, sure didn't leave any evidence."

"What about the others? Where do they fit in?"

Lanslow shook his head. "They don't," he said. "It's a puzzle."

"Maybe they were all in it together, to commit murder and burglarize the home. The black guy is with them; he has all the info; he's a look out. They enter the house, kill the Lunzers, burglarize the home, abduct the woman, have a falling out with the black man or whatever, kill him, two escape by boat across the lake, the other one takes off by vehicle. Maybe the whole scheme went bad, somehow, and everybody got away however they could. Or maybe there was an arrangement to meet somewhere later."

"Well, okay. We'll have to go with something like that for now till we prove different," said Lanslow. "One thing's for sure: that diagram points to an inside job."

"Damned strange," Wilenski said, "but that's what seems to have happened. If this is an inside job, then the first thing we're gonna have to do is find out whose gonna profit from this. I've got a hunch we'll be taking a lot closer look at the kid."

"Oh, yeah, no doubt about that," said Lanslow, picking up his notebook and turning the pages. "I'll bet ten to one he stands to inherit the parent's fortune."

Lanslow's phone rang. He lifted the receiver and answered, listened for a moment. "Okay, Chief. Welcome back. We're writing our reports," he said, looking at Wilenski. He listened for a moment then said, "Okay, Chief. We'll see you later." He placed the phone in its cradle then remembered he should call Laura.

"Chief's in?" asked Wilenski. "How was Florida?"

"His plane just landed, and he didn't say," said Lanslow. He dialed his home number and Agnes answered. "Agnes? This is Richard. Laura's still not there?"

"No, she hasn't shown up yet."

"Well … okay … I'm sure she'll be home any minute. It looks like I won't be able to make it until quite late, though. If Laura doesn't get home soon, give me a call."

Agnes didn't answer. He just heard the abrupt click of the phone dropped back in the cradle and noticed his partner making as if he hadn't heard a thing.

*\*\**

The case was well over sixteen hours old when Lanslow drove home. It was 9:00 P.M. He was only a couple of blocks away when the cell phone he kept in his car rang. It was Agnes, and Laura had not yet returned from work.

As he approached the door to their apartment, he could hear Melanie crying.

"I'm really sorry, Agnes," he said, taking Melanie from her arms, cradling her against his shoulder, patting her back. "There, there, little one. What are you crying for? Papa's home now." He turned to Agnes. "Did Laura say anything about being late this morning?"

"No, sir, she didn't," said Agnes, pulling on her coat, not saying another word and not looking at him.

Melanie had stopped crying. She had her thumb in her mouth. "Did you feed her?"

"Yes, she ate some peas and green beans I fixed. Her bottle is on the kitchen counter. It may need to be warmed."

"All right, Agnes. Thanks for staying. I'm sorry."

She turned toward him. "It wouldn't be a big deal if I knew, Mr. Lanslow, like I said. My husband likes his dinner at six and we have plans of our own, sometimes, you know."

"Yes, I know. You know what our jobs are like, Agnes, mine even more than Laura's. I never know when I can come home. Laura ... well, her school is out by three, she usually stays after, but she's supposed to get home no later than four-thirty or so as you know. It's just been lately that she seems to be so busy. We're just grateful that you've agreed to stay."

"I know, I know, sir," said Agnes, softening slightly. "Like I say, just let me know ahead of time and I can work it out, usually."

"We'll try not to let it happen again, Agnes. Promise."

Agnes's mouth set tightly once again. She opened the door and left.

Lanslow went to the kitchen with Melanie still in his arms, her head over his shoulder, and picked up her bottle, squirted a bit of the milk onto his hand. It was too cold. He placed the bottle in the microwave oven on low for just a few moments, lifting her over his head and rolling her from side to side while the bottle warmed. She smiled at him now and he kissed her roundly on the cheeks. It seemed only yesterday that Melanie had been born. But, he calculated, it was a year and a half ago now.

"You hold on now, little Mel. We're gonna give you your bottle in just a minute."

He took the bottle from the microwave, shook it vigorously, again squirted some milk on his hand. It was warm enough. As he entered the living room, he noticed the message light on the phone blinking. Agnes had probably not heard it. Holding Melanie and the bottle with one arm he punched the play button. It was Laura's voice saying she'd been held up at school, that she needed to stop by, too, on the way home for some groceries, but would be home as soon as she could. Her voice was hurried.

Not bothering to remove his jacket, Lanslow sat down in the living room, in the Queen Ann chair, cradling Melanie in his arms and fed her. He watched her face as she took the bottle hungrily and stared up at him with beautiful blue eyes, Laura's eyes. It was a complete surprise to him that he could feel the way he did about this little girl, loving her with all his heart. He hadn't thought about having children much, hadn't known what it would mean to him. As the baby drank, his thoughts turned to the message on the phone, to Laura's voice. He had always loved her voice. He loved everything about her, her mannerisms, the way she held herself, the expressions on her face. Already, he saw some of Laura's facial features in Melanie's face and it pleased him immensely.

But he didn't believe Laura's story. He felt a twinge in his gut.

The lights from an automobile entering the parking lot swept over the sheer curtains and Lanslow rose to look out, checking if it was Laura, but the car was different and passed on by. Melanie had stopped sucking the bottle, though it remained in her mouth and her eyes were closed. Lanslow took her gently into the baby's room and laid her in her crib. She protested and rolled over, pulling herself up by the sides, holding her arms up for him. Reluctantly, he put her back down and, luckily, she immediately put her thumb in her mouth again and began to settle down. He patted her back gently, then stood there looking down at her for a moment till he was sure she was going to sleep. In the dim light from the hallway, he looked at his watch. It was now nearly ten. He removed his jacket and hung it in the closet, then removed his gun and placed it in his dresser drawer in the bedroom. There was no reason for Laura to be this late.

The anxiety he'd felt when he first got home had subsided somewhat while he was taking care of Melanie. Now, the apartment was silent and he felt very alone, trying to understand the situation. He sat for a moment in the lounge chair before the TV, its screen dark, the room dark, too, except for the light from the kitchen. He stared at the sheer curtains covering the doors to the patio-deck, hoping he would see the lights of Laura's car brush across them as she entered the parking lot. But another ten minutes passed and Laura still had not come home. He looked at the phone, trying to decide if he should call. After a moment, he picked up the phone and dialed the number to Laura's school.

## Chapter Five

Asound snapped Colin Haskell's eyes open. He lay there in the bed, in the darkness, assessing where he was, trying to determine if he was really in prison. But he had been dreaming, the pillow damp with his sweat. His eyes adjusted. He turned,searching for his wife's form on the other side of the bed. He could barely make it out. She appeared to be sound asleep.

He rolled back on his side and looked through the open bedroom door up the hallway, illumined slightly by the orange night-light. He studied the shadows intently and thought he could see the outlines of some-one standing there. He lay quite still, trying to make out the form. There was no movement, however, nothing, only the forms conjured up by his imagination. He became aware of his heartbeat, of a pain in his chest and wondered if he was having a heart attack.

He rose, slowly, leaving his robe hanging across the chair by his bed, trying not to disturb his wife, and walked to the bathroom. He was dizzy. He closed the bathroom door softly, not bothering to turn on the light, and sat down on the lid of the covered stool, running his hands through his damp hair.

In the dream, two policemen had rather roughly

handcuffed him and led him to the squad car. He observed the one policeman holding his head to protect it from bumping the car, saw himself fall off balance into the back seat, becoming merely a blurry patchwork shadow through the glare of the squad car's rear window. He watched the whole scene as if he was having an out-of-body experience, observing all that happened to his organic self from on high. The police hadn't even given him time to put on his coat. In the dream, he was suddenly in a cell, a huge inmate towering over him, telling him he wasn't too pretty but he would do.

Colin looked at the clock on the wall. It was 5:00 A.M. He had to get back to bed, get some sleep, but it would be useless. When George Lunzer hadn't shown up at the office yesterday morning Colin called the Lunzer home and was told of the Lunzer's death. He'd gotten the shakes at the news and left the office to just drive around. It hadn't helped.

He was wondering now what he could have been thinking. How could he have been so foolish? While on a trip to Las Vegas he had reached the conclusion that there was no other way out. He'd driven out into the desert, pulled the .38 from the glove compartment, even held it to his head, but he couldn't do it.

He went back to the casino, had gotten drunk and then he'd met this man, had made what he thought at the time was an innocuous inquiry. They had talked. The man had made it all seem so easy. The man had assured him it could be done, for a price, of course, but he could take care of it, not to worry. The arrangement was made.

It all seemed so ridiculous now, unreal. A low moan escaped Haskell's lips. He sat there in the darkness, bathed in the ambient light from the clock, still trembling, still sweating, his head cradled in his hands.

*** 

Juanita Valenzuela lay on the mattress on the floor, staring at a spot on the ceiling, barely visible in the dim morning light. She'd been awake now for several minutes, remembering her dream. In the dream, she had been carried back to Mexico, to the poor barrio and the little house in which she had lived before leaving over a month ago to cross the border into the U.S. She had seen her parent's house plainly again in the dream, the tile roof, the attached kitchen built of cane stalks, the single window where she could look out at the plum trees in the orchard. And she had seen herself kneeling once again at the hearth, uncovering the ashes of last night's fire and fanning the still-glowing pieces of charcoal into flame.

Altogether it had not been an unpleasant dream and she found herself now half-wishing she was back. But there had been a man in the dream, too, towering over her bed, a shadowy figure, his face hidden. He kept trying to remove her clothing, to make love to her, but then something would happen and she would be transported somewhere else, doing something different.

Juanita wondered what this part of her dream meant, because she firmly believed dreams had meaning and could possibly forecast the future. That part of her dream, the part she couldn't understand, left her unsettled and she wanted to erase it from her consciousness and to think of other things.

A movement beside her interrupted her thoughts. Jimmy lay with his partially bare back to her, his breathing deep and thick, his head turned toward the east wall of their tiny bedroom. The light cotton blanket, their only cover, was now tucked beneath his right arm and Juanita could see, in the brightening light, one brown foot protruding.

Was it really only a month or so ago now that she and Jimmy had met as strangers in the little group that had been assembled and smuggled across the border into Arizona? And now, here they were, in Minnesota, sleeping together in this little trailer home, as if they were married—which they planned to do in the near future anyway—if they could make a go of it. Juanita crossed herself in the semidarkness. That was a big "if." Especially now that she had been fired from her job.

Juanita's thoughts turned to the scene from the day before yesterday, of George Lunzer confronting her with the video of her riffling through Sophia Lunzer's dresser drawers, of her lifting and trying on the ring, of her slipping the ring inside the pocket of her frock, of her furtive look around, as if to check that no one had seen her when all along the camera's eye had recorded her every movement.

"*Injusto*, unfair," she whispered to herself, as Jimmy stirred again. She thought how lucky they had been so far to make it into the U.S., to have found shelter in this trailer home, for her to have gotten a job already, and then how she had risked everything for a ring.

Other memories of yesterday came to her, after she'd lied to Jimmy about her losing her job, how she'd told him that George Lunzer had come on to her and that was the reason she wouldn't go back, and the stricken look on Jimmy's face when he stalked out the door and didn't return until nearly daybreak, his shoes soaked and muddy and his trousers wet. And he wouldn't speak.

Jimmy turned over, looking at Juanita, his face half

buried in the pillow. He reached a brown hand to her cheek and pushed away her black hair.

"*Eres despierto*," Juanita said.

"¿Cuándo es?," Jimmy replied. "What time is it?"

"Nearly eight. You've been restless," she said. "You haven't slept. Why have you come home so late?"

"I slept some ... a little."

"I felt you awake, moving. Is there anything wrong?"

"Nothing wrong, Juanita, nothing wrong. *volver a dormirse*, go back to sleep."

\*\*\*

As he drove to the crime scene, Lanslow knew he should be focusing on the case as he usually would have, but his thoughts wandered. An early snow had fallen overnight but only an inch or so, and it was already melting as the sun climbed higher.

Laura hadn't gotten home until after ten. He sat in the living room waiting, growing angrier and more anxious each grinding minute. When she'd arrived, he immediately demanded an explanation as to why she was so late, not even giving her time to take off her coat and gloves, or put the sack of groceries on the kitchen counter, and she'd repeated her message: some parents had insisted on detaining her after school; she'd stopped for groceries, the store had been busy with shoppers, she'd had to wait in line.

He knew she was lying and told her so and she had reacted by going into a huff, as if she were the one who should be offended. She'd sat across the room, silent, her legs crossed, one leg kicking up and back.

Looking at her more closely than he'd done for several months, she seemed changed, a different person than he'd known. She was looking at him coldly, a look he'd never seen from her, and it really hurt.

"What is it, Laura, what's going on?" he'd asked, finally.

"I don't know what you're talking about," she'd said.

"I called the school, Laura. The janitor said there hadn't been anyone at the school for hours."

She looked straight at him, the cold look again. "You were checking on me?"

"Laura, it was after ten when you got home. I was worried."

"I left you a message. I tried to call you again. The phone was busy."

Again he knew it was a lie. And now, driving to Manitou Island, he began to remember other things about his wife that were different. He remembered that Laura was wearing a very low cut blouse that morning and a tight skirt that hugged her well-shaped butt and stopped well above her knees. These were clothes he'd never seen her wear to work. And she had begun to spend a lot more time before the mirror, more time looking at herself from different angles, more time with her make up, and now that he thought about it, she'd seemed more eager lately to leave the house and get to school.

After he had confronted her, she had admitted stopping by a restaurant with some other teachers, "just talking shop and having a drink to unwind," she'd said, but once again he hadn't believed her and she had turned even colder, sitting silently, stone faced, swinging her foot, not looking at him, and they hadn't spoken a single word for the rest of the evening.

He'd been unable to sleep much until the early morning hours. The last thought he'd had before falling into a hard sleep was that his wife was having an affair and in his dreams he saw her making love with other men, and then the dead faces of the Lunzers loomed up and began talking to him, begging him to find their killer.

When he arrived at the island bridge, Wilenski, in his usual jeans and suede jacket, was waiting, standing beside a uniformed patrolman. For a moment Lanslow felt jealous of this young man, good looking, still relatively eager and innocent. He felt himself growing jaded already, at age thirty-four, and that occurred to him to be absolutely ridiculous, and it made him even angrier.

Wilenski slid into the car.

"They're dragging already?" Lanslow asked.

"They're out there," Wilenski said. "No luck yet. That water is getting cold, and it's deep."

"I'll bet," said Lanslow, smothering his anger, trying to turn to the task at hand. He wondered how Laura could ever think she'd be able to keep the guy's identity a secret—from a detective, for god's sake!

\*\*\*

Jimmy Jiminez sat up on the mattress, searched for his jeans and, unable to find them, arose and pulled a clean pair from the cardboard box he used as his "chest of drawers." He could hear Juanita in the kitchen. He couldn't find his shirt, either, so he slipped on a white undershirt and ambled into the small dining area and sat down heavily at the folding card-table he and Juanita used to set their meals.

"Where's my pants and shirt?" Jimmy asked, mopping back his black hair. He was short, but stocky and barrel-chested, and very brown in contrast to Juanita.

"I'm going to wash them. They were dirty. Where

were you last night? Why did you come home so late?"

Jimmy glanced at Juanita obliquely. "With my friends," he mumbled. "We played some cards."

"Your clothes were wet and your shoes were muddy."

"We went out in a boat on a lake, to catch some fish."

Juanita looked at Jimmy intently. "To fish?" she said. "It's too cold to fish." She hadn't known Jimmy that long but she'd learned now that he wasn't a very good liar. His tale was preposterous.

"You've lost your job. We have to eat."

"Where's the fish?"

"We didn't catch none."

"Jimmy, I'll find another job. You will find work."

"*Gané algún dinero anoche* (I won some money, last night)," Jimmy said, switching from English to Spanish. "*Tout à fait un peu, je pense. Il nous tiendra pour un moment.*(Quite a bit, I think. It will hold us for awhile.)"

Juanita stared at Jimmy again for a moment. "You think? Don't you know how much? Can't you count?"

He merely looked away as he was prone to do, she'd learned, signaling that the conversation was over. She turned back to the stove and dished up a plate of eggs and tortillas and placed them on the card table, got the salt and pepper shakers from the cabinet and placed them alongside his plate. She sat down then, across from Jimmy, and stared out the window.

"You ate?" Jimmy asked.

"I'll eat later," she said.

Later, When Jimmy had gone, saying he had to meet a friend but would be back in a couple of hours, Juanita heard the news on the radio of the murders of George Lunzer and his wife, Sophia, in their own home, in their bed. The sister, Jacqueline, was missing. Her baby, left behind, was okay, in the hands of relatives.

Juanita was standing at the kitchen sink. Her knees nearly buckled. She tried to understand what she'd heard. Finally, she simply sat down on one of the kitchen chairs and held her head in her hands for a few moments and wailed silently inside. Then she went to the bedroom and began to pack clothes in the battered old suitcases they'd used when they'd crossed the border.

"Jimmy, Jimmy," she whispered to herself, "*El loco, el loco.*"

***

The phone on the other end rang six times before the man in the phone booth got an answer.

"Did you read the papers this morning?" he asked. "The job is done."

"I read the papers," said the voice on the other end. "God damn it, this wasn't part of the deal! How the hell did Jacqueline become a part of this? And who the hell is that black man they found?"

"She was there. You said they'd be alone."

"She wasn't supposed to be there."

"Well, she was, and we have her."

"What?"

"We have her."

"What the ... you have her? What do you mean you have her? What the hell is going on?"

"Well, my man, we got to thinking. Seems a guy like you with a lot of money ought to be willing to pay a little more for the job since there's a woman and a little baby involved. Know what I mean?"

"We? What do you mean, we? You brought someone else in on this? Who? Was it the black guy?"

"Just my partner. You don't know him. Now, about the money ..."

"But why did you take Jackie? What have you done with her? You're nothing but an animal! What the hell have you done with her?"

"She's being taken care of. Not to worry. We'll let her go if you can just give us a little more, ah, incentive, you know? Otherwise ... well, we'll just have to take care of things, if you get my drift."

"Incentive? You got your money and you'll get the rest. What are you talking about?"

"Well, like I said, a little more cash wouldn't hurt."

"I'm not going to pay another red cent more than we agreed on! You hear me? Not another red cent!"

"'Scuse me, big shot, but did you hear what I said? We're not playin' 'round here. You ain't got no choice. We're going to kill the woman, dump her right in the cop's lap with a little note about you if you don't come up with a little more money. You dig, man?" There was a long pause. "Hey, man! You there?"

"How much? How much more do you want? I don't have a lot of money, contrary to what scum like you might think."

"Ah, big shot, the name calling is unnecessary. We know you got money, so don't shit around on us."

"How much, damn it! How much?"

"We were thinking a little round figure, like fifty-thousand might do the trick. Yeah, I think that'd do the job."

"You son of a bitch! We had a deal. You'll get what I owe you and not a penny more. You bastard! I don't have that kind of money available now. I can't even raise that kind of money."

"Like I said, man, you ain't got no choice. We'll give you till tonight. You get the additional money, you're free and clean. We'll let the woman go. She'll never know it was you, and the cops won't, either. But you gotta get the money. Now, do we get the money or do I just hang up here?"

"Wait... wait ... uh, I'll have to see what I can do."

"Much better, man. Much better. Remember: tonight. I'll be in contact then. "

"Wait! It's Saturday, God damn it! The banks are closed by noon. There are things I have to do to arrange this. I can't possibly get the money today, or tomorrow either, on a Sunday."

The man on the other end of the phone paused. Then he said, "What kind of things?"

"I have to contact some people. It's not just a matter of getting the money out of an account. There are arrangements that have to ..."

"Why can't you contact them now if you don't need the bank? There's no other way?"

"No. No. I have to use the bank but I can only get the money from these other arrangements. It's not so easy. I can get it but you have to give me time."

There was another long pause. "Okay," said the voice. "We'll wait till Monday ... Monday morning. You'd better not be shitting me. You hear?"

"What are you going to do with Jaqueline? If one hair on her head is harmed, I'll come after you."

The man on the phone just laughed. "We'll turn her loose. I'll call, give you instructions—and don't even think of bringing the cops in on this! You do, and you won't even be able to recognize her. *Entiendes Senor?* You get what I'm saying here?"

"Yes. Yes. I understand. I'll have the money by Monday. I'll wait for your call."

The man in the phone booth hung up. He turned to the other person standing just outside the booth and signaled thumbs up. "*Que va por ella,*" he said. "He's going for it!

# Chapter Six

The throbbing in her temples woke her. The spot where she'd hit her forehead as she had been thrown to the floor was still tender. There was a bump there. She'd learned that lying still kept the pain down. She turned her head a little, testing. She glanced at the stove, turned dark now. A chill had reclaimed the room. She tried to burrow deeper in the sagging bed. The red letters on the clock read 7:45. She guessed it was morning. Her thoughts returned to earlier events.

The man hadn't raped her as she thought he would. She'd thought he would kill her, too, but he'd only stood over her for a few moments, saying nothing, while she looked up at him in terror. He had something in his hands. He had turned on the overhead light and she saw that he carried a bucket and some sticks of wood. He sat the bucket next to the bed and opened the stove door and poked the wood inside. He had a fire going after a few moments.

"If you have to go to the bathroom when I'm not here," he'd said, pointing to the bucket, "this will serve as a pot. Otherwise, when I'm here, you can use the bathroom upstairs. You'll have to call me." His voice was a sonorous baritone.

She'd nodded ever so slightly, her eyes wide with

fear, fixed upon his face. She could not help but notice his appearance. On his upper lip was a moustache, and his lower jaw and chin were covered with a shaggy beard, roughly in the shape of a goatee. The rest of his face showed a short, week-old stubble. But it was the man's eyes that Jacqueline focused upon. He wore eyeglasses with square lenses and partial rims at the top. His eyes were brown and hooded, his look insolent and resentful.

"I'm going to leave you down here for now," the man had said. "I'll untie you but you shouldn't try to get away. There's no way out of here. I'll take you upstairs later, maybe. Let you walk around."

The tone of his voice, his demeanor, took away some of her terror. She looked at him more closely. Apart from the eyes, the man gave no appearance of abnormality, of psychic aberrancy, as far as she could recognize such things. In the dim light she got the impression of a medium-sized man with dark hair parted and combed to the side, a shock of it hanging over the middle of his forehead. A heavy collared sweater covered a black turtleneck shirt. His light-blue jeans were worn almost white at the baggy knees, but not frayed, and their length stretched well down over an unpolished pair of brown, scuffed, shoes. Her fear subsided a little further.

The fire in the stove had still been burning then and the overhead light was still on. She'd assessed her surroundings. There was a table with two hard-back chairs, and the objects on the table appeared to be books and some brown cardboard boxes. Near the back of the room it was darker and she could make out nothing other than empty space and shadows.

She remembered that he had pulled back the blanket and a jolt of terror shot through her. She was still wearing the sky-blue cotton flannel pajamas she'd had on when she was abducted. But he had sat down on the edge of the bed and proceeded only to remove the gag from her mouth and untie her, slowly and laboriously, for the cords had been pulled tight. It seemed to her he had lingered a little too long, fiddling with the knots, and with her hands in his. When her hands and feet were free he had rubbed her wrists and ankles and she did not protest. She could merely watch, her throat dry with alarm, but, at the same time, the relief was immense.

When he was done he had stood and looked at her once again. "I don't have any women's clothing," he said. "Perhaps I can pick up something later. I'll bring down a pair of sweat pants that might fit, and a sweatshirt." He turned to go, then turned back.

"Remember," he said, "it'll do you no good to try to

escape. You should try and get some sleep."

"Where am I?" she'd asked, tremulously. "What have you done to my baby?"

"No questions now," he said. "I'm in a hurry. I'll be back soon. You should just rest now."

He'd cut her off and left, turning off the light, enveloping the room in darkness once again. She heard him lock the door and then heard sounds only of quick steps, above, and, later, of what must have been a door slamming, a sound she'd heard before, and then silence.

She had immediately struggled up and groped her way toward where she thought the light switch was. She felt dizzy and nauseous but she kept on. She managed to find the switch and turned the light on. She was afraid to try the door because she didn't know whether the man was still around. She went back down the stairs and carried a chair from the table to where she could get up to what she could see plainly now as a window. It was, of course, locked, not only from the inside but, apparently, outside, too, and she saw bars just outside the windowpane. She could also see what appeared to be a black shiny fabric of some kind that had been stretched and fastened over the window outside on the exterior of the house. It had small holes in it, allowing pinpoints of light. The bars puzzled her, for she hadn't heard anything resembling their installation while she lay in the bed. They must have already been there when she arrived and she wondered with horror if she was in some terrible place where the capture of women was the routine. She thought that the dark covering over the exterior of the window might be to conceal the bars from strangers. She thought about breaking the glass but feared the sound—and then there was the coldness outside, and it would, besides, do her no good.

She had replaced the chair at the table and summoned the courage to ascend the stairs once again and try the doorknob delicately. It was locked firmly. She wandered to the other side of the room but it was windowless, nothing but solid concrete block walls all around, painted a sickly green. The rear of the room—the area where before, from her bed, she could only make out shadow—she discovered, was merely a hard packed earthen floor, as if the builder had run out of cement before he had finished.

She'd returned to her bed, disconsolate, leaving the light on. She had to think.

But her thoughts were muddled. Her mind was awhirl. Throughout the remainder of the night she lay awake, sobbing, anguishing over what may have happened to her baby and parents and fearing the man's return. His face kept insinuating itself into her thoughts along with feelings of fear and grief. Sometime near morning, she must have fallen asleep.

She looked at the clock again. It read 7:59. She heard a door slam above and heard footsteps. A short time passed during which she could again hear someone moving about the house. The door to the basement opened and once more she saw the man descending the stairs. He was again carrying something, a tin tray, and clothing draped over an arm, a pair of sweat pants and a sweatshirt. He set the tray on the table. He approached her, tossing the clothing on the bed. "You can put these on later, if you wish."

Before she could resist he pulled her to a sitting position on the side of the bed. She felt the strength of his hands and arms, felt as though she were a doll in his grasp. She thought it would happen now; he would rape her.

But he returned to the table and brought her the tray. There was a bowl of oatmeal cereal, with a plastic spoon, and he'd provided a cup of milk and sugar and a glass of orange juice. He set the tray on the side of the bed.

"Eat," he said. "I'll be back."

"Please," she said, in desperation, "I need to know what's happened to my baby, Erica. What have you done ...?"

But he turned and was up the stairs again before she could finish. She heard him set the lock, heard another door slam and it was quiet above. She continued sitting on the edge of the bed for a moment, chastising herself because she hadn't persisted in finding out what had happened to Erica. His hooded eyes, the sullen look, frightened her.

She rose, leaving the tray of food where it sat and quickly took the sweats from the bed and pulled them on over her pajamas. She eyed the food on the tray. She sat back down and lifted the spoon from the bowl and tentatively tasted the lukewarm oatmeal and found herself ravenously hungry. She poured the milk over the oatmeal and spooned in some sugar, then downed the orange juice and drank the remainder of the milk.

When she finished, she took the tray and set it back on the table. She took time to observe the stack of books and boxes atop the table, noting a very large volume of "The Complete Works of William Shakespeare," and another smaller volume of "The Taoist Iching." Acutely aware of the pain of movement and, growing dizzy again, she looked no further and crawled back into bed.

She pulled the cover over her, up to her neck and listened for any sound from above even as she feared hearing it. The long ride, tied as she had been and covered to almost suffocation, had taken its toll. Her head throbbed and her wrists still ached from being bound and she also had a deep pain in her lower back from lying in an awkward position against something very hard. The overly soft, sagging mattress upon which she lay was not helping either. She moaned and involuntarily drew her legs upward to her chest, only to experience a sharp nausea. She gasped and lay still and the nausea subsided, but only a little. Some time passed and despite her pain and fear, she fell into a half-sleep.

She was still asleep when he returned. She had no idea of how long she'd slept. The light was still on. She glanced at the clock. It read 10:00. She'd learned that when there was no red dot showing on the face of the clock it was morning.

He was carrying some wood, which he placed in the old stove, its door creaking as he opened and closed it. Jacqueline watched in consternation. The pain in her body and head wasn't getting any better. When he had the fire going once more he said, "I was low on wood. I hope the fire will make you more comfortable." He took the tray from the table and started to make his way back up the stairs.

"I'm in a lot of pain," she ventured, timorously.

He turned back. "I may have some medicine—some

pain reliever—upstairs," he said. "I'll have to check."

"Thank you," she said, but again he was already on his way back up the stairs.

Again, he had left the light on. She continued lying in the bed, staring at the bare floor joists above, wondering why he hadn't kept her tied. But it occurred to her she was physically powerless against him anyway. And she couldn't escape this basement, which was obviously designed to either keep people in or out. Clearly, too, he wasn't concerned with any noise she might make to try to alert neighbors or visitors. She thought the place she was in must be remote. Her assessment of her situation was at best foreboding and her hopes were crumbling and she began to tremble once again.

*** 

Viewing her face carefully in the mirror, Laura Lanslow searched her image for anything that might be deemed of note, maybe beautiful, even. Actually, she thought her face was at best ordinary. Apparently the man she had been seeing didn't think so, however. It was a surprise to her when he told her so, in the doctor's office, when they were alone a couple of months or so ago. The kiss that followed, that she had, surprisingly, allowed, excited her even now, to say nothing of the thrill of what happened a few days later.

She was in the kitchen, in front of the full-length mirror on the wall with Melanie's little handprints all over it. She turned slowly, viewing her full image, noting the smooth slope of her hips to her thighs, her thighs to her legs. Maybe not so bad, she thought. She remembered the man's smell, the feel of him, the absolute excitement. She shivered, though the room was quite warm. She became aware that she was peculiarly cold, trembling even. Not peculiar, though, when she thought about it. Truth was, she was trembling with dread, dread of what might lie in her future, of what might happen in her marriage. The thought of it left her nearly ill.

Why had she, would she (for she knew she would again), risk her marriage? She knew why. She was searching for something desperately, and she thought she knew what it was: she'd psychoanalyzed herself. All she wanted was someone to love, someone to love her, a love she felt she'd lost long ago when her father had left home and her parents were divorced, a craving that had lasted all her life.

Sarah, her mother, with whom she'd lived following the divorce, became obsessed with her own problems and often-lapsed into deep depression. Laura had missed her father terribly and had felt completely alone. She wanted more, too—companionship, romance and excitement—and, perhaps most of all, happiness.

Not that this knowledge was any great surprise, really. These had appeared to be such simple things a little over two years ago, and she'd thought she had found them with her marriage to Richard Lanslow and the subsequent birth of their daughter. That day, the day of her marriage, was the happiest of her life. Later, it was true, his job seemed to claim too much of his time, but she had managed to overlook it for a while. Melanie, for one thing, demanded a lot of attention. And at first there *was* love and companionship and certainly romance. At first she was happy. But over time, something went missing. Slowly, bitterly, love, companionship, happiness, and even romance faded and she realized even the afterglow was now gone—and perhaps she had made the biggest mistake of her life.

Captured by this desperate thought, she went about her chores in a kind of daze. Idly she plucked the dishcloth from behind the faucet where Richard kept putting it despite her admonitions to hang it across the divider in the sink—and this was just one of the many little things that had begun to irritate her increasingly about him—and she turned back to the mirror and began wiping the hand-prints off.

Melanie was asleep, taking her afternoon nap.

As she cleaned, she thought again how surprised she'd been at the ease with which she could have fallen out of love (if love was what it had been); at how her love for Richard Lanslow could tumble so effortlessly before the many little things that had grown to exasperate her: the way he sometimes ate his food so quickly and, on the other hand, his penchant for neatness and orderliness raised to a near-phobia; his constant rearranging the knick-knacks and decorator pieces around the house; his taste in music (the crooners of the 40s and 50s, or rhythm and blues—she liked rock and roll and the classics); his preferences in books and poetry (Steinbeck, Hemingway and Yeats—she liked Nicholas Sparks and Dickinson); and movies ("Apocalypse Now" versus "Terms of Endearment"); and, above all, his general pessimism and cynicism toward life. She'd loved his seemingly perpetual smile when she first met him, but she found these other characteristics, like shadows, lying behind the outward appearance.

She could, she supposed, forgive him these characteristics because he was a policeman. But that was another thing: how on God's earth could she have married a policeman, now that she thought about it? It was nearly the same exclamation her mother had made over the phone when she learned of their plans. She recounted: She and Richard had no social life; She found herself alone with Melanie ninety percent of the time; Richard's friends were not her friends and vice versa. And when he was on a case it seemed all he could think about was that case and he would go off into his own little world for days at a time — and that seemed to be happening more frequently.

She carefully folded the dishcloth and draped it over the middle of the sink, got a dishtowel and dried the mirror off.

Sarah, her mother, had warned her bluntly, as she was prone to do when giving advice: "A policeman, Laura, for God's sake? A policeman?" she'd said. Thank God Sarah wasn't here now to harp on her. She had been right. But they, she and Richard, had been full of and blinded by infatuation then, and even though she'd tasted early (during their engagement, while living together) what it could be like to be the wife of a policeman, she'd pushed her reservations aside and had somehow found herself married to one. And now, she had a little daughter that she loved with all her heart, a fact that made her situation all the worse, if that made any sense whatever. Truth was, she and her husband were practically leading separate lives and—she admitted it—she was thinking of divorce. Melanie only complicated things.

And then there was this other man ...

\*\*\*

Lanslow and Wilenski returned to the Lunzer home to do another walk through. It was nearing 2:00 P.M. Dragging of the lake had been called off temporarily due to cold. Strung together at even intervals tied to a nylon rope, the divers had searched out from the shore nearly two hundred feet around the shoreline and found nothing but tree limbs, tin cans, bottles, rubber tires, minnow buckets and even a fishing rod. But there was no body, and Lanslow suspected there wouldn't be one. The missing information they needed to fill out their theory was in the Lunzer mansion, Lanslow thought. They would call for divers again later if the other leads didn't materialize. In the meantime, they had also asked the Washington and Ramsey County sheriff's offices to conduct searches of the surrounding areas of swampland and woods and along highways, both on the ground and from the air.

Lanslow stuck a key in the lock on the Lunzer's front door and went inside, followed by Wilenski. The house was warm, too warm for the detective. He wondered where the thermostat was. It was eerily quiet.

The facets of a magnificent glass chandelier reflected the low afternoon light.

Lanslow noticed a Lysol odor, mixed with a heavy lilac-scent, in the room, as though someone had been freshly cleaning, which alarmed him for a moment, fearing that someone had tried to clean up the place despite his admonitions not to disturb anything. He looked around closely. In the living room, where the major activities of the party had occurred, the streamers still hung from the ceiling, the masks and horns and balloons still lay in their former positions. Tumblers and goblets were still sitting where the guests had left them, all now covered with fingerprint powder, as were most of the other surfaces throughout the house. On the large piano were loose sheets of music, these, too, covered in a fine dust. As far as Lanslow could tell, the clutter from the masquerade party lay as it had been on their first walk-through and the crime scene remained intact. It would stay that way until he was sure they had mined every clue.

"Let's get to work," he said.

"Where should we start?" Wilenski asked.

"Let's take another look in George Lunzer's office, see what might turn up."

The office was large, lined with built-in mahogany bookcases full of books on everything from business to philosophy and literature and numerous "self help" books. Lunzer's desk sat in front of a bow window that overlooked the backyard and the lake. A computer sat on a table beside the desk. To the far left of the room were two four-drawer file cabinets.

"I'll look through these," Wilenski said, walking to the file cabinets. With latex-gloved hands he tried the drawers, found them unlocked, and began sifting through their contents.

Lanslow sat down at George Lunzer's desk and turned the computer on. When the desktop had loaded, he clicked on a folder icon that was labeled "financial." The folder's contents contained a personal financial program. He opened it by double clicking the icon and then clicked on "reporting" in the menu bar at the top of the screen and then on "net worth." Almost instantly a report of George and Sophia Lunzer's personal assets and liabilities appeared, showing their net worth at the bottom.

Lanslow whistled through pursed lips. "Fifty-seven million," he said, more or less to himself.

Wilenski had heard him. "Fifty-seven million what?" he asked, from across the room.

"Dollars," said Lanslow. "Fifty-seven-million dollars is George and Sophia Lunzer's net worth as of this fiscal year to date."

"Hallelujah!" said Wilenski. "There's your motive, right there."

In one of the cabinet drawers, Wilenski spied a small fireproof box that was labeled "Important papers" in black felt pen. A key had been left in the keyhole and he turned it and was able to lift the lid. Inside, was a stack of papers, including birth certificates, titles to vehicles, two passports, a deed search, some bonds, and, finally, an envelope labeled "Will." He pulled the document from the envelope and scanned it quickly.

"Uh huh," he said, "guess who gets all that money."

"I'd say Sophia Lunzer, first, then their kids would share equally."

"You're right," said Wilenski, "and after mom, if either of the kids die, the other kid inherits the whole enchilada."

"And that would be Derek Lunzer at present, assuming his missing sister is dead."

"Right again—an estate worth fifty-seven-million smackers falls right into that kid's hands!"

"Including the business?" Lanslow asked.

Wilenski scanned the document once again. "Maybe not. I don't see the business reported here," he said.

"That's another possibility, then," said Lanslow. "We'll have to check out the business, see what happens to it if George Lunzer dies."

Lanslow leaned back in George Lunzer's chair, looking at the remnants of the forensic work that had been done. He began to feel overwhelmed. There would be hundreds if not thousands of items that would have to be analyzed for evidence, probably hundreds of interviews yet to be conducted, perhaps scores of leads followed, thousands of documents read, scanned and placed in the file; hundreds of reports written, and untold avenues of investigation pursued.

Len read it on his face. "We're gonna need a lot of help on this, Rich," he said.

Lanslow nodded, reluctantly. "I hate to get the BCA people in here on this," he said. "You're right, though. We're gonna need help, but I think I know where I want to try to get it first, before we go crawling to the state."

"What about the kidnapping?"

"It's not a kidnapping yet, just a missing person. And, anyway, I don't want the Feds in here either. This is our case, and we're going to be the ones to solve it. But we're gonna need a little help, and I think I know someone who fills the bill."

***

After going through as many of the Lunzer's records again, Wilenski suggested they should go through as many of Derek Lunzer's things again, too, including especially his computer. But they found nothing of any portent in Derek's files anywhere. It was clean, too clean, Lanslow thought. They would have the computer seized, however, and send it to the State Bureau of Criminal Apprehension for a search of the hard drive.

They decided to split up to do some additional interviews with neighbors. Then they returned to the station to compare notes.

The interviews had produced nothing new about George and Sophia, only the repeated gossip of a roving eye for them both. There appeared to be no problems between members of the family, though Derek was known as a wild one, his father often complaining about having to "rein him in." Jacqueline was the steady one, but it was also known that her marriage was in trouble. The Lunzers, otherwise, were well respected within their community and nothing further of any note had been reported.

After the detectives compared notes, they got a copy of the dispatcher's 911 tape and were playing it when Chief William "Bill" Bradbury walked into the room. Wilenski punched the stop button.

"How are you doing on this? Any leads?" asked Bradbury. He was tanned, even from his shortened vacation in Florida.

"We've learned that Derek Lunzer inherits a fortune with the rest of the family out of the way," said Lanslow. "Right now, he's a top suspect and we're going to hit him hard. But we need to conduct about a thousand more interviews on this, Chief, and follow up on about that many leads," Lanslow said.

Bradbury grinned. "That's all?"

"That's about it. Seriously, Chief, we need the help and I think I know just the person to do it."

"Oh, yeah? Who?"

"I'd like to get Dean Brooks back in here."

Bradbury looked at Lanslow, surprised. "Brooks? You want me to bring Brooks out of retirement?"

"We need him Chief. Len and I are not enough, even with the patrol help, and I don't know about you but I don't want this case to become the BCA's or the Feds. Not yet, anyway."

"Have you talked to him?"

"Not yet. I wanted to talk to you first. If you tell him you need him, he'll come back in, and I can't think of anyone better than Dean."

Bradbury stroked his chin. "Well, as a matter of fact, I'm getting a hell of a lot of pressure on this case already from the mayor and the council. They're, of course, afraid of the public. We need this taken care of but I don't want the other agencies in here, either, just yet. We do have the third investigative position still open. I'll think about it, Rich. Let me take a look at what we can do." He turned to leave the room.

"Thanks, Chief."

Bradbury waved a hand airily as he left. "We'll see," he said.

"I'd heard Brooks was losing it before he retired," Wilenski said.

"You heard wrong. That was the scuttlebutt, but Brooks knows what he's doing, believe me. He was with the LAPD for several years and he'll be a big help."

"How did he wind up here, anyway?"

"Wanted to come home, tone it down a little. Then Zeke was murdered."

"That's when you became partners?"

"Yeah. Couldn't have solved Zeke's case without Brooks."

Wilenski knew about Zeke Mallard's case, Lanslow's first partner, who'd been murdered in his own garage. He knew, too, about the bizarre turn that case had taken. It was a case Lanslow didn't seem to want to talk much about and Wilenski didn't press it.

"You want to listen to this again?" Wilenski asked, and Lanslow nodded.

Wilenski punched the rewind button on the tape recorder, let it run for a few moments then pressed the play button once more:

Dispatcher: White Bear Lake emergency.

Derek Lunzer: Yes, is this the police? Uh ...

Dispatcher: What's the problem?

Derek Lunzer: My name is (sobbing) ... Derek ... Lunzer, I ... "

Dispatcher: Sir, I have your name. What's the problem? What's the problem?

Derek Lunzer: (Still sobbing) My parents ... they've been shot. I came home this morning and found them. My sister, she's ...

Dispatcher: Who shot them? Are they still there?

Derek Lunzer: Yes, I think ...

Dispatcher: The people who ...

Derek Lunzer: No! Not them. My sister isn't here ... the baby ...

Dispatcher: A baby was shot? Your parents were shot?

Derek Lunzer: Morgana! Damn it! Get off ...

Second Dispatcher: Sir! What's going on? Is there someone there with you?

Derek Lunzer: No, no, it's the cat.

Dispatcher: Sir, don't get hysterical. Who is the person who was shot?

Derek Lunzer: My parents!

Second Dispatcher: All right, sir. We have your number

and address. Just hold on. We have a unit on its way. Okay?

Derek Lunzer: (Faintly) Okay.

Lanslow shut off the recorder and looked at Wilenski. "Morgana?" he said. "A cat? Not the baby?"

"No. The baby's name is Erica. Morgana is the cat," said Wilenski.

"What the hell was the cat doing?"

"She'd jumped up on the bed, according to Lunzer."

"Well for God's sake! Another suspect!"

Wilenski laughed. "A cat with a shotgun!"

Lanslow sobered. "Okay, what do you think?"

"This kid, Lunzer, drives race cars, and from what some of the neighbors have told me, he's kind of a playboy type," Wilenski said. "He doesn't strike me as the type who'd be crying on the phone, and it sounds a little phony."

"He'd just found his parents, shot, in bed."

"Yeah. I know. Still, did you notice how he got it in that he'd just returned that morning?"

"I noticed. You're right. He stands to inherit an estate of over fifty million."

"No doubt we need to find out a little more about Mr. Lunzer the younger."

At that moment, Chief Bradbury stuck his head

around the door and said, "We'll get Brooks, Rich. I'll leave it up to you to talk to him and get him in here and we'll get the paperwork done."

"Thanks, Chief. I'll take care of it."

"A couple of weeks at most, though. No more."

"You got it, Chief. Thanks."

Lanslow looked at the clock. 9:00 P.M. He'd forgotten to call Laura to tell her he couldn't make it home for dinner.

\*\*\*

The clock on the wall said 4:00 when the man came down to the cold basement once again, carrying some more clothing in his arms. The time surprised her. She must have been sleeping for all that time. She felt listless, and she wondered if he'd fed her drugs.

He placed the clothing upon the table and stoked the fire. She watched him with growing alarm, her listlessness fading. He came to the bedside where she was lying and grasped her arms and helped her upright from the bed once again. Despite her alarm she didn't resist. She felt very weak. Again, for just a moment, he held her for what she thought was an unnecessary length of time, but he released her to stand on her own.

"I'll take you upstairs for a little while," he said as

he placed a large bathrobe around her shoulders and let her sit back down to put on some heavy wool socks over the light ones she already had on. She got up and wobbled when she tried to walk, and he helped her across the floor and up the stairs—a slow process. She worried she might have suffered a concussion. She was nauseous and felt like vomiting when she stood, and she was dizzy and sometimes her vision blurred.

"I found some pain medicine in my brother's room," he said.

The steep stairway from the basement ascended directly into the kitchen. When they had labored to the top she saw a door immediately to her right and through the parted curtains on the window she could see a path that led to another adjacent building, about twenty or thirty feet away, presumably a garage. Parked in front of it was a car, though she could not tell what kind or model, or exactly what color it was. It appeared to be an old station wagon, perhaps a two-tone dark brown and tan. She could just make out an opening in the trees where she saw car tracks, disappearing around a bend. It was a road, a lane, really, barely visible.

Almost immediately to her left was a bathroom, its door partially open so that she could see a lavatory over which was a small wooden medicine cabinet with a mirror in the door. To the right side of the bathroom door there was another door, to a closet, partially open, with a coat hanging from a peg and, beneath it, a pair of high-top shoes, the ones she'd seen him wearing the first time he had come down into the basement.

He picked up a bottle from the cabinet counter and shook two pills into her hand and gave her a glass of water and she drank and swallowed the medicine. He closed the bathroom door and allowed her to relieve herself in private, though she literally quaked in fear while she was doing it. Despite her fear she took account of the room, searching desperately for something that might be of help in assisting her to escape.

The room was all male: there was a reproduced painting of a grizzly bear standing on a gravel bar at the edge of a stream, another of three wolves in a snowy birch forest, their eyes seemingly riveted on the person viewing the painting. There was a Christmas ornament of Santa Claus in fishing regalia, three large fish dangling below him, their tails wrapped around one another, hanging on the wall beside a mirror. There was nothing in all of this to possibly help her escape but she had learned something about the man who was holding her prisoner: he appeared to be an outdoorsman and she guessed she was probably the only woman around.

The kitchen was tiny. There was a row of wooden

cabinets above a short counter that ended in a stainless steel sink with one faucet. Above the sink was a relatively wide window through which she could see the forest, of birch and pine. The trees had a light snow covering and she could not help but think how beautiful they were.

The refrigerator sat next to the counter on the right of the window. On the left side of the window at the end of the counter, which turned left at a 90-degree angle, was a small apartment-sized electric stove, and near that, on the counter, was a microwave oven. On the counter top there was a wooden spool holding a roll of paper towels along with an assortment of plastic bottles containing various colors of liquids. There were no doors on the lower portion of the counter and she saw the drainpipe below, on one side, and a place for storing dishes and other things on the other. The man lived sparsely, no doubt.

He led her on through a wider doorway into the living area. Again, the furnishings were sparse, but pleasantly rustic. There was a row of French windows running around the room so that a person could look out upon a small lake, its waters now shining in the afternoon sun. There appeared to be an access road between the garage and the house leading to the lake but it was obviously seldom used. Even the light snow had nearly wiped out any sign of its existence and there were no tire tracks.

To her right, as she entered the room, was a small hallway that led back from the living room to the side and rear of the building, ending in a blank wall. As she had entered she had noticed two doors on either side of the hall, and she guessed these were the bedrooms, but the doors were closed.

Inside the living room an old grey-to-black leather couch sat perpendicular to the windows, its back pushed against the wall. At the end of the couch, near the windows, there was a round table with a lamp. The table was stacked with books. She surmised that he was a reader, too, and this was probably where he did most of his reading. She could imagine him lying there, on the couch, the light through the windows shining upon the pages.

She took it all in, absorbing the details of her prison for possible means of escape. Across from the couch was a small table covered with a checkered oilcloth of blue and white, surrounded by four metal chairs. Its surface, too, was littered with books. In the back, cen-ter of the room, to their right as they had entered the room, just before the hallway, sat a black, wood- burn-ing stove with a polished brass damper on the front of the door. A cheap and frayed short-nap carpet covered the living room floor.

He cleared away some books from the table and motioned for her to set down at one of the chairs. He returned to the kitchen and from the small refrigerator she watched him remove a covered dish. He poured milk from a cardboard carton into a plastic glass and emptied some potato chips into the dish.

She watched him closely as he set the dish and glass of milk upon the table. There were a couple of chicken legs inside. The chicken appeared to her to be from a deli, suggesting a town nearby, perhaps. She picked up one of the chicken legs and began to eat, taking the opportunity to assess the rest of her surroundings.

She looked through the multipaned windows at the small lake stretching away to her right. The water was absolutely placid, reflecting the forest around its shore. Here, in late October, the water hadn't frozen over yet. The house sat just at the east end of the lake, for she could see the fading light from the sun off to her right in the west. She noticed a high hill just across the lake, off to her left, covered in spruce, juniper, birch and aspen, the latter deciduous trees still in color though the colors had faded.

He was watching her, too.

"Taking it all in, eh?"

"Do you actually live here?" she asked. "All year round?"

He smiled slightly. "All year round," he said. "So far."

She didn't pursue the "so far" part. He gave her a blanket, for it was chilly even up here, out of the basement, and the heat was uneven and she couldn't help shivering a little. He, on the other hand, didn't seem to be affected by the cool temperature.

When she had eaten the chicken and the potato chips, he removed the dish and glass from the table and carried them to the kitchen. She hadn't finished her glass of milk and he brought it back to her.

"Finish this," he said. "You look like you need it."

She took the glass. The light outside was growing even dimmer by now but from where she sat she could see a pathway leading from a small front porch to the lake, about thirty or forty yards away, and a pile of split wood, lightly snow covered, on the shore. She could now see the rest of the other building, an unattached garage. From this different angle, she could also see that there was a red vehicle parked to the side with a tarp thrown partially over it. She shuddered. For some reason she suspected that this was the vehicle used to bring her here.

"I'll try to tend the fire a little better in the basement," he said, "keep some larger logs in the stove. And you can keep the blanket. I'll get more."

"Let me stay up here," she pleaded. "I won't try to get away."

He looked at her for a moment then smiled tightly. He was working carefully with the hot latch on the stove.

"It wouldn't do you any good if you tried to escape," he said. "You'd die in the woods on that road. No one knows you're here. No one comes out here."

"Then why do you keep me down there?"

He straightened and looked at her again. He seemed to always be looking at her.

"To keep you from trying it anyway," he said. "And to save myself the trouble of having to find your body on the road after you've died from hypothermia. Winter will be setting in up here soon. There will be a lot more snow anytime, now. The nearest neighbor or town is fifty miles away."

The way he looked at her was extremely disconcerting. She felt as though she was on a thin line, a hair's breadth from being raped and even murdered; yet his look didn't exactly support that impression. It was confusing.

She lifted the glass of milk to her lips, peering at him surreptitiously over the rim, dropping her gaze when she found his eyes still on her. She couldn't keep her hands from shaking, not just from the chilly air, but he didn't seem to notice, or chose not to speak of it. He spoke only the necessary things, in short clipped sentences.

"What are you going to do with me?" she asked.

"I can do with you what I want," he said, looking at her with amusement, a faint smile on his lips.

"Who are you? Where are we? What town were you talking about?" she asked, and again he merely smiled. "Where is that other man?"

"He's been taken care of—finally."

"Is he the man who helped you bring me here?"

"He brought you here. I didn't," he said.

"You didn't ...?"

"Wasn't my idea; you're not supposed to be here."

"What happened to that other man?" she asked.

"Like I said, he's been taken care of."

"Why were you fighting? I heard you."

"He messed up. Plenty. You weren't in the plan. You don't want to know what he was going to do to you—and to me, as far as that goes."

"You planned this? But ... "

"I didn't plan anything," he said, with obvious exasperation. "Bringing you here was his idea. You're asking too many questions, now."

"What did you do to my parents?"

He hesitated, looking away. "I'm sorry, but they're dead. According to Silas, anyway."

She'd suspected it but had held on to hope. She felt an awful swell of pain and sorrow and was silent. Tears welled up. He looked at her again, and she thought she could see true sympathy.

"Why?" she said. "Why did you kill my parents?"

"My brother killed your parents," he said, now plainly irritated. "For money. I had nothing to do with it."

"Silas? Your brother?" She began to sob.

He stared at her. "Sorry," he said again, after a moment.

"Sorry?" she said. "You're sorry?"

"I wish it could be different," he said. "But ... " He shrugged and rose. "Things don't always go according to plan—in fact, they usually don't. We got a little problem, you and I." He looked down at her. "Are you about through?"

She looked confused.

"With your milk," he said.

She handed him the not-quite-empty glass.

"What about my baby?" she asked. "What have you done to my baby?"

"Would you stop referring to me as if I did this? I

told you: you weren't supposed to be part of this, you or your baby. What happened as far as you and your baby are concerned—I had nothing to do with it."

"But you know ... about my baby? Do you know what they did to her?"

His eyes searched her face, but he didn't answer. He turned and carried the glass to the kitchen, then came back, standing near her. His refusal to tell her about Erica didn't bode well and the emotion that seized her almost made her sick with grief. Then, she reasoned, his silence might simply mean he didn't know, and she seized upon this. Maybe Erica was still alive. Her spirit rose.

"They'll be looking for me—still," she said, defiantly.

He shrugged again. "No doubt. But if my brother did as he said, they won't have the least idea where you are right now. Knowing my brother, though, that's a big if."

Referring to the other man by name and as his brother finally registered in her consciousness.

"That man was your brother?"

She was startled that he would disclose it. The thought occurred to her again that, if he had killed his brother as she now suspected, he would do it only if he wasn't afraid she'd reveal it later, and that meant ... she pushed the thought away.

"Yeah. Stupid lunatic, always in trouble—that's what he is ... was."

"Was? Did you ...?"

He didn't answer and went to the picture window, staring out, his hands folded behind his back. He stood there for a long time, without speaking. The heat from the pot-bellied stove was radiating toward her now and she felt wave after wave of fatigue and grew drowsy. She struggled to regain some energy.

"There were two men who brought me here," she said, breaking the silence. "If it wasn't you and your brother, then who was the other man?"

"Damned if I know. Just another incompetent, apparently," he said, without turning from the window. "Just another part of my brother's hair-brained ideas. He's been taken care of, too ... I think."

"Taken care of? You mean ...?"

"Yeah," he said, turning toward her. "Exactly. It's just you and me, now. Like I say, that's a little problem I hadn't counted on."

She was silent for a few moments afraid to contemplate the implications, and he just stood there,

"Where are we?" she asked, finally.

"You're a smart one, aren't you? It doesn't matter, though. You're here with me, so deep in these north woods nobody might ever know."

"North woods?"

"That's right. You can almost spit into Canada from here." He laughed, a short laugh, deep in his throat.

"You can't keep me forever," she said. "I know you're going to kill me. I want to know about my child. What has happened to her?"

He merely shook his head. "I'm not going to kill you. I have to lock you up till I can decide what to do," he said, as if in apology, and he crossed the room and took her hands and pulled her erect and helped her back down the stairs, and she sat back down on the bed. She did not even think to fight now, feeling completely exhausted once again, and her thoughts still whirled from the news that her parents were dead and she still did not know for sure about Erica.

"You can use the bucket there if you need it," he said, reminding her. "I know, it's not real sophisticated, but that's where we're at right now. I apologize."

She could only nod assent, feeling herself falling into complete despondency.

"What were those pills you gave me?" she asked.

"Tylenol. Tylenol Three. At least that's what the bottle said. "It has codeine in it. It'll help you sleep." Again, he looked at her intently, reading her face. Then he said, "There's no way you can get out of here. I've made sure of that, so you needn't even try."

She summoned what little energy remained. "What is your name?" she asked.

"It'll do you no good, you know—all these questions. You might as well get used to being here. I have to take some time, figure some things out."

It gave her some relief, actually, that he wouldn't tell her, for if he did, it would be further proof that he was planning to kill her. But she persisted nonetheless. "Then why don't you tell me?" she said.

"In time, maybe," he said.

He again stood looking down at her and she recognized desire in his face and she thought he would surely rape her, now that the "foreplay," for whatever its original reason, was over. But all he did was to say, "I'll take you upstairs again, after while, let you walk around a little, maybe get some fresh air."

She simply sat there, staring at him, beginning to feel faint. He walked away. At the foot of the stairs he paused, looking back.

"I can't be sure about anything Silas has told me, and I don't want to raise your hopes unnecessarily," he said, "but from what my brother said, the baby was not harmed. I'll try to confirm that, if I can."

She looked at him blankly for a moment then began to shake, despite her attempts at control. She tried to read his face, to see if he was telling the truth. She thought again she saw something like sympathy in his expression. Tears rose in her eyes unchecked now and ran down her cheeks. He stood there for a few moments, as if he had something further to say, but, finally, turned to go. He paused, looking back at her once more, then turned again and made his way back up the stairs.

## Chapter Seven

It was supposed to snow again today—not this: a mixture, part rain, part snow, cold but melting as quickly as it hit the windshield. Most of the half-inch of snow that had fallen earlier was gone. There were still shallow patches of it on the northern sides of the hills and knolls and in the roadside ditches. He'd heard that there was still snow in the northern part of the state, mainly in the Arrow Head region.

"Weather's all screwed up! Just like everything else," Lanslow said, out loud, to himself. He was alone in the car. The sky was a solemn gray, the sun a pale yellow orb low in the east behind the clouds.

He thought of Laura and Melanie and wondered what they would be doing while he was away. It was Sunday and he was working again. The thought confirmed what he already had concluded: his work was ruining his marriage. He knew there was more to it than that; still, he admitted, he was never at home. His hours were seldom the same from day to day. Out at night till late, social occasions missed. If it were true, that Laura was having an affair, almost certainly the marriage would be over. He hoped fervently, desperately, for it to be something else: perhaps a depression or sadness maybe, over something he didn't even know

157

about. If that were the case, with more time, he thought, maybe he and Laura could work things out. But, he feared, with this case, their problems could only get worse.

Ten minutes later the mixture of snow and rain had turned to all rain, but only a mere sprinkle. When it rained softly like this from a grey sky, he would often become melancholy and his thoughts would turn to the larger questions of life, philosophical questions, such as whether life had any purpose, and, if so, how he himself had arrived at this particular situation, traveling to one of the more terrible crime scenes he had ever witnessed, a crime that promised hard work with justice in doubt—and he facing a possible divorce, the loss of his wife and child. What purpose in life could bring him to such a state? He knew it would nearly kill him to lose Laura and Melanie. Was he to be a latter day Abraham, to be tested, not in his faith of God, but in himself?

Several years ago, while he was still on patrol, and before his partner had been murdered, he had come to at least a tentative conclusion that there really weren't any answers to the question of life's purpose, that most of the philosophical questions were rhetorical only. From that, the best he could conclude was that you were born a male or female, short or tall, fat or thin, fine looking or ugly or somewhere in between (depending on the cultural norms), with certain mental and physical capacities, and then things, events, just happened to you, both small and large, and you reacted to these things and events and you made your choices and endured the consequences—or at least you strove to endure them, stoically if possible—and on and on, and you traveled the roads to and through these experiences until you died.

Some people, he thought, might call this way of thinking fatalism. In a way they were right. But when he thought back over his life it seemed to him that things had simply happened to him, somewhat random things, mostly, but some planned things, too, things that required choices. And he'd made them and in that way he'd directed his life in some small measure. You simply did what you did, for good or ill, as you understood the situation and your life took its winding path. There was no life-script, and, he'd come to believe, no mysterious scriptwriter behind the curtains.

He'd taken a philosophy class in college where the professor had the habit of writing the names of the different philosophies on the chalk board, never erasing what he had written, even standing on a chair to reach the uppermost reaches of the blank parts of the board. On the first day the professor had written something about the "uncaused cause," and the "unmoved mover," and he had turned to the fellow student next to him and asked, seriously, if he was in the right course. As it turned out he had enjoyed the course and had tried to remember the names of the great philosophies and applied them to his own thinking. Mostly, he surmised, he was perhaps an existentialist and had *ad libbed* as he'd gone along, and life, at bottom, was just a test of will and strength, an obstacle path to be run, to win or lose. Or, perhaps, he thought, he claimed no particular philosophy but was a Darwinist. Yes, that was better, very close to the truth; survival of the fittest, win or lose.

He'd almost always won, thus far, except for the deaths of his brother and partner. But those were among that category of events beyond his control. His situation now, as he understood it, was that he was a detective and he sought out the criminals and tried to put them in jail, away from the rest of the population, to keep them from harming others. That was all it had come down to and he'd thought he'd found his niche, enjoyed his job, and he thought he'd found the woman he loved, and he'd also thought at last that he had established his family and had a beautiful little daughter whom he loved with all his heart. All that was up in the air now and he wondered what was next. Doubt was becoming the prominent player in his thoughts, now, and he was growing confused, anxious, and irritable.

It was raining somewhat harder now and he turned on the windshield wipers. The small patches of the early snow that had accumulated here and there were fast disappearing and the world outside his car was now merely wet. The reeds in the swampland along the roads had turned darker rust from the rain, and the swamp grass had turned contrasting beige.

Dean Brooks, with whom he had arranged a meeting this morning, his former partner before he'd retired about a year ago, had warned him back then: "Do you know what's happening to you, Richard? You're not paying Laura enough attention. All you think of or talk about is your work."

Ordinarily cops, his peers, wouldn't talk like that, so directly, so personally, but Dean had become a special friend. And Lanslow knew what Dean said about him was probably true. Dean was right: he shouldn't get caught up in cases like he did. But, he told himself, that was just the way he was. There was always the chance that just while thinking or talking about a case he could remember something he hadn't thought of before—some new angle, some new lead. That's how he had helped solve his former partner's murder over three years ago, when he'd become intrigued about the background of a man they had long written off, and begun to connect some things. And he and Brooks had gotten their man. When he got on a case, he couldn't let it go. He would dig so deep he began to know the victims better, even, than their family and friends, and the cases would simply nag him until they were solved. He knew now it made for good detective work but was hell on marriage.

Not that he'd had that many homicides since his partner had been killed, only one, in fact. And he had dogged it, too, until the perp was in jail, even now, serving out his sentence at Stillwater State Prison. His commitment to that case had resulted in an episode that now threw even more light on his and Laura's problem, especially since he'd forgotten to call Laura last night.

One morning, after they'd been married for almost a year, Laura had asked him to not forget to pick up some medicine and then he had forgotten and she'd had cramps and pain all night because they couldn't get the prescription filled until morning. Talk about being in the doghouse! At least, back then, she'd been angry and the making up was memorable.

As he had driven home last night he'd felt the same way, remembering he was supposed to call, and he cursed himself for having forgotten once again. When he arrived home his dinner had been set out, and it was cold, and Laura had gone to bed and was reading. And she had accepted his apology with obvious indifference. Indifference was worse than anger. This time there'd be no making up.

Lanslow's hands gripped the steering wheel a little tighter and he felt his stomach knotting up. He was tired from lack of sleep and needed a cup of coffee and was glad he was meeting Dean Brooks at the cafe rather than the station. Wilenski would be doing more interviews and they would meet later. He welcomed the diversion from his personal misery.

When he walked in, Brooks wasn't there yet and Lonnie, the waitress, greeted him warmly. "Hi, handsome. How you doin' today? Coffee as usual?"

"Hot and black, Lonnie."

"Coming up!"

Lonnie returned with the coffee and poured the cup full. "I heard about the murders," she said to Lanslow. "Quite a deal, huh?"

Lanslow noticed Lonnie's hands were heavy veined and rough, probably from hard work. She'd had a tough life, no doubt, and Lanslow thought of how little he actually knew of Lonnie, of how little anyone actually knew of the others they associated with every day. What did he really know about Laura? What did she really know about him?

"Worst I've ever seen, Lonnie."

"You know, Rich," she said, "there were a couple of guys in here three or four days ago that seemed mighty suspicious to me; one of them for sure. A real character, scary."

"Why so, Lonnie?"

"The eyes. The guy just looked spooky. The other guy was just a young kid. Struck me as strange companions."

"When was this, you said?"

Lonnie paused and thought a moment. "Last Thursday. I remember now because it was the day before that family was murdered."

"Were they with the black guy that Tony reported that day, by any chance?"

"No, I saw him, in the park. He wasn't doing nothing, really. Just sitting there. But you know Tony ... " Lonnie just rolled her eyes, then looked quickly around, as if Tony, the owner of the café, might have heard her.

Lanslow thought again, no I don't know Tony, whether he's racist or not, and neither does Lonnie. "Well Lonnie, thanks. I'll send someone over here to take a statement from you if you don't mind. We'll need descriptions of those guys, as much as you can remember. We're looking at everything right now."

"Sure thing, Rich. Anytime."

Lanslow was half through the cup of coffee when Brooks came through the door.

"You look like hell, Rich," Brooks said without preamble, as he slid into the booth.

"Thanks a lot, Partner. You seem to be doing okay, yourself, though."

Brooks did look good. Lanslow hadn't seen his former partner for several months. There were fewer lines in his face, especially around the corners of his eyes.

"Just good eating, Rich, and a hell of a lot less to worry about. And, hey, I'm working out a little, keeping it off."

"Come on, Dean! Working out?"

"You got it. I don't believe it myself. But there you go."

Lanslow noticed Brooks' hair was greyer than he remembered, cut shorter. He was wearing a black and white checked sport coat and a heavy, blue turtle neck sweater.

"Well, my Lord!" cried Lonnie when she spotted Dean. "Look what the cat's drug in. Haven't seen you, Dean, since I can't remember when." She refilled Lanslow's cup

"Just came in to see you, Lonnie. Pretty as ever!"

"Oh, sure!" Lonnie said, sarcastically, but nevertheless pulling her apron back up to her ample waistline and smiling. "What can I get you, Dean?"

"Just a little coffee, Lonnie. Thanks."

When Lonnie finished pouring the coffee and left, Dean said, "So, what's on your mind, partner? I've read about the Lunzers. Sounds like a hell of a case."

"Yeah, a hell of a case, and that's just what I wanted to talk to you about."

\*\*\*

Jacqueline once again opened her eyes to the now familiar darkness of her basement prison. Sometime during the night, the overhead light had been turned off. She was surprised she hadn't wakened.

The clock on the wall read 10:00 and there was no red dot. It was morning. The food and a little exercise, along with the codeine, had worked; she had slept. Her head felt better, her nausea was gone.

The news that her baby was alive flooded back. It released a shuddering relief in her and she now had hope. Who was attending to Erica? Derek probably had made arrangements with Aunt Alice to take care of her. She wondered what her little girl was doing now, what her brother was doing. Perhaps the man her captor had apparently murdered, whom he'd called his brother, wasn't telling the truth about her parents. Perhaps they, too, were alive. Perhaps even, the men who'd abducted her had, in fact, left clues and the police were still searching. She imagined a statewide, even a nationwide search.

She listened for sounds from above but there were none. The man spent a great deal of his time away from the house. She'd heard no sounds of a motor, so he hadn't left in that old car, or maybe she'd just missed it, if he had. He might be in the garage, outside. She wondered what he did there. She waited in silence for ten minutes or so to be relatively sure he had left.

When she was sure he wasn't in the house, she found the light-switch in the still-dark basement and took the opportunity to explore her surroundings once more. The first thing she tried again was the door at the head of the stairs and, as she expected, found it solidly locked. She tested its strength now, several times with her shoulder and found it unyielding.

She returned to the basement floor and examined the books on the table and found that the boxes contained more books, books of every description and subject, from physics and chemistry to biology, from history to sociology and philosophy—but mostly literary works: Proust, Rilke, Yeats, Hemingway, Sartre, Faulkner, Bellow, Steinbeck. They weren't new; all the copyrights were old. The books told her that the man was well read, to say the least, and probably highly educated. From the way he talked she had suspected it. There was nothing in the boxes or on the table to identify him.

She continued to look around. There was no ceiling to the room, just the bare joists and the sub-floor above, only a few pipes and electrical wires here and there. She began to explore the other parts of the room. She ventured into the darkened, floorless area. It seemed strange to her but except for that one window the rest of the basement was windowless. There was nothing else. She again felt that terrible alarm that this room was built for evil deeds.

She began to feel weak and tired again and lay back down and pulled the blankets around her. She was certain she'd received a concussion, though she was no longer nauseous or dizzy. But her head once more began to ache.

The cold was seeping through the cracks of the house again and into the blankets covering her. She reasoned that the weather must have been turning colder. The only source of heat was the old wood-burning stove. The smoke pipe ran up between the floor joists. The wood he used for fuel was pine and birch and it crackled and popped while it lasted. But the stove was silent now and there was the acrid smell of ashes mixed with the dankness of the basement. She wanted to rebuild the fire but there was no fuel and there were no matches, as far as she could tell, and the coals were dead, and she wasn't sure she could do it anyway.

She had every reason to be depressed except for the knowledge that Erica was alive and okay. But her captor was right. The security of her prison seemed complete, and even if she were able to escape she would most likely only freeze to death. But now she knew her baby was alive and she imagined she might be gaining some sympathy from the man who held her captive and she felt there might be opportunities for alerting someone to her situation.

She dozed. Sometime later, from somewhere, she awakened to the yelping and howling of wolves or coyotes. She shivered, not just from the temperature.

*\*\**

The howling had stopped but another sound had awakened her. She lay quietly, listening. The clock on the wall showed 10:00, with a red dot. After a moment she heard the sound of an engine and soon thereafter a door slamming above and the stamping of feet and, after a short time, he came down the steps. Once again he took her upstairs and let her use the bathroom and waited for her to finish. It was dark outside and she could see nothing through the bathroom window. When she came out of the bathroom he guided her to the living room and walked to a woodbin in the corner of the room and from it gathered a few sticks of wood and placed them on dying coals in the stove. The air in the house was brisk. He stirred the coals beneath the wood until he got a flame. Soon the room began to warm up.

He'd said very little during this process. He let her sit at the table again and fed her a bologna sandwich and milk and some cold stale Cheetos, offering a short apology. Again she ate ravenously. She had long since quit feeling embarrassed at her actions, despite his watching her, being simply overwhelmed at the relief of receiving food, of emptying her bladder and bowels, of being free of the bonds she'd been tied with so tightly, of not having to endure the jolts and bumps of the road. Her dignity had become less and less important.

The man sat down in the other chair but made no other reaction, merely sat and watched her eat. She would glance up now and then and their eyes would meet and she thought she saw the sullenness and anger fading, replaced by a tenderness, and she thought that what he'd told her was probably true, that her baby was alive, that he'd had nothing to do with her abduction.

It was then that he arose from the chair and walked to where he'd hung his coat on a peg on the bathroom door. From the inside pocket he pulled a crumpled sheet of newspaper and laid it before her on the table. She picked it up and read:

MURDER ON MANITOU ISLAND!
By Chester Woolridge
Pioneer Press
Friday, October 27, 2006

Sometime early this morning, according to Police Chief Bill Bradbury of the White Bear Lake Police Department, Mr. George and Mrs. Sophia Lunzer, long-time residents of White Bear Lake, were found murdered in their home on Manitou Island. The Lunzer's son, Derek, found the bodies of his parents when he returned home at about 6:00AM this morning. The Lunzer's daughter, Mrs. Jacqueline Bideau, who was apparently staying overnight following a masquerade party at the Lunzer's home, is reported as missing and the police said that Mrs. Bideau's baby daughter, Erica, had been found unharmed at the home by her brother, Derek. No further information on the missing daughter was offered. The department has asked for anyone who might know of Jacqueline Bideau's whereabouts or having information about her to call. Police report the baby as having been transferred to relatives. The police are still combing the area for clues but no further information has been released and they are asking anyone who might have useful information on the murders to come forward.

It was true, then. Her baby was safe, but her parents were dead. She laid the paper down and looked at him.

"I'm sorry," he said. "It's pretty much like my brother said."

She simply looked away, numb with emotion. The clock on the wall of the kitchen displayed 10:45.

"What day is this?" she asked.

He sat back down and picked up some of the Cheetos and began chewing on them and drinking what appeared to be black coffee. "Sunday," he said.

The article was dated Oct. 27th, a Friday. She had been abducted early that Friday morning so she calculated she'd been here at this place for over two days.

"Have you figured out what you're going to do with me?" she asked.

"Keep you here, until I find out whether my brother made any foolish mistakes."

"Mistakes?"

"Yeah ... if he did anything that might lead the

police to this place. In which case, you're a hostage that might get me out of here. You're my ace in the hole, so to speak."

"The police? Why are you afraid of the police?" she asked. "If you've done nothing wrong, bringing the police here will get you a reward."

He seemed genuinely amused at this. "It's a long story," he said.

She did not pursue it but now she knew he was a criminal. "If the police come then what are you going to do with me?" she said. "They won't quit looking."

"I know," he said. "There are other possibilities." He was looking at her, his eyes never leaving her face.

It was her turn to stare at him, now. She could not fail to consider the implications of what he'd said.

"I think I heard your brother talking about killing someone—a woman—when they were bringing me here. I thought it would be me." She looked at him, searchingly.

"You probably did," he said. "My brother was probably talking about my wife."

A look of horror crossed her face and she drew back, her hand covering her mouth. "Your wife, your brother? He killed her? He said so?"

"No, he didn't say as much, but I think he did," he said. "I've thought about it. It could easily have been him. He tried to kill me, too. You're lucky he didn't."

"Was that what I heard? The sounds? You ...?"

"Yes," he said simply.

"What happened to him?" she asked. "Is he gone?"

"You don't have to worry about him anymore," he said.

There was a bitter finality in his voice. She didn't know what he'd done to his brother and she thought she might not want to know. But she felt relief that the man was gone, no longer a threat to her. Now, though, she looked at her captor anew. I don't know this man, she thought. I don't know him at all. Who is he? Why is he keeping me here, alive? I can only bring him trouble. Her thoughts were a whorl. She'd been here nearly three days. But he had never threatened her, in fact had been overly considerate. Yet he was a fugitive from the law. And she strongly suspected he'd done harm to his brother.

She watched him walk into the living room. Once again he stood before the multipaned window, looking out, saying nothing. She felt a sadness emanating from him, seeming to pervade the room, reaching her, surrounding her. She arose and walked into the room and sat down on the couch, behind him.

"I'm very sorry," she said. "I could be mistaken about what I heard."

He turned. "No. No, you're probably not mistaken. It's the only thing that makes sense, now. I should have guessed it long ago. Christa ... " He paused and she thought his voice had choked in his throat, " ... had complained of him."

He turned to look at her and she could see his grief. She looked away. When she turned back to him he was still staring at her.

"Why do you look at me that way?" she asked.

"You're the most beautiful woman I've ever seen," he said.

She looked down, startled at this sudden eruption in their conversation. She'd seen his desire, known it was there, but his words, his emotions now out in the open, shocked her nonetheless. In that moment, however, a new thought flared in her mind: that she might be able to appeal to his sympathies and somehow persuade him to let her go. Once again she looked at him anew. She thought now that the man must not be a monster. Plainly, he thought her desirable. Yet he had not touched her sexually, had not asserted his physical control over her beyond keeping her here, and she knew how easy it would be for him to have taken her by force.

She decided to start the ruse, then and there. She could feel him still watching her. "You've never told me your name."

He turned to stare out the window again. Finally he said, "It's Jeffrey. That's all you need to know."

"I've never met a man like you, Jeffrey," she said, attempting to work on his now-revealed feelings for her, feelings that she believed she could manipulate to her own advantage. But immediately she realized it sounded so counterfeit. He turned back from the window and looked at her quickly, studying her face for just a moment, then looked just as quickly away. Instantly, she knew she'd made a mistake, had hurt him, and she felt ashamed.

He brushed something from his shirtfront and went back into the kitchen and began clearing the few dishes. She came into the kitchen and began to help him. He took her by the shoulders firmly and, thinking at last he might attempt to molest her, that she'd over-played her hand, she jerked back and struggled. He held her shoulders fast, though, and just sat her back down in a chair at the table. He straightened up and stepped back.

"I know what you're doing," he said. "It won't do you any good."

"Don't put me back downstairs," she pleaded, not wholly abandoning her scheme even yet. "I won't try to escape."

He smiled bitterly. "Of course you will," he said. "As I told you, it wouldn't do you any good. You'll freeze and die or the wolves or a bear will get you."

"Wolves ...?" Her hand went to her mouth. That's what she'd heard—the wolves, howling.

"Yeah. They're out there. Just another reason you can't get away."

After a moment, she got up again and began helping him clear and clean the table and this time, after a long look, he didn't push her away and they stood at the sink and washed and dried the dishes together.

# Chapter Eight

It was Monday. The weather had turned from chilly to balmy. The forecast for the day called for a high of nearly forty degrees. Somewhere Lanslow had read that Minnesota had the most variable weather in the world except for Siberia, Russia. October, now nearly over, was making him a believer.

The other desk in the room had been empty since Lt. Johnson, former head of the investigation division, had left for "greener pastures," and Dean Brooks took up residence there. Sunday afternoon Lanslow had a copy of the case file made up to have it ready for Brooks that morning. Brooks had spent a couple of hours perusing the file. His desk was beginning to look familiarly cluttered. As he read through the files he pulled yellow Post-It notes from a small book in his pocket and pasted them to the rim of a shelf above his desk.

By 9:00 A.M. the pathologist's report was received and numerous other lab reports as well. The detectives added this material to their files and got busy going over it. The reports promised to add to the ongoing construction of the events of the crime.

Reports on blood tests and hair that might be used to ID the perps, however, had thus far come back with no leads. Two unidentified hairs were found in the hallway of the Lunzer home but they were minus their roots and would not be able to be analyzed further. According to the pathologist's report, both of the Lunzers had died of gunshot wounds to the body from close range, Mr. Lunzer's to the chest, Mrs. Lunzer's to the back. Blood gases and tissue samples from the lungs indicated their deaths were immediate. Based on various findings with respect to their body temperatures and digestive states, the pathologist estimated that the victims' deaths had occurred almost simultaneously between the hours of 1:00 A.M and 2:00 A.M. George Lunzer, according to the pathologist, was facing his murderer when shot, the shotgun blast coming from directly in front at close range at a downward angle. Sophia Lunzer had been shot from a downward angle also, to her left side and back. It was impossible to tell who had been murdered first, though it was likely that Mr. Lunzer had probably started to rise from his bed and been shot first, then the gunman had swiveled the weapon toward Mrs. Lunzer and discharged it, perhaps even before she could have woken. To Lanslow these reports confirmed more than ever that the motive for the crime was murder as well as burglary.

The report on the still unidentified black man indicated no water in his lungs and that his death had occurred primarily as a result of severe blows to the rear right side of his head from a blunt force object. His body showed several cuts and contusions, especially to the arms and back, but it was the blows to the head that had killed him. His death was estimated to have occurred between approximately 3 A.M. and 4:00 A.M. The diagram of the house they'd found in the man's pocket, though the printing had remained legible, had deteriorated badly from the wetting and yielded nothing by way of fingerprints or any other telltale evidence.

For Lanslow and Wilenski, other than confirming motive, the reports had not yielded any further significant insights into the crime and both were dismayed. They had only been reviewing the reports silently for five minutes, however, when Brooks said, "If this report is right, the Lunzers could have been dead as much as an hour, maybe even two hours, before the third victim was killed."

Wilenski looked up from his reading, startled, and stared at Brooks curiously.

"He does that," said Lanslow, grinning. "You'll get used to it."

"Sorry, Len," said Brooks. "Sometimes I think out loud. Helps me keep things a little straighter. Hope you don't mind."

Wilenski looked over at Lanslow, who simply grinned at him again, shrugging before he went back to his reading. He was going over the statement taken from Lonnie the waitress who'd seen the black man in the park across the street and who also had reported two suspicious looking men in the café, one of whom had sat alone, for over an hour, after the other one, the younger one, had left. She said she'd never seen the black man with the white men nor had they indicated in any way that they were together or knew each other.

"What do you make of that, Len?" Brooks asked about a minute later.

Wilenski, after staring questioningly at Brooks again for a moment, said, "What do I make of what?"

"Of a full hour or two elapsing between the two sets of murders."

Lanslow kept reading the report but was still smiling slightly as he listened to this interchange between the two detectives.

"Well, seems rather obvious," said Wilenski. "The perps were hanging around the house for a hell of a long time."

"You got it," said Brooks. "Now, what do you suppose they were doing all that time between the killing of the Lunzers and the killing of the third vic?"

Wilenski leaned back in his chair, scratching his head. "Gathering the loot. And maybe the third vic didn't die right away."

"The report says he couldn't have lived very long after he'd received that blow to the head. So the time of his death, two hours later seems to be accurate. They could easily have taken what they wanted in less time, even the woman. But they hung around to finish off the black guy?"

Again, Wilenski scratched his head.

"Two hours? With a young woman supposedly about to be abducted, too?" Brooks continued, stressing his point.

"Well, Brooks, what are you driving at?"

"Two groups, not one."

"Two groups?"

"That's the way I figure it; at least a group of two and then the third man. There's too much evidence that the black man wasn't with the other two. He was spotted alone in the park down town. He was surely a transient. He wasn't seen with anyone else. The tracks show he was probably chased down and killed by two guys."

"We've been over this, Brooks," Wilenski said. "How come he had that diagram if he wasn't in on the deal?"

"I don't know. All I know is he had it and seemed to be taking advantage of it. I agree with Richard. I think he might have run into someone else, another party, who had the same idea and they killed him."

"Here's another thing," said Lanslow, joining in. "That footprint in the house wasn't found anywhere outside, where the other two were. You'd expect they would all show up if they were together."

"Doesn't necessarily mean that they weren't together on it, though," said Wilenski. "The two perps whose footprints were found outside may just not have left any footprints inside. The perp whose footprint was found inside may simply have not left any outside."

"Possible," said Brooks. "But I'd go with the probabilities. It's much more likely that the print inside would also be found outside where there was a lot of action—there were only two distinct sets of prints out there besides those of the third vic. Besides, there's the problem of the key."

Lanslow and Wilenski looked at one another. "The key?" said Wilenski.

"Yeah, the key that was supposed to be in the pot, according to the diagram. Where is it? I don't find anything on it in these reports."

"I'd forgotten about the key," said Lanslow. "No one found it, apparently."

"You know," said Wilenski, "I saw the dirt from those two pots spread across the cement. Doc says the black dude must have been digging there. Must have been for the key."

"Then where is it?" Brooks said. "Doc's reports didn't say anything about finding a key."

Brooks picked up a report. "Says here they found dirt on the black vic's hands and underneath his fingernails. He was the one doing the digging. No key on him, though."

"Nope. No key on him," said Wilenski.

They all went silent for a moment.

"Someone got the damn key and opened that door," said Brooks.

"Before the black guy got there," said Wilenski.

"Unless the black guy threw it away," said Brooks.

"Those grounds have been searched, even with metal detectors," Lanslow said. "It would be hard to find, but it likely would have turned up, somewhere."

"Unless he threw it in the lake," Brooks said. "But that's highly unlikely. I'd bet that someone else has that key."

"Okay, okay," said Wilenski. "So, we have at least two groups working here."

"Yeah," said Brooks, "at least two. If the black guy wasn't in with the others—and it seems likely he wasn't—then you have him working the scene alone. And then there's that one footprint inside the house, unlike any of the others. Someone else was in that house and I'd bet he's the one who had the key. Counting him—or them as the case may be—that makes four perps."

"There may be more than four," Lanslow interjected, looking at Wilenski. "We're forgetting the man you said Derek Lunzer saw running off the island."

"Shit! That's right," said Wilenski.

"That would be about six o'clock, wouldn't it?" said Brooks.

"That's right," Wilenski said, watching Brooks' face. "That's at least three to four hours after the Lunzer's deaths and one hour after the last guy supposedly died. That argues for him being alone, too, not with any group."

"Then it's possible we have four different sets of perps, working here," Brooks said, matter-of-factly. "The guy who left the footprint, who I'd say had the key and got in first, the black guy who was apparently searching for the key and didn't find it, the two guys who must have shown up later and whacked him, and the guy running off the island."

"That shoeprint inside the house could be the guy who Lunzer saw running off the island," said Wilenski.

"We'll need to check for those shoe prints around where Lunzer saw him," said Lanslow.

"Jeeesus!" exclaimed Wilenski. "Possibly four different sets of suspects, all working to burglarize and kill the Lunzers and abduct the daughter, following a masquerade party of almost a hundred people, over a period of four or more hours, on the same night? Jeeesus!"

"Well, we don't know the motives for sure," said Lanslow. "Maybe they weren't after the daughter, but she was there and they took her—and they were certainly after the loot."

\*\*\*

The detectives agreed to split up to do some follow-up interviews. It was about 10:00A.M. Lanslow wanted Brooks to size Derek Lunzer up. Wilenski had drawn Colin Haskell, George Lunzer's business partner.

In a call to Haskell's home Mrs. Haskell told Wilenski that her husband was on his way to work. Wilenski then called the real estate office but was told Haskell hadn't shown up yet. He decided to try to intercept Haskell there. When he pulled into the visitors' spot in the parking lot and walked toward the entryway, the door to the building opened and he recognized the man in an overcoat coming toward him down the sidewalk away from the building as Colin Haskell. The man stopped for a moment and stared at Wilenski, turning slightly toward the building he'd just vacated, as if he had forgotten something, or, on the other hand, as if he might want to avoid the detective.

Wilenski acted quickly. "Mr. Haskell? Good morning. I'm Detective Wilenski from the White Bear Lake police department. Sorry to interrupt you, Sir, but I wonder if I might have a word with you?"

When he introduced himself to Haskell, the man turned a shade of pale that made Wilenski think he might faint on the spot. Leonard almost laughed out loud but managed to keep a straight face.

"Oh, Detective Wilenski!" exclaimed Haskell. "Yes, yes, of course. They told me you'd called. Of course, I'd be glad to talk to you, but I was just on my way to a meeting and I can't be late. Could we talk later?" Haskell was carrying a briefcase, which he had shifted to his left hand as he shook Leonard's hand with his right.

"It's very important I talk to you, Mr. Haskell. I just need a few minutes of your time, Sir. It's about your partner's murder."

"Oh, my God, yes, such a terrible thing, Detective, a terrible thing; so unexpected! We're all trying to deal with it as best we can."

"I'm sure you are, Sir. Can we talk?"

Haskell glanced at his watch, plainly caught in a conundrum. "Well, I suppose so. I can only spare a few minutes. And I'll have to make a call first, if you don't mind."

"I appreciate your talking to me on such short notice, Mr. Haskell. I know how hard this must be," Wilenski said, eyeing the man closely. "I'll try to be as quick as I can."

"Oh, certainly, certainly, Sir, no problem, no problem at all. Well, of course, we'll just go back into my office." Haskell motioned toward the door of the building and he and Wilenski walked back toward the doorway from which Haskell had just exited.

Wilenski followed him by a receptionist's desk into a large office, the walls decorated with plaques and framed certificates and awards and several pictures of various construction projects.

"Please excuse me," Haskell said. "I'll just make a quick call, then I'll be back."

"Certainly," said Wilenski. "Take your time."

Haskell removed his coat and left the room, returning in a few minutes. He seated himself in the leather executive chair behind his large desk.

Wilenski had remained standing, noting that Haskell had preferred using another phone than the one on his desk.

"Please accept my apologies, Detective. We're having a heck of a time around here with George's sudden death." He motioned for Wilenski to take a seat in a distressed-leather guest chair in front of his desk. He leaned back in the tall chair, his head resting against the expensive leather, far below the chair's top; a concave bald spot inched its way toward the back of his skull. He wore a red tie against a white shirt beneath an obviously expensive black suit.

Glancing at his watch again, Haskell said, "Would you like something to drink, Detective? I can have one of the employees bring you something."

Leonard shook his head, removing his notebook from his coat pocket. "I'm fine, Mr. Haskell. I have just a few questions. Do you mind if I take notes?"

"Of course, certainly. What can I tell you, Detective?" Haskell placed his hands on the polished surface of his desk, the manicured fingers spread evenly, tapping lightly, nervously, his face a forlorn mask, either of grief or guilt, Wilenski couldn't say. Haskell kept glancing at the clock.

\*\*\*

Young Derek Lunzer appeared not to have shaved since Lanslow had seen him on Friday morning. His beard was heavy, one of those that would develop an early five o'clock shadow despite a close shave. Now, the beard was full stubble and it made him look older. He was standing in the doorway to his aunt's house, having answered the doorbell. The house was not large, certainly not the equivalent of the Lunzer estate on Manitou Island. Nevertheless, most of the houses in the community of North Oaks boasted an up-scale appearance, middle-middle to upper-middle class, with most houses set well back on acreage, the air redolent with white pine. Lunzer was wearing sweatpants and a red, pocketed T-shirt that was emblazoned with a bright yellow racecar on the front.

"Mr. Lunzer, good morning. Hope we didn't get you up?"

Lunzer shook his head. "No, no, that's all right. What can I do for you?"

"Derek, this is Detective Brooks," said Lanslow, turning to Brooks. "Detective Brooks is joining us to help catch your parent's murderers and to try and find your sister."

Derek nodded to Brooks cursorily. "Anything new?" he asked, turning back to Lanslow.

Lanslow ignored the question. "Nice of you to agree to talk to us. I'm sure it must be difficult. May we come in?"

Lunzer nodded and opened the door wider to allow them to enter. "Sure, come on in," he said.

A middle-aged woman stood at the entrance to the hallway, holding the baby Erica in her arms.

"This is my aunt," said Lunzer, motioning listlessly toward the woman. Lanslow thought Lunzer might be high.

The woman stepped forward, offering her hand, holding the baby under one arm. "I'm Alice," she said. The baby stared at the two detectives, clinging to Alice. Lanslow smiled, reaching out to touch a loose wisp of the baby's hair but she quickly turned her head and buried her face in Aunt Alice's shoulder.

"How is she doing?" Lanslow asked.

"She's fine," said Alice, smiling. "Too young to know, but she misses her mother."

She offered them drinks and Derek offered to take their jackets but they refused both invitations and the young man ushered them into a spacious sunken living room with a large leather sofa and chairs and original oil paintings hanging on the walls. There was a stone fireplace with birch logs and a crackling fire.

"We can sit here," said Lunzer, and motioned the two detectives toward the sofa while he sat in one of the chairs. Aunt Alice disappeared back down the hall with Erica.

\*\*\*

Early Monday morning she heard the sound of snarls

and growls, of shouting and the short, flat, pop of what she thought were gunshots. Then silence. The sounds seemed to have come from the direction of the lake. She waited, wondering for the moment if the time had come for her to die. But she discounted the notion for she believed she had the situation assessed properly now and it didn't include her death or her abuse.

She'd thought it all out, the things that had transpired recently, and she believed her captor had been caught in a scheme not fully his own and was now faced with the problem of having to hold her a prisoner because she had interrupted his plans. She could not imagine what his plans were. He was hiding from the police, though, that he had as much revealed. Certainly killing her could possibly solve his problems, depending on how seriously he was in trouble. Her presence threatened to lead them to him but now, she thought, there were his feelings for her; his declaration that he thought her beautiful had confirmed them.

The door opened at the top of the stairs and light from the kitchen spilled down. She heard a swishing sound and then a roll of carpeting bounded down the stairway, coming to rest at an angle against the bottom stair post, not quite on the floor. A human head with long strands of blonde hair popped out of the end of the roll of carpet and dangled over the edge of the stairs.

She could see the face and that the eyelids were tightly shut.

Jacqueline gasped and screamed, falling back onto the bed and covering her head. She heard the footfalls coming down again, Jeffrey grunting as he made his way toward the foot of the stairs. She uncovered her head and watched him place his foot against the roll of carpet and shove it the rest of the way down to the floor, the head bouncing and rolling.

He only glanced at her. His face was ashen, grim.

Jacqueline screamed again. "What are you doing? What are you doing?"

But he was intent and didn't answer. At the bottom of the stairs, he grabbed the edges of the carpet and began to pull it toward the back of the room to the dirt part of the floor. He left the roll lying near the wall.

He turned to her as he started to go back up the stairs. "I'm sorry to put you through this, but the animals were trying to get to him. The ground outside is too hard to dig a proper grave. I'm sorry," he said. He walked back up the stairs.

Jacqueline looked to where the body lay, knowing it was one of the men who had abducted her and brought her to this place, probably the man he had called Silas. And Silas was also the man who was Jeffrey's own brother and who had tried to kill him, and who had probably killed Jeffrey's wife, and in all probability had brought *her* here to be raped and then killed. Once again she was glad that he could no longer threaten her, and even with all her inner turmoil she thought that perhaps justice had been meted out in its own way.

But the body's presence practically left her petrified. She covered her head again. A half-hour passed. Her situation seemed impossible. The body lying against the far wall, which Jeffrey had so far ignored, was a horrible presence, intensifying her desire to escape, to get away from this dreadful ordeal. But she could not force herself to rise to seek a way out.

After another fifteen minutes, she heard him coming down the stairs again and she peeked from beneath the covers. He was carrying a shovel and again merely glanced at her as he walked by. He shook the shovel.

"I'm, sorry. I have to do this. I couldn't find this damned thing."

He leaned the tool against the wall beside the body then went back up the stairs and came back down carrying what appeared to be an old fashioned washtub. Taking hold of the shovel, he began to dig at the floor next to the body.

She watched him work for sometime, digging a hole, shoveling the dirt to the edges. She grasped his intent.

Despite all her previous reasoning, she realized she might be next. She became almost numb with fear.

When she opened her eyes again, for she had fainted, the light was still on but Jeffrey was gone and the room was silent. She looked toward the place where he had been digging. The body was not visible and most of the pile of dirt had disappeared, only a small mound remaining.

She heard him coming back, grunting as he came down the stairs with the tub in his hands. He merely glanced at her again as he went back to the pile of dirt and shoveled the remainder in the tub and smoothed the grave's surface and carried the tub laboriously up the stairs. He was wearing a sleeveless sweatshirt and sweat bathed his arms and face despite the coolness of the room.

Jacqueline read the clock on the wall: 4:12, with a red dot.

He came back down the stairs and picked up the shovel, leaning it against his side, and stood looking at her. The grimness in his face had not left.

"It can't be helped, now," he said. "I'm sorry. The animals ..."

She began to shake. She could read sympathy on his face. She squeezed her eyes tightly shut and turned her face into the bed and covered her head again with the blanket. She couldn't see him, but knew he was still there.

He sat down on the side of the bed.

"You know that Silas tried to kill me," he said. "There was nothing else I could do. There's no other place to put him."

She uncovered her face. His was a face of agony and suddenly she was aware of what he must be going through. He dropped his head into his hands and covered his eyes. "Yes, I know," she heard herself saying. "I don't ... can't ... blame you."

"It's over now, anyway," he said, looking up. "He would have harmed you. That's why he brought you here."

"I know, I know." She said.

"It's something that had to be done," he said, as though trying to reassure himself, to justify his actions. She could read the guilt in his voice and on his face.

"It's okay," she said.

"I'm going to take you upstairs," he said. You need to get away from down here, now. It will be better. It doesn't matter, anyway; you can't get away."

He started toward the stairs. His outward appearance was haggard, he looked worn down; the whole episode still astonished and shocked her.

He came to the side of the bed and helped her get

up and they went up the stairs. He led her to the sofa in the living room and she lay down, pulling a pillow under her head.

"I'll get a blanket," he said. He paused at the entryway to the kitchen and said, "I'll fix something to eat, if you're hungry."

She didn't say anything. She just watched him as he went into the kitchen and began to prepare their meal. There was a fire burning in the stove and she began to feel its heat seeping into her benumbed body.

## Chapter Nine

You say your father had fired the maid?" Lanslow asked. Derek Lunzer nodded. "Yeah, he has her on tape taking a ring."

"Taking a ring? On tape?"

"Yeah. George had a video camera hidden in the TV set in their bedroom. Caught her red handed."

Lanslow and Brooks glanced at one another. "You're telling us now, Mr. Lunzer? Why didn't you mention this before?" Lanslow asked.

"I told the black guy, the other detective—what's-his-name."

Lanslow remembered Wilenski mentioning a maid being dismissed. But that was all.

"What's the maid's name?" asked Brooks, his pen poised above his notebook.

"Juanita. Valenzuela. She's a Mexican. I suspect she's an illegal."

"You know where Miss Valenzuela lives?" Lanslow asked.

"Not really. I think around here, somewhere."

"Around here? Where around here?"

"In White Bear Lake, or maybe Hugo. North of White Bear, I think."

They could hear the baby, Erica, crying somewhere

in the back of the house, but Derek paid no attention to it.

"You know," Lunzer said, out of the blue, "It occurs to me that the man I saw running as I was coming home Friday had very black hair and was short. Yes, I remember that."

"And ...?" said Lanslow.

"Maybe that was Juanita's husband. I saw him once. A real shabby character."

"And you think this guy might have something to do with the murder of your parents?" asked Brooks.

Lunzer hesitated for a moment, looking at them in astonishment." Well, Detective, you tell me. That's your job isn't it? It's just a thought. I'm not sure it was Juanita's husband. As I said, I saw him only once."

"And why would this man want to murder your parents?" asked Brooks.

Derek shook his head as if wondering why the detective couldn't see it. "Geese! It's obvious, isn't it? George caught her stealing and fired her. Maybe he was angry. I don't think George liked her husband, anyway, but I don't know, actually. As I say, it's just a thought."

"Well, Mr. Lunzer," said Lanslow, "you've been very helpful. If you think of anything else please let us know. You still have my card?"

"Yes, I think so. Somewhere."

"Here's another, in case you've mislaid it. Detective Brooks will give you one, too. You can contact either one of us."

"Sure," said Derek, indifferently, as he took the cards, placing them in his pants pocket.

After the interview, as they got into the car, Brooks said, "A real cool smart ass, that."

"Yeah, maybe too cool," said Lanslow. "I'm thinking we should put surveillance on Mr. Lunzer." As he slid into the passenger's side he made a call to the station.

Brooks said, "You notice how he refers to his father as 'George'?"

"I noticed," Lanslow said. "And he calls his mother by her first name."

"Yeah, but she's his stepmother," Brooks said. "Maybe nothing so unusual about that. Unusual, though, to call your biological father by his first name."

Manitou Island had by now been opened to its residents without restriction; only the home and grounds of the Lunzer estate were still being secured by police tape. Brooks parked the car at the front of the garage building and they made their way to the house.

"It's funny," said Brooks.

"What's funny?"

"In the years I was on the force, I never once got over here."

C. C. Canby

"This thing has rocked this whole community pretty good," said Lanslow. "First of anything like it."

Brooks hesitated, gazing off across the lake. "Beautiful," he said. "Just beautiful."

The day was cloudy, casting a stainless steel gray over the water. There was still plenty of fall color to the trees, muted by the gray skies, but still quietly bright.

"Winter'll be coming soon," said Brooks.

"No doubt," said Lanslow, amused.

"See the shadows of the reeds in the water over there?" Brooks asked.

"Sure," said Lanslow.

"You get older, you begin to notice that kind of stuff. You know? You're so busy when you're young, you don't think about it, you don't stop to enjoy it."

"You're not that old, Dean," said Lanslow. "How old are you now, by the way?"

"I'm reaching for sixty-three, young man," said Brooks.

Lanslow smiled and motioned toward the Lunzer house. "Come on, old man. We've got work to do."

As they were walking in, Lanslow decided to call Wilenski, to check how things were going.

***

201

As he left the real estate building Wilenski was suspicious. Colin Haskell had seemed too nervous. He'd kept averting his eyes as Len asked him questions. He seemed jittery, unable to concentrate, in a hurry to get the whole thing over with, checking the time. Then, to cap it off, Leonard wondered what the phone call was about. It was enough to cause the detective to simply pull the unmarked car across the street and park where he wouldn't be noticed, where he would have some time to think things out, perhaps update his notes, and simply watch the building for a bit to see if Haskell went to his meeting.

Wilenski saw Colin Haskell come out of the building almost immediately. Haskell opened the rear door of his car and put his briefcase on the backseat. As Haskell's white Mercedes exited the parking lot, Wilenski pulled in a good distance behind, staying within eyesight but far enough away that he shouldn't draw attention. Haskell had turned east, on State Highway 96, moving toward downtown White Bear Lake. When he got to Highway 61, though, he turned south, heading away from the city, toward the cities of Vadnais Heights and Maplewood.

Haskell's destination proved to be the Maplewood Mall shopping complex. He steered the Mercedes into the large rear parking lot. Wilenski hung back at some distance, in a position to follow should his quarry leave. Haskell seemed to be cruising, looking for a place to park nearer to the mall entrance. Wilenski watched Haskell's car circle once, then again, ignoring several open parking places, eventually backing into a spot with the front of his car pointing toward the lane. Haskell got out of the car, closed the door and looked around as if he was trying to spot something. For a moment, he simply stood there, staring out over the parking lot. He looked at his watch, turned, promptly, and got back into the car behind the steering wheel and just sat there, staring straight ahead.

Haskell was still sitting in his car when Wilenski's cell phone rang.

"Wilenski."

"Len, Richard here. Are you still with Haskell?"

"I've interviewed him and I've tailed him to Maplewood Mall. He's acting suspicious."

"Suspicious? How so?"

"Seemed evasive. He told me he was on his way to a meeting, didn't want to talk. He agreed to talk to me, though, said he had to make a call first. Now he's come here, to the Mall. Just sitting in his car right now. He keeps looking at his watch and looking around, like something might be going down."

"Where are you exactly?"

"In the upper rear parking lot, near Macy's west entrance."

"Listen, Len. We found out that Colin Haskell will become sole owner of the business if George Lunzer dies."

"Uh huh. That figures. More the reason to keep on his tail, then," said Wilenski, watching Haskell still sitting in the car. "I got a feeling about this, Sarge. I may have to have some backup here. Where are you?"

"We're heading toward the Lunzers. We found out that George Lunzer had a Mexican maid, probably an illegal, and that Lunzer caught her on videotape stealing a ring and fired her last Thursday. Derek Lunzer mentioned her husband might have something to do with the murder. He thinks that's the man he saw running off the island the night of the murder. Says he told you about the tape."

"No, he didn't mention any tape to me," Wilenski said. "But, anyway, I'm betting on Haskell. He looks like he's about to move. If he does, I'm going with him. Like I said, I think something is about to go down here, so I could use some backup.

"Alright, then. We're just outside the Lunzer estate. Stay on him, Len. We'll find you when we get there, five minutes."

"Copy that, Sarge. He's in my sights."

\*\*\*

Wilenski recognized Lanslow's unmarked car as it pulled into the parking lot and he nodded to the two detectives as they drove by.

His cell phone rang. "Wilenski."

"Where is he?" It was Lanslow's voice.

"Just down to your right, the white Mercedes. I'm sure something is going down. We need to clear this with Maplewood?"

"I've alerted them, and Mall Security. Security will lend a hand if we need it," Lanslow said. He put away the phone and pulled the car on farther down, passing the white Mercedes. Neither man looked at Haskell as they went by. Lanslow found a parking space several cars away and backed into it, effectively placing Haskell's Mercedes between their car and Wilenski's.

Lanslow's phone rang.

"Something's going on," Wilenski said. "He's getting out of the car."

They all watched as Colin Haskell exited his car and began walking at a hurried gait toward the entrance to the Macy's store. Again, he kept swiveling his head in all directions, obviously watching for something, and glancing at his watch.

"I'm going to go with him," Wilenski said. "He doesn't have his briefcase with him."

"Alright," Lanslow replied. "Brooks will back you up. I'll stick here with the car. Keep in touch and let me know how things are going."

"Copy. I'm on him."

Haskell trudged toward the entrance to Macy's, followed by Wilenski. Brooks exited the car and followed them both at a discreet distance.

Haskell had entered the store and disappeared for the moment. When Wilenski entered behind him, he spotted Haskell just off to his right in the men's clothing department. Haskell had appeared to glance directly at Wilenski when he first came in and Len thought he'd been recognized. But Haskell just turned back to examining the clothing, ignoring him and continued moving from rack to rack. He kept checking his watch. Haskell turned and walked on through the clothing department to where the suits were displayed, again looking at his watch and appearing to survey the store. Wilenski had stationed himself unobtrusively behind a clothes rack, casually examining the shirts and trousers, and Brooks was doing the same, not far away. They, too, kept watching for anyone who might be acting unusual.

"He's up to something," Wilenski muttered into his cell phone. "Nothing yet, though."

"Just stay with him, Len," said Lanslow. "Don't let him get away.

\*\*\*

Lanslow had been sitting for about fifteen minutes when he saw a blue Ford van pull slowly into the parking lot and make its way down the lane in which Haskell's car was parked. When it reached Haskell's Mercedes, it stopped and one man got out from the passenger side and walked to the car and opened the rear door.

"Someone's at Haskell's car," Lanslow reported into his cell phone, at the same time throwing the car into gear and turning on his flashers, accelerating down the lane toward the van.

The men had seen him. The one at Haskell's car had jerked a valise from the backseat and plunged back into the van. The driver rammed the van in reverse, its wheels squealing, throwing up blue smoke, swerving backward, ramming another car, then darting through an open parking spot to another lane on the right. It headed down the lane, southward.

Lanslow cursed, wheeling his car through the same spot, grazing one of the parked cars to his side as he steered through the empty parking space.

At that moment a Maplewood security car pulled into the lane at the far end, effectively blocking the getaway vehicle. This time, there were no openings to get out. The security guard jumped out of the vehicle but just stood behind the open door of the car, holding up his hands. He had no gun.

"God damn!" exclaimed Lanslow, seeing the actions of the guard. He's liable to get himself killed, he thought. But he was grateful. The guard had probably brought the chase to an end.

Lanslow screeched to a halt behind the blue van, jumping out, gun pulled. Neither man inside the van was making any attempt to get out. He contacted Wilenski on his cell phone.

"I've got two suspects right here, Len. Gottem' trapped with help from security. Arrest Haskell and bring him on out, send Brooks on out as quickly as you can. I'm going to need some help in getting these two out of their car."

"Ten-four, Sarge. Brooks is on his way. Haskell is not going to be any problem."

## Chapter Ten

They had all three of them at the station: Haskell, in the interrogation room, a man who'd given his name as Donald Bellinni, and another by the name of Patrick Maher, both the latter in separate holding cells distant enough to not allow them to talk to one another. Already, computer checks on Bellinni and Maher had come up with rap sheets: petty misdemeanors, theft, etc. Neither man was talking yet, but Haskell was telling his story, sweating as if he was in a sauna even though his face was devoid of color. It hadn't taken long for him to break down and confess.

While on a business trip to Las Vegas, he said he had hired Bellinni to kill George Lunzer. Bellinni brought Maher into the deal with him without his knowledge. That was it. Sophia Lunzer was not to be killed, nor was Jacqueline Bideau. He'd understood that Jacqueline wasn't even supposed to be at the Lunzer home, following the party. Only George was the target, and then he, Haskell, would inherit the business. And, he confessed, his pilfering of the business till had brought all this about. He even told them how he did it, by placing white-out tapes over the spot on checks where the name of the recipient would appear when they were printed out via the computer, then he would substitute his own name on the check and cash it. When a vendor who'd then not been paid sent overdue invoices to the company, Haskell simply cut another check to the vendor, made out this time in the company's name. Being in control of the whole accounting process, Haskell would remove the checks with his own name on them when the bank statements arrived. He had bilked the company of several thousands of dollars.

George Lunzer had, for reasons unknown to Haskell, become suspicious and had ordered an audit. Haskell knew the missing checks would be noticed and his fraud would be discovered and he would be sent to prison. He took the only way out he could think of. According to Haskell, Bellinni had received an initial payment of fifteen thousand dollars, and was to get another fifteen when the job was done. But now the they were blackmailing him, demanding more money or else they would kill Jacqueline Bideau and squeal to the police. Haskell swore over and over he knew nothing about Jacqueline but had believed Bellini when he told him over the phone that they'd taken her. That was when he first became aware that Bellinni had brought in Maher.

Bellinni, a sun-darkened raffish type, and Maher, a sober, tough looking Irishman, had denied everything, but they had in their possession, when captured, a satchel with sixty-five thousand dollars in small bills.

Both men had been booked for breaking into and entering a car in the Mall parking lot and stealing the bag of money, using a firearm to commit a crime, fleeing the scene and resisting arrest, reckless driving and a whole bunch of other charges that would be rendered eventually, including swindling, fraud, blackmailing, kidnapping and attempt to murder. Impressions of their boots had been taken as well as samples of DNA and sent to the lab in St. Paul. Now, both men were cooling their heels in holding cells.

\*\*\*

Wilenski had missed all the real action except for arresting Haskell and perp-walking him meekly to the squad car to be taken to the station. So far, Bellini and Maher weren't talking. Now, Wilenski and Brooks found themselves visiting the local hotels and motels, showing the desk clerks photos of Bellinni and Maher. Phone-checks, using the two men's names, had yielded nothing. But they struck pay dirt on the third visit.

"Yeah, they're staying here," said the clerk, a young woman with a face that looked like someone had pinched it real hard, pushing her eyes and nose together and puckering her mouth. She wore glasses, which kept slipping close to the end of her nose.

"We need to see their room," said Wilenski, placing his badge on the counter. "Is the owner or manager around?"

The woman punched a button beneath the counter. A door opened and a small man in a dress shirt and tie came to the counter. He had a harried look on his face and was plainly bothered by the interruption.

"What is it, Leslie?" he asked.

"These men want to see a room. They're policemen."

The man looked at them warily. "I'm Donald Sager, manager," he said. "What can I do for you?"

Brooks showed Sager his badge. "We need to take a look at these men's room," he said, extending the photos so Sager could see them. "We're holding them now as suspects in a murder. This young lady has told us they stayed here."

"Which room?" Sager said to Leslie and the woman turned and plucked a key from where it hung on the wall and handed it to the manager. He came around the counter and motioned them to follow him, marching ahead of them to the stairs, ascending, then turning left down the hall. He stopped, knocked on the door several times and when he received no answer inserted the key and Wilenski and Brooks went in.

***

Jacqueline came into the kitchen area and offered to help fix dinner. She set the table with plates and glasses and, at his direction, peeled some potatoes and sliced them. She was again aware of him watching her. She tried to still her tremors when she thought of the dead man downstairs. She had no illusions about what could happen to her, even now that she fancied their relationship had changed. But, she thought again, she really didn't know this man. He might be psychotic—bipolar, schizophrenic, or something she'd never heard of. A Dr. Jekyll or Mr. Hyde. And what were his plans for her, to keep her here in this wilderness? She'd been held here for over three days, now. It couldn't last.

She was growing a little stronger from better treatment. How much time did she have? Not much, she was sure. She decided she must restart the ruse, more subtly, this time. She'd concluded, as absurdly as it appeared, that her only hope was to make him fall in love with her, to make him at least have pity for her until she could get an opportunity to escape. She had no idea what that opportunity might be. Perhaps he would leave the car keys lying somewhere; she could pick them up, get in the car and drive as hard as she could to the town he'd said was fifty miles away. Maybe the town wasn't that far; maybe he was lying. Or perhaps she could leave some signal somewhere that someone might notice. She imagined her being able to somehow find a weapon with which she could kill him—but the thought was revolting to her. She knew she might not be able to do it.

"I saw all of your books," she said, trying to smile naturally. "Are you a professor?"

He smiled, too, an enigmatic smile. "You could say that," he said. "Do I look like a professor?"

"Not really," she said. She could see he was amused. "What did ... do ... you profess?" she asked.

"What do you think?" he said. He opened a package of hamburger that appeared to be fresh and unfrozen. She guessed he'd bought it a day or so ago and that confirmed what he had said about a town somewhere.

He squeezed two balls of meat from the package and flattened them into patties between his hands and placed them in a skillet with a little oil.

"Most of your books were in literature, quite a few in sociology; some philosophy."

"Ah, and what do you conclude from that?"

"I'd say literature," she said.

He smiled at her. "Well, well. You would be correct."

"Where do you get them—the books?"

"There's a small bookstore in the town."

His mention of the town registered solidly once again but she tried to hide that she'd noticed. Was the town nearby? How far was it, fifty miles, as he had said? Could one get there by walking? But she decided not to remark upon it.

"Did you know that I'm writing my dissertation in philosophy on Pascal and natural theology?" she said.

"Is that a fact? Why am I not surprised?"

She looked at him quickly. "You knew?" she said.

"Actually not," he said. "A smart woman like you? It follows." He pointed to another smaller skillet he'd placed on the stove. "Just put a little oil in there," he said, "then the potatoes, a little salt and pepper."

"I know how to cook," she said, annoyed, then amused that she would be so. "I'm not helpless."

He seemed to get some enjoyment at her pique. She had not grown up in as cosseted circumstances as he might be thinking. She had been camping and mountain climbing with her father and had even driven her brother's race car. But she kept these things to herself. Despite his warnings, she thought she could, if she had to, make it down that little lane to a main road and from there to a town.

She dumped the potatoes in the skillet, salted and peppered them lightly, stirring them with a wooden spatula. She was aware of him watching her again as she opened a can of green beans with a hand held can opener and dumped them in a saucepan and added a pat of butter. She eyed the sharp lid of the can as she put it into a wastebasket. Could it serve as a weapon? She imagined cutting his throat. He would break her into little pieces.

It seemed to her that he had actually relaxed, that for the first time he might be having a pleasant time.

"Have you ever tried onions in your potatoes?" she asked.

"Of course. Very good, but, I have no onions, unfortunately."

He extracted some plastic spoons and forks from a bag he'd taken from below the sink, placing them on a paper napkin beside the plates.

"Why Pascal?" he asked.

"What do you mean?" she said.

"Why did you choose philosophy, especially Pascal's?"

"You know of his work?" she asked.

"Slightly," he said, and she noticed a slim play of displeasure across his face.

"You have something against Pascal?"

The potatoes were sizzling, turning brown. She turned them with the spatula and they sputtered even more. The two of them stood at the stove, side by side in silence for the longest moments. He stirred the green beans, seemingly ignoring her question. She was extremely aware of his presence.

He took the spoon from her and scooped steaming potatoes from the skillet into a bowl, stirred the beans once again and emptied them into another bowl and set them on the table. He placed the two hamburgers upon a platter at the center and added the salt and pepper shakers.

"Voila! Dinner's ready," he said. "Sorry, I don't have any wine. Even Pascal might grant we can find a little happiness in eating, though such happiness would be at best be temporary."

She looked at him perceptively. "I would think so; but, you're right, not a lasting happiness. We find that only in belief in a higher being—according to Pascal."

A look of outright disgust was on his face now as he passed her the meat.

"What?" she said. "You are an atheist, then?"

"I'm aware of Pascal's so-called wager," he said.

"Repeat it, then," she said.

He smiled at her. "You're questioning the professor?"

"Yes," she said, defiantly, playfully.

He paused for a moment, took a bite of potato, chewed. "Well, let's see," he said. "I believe it goes something like this: Pascal agrees there is no proof of God's existence, but one is better off to believe He exists, nevertheless, than not to believe, for if our belief in God is correct, then we gain eternity; we win. If God does not exist, however, we've lost nothing, for we wouldn't have gained eternity in the first place. In the meantime, it's a better bet to live as though God exists."

"Very good," she said. "You pass."

"And you believe this?" he asked. "That it is better to follow the Godly life that Pascal espoused whether or not God actually exists? Of austerity, self-denial, absolute obedience to the Word of God, without doubt, without reason?" He took another bite of potato, looking at her over his fork. "These are good," he said.

"I don't know what to believe," she confessed. "I'm hoping to find out. Do you believe in anything?"

"Anything?" he asked.

"You know what I mean."

"Well, there's always Buick," he said, laughing outright.

She looked puzzled.

"You know," he said, "the advertisement, the slogan? Buick: something to believe in."

She, too laughed, and she could tell the sound of her laughter pleased him.

They both looked at one another now and then with

a new attitude, and they ate in silence for a while. Her glances sideways at him from time to time astonished her at the feelings he had begun to arouse: an ineffable something she dared not admit.

What am I doing, thinking this way, she thought. I must be crazy. I have to see Erica, hold my baby in my arms again, and see my brother. Escape must still be my uppermost goal. Her attitude turned desolate.

When he finally spoke, she was startled for it had nothing to do with what they'd been talking about.

"Like I said. We'll move you up, now, to my brother's room. He no longer needs it."

"Aren't you afraid I'll try to escape?" she asked, and immediately regretted it.

"It'd do you no good to try. We have several winter months ahead of us. You would freeze to death. It's already cold, turning colder, and there are wolves and bears out there."

"I won't try," she said, and once again he just smiled, faintly.

"Why are there bars on your windows?" she asked.

"They were here when we moved in. I really don't know. I think that was part of why Silas brought you here, to have the convenience of a safe place to keep you, where he could use you without fear of your escape. I think he planned to kill me, get me out of the way. You would be next."

She shuddered, and he reached over and patted her shoulder, which, to her amazement, didn't bother her at all. "Not to worry, now," he said. "It's over."

After they ate he led her by the hand down the short hall to what had been his brother's room. She was aware of the strength of his hand, the muscular feel of it. Silas' room was plain, with a twin bed, neatly made, no pictures on the walls, one spoked wooden rocking chair and a nightstand with a lamp. The closet contained only a few garments on hangars at uneven intervals (some hangars empty) and there was a small chest with underwear and more sweatshirts and sweatpants, unfolded, in the drawers.

"You might be able to use some of these," he said, lifting some of the sweatpants and shirts up so she could see. "I'll leave his stuff here. You can use any of it you want."

"Are these clothes I have on his?" she asked, with revulsion.

"No, they're mine. My brother is taller. I thought mine might be a better fit." He smiled amusedly as he looked her over, the sweatshirt falling loosely around her shoulders, the sweat pants drooping around her ankles.

She saw him looking at her and then she looked

down at herself and couldn't suppress a smile of her own.

"I haven't had a chance yet. Perhaps I can pick up some women's things later."

"In town?" she asked. "How far is it?"

He grinned at her. "Far enough you'd freeze if you tried to make it there. Don't be foolish."

He turned then to leave. He said, "You can move about as you please. Remember, it will do you no good to try to escape. No one knows you're here. If what my brother said is true, no one will have any idea where you are—not the slightest. In the meantime, I have to figure out what to do. There are books you can read. Not on Pascal, I'm afraid. Make yourself at home."

He closed the door then and left her to her thoughts.

# Chapter Eleven

To his surprise, Lanslow found Laura at home when he'd phoned on Monday evening, around 9:00 P.M. He had fully expected her to be late again. Nevertheless, when he got home she was there. It had been strained, however, and they'd passed the remainder of the evening with her doing some ironing, the TV going, and they talked little. Melanie kept him busy enough to avoid the argument that would surely have developed. He laid down on the carpeted floor and let her tumble over him, and Laura had even softened after a while, seeming to become amused at their antics.

He looked at her from time to time, without her noticing, as she pushed the iron across a shirt or a blouse, and his heart split. She seemed unusually melancholy and her face showed lines of tiredness and worry. Once again, he suspected he was about to lose her, and perhaps Melanie, too.

The weight of these thoughts draped over him as he drove toward the scene of the crime early Tuesday. He tried to shake it off, knew he had to. Working our butts off, practically around the clock, he said to himself. And things didn't look like they would change. He'd made up his mind he was going to have to call a private detective he knew to check on Laura, a man who owed him a favor. He was pretty sure of what the detective would find.

He looked through the car windows at the fall colors and blinked back the wetness in his eyes. The outside temperature was a balmy forty-five degrees. But inside he ached. A dull, hopeless misery had overtaken him. His life seemed to be emptying of all that mattered: even his job, his work seemed to be fading in importance. But he knew he could never give it up for the eight-to-five existence of most other people, or even return full-time to teaching at the community college where he'd taught a night class until his partner had been murdered. He loved police work. He'd even gotten the same satisfaction when he was on patrol.

Back then, after Zeke had been promoted to detective and he'd remained on patrol, unlike a lot of his brethren (judging from their complaints), he had often found solace in merely driving, alone in the squad car, a time that he could use to forget the more pressing problems, whatever they might be—or when he could, oppositely, mull them at deeper levels and hopefully gain some measure of understanding and solution. For the first time in his life now, he felt adrift and in limbo, with events moving him to places he didn't want to go. For the first time in his life he began to feel an overwhelming loss in the face of things beyond his control and he fought it, just couldn't let that happen. A determinist he was not, a fighter he was. I'm going to have to get some help from Mick, he told himself. It couldn't be helped. Mickey Spiel, a private detective whom he'd befriended, would be eager to offer assistance, probably. So he would do it, as reluctant as he was.

He forced his thoughts back to the case.

Wilenski and Brooks had found plenty in Bellinni and Maher's room: clothes with blood spatters, more cash, some antique decorator pieces that belonged to the Lunzers, and a short, bloody crowbar in a bag with patches of hair still clinging to the curved end. He was sure both the blood and hair would turn out to be that of the unidentified black man's and not Jacqueline Bideau's nor George and Sophia Lunzer's. And the plaster molds of the footprints on the beach, he was also sure, would match the boots of the two men. Derek would have to make a definite identification of the decorator pieces the men had probably lifted from the Lunzer mansion.

Confronted with all the evidence, the men had confessed to the murder of the black man, in self defense they claimed, but both vehemently denied having abducted Jacqueline Bideau or murdering the Lunzers. Bellinni said they had used a boat they'd rented to cross the lake to the Lunzer home. They'd merely pulled the boat ashore at a relatively unoccupied, reedy part of the lakeshore earlier in the day and left it there until the early A.M.

They'd found the house in disarray, he said, and the Lunzers dead. Startled and frightened, thinking they'd been set up or that the killers might still be around, they had left "immediately" only to find the black man "waiting" for them and they'd killed him in the ensuing struggle. (They'd had a little trouble explaining the fact that the tracks indicated strongly that they had been chasing him.) They'd assumed that the real killers of the Lunzers, whoever they were, would be blamed for the black man's death. After their confrontation with the black man, Bellinni said, they'd motored back across the lake and abandoned the boat where they left it. They'd read about the abduction in the papers later that Friday and concocted the story of Jacqueline's kidnapping, and Bellinni had called Colin Haskell and told him they had her, they said, to get even more money out of him; both men had told the same story, more or less, without any apparent opportunity for collaboration.

"What did you do with the keys to the house?" Lanslow had asked Bellinni.

"Keys? What keys?"

"The ones you must have taken from the black man. He had the diagram of the house, showing where the keys were."

"We tried to find them. There weren't any. We had tools. But the door was open. We didn't need them."

Bellinni and Maher's accounts seemed to absolve them of the murders of the Lunzers. Colin Haskell had identified the container of cash found in the motel room as part of the money he'd paid for the murder of George Lunzer, $15,000 dollars. Haskell had confirmed their telephone call demanding more money. Both had sworn the ransom was a ruse and no evidence had turned up indicating the two had been in contact with Jacqueline Bideau. They could, of course, have snatched her for a real ransom, and Bellinni and Maher could even have murdered her, dumped her body somewhere and tried to cash in on it with Haskell. The time line made that possible. But the muddy print left on the rug in the Lunzer's bedroom was different from the shoes the two were wearing. Their account of when they'd arrived at the Lunzer mansion was after the Lunzers had probably been killed. The gist of their story, the times they had given, and other facts, seemed to check out with what he knew. Haskell had had the misfortune of teaming up with Bellinni, and Bellinni had then brought Maher in. Two dumber, more careless criminals,

Lanslow thought, would be hard to find; But the bottom line was that Lanslow was certain they'd killed only the black man and taken some valuables and he was still left with finding the true murderers of George and Sophia Lunzer and the abductors of Jacqueline Bideau.

This morning, he and Wilenski would go through the Lunzer home again, a task that had been interrupted when Lanslow had called Wilenski yesterday and he and Brooks had gotten caught up in the arrest of Haskell, Bellinni and Maher at the mall.

A preliminary check of most of the local phone books yesterday, as well as other records, before they'd gotten caught up in the arrests, had yielded no one by the name of Valenzuela. No surprise.

So, here they were again, at the Lunzer's home. Brooks, in the meantime, would be continuing interviews of the persons who'd attended the Lunzer's party.

\*\*\*

Jacqueline thought she heard soft thudding but it faded. After a while, when she listened very closely, every so often, almost rhythmically, she could hear the sound again, coming from outside.

She arose from the bed. She tried the door to her room and to her surprise found it unlocked. She opened the door guardedly, wondering if she should test the door to his bedroom. She summoned her courage and slowly turned the knob. It resisted, apparently locked. But she heard the soft thud again.

She made her way down the short hall to the living room and found it empty. A clock on the wall showed 7:00 AM. She calculated: it must be Tuesday.

She walked to the kitchen, found it empty also, and peeked through the curtains on the door. With a start she saw the brown car sitting before the outside garage. That meant he was around, somewhere. She heard the thud again.

She stole back to the living room and peered out. The red car was still parked by the side of the garage. She had thought previously that the cars represented a possibility of escape, though she was sure Jeffrey had taken care of that. She doubted the keys would be available anywhere, and the road out, she knew, would be barely negotiable—especially if it should snow further.

She heard the sound again, this time more like something cracking. She peered out the picture window. Jeffrey was down by the side of the lake, swinging an axe, pieces of wood splintering away and tumbling from the chopping block. Standing just inside the curtain where he couldn't see her, she could watch him.

After he had chopped several pieces he would pause, dropping the axe, leaning it against the chopping block. He would remove his pullover cap and run his fingers through his hair and over his face and stand there for a few moments, peering across the lake. He would pull the cap back on, select another piece of wood from the pile, position it, and swing the axe expertly, cutting the block into two, then four wedges. She stood there longer than she had intended, appraising his physique, and she became conscious of what she was doing and was surprised again at what she was thinking. Her thoughts contained more than the possibilities of the axe, which she knew he would hide anyway, or put somewhere where she'd never be able to get to it. Had she really envisioned the two of them ...?

She turned the thought off immediately and returned to her mission. This was taking a great chance but now she was confident that she held some womanly power over this man, though she knew it was fragile, tenuous at best. One false move on her part and he might turn against her. But he seemed to be softening more and more and she felt that, even should he return and catch her, she could talk her way out of it. It would take something more serious, she believed, for him to savage her. He'd said it himself: There wasn't much danger in her escaping by simply running into the woods or dashing down that rutted lane. Such an act would bring its own brutal reprimand.

She went again to the kitchen and pulled open the drawers one by one, looking for knives, but found none. Even the forks and spoons were gone, except for the plastic ones. He had anticipated what she might do with the silverware, too, she guessed, or perhaps he had none. She knew then, in a less emotional moment, that he would be anticipating whatever she might try, physically. The more she thought about it, to do harm to him physically was practically out of the question anyway. No matter what kind of weapon she could wield, short of a gun, he could squash her easily; break every bone in her body. And what, indeed, could she do if somehow she was able to subdue him? Well, she would have to think about that later.

A gun. Yes, that was what she needed. She was growing desperate now. Perhaps she could perform the reprehensible act of shooting him. He had one, hidden somewhere. She'd heard him use it. She began to believe, under the circumstances, she could, too.

She strode back into the living room to the hallway, making sure he could not see her from where he stood. His bedroom would be where he might hide a gun, probably, in such a small house. There was no attic, as far as she could tell. Somehow, she must find a way to get Jeffrey's bedroom door open.

But now the sound of chopping stopped. She returned again to the window and saw him making his way slowly up the path toward the house with an armload of wood. She turned and hurried back to her bedroom, closed the door behind her, and got back into bed.

*** 

Lanslow and Wilenski found the camera still inside the television set in the Lunzer bedroom. Even the crime scene technicians had overlooked it. They removed the videotape, rewound it and replayed it right there.

Juanita Valenzuela was a small woman, obviously of Hispanic decent. She had looked right into the camera as she was dusting. She took a ring from Sophia Lunzer's jewelry box that was inside a drawer, slipped it on her finger, considered how it looked, slipped it off her finger and dropped it into her pocket, even looking around guiltily as she did so.

They now knew what Juanita Valenzuela looked like but that was about all, so far. They would send the tape to the BCA lab and get a picture of her and send out an APB. And they would try to collect her fingerprints and check them against their files.

They began once more to go through George Lunzer's records. They found no references to Ms. Valenzuela in his address book, nor any in his desk calendar. Juanita Valenzuela was, in all probability, an illegal alien, as Derek Lunzer had said. There wasn't even any record of bank checks George Lunzer might have written to pay her—not that those would have yielded any address, but if she had cashed any of those checks, they might have been able to trace them to a bank account and an address from there. George Lunzer apparently paid her in cash to avoid Social Security payments and to keep her incognito. The detectives could find nothing in their further searches. It was as if Juanita Valenzuela was a ghost in the Lunzer home.

They conferred and decided to talk to the neighbors once again. But none of the neighbors wanted to talk much and those that did knew nothing about her. Brooks was already tracking down the remainder of the hired help to interview, but they hadn't heard anything from him. They decided to follow up on the lead that Derek Lunzer had mentioned and checked around the bridge to see if they could find any shoeprints of the man he had said he'd seen running. There were plenty of tracks and they would need help lifting them and attempting to find their owners.

Returning to the station, a check of the department's internal records yielded nothing on Juanita Valenzuela. Nor did any other records yield information about her; no social security record, no voter registration record, no driver's license, no birth record, no marriage license. As an illegal immigrant, this was not surprising.

That Juanita's so-called husband, or Juanita herself, could have anything to do with the murder of her employers, was growing more and more implausible to Lanslow. It was true Juanita might possibly have set it all up, somehow; she could even possibly have drawn the diagram. But to Lanslow it was very doubtful. All they had to go on in this respect was Derek Lunzer's memory of sighting a short man with dark black hair running into the darkness near the bridge to Manitou Island. Come to think about it, it was Lunzer's statement that suggested this man might have been Juanita Valenzuela's husband, or boyfriend or whatever. This might not be true at all. Was Lunzer trying to mislead them, he wondered? Lunzer was still their prime suspect. Yet they couldn't rule out the possibility that Juanita and her husband might have played some role in the affair.

Wilenski was putting in a call to the electric company when he picked up his pencil and began scratching on a writing pad. After a moment he thanked the person at the other end of the line, placed the phone in its cradle and looked at Lanslow.

"Guess what? There's a Juanita Valenzuela who pays her electric bills from this address." He tossed the pad to Lanslow. "I know where it is," he said. "It's a trailer park, north of town."

\*\*\*

Jacqueline smelled bacon frying and when she came out of her room and into the kitchen, Jeffrey was ladling scrambled eggs and bacon onto two plates. They ate breakfast but he'd said he had errands to run and had left. She watched the old two-tone brown Buick station wagon labor its way down the lane and disappear around the corner through the pines.

Immediately, she returned to his bedroom and tried the door. This time, to her surprise, she found it unlocked. She entered the room feeling almost as though she was trespassing on sacred ground. She just stood there for a moment, looking around.

Jeffrey obviously used the room also as a kind of office. There was a multipaned window similar to those in the living room on the south side overlooking the lake, and before the window there was a small desk.

Upon the desk was a lamp, a gold colored pen-set of heavy weight, and a desk calendar. In the middle of the desk's surface lay a wire-bound tablet. Across the otherwise blank cardboard cover of the tablet the word "journal" was written in bold, black, felt-pen lettering.

Forgetting her mission for the moment, She flipped the tablet's cover over to the first page and began to read:

Journal: November 1, 1969:

I've decided to start this journal today to record my thoughts and experiences and to practice my hand at writing, since it seems I won't be doing it any other way. You see, it's been nearly six months since I graduated and I'm still without a job, so, having determined that a new graduate with a B.A. in literature isn't in much demand right now, I've done it: up and joined the army! I'm going to be an officer ...

Jacqueline stopped reading right there. These entries were going to be his innermost thoughts and feelings. She couldn't help feeling guilty and a little embarrassed. But her eyes almost involuntarily returned to the page.

Journal: November 15, 1969

As you can see, Journal, I've shirked my duty already, haven't written for a while; haven't had the time, frankly. This is some real shit I've gotten myself into ... not sure I did the right thing!

Journal: February 20, 1970:

OCS, following boot camp, has been a rough experience for me but I made it through. Next Friday will be our last day. There'll be a parade and a ceremony ... I'll take a short leave home before my next assignment ... I'm being sent to Viet Nam. Not a surprise, but I was hoping to remain stateside...

She was into it now. This was the life of the man now holding her prisoner and she wanted to find out more. She cast her reservations aside and read quickly, turning the pages:

Journal, March 19, 1970:

Well, once again, I haven't written for a while. Just as I thought, we'll be sent to Vietnam in a week or so. Going home was great, but very sad when I left ... Christa and I will wait till I return home to get married ...

Catch you later,
Jeffrey

Journal: March 30, 1970:

Well, I'm in Vietnam now. It's not as hot as I thought, but still a humid 86 degrees. I've seen worse in Texas. But what a mess this war is! I've met the members of my platoon; have gotten to know them pretty well. My NCO, Sergeant 1st class John Howard, believes I'm a little naive, a little too idealistic, being new to the war and all. He may be right ...

Jacqueline read more quickly now, only certain parts of the journal popping out at her:

Journal: April 20, 1970:

Not too hot today, about 84 degrees. Still it's very humid, sticky, especially in the jungle ... This war is just one fucking patrol after another ... We get a report of Viet Cong and we copter in and find nothing, nothing but old women, children and old men. But they are dangerous, too ... They wrap the explosives around their bodies beneath their clothes. We order them out ... the women are wailing and the children are crying and screaming, and the old men are beseeching us with absolute fear on their faces to not shoot them ... it sort of tears at my guts to ransack their houses and tear everything apart ... This is not the America I believe in.

Jeffrey

P.S. I just got a letter from Mom. Silas is in trouble. She said he'd been accused of raping a woman he'd picked up in a bar. The woman identified him to the police and he was arrested. Damn that brother of mine! As if Mom and Jacob didn't have enough to worry about. Silas has always been so goddamned inconsiderate! Mom said she'd send more information later.

Jacqueline paused. Again she felt guilty. But this man who was her captor, who aroused in her feelings she refused to fully admit, was beginning now to be known. She was beginning to understand him better. She was literally seeing his metamorphoses from the idealist to the realist in these printed lines. And now, his relationship to his half brother Silas was becoming clearer.

She took a moment to look around at the rest of his room. There was a small wastebasket beside the desk half full of wadded and crumpled yellow paper. She took it all in. She guessed he was trying to write again even now, but having trouble. She returned to her reading:

Journal: May 25, 1970:

Got another letter from Mom, today. Silas's trial begins sometime next month. I've written to him but he hasn't replied. Not so strange, knowing Silas. I just hope Mom and Jacob can handle this. Damn that stupid-assed brother of mine! Why can't he straighten up, stay out of trouble? I have a feeling Silas is headed to jail. What a kick in the butt ...! But life here goes on and I have to cope.

Went on another patrol today. Unlike most, we saw action, but it was minimal. A sniper tried to get Casey, our point man but, miraculously, missed ... We searched but couldn't find the sniper. He was probably hiding somewhere where he couldn't get a clear shot at us and could get away quickly and that's what saved Casey's life. We stopped at nightfall and set up camp, digging in, and set the trip wires, flares and explosives, around the perimeter. The men were all sleepy and tired. There is danger of dozing off while on guard. The VC are very quiet. This is their territory; they move through the jungle as mere shadows. I reported our position to base camp and we settled down, completely miserable. It's raining a downpour, and even the ponchos can't keep us dry.

Jeffrey

\*\*\*

The pink trailer home in which Juanita Valenzuela apparently lived was old and shabby with a rickety, stuck-on front porch built of two-by-fours and one-by-four planks, obviously put together by someone with little experience as a carpenter. The porch had weathered and the paint—what little was used, had been applied on the first and only coat it had probably ever received—had flaked and peeled almost to vanishing. Someone had hung a bed sheet loosely over the small picture window in the living room, probably to keep the western sunlight out as well as to secure some privacy.

Lanslow pulled the unmarked car into the graveled driveway and came to a halt at the end of the trailer. A walkway, also graveled but only sparsely so, led to the porch. There were no cars parked in front and no sign of life from the trailer. Weeds had grown up around the periphery of the home. The other trailer homes seemed ramshackle, about in the same condition, the park empty of visible residents for the moment.

The detectives exited the squad car, still feeling a little wary after what they'd been through just yesterday. They walked cautiously up the porch and Lanslow, standing to one side, knocked. There was no answer. He knocked several more times but got no response. They walked around the trailer to the rear. There was no rear exit. He peered in the windows, but couldn't make out anything of interest.

Lanslow looked at Wilenski who just shrugged.

"Maybe we should talk to some neighbors, or the manager or owner," Wilenski said, "see if anyone might know Ms. Valenzuela."

"Sounds right to me," Lanslow said. "Let's take the manager first. We need to get inside."

A man driving into the park stopped when they motioned him to pull over and he informed them of where the manager stayed. When they contacted him, he informed them that the trailer home was not owned by Juanita but had been rented by her nearly a month ago. Juanita hadn't paid her rent for November yet, he said, and he hadn't seen her or the man living with her, whose name was Jimmy Jiminez, for two or three days. Lanslow and Wilenski went through the trailer home with the owner's consent but nothing, as far as they could tell, had been left behind except the sheet covering the window; nothing else that would tell them where Jimmy and Juanita had gone. The trailer had been stripped of all personal belongings. The manager told them the furniture, what little there was, was part of the rental.

"Maybe we should talk to some neighbors," Wilenski suggested.

"Okay. Let's meet back here, say, in thirty minutes."

"Gotcha," said Wilenski, checking his watch, and ambled off in the direction of the first trailer home.

When they met thirty minutes later they had only the next-door neighbor's estimate that Juanita Valenzuela and her man had left two or three days before and he hadn't seen them since. The man was retired and looked frail. He was hard-of-hearing, often cupping his ear to hear their questions.

Back in the squad car Wilenski said, "Looks like we may have lost them. No telling where they are now."

Lanslow could only nod assent: one more broken lead, one more day that the murderers of the Lunzers and the black man would go free. And he could only guess about Jacqueline Bideau. And he even dreaded going home now.

## Chapter Twelve

Laura had been late again on Tuesday evening. A doctor's appointment she'd said that morning, as he'd left for work. He'd made a call to their doctor's office and had learned there was an appointment; and Laura hadn't been more than an hour late that evening. But Lanslow's suspicions were not allayed. Reluctantly, he punched Mickey Spiel's phone number on the keypad.

"Spiel's Detective Service, can I help you?"

"I hope so, Mick. I got a favor to ask."

"Hey, Rich! How's it going, buddy? Read about your latest. You need a really good detective, huh?"

"I wish it was that simple, Mick."

"Ah, complexity. Right down my alley. What's up Rich?"

"Mick, this is something personal and I don't want anyone else to hear about it, okay?"

"Hey, man. I owe you, and you can bank on old Mick. Mum's the word if it's you that's asking."

"It's me that's asking, Mick."

"Shoot on, Rich. What can old Mick do?'

Lanslow had supplied Mickey Spiel with information several times in the past that a private detective would otherwise find hard to get. While all the other officers in the department seemed simply to want to poke fun at him or just didn't want to be bothered, Lanslow had liked Mickey right off, mostly because he was authentic. Speil seemed to take life in stride, "laid back," as the saying went, but he knew his business. In the course of their further interactions, Lanslow had learned to admire Mickey's investigative prowess and had come to like him even better. Over time, Mickey had built up considerable IOUs and, though Lanslow had never really intended to collect them, the detective found he now needed Mickey's help.

"Like I said, Mick. It's personal. I want you to do a little undercover surveillance for me for awhile."

"Right down my alley, Rich. I got my pencil poised. What's the scoop?"

"It's my wife, Mick. I want her watched for a bit."

"Ah, your wife," murmured Mickey. "Hope it's not what I think."

"I'm afraid so, Mick. I'm pretty sure. I need it done as soon as possible."

"Hey, Rich. For you, like, I'm on it right now. Anything special you need?"

"Just the usual, Mick. That's all. Where she goes, who she's seeing ... "

"I gotcha, Sarge. How should I contact you?"

"You have my private cell phone number still?"

"Right here, Richard."

"That will be fine, then. Remember, Mick. Not a word."

"You got it Rich."

"Thanks Mick.

"No sweat, Rich. No sweat. Sorry to hear it. See you around."

\*\*\*

When she woke Wednesday morning she listened for the sounds that would tell her Jeffrey was present, but the house was silent. She arose from her bed and donned her heavy robe and tested for his presence throughout the house. She went to the kitchen window and saw that the station wagon was gone again. He was not down by the lake as far as she could tell. Strangely, he hadn't wakened her as he usually did. There was no sign he'd even eaten any breakfast.

She crossed the living room to his office and to the desk and sat down in the hard backed chair. She'd forgotten her quest for a weapon for the moment, engrossed in the journal. She'd been able to read quite far yesterday before he'd returned but the entries had been sparse and not very informative. She was anxious to continue, to find out more about him and his past.

Journal: August 14, 1970:

A long time since I've written. Haven't felt like it, nor had the time. I'm in kind of a state of shock, actually. Mom sent me a newspaper account of Silas's crime. As I suspected, it was much more brutal than she'd let on. I've seen this brutal side of Silas. It scared the hell out of me when we were growing up.

Silas got twelve years! Twelve years! I can hardly believe it. Mom says Jacob is taking it really hard and says he's sick, too. She said he'd fallen and hurt his back. I feel sorry for Jacob; he's been like a real father to me; I can't complain. The last time I heard from my biological father was when I graduated, from high school, back in 1966. He asked for money. I have no idea where he is now or what he's doing. Someday, maybe, I'll look him up — but I doubt it.

Silas still won't answer my letters.

Our platoon is back at base camp now, for a little R&R. We've now been on many patrols. Strangely, we haven't seen any significant action. But just being out there takes its toll. The men are more than ready for some rest and they're just kicking back. Their tents reek of marijuana, but I don't give a shit any more.

I'm taking the time to catch up on some reading. I read a speech today by President Johnson he'd given back in January 1966, four years before I got here. I find repeating it here somewhat therapeutic, I don't know why except that it shows the craziness of this war and I need to vent a little. Here's the way it went:

"How many men who have listened to me tonight have served their nation in other wars? How many, very many, are not here to listen? The war in Vietnam is not like these other wars. Yet, finally, war is always the same; it is young men dying in the fullness of their promise. It is trying to kill a man that you don't even know well enough to hate. Therefore, to know war is to know that there is still madness in this world."

And that is what it is! Sheer madness! After that speech, President Johnson should have ordered the troops all home. The worst thing a president can do, in my opinion, is to order young men and women into harm's way on a pretext. This is a war we can't win. I see it more clearly every day. We are dying for nothing. What do I give a shit whether the Viet Cong have this or that hill, this or that spot on a map? It is a matter of indifference to me. The president says if we lose Vietnam then we'll lose the others, too: Laos, Cambodia, and Thailand. As if they are ours to "lose" in the first place, as if these countries, even if they turn communist, are a danger to us. I used to believe this, but not anymore. President Johnson has said they threatened our security and challenged our beliefs and values. I thought that once, too, but it's a crock of shit. Nixon now says we must stand or see the promise of two centuries crumble. I don't know what the hell he meant by that. Establishing "democracy" in this country goes against the very grain of their culture. Besides, democracy is a code word for capitalism. It's easy to spout such pronouncements when you're not fighting in this fucking jungle. And so, from on high we are told to take the next hill, raid the next village, and kill and kill again.

I know I'm walking a thin line between sanity and insanity right now. All of us feel like we've been abandoned by our government. It's the politicians who are fighting this losing war, but it's us who are paying the price.

I ask again, where do I find the therapy in writing this? I guess it's in the sheer writing, the sheer telling, the relief that comes from at least expressing my bottled up frustrations, fears and anger, if only on the yellow pages in this journal. I have a lot of stories to tell when I get home, if I do (get home)—and I hope to finish my graduate degrees in literature and write the truth about this war. I've decided I'm going to propose immediately to Christa and I want to teach in a small college, somewhere, somewhere quiet, away from all this, and write a book. This hope is about the only thing that carries me through this bullshit (and, of course, the anticipation of seeing the rest of my family again: Dad and Mom, even Silas). But this hope is still not enough. Sometimes I just feel like smashing things, just going berserk. I can see these same emotions in my men. It gets tougher and tougher to keep them under control, especially when I'm fighting it myself, and especially, too, on the patrols. Not even the dope helps.

Later,

Jeffrey

Very carefully, Jacqueline closed the journal, mentally marking the place where she had stopped. The room was quiet. It seemed to her she became more aware of the things around her. Just outside the window she heard the raspy scream of a blue jay and the almost-always present raucous call of the crows. When, from somewhere on the lake, she heard the mysterious wavering call of a loon drifting across the water, she sat for a long time just staring out the window, as she knew he must have done, too, on many days – before Silas had brought her here.

She presently arose, answering the call of hunger, hoping there would be something in the refrigerator for her to eat.

\*\*\*

"Is that one of them?" Vickie asked as Derek Lunzer

backed his Jaguar out of Vickie's parent's driveway. Vickie was looking at a car parked just across the road.

"Yeah, they watch me constantly."

"They think you had something to do with your parents' deaths?"

"Vickie, along with my sister, I inherit my parents' estate. They have good reason to suspect me."

"How could they think you had anything to do with it?"

Derek looked at his girlfriend patiently. "Vickie, they don't know me like you do. You and I know I could never do anything like that. Unfortunately, they don't."

"It's disgusting!" Vickie said.

"Agreed, but they're just doing their job. I just want them to catch the people who murdered my parents and get Jackie back here and get this over with."

"You were with me," said Vickie. "Don't they know that?"

"Of course they do, Vick. They probably think I arranged to have my parents killed. They're probably just looking for me to make a mistake or something."

"Well, they're stupid, then. How can anyone make a mistake over something they haven't done?"

"I'll agree with you there. They don't impress me one bit. They should be directing their investigation somewhere else. They're wasting time. Like I say, I just want this to be over, as soon as possible."

Vickie leaned across the seat and kissed him. "You're such a sweetie," she said. "You couldn't hurt a fly."

"You think you might be just a little prejudiced, Vickie?" Derek asked, smiling.

"No way, dear boy," she said, kissing him again. "I'm completely objective where you're concerned."

\*\*\*

She'd found some cereal and ate it, along with an over-ripe banana. Jeffrey was still gone. She wondered where he went, what he did during the hours he was away. She had no idea.

She'd read all morning. It was midday, now, and she wasn't hungry. She was feeling better as each day went by. She felt she needed exercise, so she got up from the hard chair and walked about the house, even outside to the porch and down the steps, though the cold soon drove her back in. Stretching to get the kinks out, she returned to Jeffrey's room and once again began to read:

Journal: September 20, 1970:

Something has happened. I'm even reluctant to

write about it. Yesterday we reconnoitered this little village. There had been sightings of some Viet Cong in black pajamas. As usual, our unit was in a terrible mood. Two of my men had been killed a couple of days before as we were crossing a stream. We were ambushed. Sergeant Howard talked me into crossing this stream; said we needed to be on the other side, and he was right. But I hated putting my men in the open like that. Sure enough, we took fire and Conyers, on point, and Selby, who was right in the middle of the stream, were shot. Both died right there.

I'm still trying to get over it. The look on Selby's face before he died! He knew. He knew he'd never see another day. A real soldier, but when you're shot and dying—what can I say?

FUCK THIS PLACE!

Entering this village we still carried the terrible sadness and anger over losing these two men. I had a very bad feeling something else was going to happen and it turned out to be true. My men were in a terrible mood. I was remembering the My Lai incident I'd heard of a couple of years ago. I didn't want that to happen again but I had no confidence I could stop it if it did.

We went into the village quick, with the Huey's, to trap the Viet Cong, but our bird wasn't the first to land. As I jumped from the Huey and deployed our platoon, I started hearing firing immediately. As we approached a hootch I saw this young soldier from another platoon come out dragging an old woman by the hair of the head. These are small people and they are flung about like rag dolls. Before I could react the soldier had hurled her to the ground and shot her twice. I grabbed him by the shoulder and shoved him back and he looked at me as if he was a wild man. I thought he might shoot me, too. I ordered him to stay where he was and put two of my men to guard him and I went into the hootch. In the hut was the body of an old man the soldier had shot, probably seventy or eighty-years old. Five kids, some no more than five or six years old, cowering back in the corner, and when they saw me they started screaming, kneeling down. Their parents had left, obviously, leaving the kids with grandpa and grandma. Outside, I heard shooting everywhere, just random, shots in volleys coming from all directions. The guys had just gone mad, literally mad. These Vietnamese had become no better than animals to the soldiers. I ran from hootch to hootch and all I saw were bodies, young, old, male, female, but none of them Viet Cong, I am sure of it. It was unbelievable. I swear, I just broke down and cried and I didn't give a damn about who saw me. Everything happening around me reminded me of the pictures I'd seen on TV of the Holocaust. And that, to me, was what it was: another Holocaust, and it was us, the Americans, not the Germans, who were doing it this time.

I've come to feel as if I'm just being used here, and for what? We're supposed to be doing good here, stopping Communism, but I've come to realize that these people view us as outsiders, as the enemy, and they hate us. I have just grown sick of it; it is like all order has broken down and there is just this chaos. I can't believe how I've changed my mind about all this war crap. Yes, I'll admit it: I've even thought of deserting—but I stay and fight—mostly for my men. Got to hang on ...

Later,

Jeffrey

Jacqueline laid the journal back on the desk. There was tightness in her throat and her hands shook. What he'd been through must have been pure hell. The thought of his misery aroused feelings that had intermittently come and gone over these seven days he'd held her captive in this little house, despite her desperate struggle against them; opposite feelings of sympathy and, yes, even romantic mystery—but of impending doom, too.

Through the panes of the window, whose frames appeared jagged and uneven from many years of sloppy paint, she could see the trees on the other side of the lake just as she could from the living room windows. The deciduous trees were still in color, though diminished—the tint of yellow, ochre and red of their leaves reflecting in the glassy water except for a patch of mist that lay languidly close to the surface, partially obscuring the far shore such that only the tops of the trees were mirrored.

She was all of a sudden very tired, realizing she'd been reading all day. She looked at the clock on the wall. It was nearing 4:00 P.M. and Jeffrey had not yet returned.

## Chapter Thirteen

The three of them, Lanslow, Wilenski and Brooks, were at the station, at their desks, and they all looked exasperated. Lanslow had his feet up on his desk, hands behind his head. Wilenski was slouched in his chair. Brooks was leaning forward, his elbows on his desk, hands cradling his head, his toes tapping the floor in a non-rhythm that was beginning to get on Wilenski's nerves.

Over the past week, they had interviewed everyone they possibly could who'd been at the masquerade party, but they could easily have missed someone. There was no real record of who was there other than the pile of RSVPs they'd found in Sophia Lunzer's desk drawer. Some of those people, though, claimed they had decided not to attend. And then the detectives had been given names of people who were supposedly at the party that were not among the RSVPs. These, too, had been checked out. Lanslow was sure there were others who wanted no part of the investigation and wouldn't come forward. This was a messy part of the case but they had done what they could. The fingerprinting, an ongoing tedious process, had been almost hopeless. They had gotten hundreds, the Lunzers being the social types that they were over the years. They'd had to concentrate on the immediate crime scene for the most part, in the Lunzer bedroom. But all the prints found there had been linked to family members, or to what they suspected were the maid's. Lanslow guessed the intruders had worn gloves. There were no unknowns, otherwise, except for the boot print.

They'd also checked out Louis Bideau, Jacqueline Bideau's husband, and he had what seemed to be an airtight alibi, being in France. Like most of the others— Haskell, Bellinni and Maher, —Lanslow had not ruled him out completely. The couple's divorce appeared to be imminent. As Jacqueline's husband, Bideau might benefit from her death, should he somehow inherit her estate— though, according to the will, he was out of it. But he would also obtain sole custody of the baby. It was another loose end.

And it seemed, too, that Juanita Valenzuela and Jimmy Jiminez had simply vanished. Lanslow checked with the Immigration and Naturalization Service, who had then checked with Mexican authorities, but he had learned little of any use. Valenzuela and Jiminez were most likely not using their real names. Lanslow realized there was nothing much they could do now, locally, except to put Juanita and Jimmy's faces in the news-papers and on television and hope they might be seen.

In short, the three of them had worked their butts

off, almost sixteen hours every day, and the case file had grown to three heavy volumes along with numerous boxes of evidence—and they seemed no closer to solving the murders or the abduction.

Sighing heavily, trying to ignore Brooks' tapping shoes, Wilenski said, "My guess is that we should increase our focus on young Mr. Lunzer, now. Valenzuela and Jiminez are underground by this time, and besides, I don't think they had anything to do with it."

"Well, maybe," said Brooks. "They do have a motive. George Lunzer fired her for stealing a ring; they had the opportunity. They sneak over to the Lunzer's home, murder them, and pick up a few more baubles in the meantime. I've known people to do things for a whole lot less. I wouldn't rule them out just yet."

"Derek Lunzer reported seeing this Latino-looking man running from the island at about 5:30 to 6:00AM," Lanslow said. "If it was Jiminez, that puts him there hours after the Lunzers died. Perhaps he was there, but why was he afoot? He must have left a car on the mainland, or something, and then he would have had to walk to the house, a good ways away. I can't find anyone who saw him. It seems to rule him out as the perp. We know there may have been as many as four groups in on the action. We know that Bellinni and Maher got to the scene after the murders, found the black man, who was intent on robbery, too, and whacked him. That part of the case is over. Someone else had already murdered the Lunzers before all these other characters even got to the house. If we rule out the Mexicans, we follow the money, and with the sister out of the picture, the money goes right to the Lunzer kid."

"Anything from surveillance?" asked Wilenski.

"Nothing, so far," said Lanslow. "Lunzer's staying around here, not going back to college, apparently."

Brooks grunted. "Why should he? He's got enough money to live on now for the rest of his life."

To Wilenski's relief Brooks allowed his chair to drop, resting his feet on the floor. By now, Brooks' desk looked like a cyclone had hit it. Wilenski wondered how he ever found anything, or even knew where anything was.

"He's living it up pretty good, too," said Lanslow, "but he did that before, according to neighbors and his friends."

"At least he did as far as his dad would let him," said Wilenski. "Some of his friends say he was pissed at his old man for not shelling out enough funds. Especially lately."

"Maybe we should tap his phone," said Brooks.

"We probably could get the judge to allow that, with

what we have," said Lanslow. "But I'd bet Lunzer only uses a cell phone."

"We can tap that, too," said Brooks. "You just get the phone company to cooperate. We listen in, and the phone company keeps a record of the calls, too. They not only keep a record of who he calls, they know the time and duration of the call and the geographical location, as well."

Lanslow nodded. "I'll talk to the Chief," he said.

\*\*\*

Mickey Spiel watched Laura Lanslow exit her car and look around, surveying the parking lot. He'd followed her from her school. She couldn't see him and from this vantage point he was able to get a closer look at her. They'd never met.

"Damn!" he said. "She's a looker. Little wonder ... "

Laura closed the car door and walked toward the building, a red brick structure with a cantilevered overhang and a sign on the front reading "Sheldon Professional Building." She'd gone only a dozen steps when she abruptly turned and pointed her remote keyless transmitter at her car to lock the doors. Mickey smiled to himself. In a hurry, he thought. Got other things on her mind. Still, the building was a medical building. She'd just gotten off work. Maybe the visit was on the up and up.

He watched her go in before he maneuvered his three-hundred pounds out of the Lincoln Town Car as best he could and sauntered toward the building.

\*\*\*

Jeffrey had returned very late Wednesday evening. She'd noticed a tension about him, but when she'd inquired he said he was fine. She had prepared some dinner and he thanked her and they ate together quietly and he had gone directly to bed, thanking her again for her consideration, just before he said goodnight. She could see plainly that he was worried, and that worried her.

She had heard him get up early this morning and he'd left without looking in on her.

She was beginning to become quite restless. She mourned the death of her parents and she often thought, resentfully, of Melanie being "mothered" by Aunt Alice.

Now Jeffrey was gone again and she could not help herself. She had to finish reading his journal. There was no reason for her to continue reading, but she did, for it filled in the gaps of his life, gave her captor a background from which she might better understand him. Not that this was going to help her escape, necessarily, but there was the burning question as to why he was holding her, why he didn't just let her go and himself escape to some other remote place where he might resume his search for the peace and solace he seemed so desperately to be seeking.

She'd been reading all morning. Abruptly there had been a large gap in the journal. Three years had passed before he had begun to write once again. A lot had happened in the meantime.

Journal: March 1973

Taking my pen up again, it is difficult to believe the length of time since I wrote last. Has it really been three years since I wrote? Rereading my last journal entry, I might have been better off, perhaps, had I never picked this journal up again. It has all come back, the events of that day. It seems from then to now I've not been able to recover from what went on in that village in Vietnam. It has gotten even worse. Those who would chance to read this might forgive me, but, somehow, I can't forgive myself.

All I can say is, I did manage to get through that fucking mess called Vietnam and I'm stateside now, staying with Mom and Jacob. When I disembarked at the airport, I was still in uniform and some young kid, probably in his late teens, looked at me with absolute disgust. I could have killed him easily. That's what I was trained to do. Little did he know that I probably felt the same way he apparently did.

The transition from military to civilian life has been a little tough, and sometimes, I just feel like quitting everything. Our situation is pretty depressing right now. Jacob is still in pretty bad shape. Jacob, the only father I've ever known, is dying. I'm sure of it. We don't say much to one another. He asked me to forgive him one day, for the beatings and the way he treated me, but I just walked away. I couldn't do it. I can't blame Jacob for the way he is. He sees me as the result of one of Mom's affairs. And he might be right. Why these two people stayed together for this long escapes me. There must be some kind of love there. Mom seems to be in pretty good health but she worries. I think she knows Jacob is dying but she refuses to talk about it. Silas is serving his third year in prison. Christa is standing by me, but I don't know how long that will last. I could not blame her for leaving.

But I'm not going to indulge in self-pity here, though I feel like it. I've decided to go back to school on the GI Bill, get a master's degree in literature, even, perhaps, a Ph.D., and try to get a teaching position at a small college somewhere, like I've wanted to all along. This will be a sort of retreat for me if I can carry it through, and I've always wanted to teach and write.

Since no one will ever read this but me, maybe I can indulge in a little self-pity after all.

I'm not the same person I was before Vietnam; my family can see it. They treat me differently. Christa wants to get married, and I do, too. But I'm still living with my parents, can't even support myself, so we made plans to wait for a while. I'm almost twenty-six years old and I just don't know what the fuck is going on anymore. Mom wants me to go to church but I can't stand the thought of meeting all those people. Truthfully, I've lost any belief I ever had in God, which wasn't much to begin with, I admit. I just can't reconcile the contradictions I've seen—the carnage, the unspeakable horrors people have suffered, the thousands of GI's and Vietnamese dead—with a "loving" God. All because Eve ate an apple and enticed Adam to do the same? It's beyond me.

I visited Silas in the prison yesterday. It's about a three-hour ride from home. It was very uncomfortable for both of us. In the end I tried to hold his hand but he wouldn't let me touch him. He's bitter as hell, even at me—I guess because I'm out and he's in that hellhole. Silas has always been jealous of me, for some reason. He has no idea what I've been through and I didn't want to further burden him. He wants me to pursue another appeal. But the money isn't there. I tried to tell him, but he wouldn't hear of it; doesn't understand my situation. There's nothing I can do.

Later,

Jeffrey

That entry was the last. There were only blank pages in the tablet now. Jacqueline closed the journal. The last few words haunted her. "There's nothing I can do." That entry was entered in 1973. He'd been twenty-six years old, then. In that last sentence she had noted a sense of hopelessness and despair. She calculated. Thirty-one years had passed since he'd written that. It came to her with some shock that he must be nearly fifty-eight years old. She had not thought of him in that way. He didn't look it. She wondered what had happened to him in the meantime, to bring him to this remote wilderness.

But she'd read enough now that she saw the man differently, almost completely transposed from what he'd been when he'd started writing in the journal. She could only wonder what had happened in the years intervening between 1973 and the present. When had he married Christa? When did Silas murder her, if he, in fact, had?

But she knew, now, why he hadn't molested her. She'd seen his desire, had even, to her shame now, played upon it. He could have taken her anytime. But violence had become anathema to him. He was now in a struggle to free himself from the experiences he'd had of it in the jungles of Vietnam over thirty-four years ago. Was he winning? She didn't think so.

*** 

Over at the other desk, Brooks was at the phone. When he hung up, he said, "That was a pawnshop owner over on University in St. Paul. Someone just hocked a piece of the missing Lunzer loot."

"Alright. This may be our break. Let's have a look," Lanslow said, wearily, rising from his desk. "Go on home, Len," he said. "We can handle this."

"I just have a few details to clean up here," said Wilenski.

Lanslow nodded and held a "just a moment" finger up to Brooks. He lifted the phone and called home and Agnes answered.

"Hi, Agnes. Laura isn't home yet?"

"She called, Mr. Lanslow. Said the doctor's appointment was taking longer than she had expected, but that she was on her way."

Lanslow let his breath out slowly. "Alright, Agnes. How's Melanie?"

"She's fine. We've had a good day today, playing. I'm feeding her now."

"Alright, Agnes. We appreciate it. Listen, would you tell Laura, when she gets home, I'm going to be about thirty-minutes, an hour maybe, late?"

"Alright, Mr. Lanslow. I'll tell her."

He heard the phone drop heavily into its cradle. Laura late again, Lanslow thought. She hadn't been late since last Friday, seven days ago, the first day of the Lunzer case, and the night they'd had their first serious confrontation. This time, though, he wouldn't have to call to check up on her. Mickey Spiel would be doing that for him. He dropped the phone in the receptacle.

"Okay, Dean. Sorry. Let's go."

It was nearly dark, around 6:00PM, when Lanslow and Brooks turned onto University Avenue in St. Paul. This area was definitely for hard cases. Even the streetlights seemed dimmer here and the passing cars appeared to be hurrying to get away. Seedy bars sat practically on every corner of the blocks, side by side with Asian-American mom-and-pop grocers offering in large block lettering on their storefront windows to cash checks, along with their "specials." Used furniture and clothing stores and laundromats fought for their own space along the busy, four-lane street.

The owner of the pawnshop met them at the door. It took him awhile to unlock it. He was a man who had the hardened, matter-of-fact look of dealing with down-and-outers every day, people scrambling and clawing to make it, some obviously just on the edge of oblivion, others, as obviously, wending their way routinely through petty thefts, and drugs and perhaps to felonies, to their pitiful end. Lanslow could almost see the calluses on the man's psyche through his eyes. The windows of his store were completely barred and the door was triple locked.

The detectives had cleared their visit with the St. Paul police. They flashed their badges and Lanslow told the proprietor they were responding to his call. He ushered them into the interior.

*** 

Jacqueline heard a sound. Quickly she arose and went to the kitchen window and looked out. A soft white powder of snow had fallen. Heavy fluffy flakes continued to scurry downward, accumulating quickly, turning this northern world whiter. Jeffrey's car was gone. She did not know where the sound had come from. She went to the front window to peer out at the lake, but saw no one. She returned to Jeffrey's bedroom. She began to go through the rest of the desk drawers.

There was a shoebox and inside were old paper clippings. She carefully lifted the box from the drawer and began to go through its contents. Immediately, one clipping's headline caught her attention:

PROFESSOR FOUND GUILTY!
SECRET LIFE REVEALED
11/05/1999 02:16 A.M. CST
John Higgenbottom
Dallas-Express Staff Writer

She read on:

> After nearly 40 hours of deliberations, a Cameron County Texas jury found Jeffrey Stone, a former university professor of literature at Hogan-Simpson University in Albemarle, Texas, guilty of the murder of his wife, Christa Stone, whose body was discovered March 31, 1997, in a field near the couple's home not far from the university. She had been strangled, according to police. After a lengthy negotiation for a plea bargain, Stone has been sentenced to life in prison without parole.

She read farther: The former professor's tenure at the college had been politically controversial. Dr. Black, the university president, in an interview, suggested that Professor Stone had advocated the violent overthrow of the U.S. government in his classes, and some senior officials at the school viewed the professor as an annoyance and a troublemaker. His colleagues in the English and literature department and the university as a whole, the article said, were not enamored of him, either. The news story reported that he had written several articles in the local newspapers on the Gulf war in Iraq, on the similar practice in Vietnam of rounding up the population of towns and villages and placing them in "gated communities," as the military called them. What had gotten him in trouble, though, mostly, the article reported, was that he had focused his anger locally. The article reported that he had written of the administration's "racism" in the school and on what he deemed to be financial misconduct on the part of administration officials. "He was like a dog on a bone, agitating on some of these social issues," Mr. Black, president of the college, said the article. "That's enough to raise serious questions about his contributions to the department. But Stone's allegations of financial misconduct on the part of this administration have no basis in fact whatsoever," he declared. The article went on to say that the Professor had continued to maintain his innocence, claiming he had not seen his wife since she had gone for a walk. Prosecutors argued that Stone killed his wife because the couple's marriage was deteriorating, that she'd found out about an affair he'd had with one of his students. The article didn't elaborate on that aspect of the story

According to the article, prosecutors said Mrs.

Stone had also discovered evidence that seemed to implicate the Professor, along with his half brother, Silas Halladay, in a plan to build a bomb and set it off in a county government facility. Mrs. Stone, the prosecutors claimed, was about to reveal the brother's intent and Stone killed her. Prosecutors wouldn't reveal the exact nature of the evidence against Stone but said it would be enough to prosecute him and his brother and send them to prison. The professor's alleged connections to the bombings and the murder of his wife, the article reported "have shocked members of this small college community, especially his neighbors and colleagues."

The next clipping's headline read:

INMATES OVERPOWER CORRECTIONAL
OFFICERS, ESCAPE, ONE OFFICER DEAD
10/10/2005 02:16 PM CST
John Higgenbottom
Dallas-Express Staff Writer

Middle Village Texas: In one of the biggest prison escapes in Texas history, five inmates made their way out of the state prison in Middle Village, Texas, Saturday night, killing one of the guards and overpowering and restraining the others. The reported ringleader, former Professor Jeffrey Stone, age 57, suspected of being the guard's killer, was serving a life sentence without parole for the murder of his wife while most of the other inmates, including his half brother, Silas Halladay, were serving sentences of fifty years to life.

She continued reading. The article reported that three of the escaped convicts had been captured peacefully while Stone and his brother were still on the loose and considered to be armed and dangerous. The article reported further that the ex-professor was also a former army officer and had served a tour of duty in Vietnam. Friends of the professor had reported that he had returned home from Vietnam disillusioned and embittered, having come to believe he and the citizens of the U.S. had been deliberately deceived into a war that couldn't be won and in which thousands upon thousands had died needlessly. Complaints had been lodged against the professor for "railing and ranting" against the federal government's policies, especially with regard to the Gulf War in Iraq. But it was his articles in the local paper, accusing the college administration of racism and of questionable budgetary practices,that seemed to have gotten him in trouble. There had been questions raised about his loyalty as a U.S. citizen, even, and accusations of actions against the local government, whom he considered scandalously corrupt, and had written so. The administration had accused him of stealing documents and a computer from the administrative section and had filed a complaint. The professor's home had been searched. Papers had been found, officials said, showing plans for building a bomb, presumably to be used against authorities in the future. Silas Halladay, his half brother, had been implicated in this plan, too, and they both had been tried and convicted.

Jacqueline paused for a moment, returning the clippings to the box. She stared out the window, across the lake. She had her answer, now, as to what had happened in the intervening years since the last journal entry. She reviewed the events that had brought her here and the information she'd just gleaned.

Everything, from what she knew so far, seemed to point to Jeffrey's innocence in her parent's murders and her own abduction. But now she knew why he was on the run, with his brother, hiding from the police in this wilderness. Silas and another man had brought her here. And Jeffrey had objected. His brother had tried to kill him only to be killed himself. And Jeffrey found himself stuck with her, unable to let her go.

That was the dilemma. He couldn't let her go. But again the question: why not? Why didn't he just get away from this place, find another hiding place? She'd seen him looking at her. Were his feelings for her keeping him here? Or was it something else that he had in mind?

She returned to her mission, searching for a gun. Quickly she carefully placed the box back where she'd found it. She opened other drawers but they seemed to contain only the normal desk accessories.

She turned to Jeffrey's closet. At first she saw nothing, but then, farther back, she spied another box and she knelt and pulled on it. It was a long box and it was heavy. She pulled it out farther to where she could lift the flaps. The first thing she saw was what appeared to be a hunter's vest but when she lifted it up she knew it was more than that, perhaps a bulletproof vest. Beneath the vest she saw what was unmistakably the black-steel barrel of a rifle. Her heart beat faster. Not just any rifle, but one with a curved magazine, like the ones she'd seen so-called terrorists in the Middle East brandishing on TV.

At that moment she heard the sound of an automobile motor and she hurriedly stuffed everything back in the closet and fled back to her room.

She heard him come through the door. He paused in the kitchen and she could hear sacks rattling and being folded. She arose and went into the kitchen. He was putting away some groceries.

"I thought I'd liven up dinner a little," he said, holding up a bottle of wine and some fresh fruit.

"That will be good," she said. "I'm hungry already."

Over dinner, they'd had another conversation.

"I read your clippings," she said. "I don't think you killed your wife. I don't even think you killed that guard. You're innocent. I know you're not a murderer. You should give yourself up and fight this."

His fork paused halfway to his mouth. "You read about the guard? Silas killed the guard, against my orders. But I didn't care, really. Anyway, it's not as easy as you make it out to be. They'll send me back to prison. I've killed my own brother. They'd get me for that, too."

She had stopped eating. "That's self-defense. It's so unjust," she said, but he merely kept eating.

"Why are you keeping me here? Why don't you just let me go and get out yourself?"

He finished taking his bite of egg, laid his fork down, and wiped his mouth with a paper napkin.

"That's rather obvious, isn't it? I can't let you go," he said. "First thing is, you'd lead the police to me. You're being here has screwed up the whole plan. I have to figure out what I'm going to do. Leave it to Silas to do that—always the screw-up." He began to eat again, then stopped, pushing his plate away.

"Are you through? I'm sorry if I interrupted your dinner," said Jacqueline.

"No. I'm finished," he said, and he pushed his chair back from the table.

Jacqueline got up and began to clear the dishes. "But you can't keep me here," she said. "You can trust me. Just let me go. I will not tell them where you are."

"I have some time yet to figure things out. You're right. Probably I'll have to run again. I can get to Canada from here pretty easily. It's what we'd planned to begin with, then on to Europe, or somewhere else. But I'm tired of running. I'm tired of the whole damned thing, to tell you the truth."

He arose from his chair, swallowed the last of the wine from the plastic cup and began to help her clear away the dishes.

"I'm sorry," she said, "I really am."

"I know," he said. "Not half as sorry as I am, though."

## Chapter Fourteen

Following the unusual balmy weather, it snowed overnight in the Twin Cities' area, a light, wet, soft snow that drifted down gently and clung to the rooftops and tree limbs. Weather reports said the snow was especially heavy in the northern part of the state and was continuing. Around the White Bear police station, the oaks, maples, aspen and birch held the snow gracefully, their colors still peeking through the whiteness here and there. The crusted boughs of the pines drooped a little as if in lamentation of the passing of summer and fall, though officially winter was still a month away.

The computer screen on Lanslow's desk glowed a soft blue in the early morning light of his office. He hadn't turned on the office lights. It was about 7:30AM. Lanslow usually transferred his notes to a file on the computer's word processor, then he would begin to organize them into what he thought were certain salient points. He liked the efficiency of the search-and-find function and even the process of entering the notes, for it helped him to assemble the facts and to get a better perspective. He stared at the screen now, however, in frustration. He'd gone over his notes and the files in the case a dozen times.

Eight days and they were not much closer to solving the case. The cases of Bellinni and Maher had cleared up some things, though. There was still the possibility that these two men had murdered Jacqueline Bideau but Lanslow's gut feeling was they hadn't. As careless as they had been about the murder of the black man there wasn't a shred of evidence that they had anything to do with Bideau. Their cases were just beginning to wend their way through the court system. Jiminez and Valenzuela were still at large and Lanslow's gut once again told him they'd had nothing of any consequence to do with the murders or the abduction. The department was still treating the woman's absence as a missing person case, not a kidnapping or homicide, which, if it did, could bring in BCA agents, and perhaps even the FBI immediately. Out of frustration, he was half-way considering asking the chief to get BCA help anyway.

Lanslow's fingers thrummed a soft staccato on the top of his desk. He had little doubt that Jacqueline Bideau was dead by now. The ruthlessness of the people who had killed George and Sophia Lunzer left sparse room for thinking she was still alive. One could only hope.

As Wilenski had suggested, their attention had become even more focused upon Derek Lunzer. Derek's actions, from what they had observed, were nothing more than normal. He'd asked to enter the house to pick out clothing for his parent's funeral and to pick up other things, including papers he needed to adjudicate his parent's will. He'd complained about not being able to move back in. But Lanslow was in no hurry to clear the crime scene. They had secured authority to tap his phones but so far the conversations they'd picked up were innocuous blather, mostly between Derek and Vickie, who declared their love for one another about every five minutes. Derek had a lot of friends and he seemed to be on the cellular phone with them a lot. Most of these friends had already been checked out.

Unenthusiastically, Lanslow began going through Lunzer's phone records once more. About fifteen minutes later he noted that, aside from Vickie Holland, one of Derek's more frequent contacts was someone by the name of Curtis Nelson. Why had he not noticed it before? A quick check backwards in the files revealed that Nelson's name hadn't appeared on the list of friends furnished by Derek Lunzer. He'd simply overlooked it. Lanslow focused in on it noticing that Derek Lunzer's calls to Nelson had been frequent up to the day of the murders of his parents then stopped. There'd been a hiatus of three days. Lunzer had once again begun making frequent calls to Nelson on the following

Monday, but the log showed that no one had answered. Lanslow decided Nelson deserved further attention.

He decided first to check on Nelson's number that Derek had called, but he got no answer. Checking with the phone company, Lanslow learned that the number was to a phone in a dormitory room on the college campus that Lunzer had been attending as a graduate student. Because Eastern Standard Time was an hour earlier, Lanslow was able to contact officials at the college who told him Nelson and Lunzer were roommates and that their room had been paid for, that Nelson and Lunzer were enrolled for courses. A check with their professors informed him that neither Lunzer nor Nelson had been showing up for their classes during the last week or so.

He next called Nelson's parents, who, he learned, ran a car dealership in a little town by the name of Trane, in northern Minnesota. They informed him that Curtis told them a week or so ago that he was going to take some time off from his readings classes to go skiing in Colorado and had left last Friday.

Lanslow immediately figured this story was somewhat unlikely. The ski resorts weren't usually open this early in the year. If Nelson had, in fact, left for Colorado, he probably would only be hanging out in Vail or Aspen with other rich kids, drinking beer and waiting for the ski season to begin. Since Curtis had left, the Nelsons said, they hadn't heard from him. They didn't really know at which resort Curtis was staying, that he'd said he would call them after he arrived. They thought it might be Vail, where he usually went.

Lanslow was growing more suspicious. He noted the day the Nelsons said their son had left for Colorado: October 26, Thursday, the day before the murders. The phone calls from Derek Nelson had stopped then, also. A coincidence? How had he gotten to Colorado, he asked them. They told him he'd said he was driving to White Bear Lake that day and would meet with Derek Lunzer and would probably fly out, but they weren't sure. At no time had Lunzer mentioned this to them in their interrogations.

"Your son owns a car?" Lanslow asked.

"He drives a red Chevy Tahoe, Z71" Tom Nelson told him.

He thanked them and put in a call to Vail Ski Resort. The call to the resort and others failed to turn up any information as to the young man's whereabouts.

Lanslow thought he was on to something, though. He didn't quite buy the parent's explanation. Not that he suspected them or thought they were lying, because they said they'd been genuinely upset about the

Lunzer's murders and of Jacqueline's disappearance when they'd read about them in the papers, and had expected their son would call them and come home with Derek Lunzer shortly. They told him they had never, in fact, met the Lunzers, but had heard quite a bit about them. They said they were surprised that their son hadn't called after the Lunzers were murdered, or hadn't returned from out west. They had assumed that Derek had already come back to White Bear Lake and their son had stayed behind. They indicated they were a little worried about their son, also.

Lanslow decided he should give Derek Lunzer another call. Pretending to be merely tying up some loose ends, he questioned Lunzer about his roommate and Derek said he simply didn't have any idea where Nelson was; that he himself had been trying to reach Nelson to tell him that he was trying to clean up his parents' affairs and wouldn't be back to the campus for awhile. And, no, he hadn't planned a ski trip with Curtis, had no idea where he was.

Hanging up the phone, Lanslow considered Lunzer's story. It jibed with the phone records. Lanslow thought it was possible that Lunzer was telling the truth, though the number and frequency of the latest calls did seem out of the ordinary. And, he thought, it was also even possible that the Nelson's story of their son going skiing at approximately the same time as the Lunzers were murdered could be mere coincidence. Except, why had he told them he was going with Derek? Was he trying to hide something from his parents? And a check of the college's calendar indicated classes would still be in session and final exams would be scheduled soon.

Lanslow had long since learned that there were few pure coincidences in investigating crimes, but the fact that Derek Lunzer had not called Nelson immediately following the murders would be understandable, his being preoccupied with his parents' affairs. But Nelson's disappearance into the mountains of Colorado, if that was where he was, coupled with Lunzer's latest calls to their dormitory, was suspicious. Lanslow could only conclude that Curtis Nelson had become central to their investigation and had to be found.

Lanslow jumped when his personal cell phone rang. "Hello," he said.

"Hey, Richard. This is Mick. When can we meet?"

\*\*\*

Lanslow left a message on Wilenski's desk asking him and Brooks to continue checking out Curtis Nelson further, especially how he might have gotten to Colorado. They should check if he had a car, a 2006 Chevy Tahoe, whether he'd used a credit card that they might be able to trace, whether he'd flown, taken a bus or a train. He asked them also to be sure to check again with the authorities in Colorado around the resorts; to send them a picture; to have them alert the resort personnel. And, he asked them to do a little checking into Curtis Nelson's family: their financial situation, family background, etc.

He glanced at his quickly scribbled notes and hoped Wilenski and Brooks could read them. He was in a hurry. Then he remembered the unidentified print they'd found in the Lunzer home, at the foot of their bed. Could it be Nelson's? Quickly he scribbled further instructions to send a fax-image of the print to the Cook County sheriff's office and ask that they try to obtain a search warrant for the Nelson's home, that they check to see if Nelson had a pair of boots that matched, or at least that they get a confirmation of the print from the parents, if possible.

He pulled on his jacket and overcoat and checked out of the station. He and Mickey Spiel had agreed to meet at the Down Towner restaurant in St. Paul. If Lanslow knew Mickey, it would involve lunch.

***

She had heard the sound, had gone to the kitchen and saw the vehicle coming down the rutty lane, its motor revving and whining. It was not the red one, but the brown one, the Buick station wagon. She'd watched through the curtain as Stone pulled it in front of the garage, through the now deepening snow, then got out and came toward the house. She did not want to confront him just now. What he had said the evening before, following dinner, had set her to worrying.

From her room, she heard him open a door and close it. After an interlude, the door opened and closed once more and he had left again, the whine and growl of the motor fading in the distance.

She found herself once again inside his room at the closet door. With quickening pulse, she saw the gun, pulled it out and marveled at its weight. Quickly, she shuffled through other boxes, hoping to find the shells but they weren't there. She'd suspected it.

A half-hour later she thought she heard the whine and groan of an engine again. She hurried to the kitchen window and peered out cautiously between the curtains. The sky was darkening. She saw Stone's old Buick station wagon bucking and plunging down the now rutty, snow covered road once again in the grey light. She quickly returned to his room and stuffed the box back in the closet.

Back in her room, she heard him come inside, stomping and wiping his feet. He moved to the kitchen closet where she knew he'd be removing his coat and hanging it on the peg. She heard him remove his high top shoes and drop them on the floor. He would be putting on his sneakers.

She looked at him anew when he came into her room and sat by her on the bed. She'd seen a quite different side of him in the journal. She was still worried. He seemed to be at some breaking point. He didn't say a word, though, simply sat there, looking at her. This time she stared back and it was as though they needed no verbal communication. She saw the lines in his face, the cast of far-away sadness in his eyes.

"Something has happened?" she asked, finally.

"Doesn't it always?" he said. He noticed the book on her nightstand that she'd brought up from the basement, Emile Durkheim's "The Fundamental Forms of the Religious Life," and he picked it up and thumbed through it. But she could tell his mind was somewhere else, that he was irritated.

"What happened?" she asked.

"Nothing, really. I'm just beginning to suspect that Silas probably screwed up, somehow. Perhaps we don't have too much time."

She ignored the "we." "What makes you think so?"

"Just a feeling, nothing specific. I saw more cars than usual in front of the sheriff's office at the police station. It might not mean anything. I don't think we have to worry just yet. We'll see."

He got up and walked around the room, thumbing through a few more pages. He sat back down. He was looking at her again, the book still in his hands. "You understand this?" he asked, alluding to the book.

"I haven't gotten that far," she said.

He dropped the book to the table carelessly. He took her hand and caressed the back of it. She was tense, but she did not pull away.

Now, she dropped her gaze and he continued looking at her, clasping her hand gently, but firmly.

"You know," he said, "it's a wonder to me how a woman as beautiful and as intelligent as you are can believe in the crap that some men—even those as obviously brilliant as Pascal—write, about God. You're a contradiction, a contradiction of beauty and brains."

She smiled wanly. "I know you," she said. "I've read your journal and the articles. You're not an evil man, Professor Stone. Some bad things have happened to you, I know that. But you've handled them poorly."

Again, that penetrating stare: "Uh huh. Now we have the student lecturing the professor? And what would your Mr. Blaise Pascal have had me do, Ms.

Bideau," he asked indignantly. "Prostrate myself before that incredibly dumb jury and judge and beg for mercy, over something I didn't even do? And failing that, throw myself down upon the earth and pray to a God I doubt even exists?"

She could see that his exasperation ran deep. The anger, even fury, in his voice alarmed her and she remembered what he'd written in his journal; but she said, "There are many who have turned to God in prison, Professor Stone."

"Ah, yes," he said in a bitter low voice. "They turn to God just before they are to be executed, Ms. Bideau. At least they're logical: just like your Pascal. How can you lose such a wager? If there is a God, perhaps you win. If there isn't, so what? You lose nothing by trying. You're going to die anyway."

"I'm sure there were those who would have worked to get you free," she said, sensing she'd lost her argument already.

"Oh, my lawyers did their work. I have no complaints there. The locals and the feds wanted me in prison, however, because I was saying some embarrassing things."

"I know what they've said. I don't believe it."

"I think they knew I didn't murder my wife. But they could get me out of the way, remove this thorn from their side, and close a murder case. Very efficient, don't you think?"

Despite the fact she knew he'd possibly killed a prison guard and his half brother, even, she shuddered to think, his wife as well, she could not help it but her heart went out to him. It befuddled her, how she could feel this way about this particular man, with all the supposed baggage he carried with him. She put it down to the feeling—not an understanding, perhaps, but a feeling, an intuition—that she somehow knew this man deeply, more deeply than others, and could not fathom him as a killer of his wife, nor even the killer of his brother, except as a matter of saving his own life or, perhaps, more importantly, of her own.

And this last thought came crashing into her consciousness. She remembered what she had said a moment before: here was a man, she surmised, who was not evil but who, in fact, fought evil, who was fighting it (if not evil, at the very least wrong doing) even as he was being accused of it. And he had fought for her, no doubt saving her life. And somehow, evil had won out, and through a crazy quirk of circumstances, they'd found themselves thrown together, in this northern wilderness of Minnesota.

"I wish we might have met at another time, under different circumstances," he said, before she had a chance to speak further.

She remained quiet, leaving her hand in his.

"But, who am I kidding," he said. "I'm fifty-eight years old and even if you and I were about the same age, a man like me, from the wrong side of the tracks, would never make it to first base with you, would I?"

"I ... I ..."

He smiled wistfully and looked away. "Not even to first base."

\*\*\*

Mickey Spiel sat in a corner booth on the far west side of the restaurant near a gas fireplace. He'd managed to wedge his body in between the table and the seat. A large brown envelope lay on the table surface before him, unopened. It was after 2:00 PM and the restaurant had only a few customers.

Lanslow slid in on the other side. "Okay, Mick. What do you have?" he said.

Spiel pushed the envelope toward him but at that moment a waitress approached and asked them for their order. They each took coffee. Lanslow waited anxiously to remove the contents of the envelope until the coffee was served and the waitress had left. Before him was a stack of photographs, some in color, some in black and white.

The first photo showed Laura and a man coming out of the door of a medical building. The other photos showed them in a car, talking, kissing. Another photo showed the face of the man, up close. Lanslow studied it, trying to hide his devastation from Mickey. He took his time, trying to gain control.

"I've seen him somewhere before. Who is he?" Lanslow asked, finally.

"Frederick Thomas Zell," said Mickey, and he pushed a fact sheet across the table. "He's a doctor."

Lanslow scanned the piece of paper: Dr. Frederick Thomas Zell, it read, Doctor of Pediatrics, University of Minnesota, Age 35, Present employment, St. John's Hospital, Maplewood, MN.

"This is the guy Laura went to see when she thought she was pregnant again, a couple of months ago," Lanslow said.

"Uh huh," Mickey grunted. "Figures."

"What else?" Lanslow asked, turning back to the photos.

"I started watching Laura right after your call on Wednesday. Drove to the school, waited till she left. She picked up groceries at the Cub store then went on home, same thing on Thursday. Last evening was different. I followed her from the school to this clinic, followed her in until I saw her go into the pediatrics office. I knew she wouldn't know me if we met. A nurse took her back to Zell's office, I presume. I came on back to the parking lot and waited in the car till she came out with this guy. I got the phone number of his office and pretended to be you and asked if Laura had made her appointment. They said she hadn't made an appointment."

Lanslow nodded and continued sifting through the photographs. "What's this?" he said, pushing a photo toward Speil.

"That's where they ended up," Speil said. "It's a motel." He pointed to the next photo that clearly showed the motel, with its name, from a distance. "He drove her there in his car. They stayed a little over an hour, then he drove her back to the clinic." He pushed another photo toward Lanslow. It showed Laura and the man kissing inside the car, back at the professional building. The next photo showed Laura standing on the driver's side of the doctor's car and leaning through the window, kissing again.

"She left, then, and drove home," Spiel said. "Zell left, in his car."

Lanslow leaned back in the booth. He stared at the fire in the fireplace. Speil shifted uncomfortably. Lanslow turned back to him. He had regained most of his composure, now.

"Okay, Mick. You've done a good job. I'd like you to get as much more information on this guy as you can. Can you do that?"

"Sure, Rich. Like I say, anything for you. Sorry, buddy. Real sorry."

"Yeah, Mick. Me too."

# Chapter Fifteen

Saturday morning, November 4, Jacqueline woke to the very beginning of the day. The window above her bed was barely alight, etched in icy fingers. She felt the mystery of the early northern dawn, smelled the pine out of which this little house had been built. The atmosphere, for her at least, was almost spiritual. It would not be, she knew, for the man who was her guardian and keeper. Jeffrey, she knew, was not of a religious bent. As usual, it was chilly in the room. It seemed the house was always cold. She nestled deeper in her covers.

Her thoughts returned to the events of yesterday. Once again, to her utter surprise, when he'd held her hand and she'd looked into his eyes, sullen eyes that spoke of resentment, of misery and shame and sorrow, she'd felt something for him, not quite sympathy—well, there was that—but there was also something else. It was totally preposterous she could care (or whatever it was) even a whit. He was a killer, had killed, though the Army had trained him for that. There were times, too, during their discussions, when his eyes became fixed points of hatred and were frightening. He'd no doubt killed innocent Vietnamese, though he'd said he came to bitterly regret it. He'd perhaps killed a prison guard, even his own brother, though the latter was probably in self-defense. This man may even have killed his wife, for in the back of her mind there was this slight lingering doubt, the slender possibility that he had, in fact, done all these things—though he'd seemed sincerely distraught about his past. And he may have been responsible for the whole plot to murder her parents and kidnap her.

But deep down she couldn't believe it, none of it. She'd looked into his face, his eyes that could be so riveting and cold yet warm and compassionate. He'd saved her from rape, perhaps even torture and death, and he hadn't himself touched her in any way she'd felt suggestive of harmful intent, only of a kind of venerative appreciation; and she'd seen the depth of his misery and his reaction to the Vietnam War and its reenactment in the Gulf War and now the invasions of Afghanistan and Iraq. He was a man bitter at the evil around him, bitter at the way in which the simple people of the U.S. had been duped, bitter at the way their president, the man supposedly representative of the highest values of the country, had lied, had squandered the U.S. treasury on a grandiose quest to change the Middle East into a version of Western, capitalistic, Christian dominated culture, and to secure the U.S.'s access to its vast deposits of oil. And, not least (by far), to leave what Jeffrey condescendingly referred to as "his legacy."

Jeffrey was a good man, she said to herself, a patriotic man, concerned for his country, a kind man she thought, despite all that he had done and all that had happened to him.

Across the hall she heard him moving, opening his door, treading quietly to the living room, and she heard him place wood in the stove, then she heard the kitchen door pushed shut and the house was silent once again.

She continued now lying in the bed for awhile, still, even now, luxuriating in it, her memories returning to the pain she'd been through in the vehicle that had brought her here and the dark confinement in the basement. Her thoughts turned to her "jailer" once again.

She wondered how he made his living. He didn't work, she was sure, even though he left often and was gone for lengthy periods of time. Of course, he barely subsisted here, in this little house in the woods, with only the slightest electrical amenities. His life style wouldn't require much money.

Perhaps he did something part-time. But she doubted it. He had no radio, no television. As far as she could tell, he did not subscribe to any newspaper. Obviously, he was taking every precaution not to be found or to draw attention to himself from the outside world.

It occurred to her that Jeffrey's brother Silas must have brought the money and valuables he'd stolen from her parent's home with him to this place. How much was there? Where was it? Was it her parents' money and valuables that Jeffrey was using to live on? If so, it didn't matter to her, somehow, not in the least.

As he had hinted, her arrival must have set his plans completely awry. The simple answer to his plight, she reasoned, would be to kill her, as he had his brother, and to scurry across the border into Canada. But he hadn't; he wouldn't, she was now sure. He had said it, that he was tired of the whole thing and his words carried a dreadful finality.

She just lay there, wondering about these things. She wondered how Erika was doing, if Aunt Alice was taking proper care of her. Tears came to her eyes at the thought of her baby, wondering if she'd ever see her again.

The house was still dim in the early morning. There had been no sound since Jeffrey had left. She had no idea where he'd gone.

She rose, pulling on the heavy robe, and moved alertly to the living room where she peered through the picture window. The sun was getting higher now, a yellow gold background to the jagged black pattern of the pines. She was startled to see him down by the lake through the wispy fog rising from the water. He was standing beneath the snow-laden boughs of a pine, near the trunk of the tree, a rifle cradled in his arms—not the one she'd found in the box, but a smaller one, the one he'd probably used to frighten away the wolves. She drew back into the room, fearing he might see her.

He continued standing there, looking out across the water, a dim grey silhouette. What was he looking at, maybe the wolves? She saw him turn and begin trudging back. She went back to the bed and lay beneath the covers again and stretched out. Momentarily, she heard his steps upon the porch, heard him open and close the front door and then the door to his bedroom, then, moving on light feet, back to the kitchen; heard the faint rattle of the dishes they'd left to drain yesterday evening. She just didn't want to talk to him now, so she made no attempt to get up. Later, she heard his footsteps again, heard the outside door close.

She heard no sound of the engine starting. Curious, she made her way to the kitchen and peered through the curtains. From the garage door window she could see, just faintly, the shaft of yellow light upon the snow, his footprints leading to the door.

She wondered again what he could be doing in that garage. Perhaps what he did there was the answer to how he managed to subsist or how he intended to end his life in some flaming glory he'd written about in his journal. She became determined to find out.

***

When Lanslow got to the station, Wilenski had the phone pressed to his ear and Brooks was staring at his computer terminal. Wilenski talked on the phone only a bit longer then swiveled his chair around to face Lanslow.

"Anything on Nelson?" Lanslow asked.

"Nelson has a Minnesota driver's license and he owns a car," said Wilenski. "A 2006 Chevy Tahoe, red, like you said. They look like this." He handed a glossy photo to Lanslow.

Lanslow studied the photo for a moment, handed it back to Wilenski. "Good work, Len," he said.

"Nothing on Nelson at the resorts, so far," said Brooks. He crossed the room and handed a faxed sheet to Lanslow. "We got Nelson's picture from his driver's license, faxed it to all the Colorado resorts and to the jurisdictions out there. Nobody's seen him. I'd bet Nelson isn't out there."

"Then he told his parents a lie," Lanslow said, more or less to himself, studying the picture. "How about the boot print? Anything?"

"Cook County said they'd try to get a search warrant but they seemed reluctant," Brooks said.

"How so?" Lanslow asked, in surprise.

"Well, they said the judge wouldn't sign the warrant, said there wasn't enough justification. I got the impression the judge and Tom Nelson are thick, hunting partners and all that."

"That's a bunch of crap!" Lanslow declared. "What the hell's going on up there?"

Brooks shrugged. "Politics," he said.

"What about the Nelsons? Anything on them?"

"They're not nearly as well off as the Lunzers. Like you said, Tom Nelson, the father, owns a car dealership in Trane, Minnesota. The town is just south of the Canadian border, just up highway 61, a little north of Grand Marais. Marie Nelson doesn't work." Brooks was looking down, reading from a list lying on his desk. "Their home is worth about five, six hundred thousand, their bank account shows a savings of a couple hundred thousand and the checking account is some nine thousand. The Nelsons also have considerable debt, and the checking account shows some rather large sums of money in checks to Brown University, a private college—part of the Ivy League. They belong to a private golf club and I get the impression they try to live the small-town elite's life style but have a little difficulty making it."

"Where'd you get that? Who'd you talk to?" asked Lanslow.

"The club manager. Oh yeah, a couple of other interesting little tidbits: I talked to Mrs. Nelson, too. She tells me that her son didn't know Derek Lunzer till they met at the college last year but they had since become good friends. And she said she'd been told that he and Derek were going skiing together and she was surprised that her son hadn't come back from the trip when Derek's parents were murdered. Said he hadn't been home since he'd left."

"Yeah, that's what they told me, too. Sounds more and more like he's lying to his parents," said Lanslow.

"Creating an alibi," said Wilenski.

"Did either of you by any chance try to see if Nelson has a credit card account or a checking account of his own?"

"Haven't had time," said Wilenski. "But I can do that next."

"Dean, how about you checking out Derek Lunzer's credit card account, too, if he has one, and a checking account."

"Sure, boss," said Brooks, grinning. "I'll get right on it."

Lanslow caught the irony of Dean's use of the word "boss," of telling his old superior what to do, but he let it pass. He wasn't in a joking mood. "And maybe we should also check on Nelson's ..."

"Phone records?" Wilenski said.

"Yeah. His phone records," said Lanslow, "and let's get an APB out on the car and on Nelson, get him in here for questioning if we can."

"Sure thing," said Brooks.

"I appreciate it, guys," Lanslow said, as he turned to leave.

When the door to the office closed, Wilenski and Brooks just looked at one another for a moment, questioningly, then Brooks shrugged and they both went back to their investigations.

***

When he came back into the house, she was preparing breakfast, but he'd left after they'd eaten saying he had some important errands to run. She didn't inquire further. She watched the old brown station wagon buck its way up the lane and disappear around the curve. When she was sure he was gone she put on a pair of his sneakers she found in the closet and let herself outside. The sneakers were too big, but she plowed through the snow over to the garage, surveying the red vehicle only cursorily as she went by it. She tried the garage's side door first, but it was locked and there was no window.

She went back around the front and tried the large door, but it was locked, too. At the top of the door were three small windows and she looked around to see if there was something she could use to reach them. Seeing nothing, she walked around the garage and found a metal stepladder leaning against the side at the back. Snow was filling her shoes and her socks were getting wet and her feet were getting cold as she carried the ladder to the front and unfolded it and pushed it to the side of the door. The ladder was just tall enough so that she could climb to the small windows and peer inside.

The interior was very dark. At best she could make out a workbench and what appeared to be large sacks like those she'd seen for birdseed. Very dimly, she made out bottles and cans and a long tarpaulin partially covering what appeared to be barrels arranged along the back wall. Off to the side she spied two snow mobiles, and hope flared for a moment. Maybe, just maybe he had forgotten and left the keys in them.

The problem was to get in. She thought about breaking the garage door windows but they were too small for her to get through and would not allow her to reach the lock anyway. Thinking about it, she was sure Jeffrey would never leave the key in the snowmobile. She abandoned the idea.

She trudged through the snow back around to the side of the garage and put the ladder back where she'd found it. On her way back she pulled the tarpaulin away from the red pickup truck and peered through the window. The door was locked and she could make out only some sleeping bags and rugs inside the rear bay. She felt the terror again, of that painful long ride.

Her feet were now completely soaked and freezing. The snow was well over a foot deep and fluffy white flakes were still falling lightly. She replaced the tarpaulin over the truck hurriedly as best she could. She was shivering. She had to get back inside.

She returned to the house, looking back at the tracks she'd left, and the tarpaulin only partly covering the vehicle, but now she didn't care. She went to her room and crawled in bed to try to get warm. Later when she thought she heard the whine of the engine she replaced the book she'd been reading on the nightstand and moved to the kitchen. Through barely parted curtains she saw the station wagon come bouncing and plunging down the road. This time she watched the automobile as it stopped and Jeffrey exited. She even contemplated going to meet him. Why not? What could he do? And she would get a better look of what was in the garage. But she paused. She had seen the anger in his eyes before when provoked and she knew she had to tread lightly.

He raised the upper half of the rear door of the station wagon and let the lower half down and began removing items in brown paper sacks similar to those she'd seen in the garage. He carried two of them into the building through its large door. He slammed the garage door down, locked it and locked the car and turned toward the house. She watched him put the keys in his jean's pockets. He stopped, looking at her tracks, following them to the back of the garage. He came back around to the front and readjusted the tarpaulin over the truck, though it did not cover it completely.

She stepped back, ready to greet him. She recognized the incongruity of her actions. Strangely, she felt some excitement in meeting him like this. The thought occurred to her she was acting like some middle-class housewife waiting for her husband to come home from the office after a long day with no one to talk to. But there was more to it than that.

But he apparently had changed his mind for he turned and began walking down toward the lake. She went to the living room where she could follow his progress. He walked slowly, his shoulders slumped, his hands jammed into his coat pockets. It was still cold, getting colder. She could see his breath. Once again he walked to the side of the lake, stood beneath the bough of the pine tree, and stared across the water. Now and then he would turn and look back at the house, then back across the little lake. He seemed to stare for an eternity. Then, at a snail's pace, he turned and began plodding back toward the house.

She decided she wouldn't back out. She would meet him as he entered the room.

***

That evening, over the phone, Spiel filled Lanslow in a little more on Dr. Zell. The doctor was married, with two children, a boy and a girl, ages eight and six, respectively. Spiel gave Zell's address to Lanslow. The PI had kept watch on Laura earlier in the day, but she had stayed at home.

Lanslow was curious as to where the doctor lived, the man who was stealing his wife, wrecking his marriage. He sat now a few hundred feet from the house in his unmarked squad. For some reason he felt some trepidation doing this. He didn't want to be seen. The streetlights were on, but his car sat farther back, in the shadows. It was about 8:00 P.M. when he saw a new silver BMW pull up next to the mailbox by the driveway and the car's driver reach through the window to retrieve the mail. He watched as the vehicle pulled on into the driveway and then into the garage. He could see that the interior of the garage was finished off with sheetrock, and everything in it—tools, boxes, etc.—was all neatly arranged on shelves along the walls. The garage door descended, leaving Lanslow to stare at the house, to wonder how the doctor greeted his wife and children, what his house looked like on the inside, what his marriage was like.

Zell's house was huge, sitting on a wooded knoll that abutted a golf course—a red brick and wood structure with a large deck and patio. No doubt, the doctor lived the good life; no doubt the good doctor belonged to the posh private golf club that sat only a half-mile or so down the road; no doubt the doctor took expensive vacations, adorned his wife with expensive clothes and jewelry, sent his children to private schools, provided them with—as Lanslow had actually observed—an in-ground swimming pool and every playground contrivance in the backyard one could think of. No doubt the good doctor had most everything a man could want, and now he wanted Laura, too.

A slow rage boiled up in Lanslow's chest and he felt

himself shaking. He reached to his side, fingering the gun and holster strapped to his belt. Immediately he became conscious of his action and was amazed at the momentary loss of control. What was he thinking? What on God's blue earth was he thinking, he repeated to himself.

He tried to settle down, to consider what he was to do. But his thoughts flitted around wildly.

What a waste! How could this man endanger his marriage and family; how could Laura endanger hers? Was this affair a fling on the part of the doctor? And what about Laura? Was it a mere flirtation for her also, or something far more serious, something that would suffice to wreck their marriage anyway, no matter what? He'd noted over their time of marriage what he believed to be a certain kind of vulnerability about Laura, the way she sometimes looked down and then sideways, her eyes almost saying "love me, don't hurt me," a sort of plaintiveness that had made him want to take her into his arms immediately and soothe her. No doubt Zell had taken advantage of that trait. Had he himself failed her?

He had no sure answer to that question. Perhaps he didn't really want one. If the affair was mere dalliance on the doctor's part but not on Laura's, then there was tragedy afoot. Laura would have sacrificed her marriage for a man whose intentions were dishonest at best, it seemed, mere lust and conquest, and the doctor would abandon her when it was over and she would lose not only the doctor, but her own family as well. Lanslow thought he knew Laura well enough that the affair, for her, was not merely frivolous, that the loss of her marriage had been conceived, and even that thought had not kept her from Zell's embrace. Either way, for himself, he figured their marriage was over. He had his pride and would not put up with being a cuckold.

At thought of the collapse of his marriage he felt an agony that seemed to actually physically wrench his insides. A fury boiled in him again toward the man in that house. The lights from its windows now shone warmly upon the snow covered shrubs and bushes, reminding Lanslow, ironically, of a scene from a Christmas card. Inside, the man who had no doubt made love to Laura, his wife, the woman he loved, was having dinner, or perhaps watching TV, or having a drink by the fireplace. And he deserved none of it, this callous man, this adulterer, who was so willing to ruin another man's marriage, to make love to another man's wife for his own egotistic and lustful purposes, to cheat even on his own spouse.

But what was he to do? In the wake of his agony and rage, helplessness overtook him. He sat, staring at the house.

Curiously, Lanslow's thoughts filtered backward to conversations he'd had with Zeke Mallard, his former partner and mentor, first when they were together on patrol, then when he'd made detective and joined Zeke once again in the investigative unit. Zeke had a genial personality, a happy-go-lucky demeanor even after nearly twenty years on the force, and Lanslow had asked him how he could remain that way in the face of the petty, sometimes even heinous behavior they encountered almost every day.

"You take the bad with the good, Rookie," Zeke had said. "Justice here on earth is an ideal as often as not, anyway. Most of these shit bags get away with it. You do what you can and gamble that the ones you can't catch will get justice in another world."

He'd never thought of his partner as particularly religious. But he'd been wrong about Zeke in many ways. Lanslow himself had lost his belief in another world. For him, it was justice here and now or no justice at all.

Ironically, Zeke had made his own gamble, to dally with another woman and to risk his own marriage. He'd paid the price for it in a bizarre way: murdered in his own garage by a demented man he'd met for the first time that very day and who'd had nothing whatever to do with Zeke's affair.

Lanslow shook his head in stupefaction. Life is a crapshoot, he thought. You rolled the dice and hoped for sevens but just as often you got snake eyes. He lowered the window of the car and felt the cold air bite at his cheeks. It felt good. He could see clouds gathering in the pink glow of the lights of St. Paul, a few miles down I-35. Another snow was forecast and this one would probably be bigger and stick around for awhile as winter gathered its forces. He made out the serrated silhouettes of the pines around Zell's home as the light from the rising moon sifted through the wafting clouds.

The question was what he was to do now. All that came to him were Zeke's words echoing in his ears: "You do what you can, buddy. You do what you can ...

\*\*\*

When Jeffrey Stone was about to open the kitchen door Jacqueline opened it for him and his face registered mild curiosity.

"What's this?" he asked, and stepped inside.

It surprised even her, but she took his face in her hands and kissed him; not long, but not short. His reaction to the kiss startled her almost as much as her kiss had apparently startled him. He actually lunged backward, striking his head against the door and just stood, body flattened against the wall as if he'd been glued there. She laughed. Once again he stared at her and she came to him again, kissing his lips softly and tenderly, looking up into his face, running her fingers under his cap and through his hair. Still, he said nothing, though his arms now had naturally fallen around her waist. He looked into her eyes and face for clarification.

"You've made it to first base," she said.

## Chapter Sixteen

Another Sunday. The case was now ten days old and he was on his way to the station. Laura had merely nodded when he told her he had to go in. He could see it didn't matter to her where he was or what he did. "As long as she can find time for her lover," he said bitterly to himself. Images of the doctor and his big house reemerged. The snow had been lighter than forecast, and most of it had now been cleared from the roads. He passed an old man shoveling the snow that had been thrown there by the passing snowplows. There was not much of it and it would be gone in a few hours, melted by the sun. The action appeared so futile to Lanslow at that moment. He wondered what difference it would make to the old man, shoveling this small amount of snow from his drive. In the long run, it would make no difference: But that was the key, he supposed. Here, now, at this moment, it made a difference. Not to anyone else, perhaps, but to the old man.

Perhaps all of one's actions were of this nature: momentary satisfactions, momentary disillusions. Perhaps this realization was the key to true happiness. They melded to make life what it was. Like Zeke said, you take the bad with the good. Cognition triumphed sometimes over emotion—but only briefly, he was coming to believe. It was emotion that was in control of his life, now. For him, presently, in this moment, he felt as if his life was falling apart. Lack of control went against the very essence of his being.

For his part, he could not bear to be around Laura for very long, the temptation to bring up the affair was so strong, to have it out, then and there. But he'd bottled it up, hadn't said anything yet, struggling for a little time to figure things out. Cognition won out over emotion in that case. Melanie was on his mind now, mostly. He might lose her, despite the fact that a judge probably wouldn't look favorably on Laura's transgressions and might even give him custody. But that would solve nothing. He knew he could never take care of Melanie properly as a police detective.

He was miserable.

Brooks and Wilenski were both at the station when he arrived. He'd seen the looks on their faces when he left yesterday. There was nothing he could say to them, though, not now. They'd find out soon enough. It was none of their business, anyway.

They greeted him too pleasantly when he sat down at his desk. He merely shrugged and tried to get control of himself.

"Okay, guys, what did you come up with?" he said.

Wilenski went first. "Funny thing," he said. "Sure

enough, Curtis Nelson has a credit card. The last transaction he had on it was on October twenty-seventh, the day of the murders. And, guess what? It was probably for gas in Grand Marais."

"Grand Marais? Nelson was in Grand Marais on Friday?"

"That's what the record says. He bought something at a service station, about 9:30AM," Wilenski said.

Lanslow paused in thought. "Grand Marais is not far from where he lives," he said. "He could have just been stopping for gas."

"If Nelson is connected to this, that means he could have been taking the woman up north. Perhaps even to Trane, where his parents live. The pathologist's report said the Lunzer's murders occurred between 2:AM and 3:AM," said Wilenski. "Nelson would have time to get back up there by 9:30 or 10:00. "

"Why in hell would he do that?" Brooks said. "You'd think he'd want to stay as far away from that area as he could."

"You would, ordinarily," said Lanslow, addressing Wilenski. "But you've said it yourself, he may have had other things in mind. Maybe it's more convenient for him up there. Maybe he's got a place to stash her, hold her for awhile. You said there were no other credit card transactions?"

"None."

"All right," said Lanslow, wiping his face wearily with his hands, his fingers probing around his temples and eyes. He wondered if the Nelsons might be lying about their son not returning from the ski trip, after all.

"You checked Lunzer's credit?" Lanslow asked Brooks.

Brooks nodded. "Nothing unusual there except the amounts. The kid spends money up the gazoo."

"Alright," said Lanslow. "You guys have done great work. We need a complete biography on Nelson, ASAP. We have to know if he's been in any trouble, with women especially. I'll get some more help to try to pull that all together. Now, you'd better be on your way to Grand Marais."

Brooks and Wilenski glanced at one another.

"You're not coming?" said Brooks.

"You two can handle it," said Lanslow. "I got a little business to take care of down here."

\*\*\*

They lay in one another's arms. She'd been surprised at the firmness of his body but she had to admit she knew nothing of fifty-eight-year old bodies.

"I work hard," he'd explained. "It's a different life,

316

living out here, making do on very little. Physical stuff, mostly. Keeps me in shape and helps keep me from going nuts with that crazy world out there."

"You have your books, though," she said, "and I see you've been writing."

"Not so much, any more. You know what I've been through: the mindlessness of the war, the very horror of it; the murder of my wife, the trumped up charges and the trial; prison life—unbearable. I know there are others who've been through far worse things than I, but knowing that does me no good. My life has been made a shambles. I thought teaching and writing might change things. Now I know that's sheer idealism, a pipe dream. I'm no longer an idealist; I'm a revolutionary. All I yearn for, the thing that pushes me on, that has kept me going, is the thought of striking back, even if it means I die in the process. At least that's the way it was up until recently."

"Recently?" she asked.

"Until I got out here, in this place—and, of course, especially when you dropped in," he said.

She rose up a little and kissed him on the mouth, on the tip of his nose, on his forehead and chest.

"I still can't believe it," he said, and she remembered the withering inquisition he'd given her after the first kiss, his almost brutal attempts to uncover the truth behind her action, the wavering way he'd only slowly succumbed to her advances, as if in fear of opening himself to yet another wound in his psyche, or of yielding to temptation when she may well have had ulterior motives. She could not blame him.

"You can believe it," she said as she thought of her husband in France, probably making love to some French woman at that very moment, though she couldn't remember now what time it would be in France, as if that mattered.

What a difference in these two men, she thought, the older and the younger! He'd been so tender, so delicate, as though she were a fragile flower so easily crushed. Then there was Louis, with his rambunctious ways, his on-and-off love making, totally self-engrossed, his sexual style resembling the capture and submission of prey.

There was nothing to fear any longer, she thought. She knew him, now. He would not hurt her. But she was worried what their future might now have in store, especially with her baby Erika, and she began to cry. He held her tightly, in silence.

***

"Something's going on with Richard," Wilenski said as

he maneuvered the unmarked car deftly through traffic. He and Brooks were headed west on State Highway 96. They would pick up Interstate 35E northbound and stay on it till they reached Duluth then they would take Highway 61 to Grand Marais. It would be about a six-hour drive if the weather held. The roads were clear of snow, so far.

"Woman problems," said Brooks. "He and Laura have had problems right from the very start."

"What kind of 'woman problems'?"

"The usual, him gone all the time, no home life, wife wants to talk, he doesn't, etc., etc. Police work's not a job that promotes happy marriages."

Wilenski nodded. "How did you manage to stay hooked all this time, Brooks?"

"'Hooked' is probably the right word," Brooks said, grinning. "But, it's true. Thirty-nine years now."

"God! It's hard to imagine. I haven't even lived that long. So, how'd you do it? I might be able to use the advice one of these days."

"You got a gal tucked away somewhere, Leonard?"

"No, not really. I'm trying to stay unmarried right now."

"Good boy. But, well, to answer your question, I was just lucky, I guess. I don't have any formulas. Women are different. Take Richard's wife, Laura. She's a socializer and she wants Richard to be around. Alma? She just puts up with all the crap, doesn't mind me not being home."

"So why did you retire. You're not that old."

"Interesting question," said Brooks, "Alma wanted me to retire, but when I did, I just became a nuisance. I think she was a little surprised, but glad I decided to come back to work, even if it is just a short stint. See, that's the difference between her and Richard's wife."

Wilenski turned onto the interstate and pushed the car to seventy miles an hour. Other cars began passing, going at least eighty and eighty-five, ten to fifteen miles over the speed limit.

"Look at that shit, will you?" Wilenski said to Brooks. "Just for a little I'd pull some of those buggers over."

"No harm, no foul," Brooks said. "We've got other things to do." He settled back in the seat and stared out the window and they both grew comfortably silent.

\*\*\*

"Hello?"

"Hi, how are you doing?" the doctor's voice said.

"I'm doing great, Tom. I'm so glad you called."

"Safe to talk?"

"Sure, Richard's out, as usual. Where are you?"

"I'm at home, my wife's out doing some early Christmas shopping. What are you doing? Can you get away?"

"Oh, I wish I could, Tom. I'm here with Melanie today. I can't leave now."

"Yes, of course. I'd like to see you, though."

"I can hardly wait to see you too, dearest. I just can't, can't do it now."

"Well, that's okay. Don't worry about it. I'll call you later, okay?"

"Not today, Tom. I'm not sure how long Richard's going to be gone. Call me at work tomorrow."

"Okay, dear. You be a good girl, now. Have a good day. Love you."

"Love you, too, Tom. I'll talk to you tomorrow."


Lanslow switched the recorder off. He could only sit, his head down, attempting to ride out his swirling emotions. He kept hearing the way she'd spoken his name, her husband's name, like he was an impediment, a stranger, like he was some *thing*, not her lifelong companion. And she'd called Zell dearest and told him she loved him.

Before him, on the table next to the tape recorder,

were the pictures of Zell and Laura that Spiel had given him. To his right were some other photos, in an album, that he had retrieved from a bookcase on impulse. He opened the book to his and Laura's wedding pictures, turning through the pages to the pictures of Melanie in the pediatric's ward, her eyes half open, his big hands practically engulfing her tiny little body. He turned the pages to the pictures of her first birthday, and shots of her first waking in her crib, of shots showing Melanie on the living room rug midst a panoply of toys, shots of Laura teaching her to walk, of Melanie beaming at the camera. He lingered over a close-up of his daughter, her untrimmed bangs hanging over her eyes, her little hand grasping her foot as she seemed to be laughing uproariously at the photographer.

There was a picture of Laura, young, vibrant, laughing. He looked at her hair, thought of how he used to run his fingers through it as he held her face between his hands and kissed her on the tip of her nose. The photo was one taken when they had returned from a park, where they'd made love in the dark, on a blanket. Passion had overridden the possibility that they might be discovered. He remembered her skin, smooth to his fingers, and soft lips, and her sweet smell. It was his first time and she'd said it was hers, too.

He closed the album and stared through the sheer curtains. He felt the pain slowly twisting through him. He was losing everything. How different they were. They'd both known it, even before they were married. But rapture had carried them on. Now, rapture was gone, for Laura it seemed, and there was apparently nothing else to hold them together, indeed, the opposite; there seemed to be everything to force them apart.

He couldn't blame Laura. He'd become cynical, pessimistic, and, above all else, faithless—or at the very least agnostic. Laura saw these changes, but was indifferent. In that respect, he had begun to see her as selfish, unwilling to see his side or even to try to understand his feelings. Ironically, he thought, his loss of faith made him love life even more. Life appeared so tenuous to him now and this tenuousness only served to increase its value. Why waste time on religious beliefs that lacked the slightest bit of evidence to give them reality, most of them downright absurd. But this loss of faith, he was sure, was one more wedge driving him and Laura apart.

On an intellectual level, when they rarely discussed it, Laura would agree with him, but there was a layer in her character—an emotional layer—that she couldn't, didn't want to, ignore. He struggled going to church, felt hypocritical when they went, could hardly wait for it to be over. The greatest irony for him now, however, was that Laura, the supposedly upright one, was carrying on an affair. Their differences had come to a head and demanded action. Laura had taken hers.

He took a deep breath. Rising from the chair, he walked to the bedroom and pulled out a large suitcase stored overhead in their bedroom closet. He began to pull clothing from the closet racks and chest of drawers and place them in the bag. He took only what he would need in the short term, still half hoping he wouldn't need to get the remainder. But it had come down to this. He had his pride and he was an officer of the law. And, above all, he had to be careful not to act toward Zell on his emotions. He was different from his comrades that way. Other cops, he knew, might take another path; take Carnahan, or Cordova, for instance, just to name a couple of his fellow cops. Dr. Zell would find himself in some kind of deep shit with those two. In a way, he was envious.

Next, he wrote Laura a note. She had taken Melanie with her to the grocer. Standing over Melanie's photo once again for a moment, he finally turned away, tears wetting his cheeks. Here in the privacy of his home, he could cry, he could weep, deep agonized moans. He went to the bathroom and dried his face. In the mirror, staring back at him, his face appeared haggard, circles beneath his eyes. He noticed he'd lost weight. His face appeared almost craggy. He stood there, observing himself. What next? he thought. Then he picked up his bag, looked back at the room for an instant, and left, closing the door firmly behind him.

# Chapter Seventeen

Cook County Deputy Sheriff Investigator Bill Herzog got the call through dispatch Sunday evening just as he was leaving for home. For Deputy Sheriff Herzog, working Sundays was not unusual. There was always paper work to clear up and he'd found Sunday evenings quiet and helpful in getting the work done.

He was in an unmarked car, in Grand Marais, heading west on highway seven toward his home when he heard the dispatch. According to Deputy Bob Kellerman, who'd called, a man had found a human body on a side road leading off Highway 12, otherwise known as the Gunflint Trail. Herzog spoke into his radio.

"Where's the body, Bob?"

"Just off The Trail, Sheriff, on NF-1314. Looks like foul play."

"Like how?" Herzog asked.

"Well, he was covered with snow so it's a little hard to tell. I cleared a little of the snow off his head. He's been here a long time. Frostbite. Skin is almost black. It looks like he's been stabbed or hit hard with something 'cause there's frozen blood on the ground underneath the snow, around his head."

"Shit! Yeah, I'd say that's foul play, all right. Don't do anything else. Just keep the public away till everbody else gets there—and don't go tramping around the body or clearing any more snow yourself, either, hear?"

"Copy that, Sheriff. There's no one here anyway 'cept me and the guy who found 'im."

"Who would that be?"

"Dr. Morrison. Henry. His dog found the body, pretty deep in the woods. We probably wouldn't have found it till spring, if then."

Herzog knew Dr. Henry Morrison, locally known as "the Bear Man." Morrison was a zoologist and an expert on bears and he spent most of his days observing the creatures.

"Okay, Bob. Like I said, just keep the scene under control. Go ahead and see what you can get out of Dr. Morrison. I'll be there as soon as I can. Meantime, I'll call dispatch and tell'em to alert the sheriff and other deputies and we'll get the coroner out there."

"Copy that, Sheriff."

Herzog checked his watch. Almost 7:30. Daylight had already long since faded. He picked up his cell phone to call his wife. Once again, he'd go without dinner until late into the night.

\*\*\*

At about 3:00 P.M., Brooks and Wilenski approached Duluth. It was Wilenski's first time to see the city. The view was spectacular, if industrial. Duluth was once a bustling center of commerce centered upon the production and shipment of iron ore pellets to the major American steel producing companies. Most of that economic activity had waned with the rise of Japanese steel production, but the city was still an important port for trade in the great lakes region. The water of Lake Superior, still unfrozen, shimmered in the afternoon sunlight, stretching in a vast expanse as far as the eye could see. The city itself was situated on the shoreline of the lake, extending up the sides of the low-lying hills. A great jumble of railroad switching tracks and multiple buildings and gantry cranes, rising here and there, lay at the southeast of the city. The buildings' roofs were now snow covered. Wilenski saw several freighters, painted black and brown and red, lying at dock in the harbor.

Wilenski saw the lake as a possible escape route for their perp.

"Does the lake ever freeze so that these ships can't get in and out of here?" asked Wilenski.

"I'm not the one to ask," said Brooks, " but I don't

think the lake ever freezes over completely. I think I heard it almost did one time. I've heard it freezes enough to keep most shipping out of here till spring. It's been pretty warm this fall, but these ships will be leaving soon, before the ice sets in."

They were hungry and decided to eat at Grandma's Restaurant. By the time they'd finished their meal and gotten out of Duluth it was nearing 5:30 P.M. They pulled into the all-night service station on the outskirts of the town of Grand Marais where Curtis Nelson had used his credit card. They showed their badges to the young man behind the counter and he introduced himself as Harry Lezalla.

"We're trying to find this man, Mr. Lezalla," said Wilenski, showing him Curtis Nelson's photograph. "We believe he might have stopped here for gas, or some other purchase, on a Friday—back on the twenty-seventh of October, to be exact. His parents own the auto dealership up the road in Trane. Just wondering if you might have seen him."

Lezalla took the photograph and examined it. "Yeah, I remember this guy. I was working that morning. They got some gas and some other things."

"They?" said Wilenski.

"Yeah. There was another guy with him. Kind of strange looking. I was suspicious of him. He wandered around the store a little bit. I thought he might be gonna, like, lift something, you know?"

Wilenski glanced at Brooks. "What did this guy look like, the suspicious one?" he asked.

"About your height, I'd say; stringy, blonde hair, maybe a little lighter than you … " Lezalla looked quickly at Wilenski. " … I don't mean complexion, I mean he was lighter in weight, a real rough looking character. Had a kind of bad look in his eyes. That's why I remember this other one, too. They just didn't fit together, seemed like."

"What kind of vehicle were they driving? Did you get a good look at it?"

"Sure. It was a red Chevy Tahoe. Pretty late model, I think."

"License number?"

"No, afraid not."

"Do you have any idea where they were going? Did they say anything?"

Lezalla shook his head. "Seemed like they were having an argument about something before they left. Looked to me like this mean-looking dude kind of forced the younger guy into the passenger's side when they left, then he got in on the driver's side and they turned and went on up The Trail. That's all I know."

"Forced? What do you mean?"

"Well, seemed like he was kind of guiding him, holding him by the arm, and the guy was resisting a little."

"Then they went on up The Trail?" said Wilenski. "Highway twelve?"

"Yeah. The Gunflint Trail."

"Was there anyone else with them, a woman?" Wilenski asked.

"No, I don't think so. If there was, I didn't see her."

Wilenski extended his hand. "Thanks, Mr. Lezalla. You've been a great help." He handed Lezalla his card. "You think of anything else, give us a call, okay?"

They exited the store and each took in the situation, as if there might be another clue or something. But neither man saw anything that looked suspicious. It was totally dark now. Large piles of snow had been pushed to the side of the station out of the driveway.

"Well, now we've got two suspects," said Wilenski, as they walked to the car. "It fits."

"Yeah, Nelson had to have help, no doubt about it."

"And it wasn't Derek Lunzer."

"Nope, Lunzer's got the alibi. There's another man in on this, somehow."

"You think they had the woman?" asked Wilenski.

"Yeah, probably. Maybe had her hid in the Tahoe somehow." But Brooks was also thinking the perps could have dumped Jacqueline Bideau's body already.

It was even likely they'd done what they were going to do to her and she was dead, her body lying somewhere along the highway between Grand Marais and White Bear Lake, or, perhaps, somewhere farther up the Gunflint Trail.

"What now?" asked Wilenski, once they were back in the car.

"Damned if I know," said Brooks. "Think of this," he continued. "All we know for sure is that Nelson was Derek Lunzer's roommate in college and that they called one another a lot up until about the time of the murders. After which Derek Lunzer attempted to reach him by phone several times and never could get him. We know Nelson and another man stopped and bought some gas here at this station on the morning of the murders within a time-frame that could have put him at the crime scene and then back up here. That's all we know. Maybe Nelson had nothing to do with any of this, especially taking Lunzer's sister. They were friends, roommates. We've made a mighty big assumption. Hell, we could be on a wild-goose chase, for all we know."

It was a long speech for Brooks. Wilenski sensed his partner's frustration and he thought Brooks might be upset partly because, for some damned reason, Lanslow hadn't thought it important enough to come with them. They just sat there in the car, both thinking hard.

"Well, it is a lead," Wilenski ventured. "If that clerk is right, this other dude seems to have been forcing Nelson to go with him on up the trail. What do you make of that? Maybe taking the woman, like you said, was the other guy's idea and Nelson was resisting."

There was a long, palpable silence.

"Well, if they did have her in that Tahoe," Brooks finally said, "and haven't killed her already, they would have to find a place to stash her and hide for awhile."

"Yeah, that's true," said Wilenski. "Damned strange that Nelson and this other dude—whoever he is—would even bring her up here, so close to Nelson's hometown. Maybe Nelson was coming back from his ski trip and picked up a hitchhiker. Maybe the other guy decided to get in on the act. Or maybe he's from around here, too. And maybe they're just more comfortable in familiar territory."

"That's a hell of a lot of maybes," said Brooks. "If Nelson is in on this, I'd bet they were in it together, all the way, had a falling out, probably, like you say, over the woman."

"It's a loose end," Wilenski said, "got to be tied up."

"Afraid so," said Brooks, glancing at his watch. "Let's get on with it. Maybe we can go on up The Trail, see if anyone else might have seen the Tahoe—or maybe we might spot it."

Wilenski started studying the road map. "That trail looks pretty uninhabited on up north, except for a few lodges. I hope we can find a place to sleep."

"We can always come back to Grand Marais, if we have to," Brooks said. "Or get a room in a lodge or sleep in the car."

Wilenski grimaced. "Temperature's supposed to fall to below freezing tonight," he said. "Sure would hate to have to sleep in the car."

"Don't worry," Brooks said. "I'm not keen on that idea, either."

***

The two detectives saw the cherry lights in the distance.

"What have we here?" said Brooks, who had taken the wheel.

"Looks like an accident," said Wilenski.

An officer in brown uniform was in the middle of the road, waving them to a stop. From far behind, Brooks heard the sirens and saw the swirling, flashing lights of another responder in the rearview mirror. He pulled the car to the side of the road and let the vehicle pass. While they waited, the officer waved the automobile on by them. It was an ambulance. He walked over to their vehicle.

They showed their badges to the officer.

"Oh, yeah," said the deputy. "The sheriff told me about you boys. Let me give him a call."

He spoke into his radio and they heard a loud gruff voice that Brooks recognized as Investigator Herzog, whom he'd spoken to that morning. Herzog had related over the phone that he knew of the Nelsons, but didn't know their son Curtis. He said Curtis had never been in trouble as far as their records showed. Once again he'd stated that they'd been unable to secure a warrant to search the Nelson home and he'd apologized.

The officer turned back to them. "Yeah," he said. "Go right ahead. He's down there, by the ambulance."

The two detectives drove on only a little farther, parked their car at the direction of another officer and were sent down the trail to another road.

"Just walk on down there," the officer said, pointing toward the flashing lights of the ambulance.

The big man was easy to pick out among the gathered group. They introduced themselves to Bill Herzog whose grip matched his size. He dwarfed the other officers and responders around him. His voice matched his bulk.

"Well, boys, I see you got up here right in the middle of things. Welcome to Cook County."

"What've you got here, Sheriff?" Brooks asked.

"Just a little homicide, Detective," Herzog said. "Maybe you boys might wanta take a look? We haven't disturbed anything, or at least we've tried not to. We might use the help."

"Sure, Sheriff," said Wilenski.

"Just be a little careful," said the Sheriff, unnecessarily. "The coroner is on his way."

They made their way to the side of the road where spotlights from a couple of squad cars had been pointed down a steep embankment into the woods. The sheriff guided them well off to the side of a set of tracks in the snow, down the embankment.

"Those tracks there," said Herzog, pointing to the human ones, "are from the guy who discovered the body, and from my deputy. Those animal tracks are from the guy's dog. It was Dr. Morrison's dog discovered the body. Morrison is a zoologist, studies bears." He was grunting with exertion.

The heavy scent of pine filled the air and in the light from the squad cars the shadows of the trees loomed over the scene. The detectives could barely make out the two sets of shoe tracks leading to the body.

They continued on down the embankment, slipping and sliding.

"From what we can tell so far," Herzog wheezed, "the

vic has been here for a long time. The body is frost bitten, lying on the bare ground. So the vic was put here before the snow last Thursday, or sometime thereabouts; nothing in the snow to suggest anything else. He must have been dragged down this embankment and left down here by the perp. Like I say, it's been here a long time, but the forensics people will be able to tell us more about that, later."

They came upon the body a few moments later. Brooks and Wilenski stood, surveying the scene.

Herzog spoke: "What do you boys think?" he asked.

"You think he was dragged down here? So he was killed before, up near the road?" Wilenski asked.

"No way to tell, really. My guess is he was strangled up near the road. I'm just thinking the perp would probably drag the body down here to hide it. That's what I'd do. We won't know much more till the coroner and his team get here, though. They're on their way."

"There's no blood here," said Brooks. "Is it covered by the new snow?"

"Yeah, must have been. You have to look close. Hard to see in this light, but there's blood around his head. I got down close as I could, looked at his neck," said the sheriff. "There are marks; looks like stab wounds. But him freezing like this, it's hard to tell. I'd say he might have been strangled up near the road and left for dead, but he was still alive. There's no sign of a struggle up there, but a hell of a struggle went on down here. Perp must have come back, followed him down here and finished him off."

"You said the vic was local, Sheriff? Who is he?" Brooks asked.

"Didn't say that. We don't know yet. He's just a kid, though."

"Curtis Nelson is the guy we talked about this morning, Sheriff. Think it might be him?"

"Well, it could very well be him. We got your fax but I can't remember how he looks. You know what Nelson looks like?"

The body was bent in a fetal position, the hands thrust between the legs, the face, now almost completely black, turned upward, partially covered with snow. Wilenski imagined the young man realizing he was about to die, fighting for his life. Perhaps it had dawned upon him that his life was over and that he would never see or hear or feel again, the stillness of the forest, the darkness of the night, the coming dawn, the coldness of the ground upon which his blood was spilling.

They both bent down to examine the face closely. The skin had dried and shrunk to the skull, almost mummified, but it was recognizable.

"Yeah, I think that's our guy," said Brooks, finally.

"That's Curtis Nelson."

Herzog began swearing. "God damn it," he said, "Somebody's going to have to notify the Nelsons. They're gonna have to ID him from the photos first, then at Duluth, just to be sure. God damn it," he said, again, pounding his fist into his palm. "I hate this fucking part!"

## Chapter Eighteen

Lanslow stood before a table in front of Deputy Sheriff Investigator Herzog's desk reading the letter dated October 26, 2006, from Sabriga Quill. Wilenski and Brooks stood just off to the side. He handed the letter to Wilenski.

"You got this letter on October twenty-sixth, Sheriff?" Lanslow asked and Herzog nodded, somewhat shamefaced.

Wilenski read the letter and looked up. "This describes our case," he said.

"Looks like it," said Lanslow.

Wilenski handed the letter to Brooks. "Amazing," Brooks said. He handed it back to Lanslow who couldn't help scanning it once more.

"I gotta tell you, boys," the sheriff-investigator said, resting his ample bottom against the front of his desk, "I'm sorry. But I didn't connect this to what happened down in the cities. Sabriga has her quite a reputation 'round here, and most people just think she's a little nuts. I just chucked this in my hold file and forgot about it."

"I'd probably have done the same thing, Sheriff," Lanslow said, trying to be diplomatic, continuing to scan the letter carefully. "Hard for you to have known."

Secretly, he was still miffed at Herzog for not pushing their request for a search warrant of the Nelson's home.

Lanslow looked at the date on the October letter again: the postmark was one day before the Lunzers had been murdered, and it had been sent through the Trane post office. There was no way that Sabriga Quill could have gotten some of the details of the murders she'd described in the letter. They hadn't even happened yet!

Lanslow shook his head in disbelief. He sat down at the table on which the crime photos and reports had been laid, trying to focus.

"How would Miss Quill pick up this information, Sheriff? How could she know about the Lunzers' murders even before they happened?"

Herzog shifted his weight uneasily. "All she has to say about that is that she has both kinds of visions, things that have happened and things that are about to happen. Had the ability since she was a child. Sabriga says she got bad vibes from the man she saw in a grocery store up in Trane and she said she got the visions sometime after that."

Lanslow was trying to focus, to clear away the cloud in his brain. He rubbed his eyes, massaged his cheeks.

Brooks and Wilenski exchanged glances.

Lanslow had started the drive to Grand Marais

almost immediately after receiving Brooks' call. He'd arrived at the motel where the two detectives were staying about an hour ago. It was now 3:A.M.

He wasn't thinking about the crime much on the way up. It was as though the energy had been sucked out of him. All during the drive up he was thinking about his and Laura's situation and he couldn't come up with any other alternative than to do what he had done, move out of the apartment, perhaps just to give him time to think. But he was drowning in sorrow— agony, actually. He'd felt almost the same way years ago when his brother had been killed in a car accident, totally despondent, and again when Zeke, his first partner, had been murdered. But this marital problem was worse, like a weight on his chest, a heavy weight of grief and loss that threatened to crush him.

The room he'd taken after he'd left his and Laura's apartment only made him feel worse: sparsely furnished, the bed with dilapidated springs, the laminated wood chest-of-drawers with worn, faded finish, an old hardback chair, a warped folding closet door that wouldn't quite close. The room was the only thing he could get quickly. He would try to get something better later.

He'd dropped his bags heavily onto the floor and fell, fully clothed, emotionally drained, on the bed and attempted to sleep, grateful to escape his torture, if only by giving up wakeful consciousness for a while. But sleep wouldn't come and when he took Brooks' call on his cell phone only an hour or so later he had actually felt relief that something else could claim his time and attention.

Lanslow tried to hide his grief as best he could. He put the letter down and began going through the crime photos. Brooks and Wilenski had briefed him already about the prominent theory of the crime.

The man who'd killed Curtis Nelson was evidently in on the killing of the Lunzers. Sabriga Quill had described him in her letter only briefly — yellow hair, smokey, angry eyes, a beard. This man and Nelson had most likely abducted the woman following the murder of the Lunzers, and made their escape to here, in this northern part of the state, where Curtis had been killed for whatever reason. Curtis had probably first been choked, left for dead along that lonely road. The killer had then, probably, returned for some reason, perhaps finding Nelson still alive. The signs indicated that Nelson had struggled to get away, maybe running into the woods, but was caught and stabbed to death. The killer had then proceeded to drag the body on deeper into the woods in an effort to hide it. He then continued to wherever he was going, in Nelson's vehicle, with or without the woman. A new APB was already out on the red 2006 Chevy Tahoe.

Lanslow continued going through the crime photos. The identity of the man who'd apparently murdered Curtis Nelson began to gnaw at him. Who was he? And how did this man connect with Derek Lunzer, their prime suspect? Did he have the woman? Would they find her, too, alongside some remote road? Was it Curtis Nelson who'd drawn the map of the Lunzer home? Was Derek Lunzer innocent, afterall? And, back to the nagging question: how had the black man gotten that map?

Lanslow looked up at Brooks. "Didn't you say that Curtis Nelson lived in Trane, with his parents?"

"That's right, Rich. He's a college kid, back east."

"Trane's not far on up highway 61," Herzog said. "I've had the parents notified. They'll be ID'ing the body in Duluth sometime later today. I got a deputy, who'll take a statement, going with them."

"This woman—Sabriga Quill—is a psychic, Sheriff?" Lanslow queried.

The sheriff nodded. "Claims to be."

Lanslow glanced skeptically at his two detectives.

Herzog saw the exchange. "Yeah, I know," said the sheriff. "I've got my doubts, too," but there's the letter. How do you explain it?"

Lanslow put the crime photos back in the envelope and handed them to the sheriff. "Can't say as I can, Sheriff. And I'm just about ready to try anything at this point." He began rubbing his temples again, as if to stimulate some kind of belief in the woman called Sabriga Quill and her strange powers.

"Sheriff," said Wilenski, "if this perp was headed on up the Gunflint Trail, where might he be intending to go? I've been looking at the map. It doesn't look like there's anything up there much except resorts."

"Well, that's true when you get farther north. The country around the trail that far north is mostly wilderness. Some people live along the trail up there, but not many stay all year long. It's paved highway all the way to the end of the trail and there's a turn-around there, several campsites along the way."

"These resorts, would he be likely going to any of those in particular?" Wilenski asked the sheriff.

"In particular? Well, you got me. But I have my people calling every resort and business up that way. I don't give a damn if I have to roust them all out of bed. I think time is important here. Some of the resorts have faxes as well as phones. We're asking them if they've seen anyone and we're sending Nelson's picture to those that have fax machines, just in case they might have seen him with this other fellow. I have some cruis-

ers on the trail, too. Oh, yeah, and we'll have a helicopter searching that area by light of day and we'll try to
organize an on-ground search as soon as we can. That's
wild country. A person could hide in there and maybe
never be found."

"Could he be living up that way?" Brooks asked.

"Could be. We'll check on the residents up there, get
their names."

"We know you're doing everything you can, Sheriff,"
said Lanslow. "We appreciate it."

"Well, look, boys, this is our case too, you know. We
want this guy as much as you. Now, you guys better
catch some sleep if you can. I got a couple of reporters
pestering me."

***

Early that Monday morning, Sabriga Quill saw the
news report on the TV and was immediately seized by
visions. She staggered to her living room and sat in the
big overstuffed chair. She saw a dark place. There was
a terrible struggle, terrible fear, and a sound of someone moaning in pain.

She saw a cold, cold place, again a place of struggle, and wrenching, tearing fear.

She saw showers of white against white, slashes of

346

green, sounds of strenuous effort and, again, fear and terror, and heavy jagged shadows. Then she saw a human figure appear briefly. The image was blurry, but she recognized it as much like the one she'd seen in a vision over a week ago, strands of hair flying, an arm raised, a contorted face. That was when she knew her earlier vision of a terrible event was connected to this one. It was the same figure, appearing in both visions. And, this time, she remembered again, having seen him in person, at a grocery store on a Thursday morning, on October 27, 2006.

This time she decided not to write. She picked up the phone and dialed Under Sheriff Herzog's number.

*** 

Herzog leaned back in his chair, turning his gaze upon the men standing around his office. All their faces were haggard. Most had slept for no more than two or three hours.

"That was Sabriga Quill," he said, looking up at Lanslow. "Says she had visions about the boy's murder. I'm going to send a squad over to Trane to get her. Shouldn't be more than about a half-hour. We'll get a statement from her."

"How do you think she got wind of Nelson's murder,

Sheriff?" Lanslow asked.

"Well, she saw the visions when it was reported up here on the TV on the early morning news this morning. I talked to a couple of reporters late last night. They reported the crime this morning."

\*\*\*

Sabriga Quill, wearing a long black coat over a red dress, with black hose and leather boots over her slim legs, was ushered in to Sheriff Herzog's office. After the sheriff had taken her coat, Sabriga sat down imperiously in the chair offered to her and placed her purse on the floor beside it. She appeared only remotely aware of the other officers leaning along the sides of the office against the walls. Folding her translucent hands across her lap, she fixed her gaze on Sheriff Herzog, waiting.

Herzog cleared his throat. "Sabriga, these gentlemen are from the cities. They are detectives and they're working on a case that appears to be very similar to the events you described in your letter to me back in late October."

Sabriga shifted slightly. "Yes, I know."

The officers all exchanged glances.

Sabriga shifted her small prim frame on the chair. "You said you got my first letter in late October, Sheriff?

Did you even read it?"

"Sabriga ... "

She waved him off. "Never mind," she said. "I'm here to help, not to blame, although ... " She didn't finish.

"Sabriga, this is Sergeant Detective Lanslow, this is Detective Brooks, and this is Detective Wilenski. As I said ... "

Sabriga nodded to the detectives, then turned her attention back to the sheriff. "I saw the vision of this latest murder, too, Sheriff, like I told you on the phone. And I believe the same men, at least one of them, are involved in both incidents. Do you want me to describe what I saw?"

"By all means, Sabriga. Do you mind if we use the recorder, and a sketch artist? And we'd like for you to give us a written report later, too, if you could. "

"Of course. That's fine, Sheriff, thank you," she said, appreciatively. "I can begin anytime."

"Do you need anything?" the sheriff asked.

"If you have something from the scene—something which might have been touched by the killer or the victim—that might help."

There was an exchange of glances all around. Sabriga saw them, but only smiled slightly.

"Sabriga, I'm afraid the items collected at the scene

on their way to the lab in Duluth. I can call and get the boys back back here if we have to."

"That may be necessary, Sheriff. I can wait."

Herzog nodded, then picked up the phone and instructed dispatch to contact the cruiser on its way to Duluth and have them turn around and bring the evidence back.

In the meantime, to hurry things along, he then went to his desk and picked up the case file and pulled some of the crime scene photos from the envelope. "We don't usually show these around," he said, "but in this case, would these perhaps help?"

Sabriga took the pictures gently in her hand, a look of consternation spreading across her face when she began to scan them. "Yes, I've seen this man before, Sheriff," she said, pointing to the closeup photo of Curtis Nelson's face. "He was the man with the other one, the bad one."

*** 

Jeffrey Stone was still euphoric, but he was worried, too. The two emotions mixed inside him like oil and water. At last he'd found something to live for rather than die for. He was like a man reborn. He was jubilant.

But underneath these emotions, there was still the

concern, the anxiety, the unease, the apprehension and, always, always, the seething anger.

On his way into Grand Marais he listened to the news on his car radio. It was the only time he ever had contact with the wider outside world beyond the house and the drive into Grand Marais. He had long since stopped listening to the blather of the talk shows and the blare of the rock and roll and hip-hop bunch. It was the news he listened to, and especially the steady stream of opinions from the so-called "experts" on the death and destruction in Iraq "for democracy and freedom." He couldn't avoid it. He was attracted to the news in Iraq like a moth to a flame and, ultimately, he thought, probably with the same consequences.

As far as Iraq was concerned, to him it was all the same as before, the same as what he'd heard and seen happen in Vietnam. On the radio now was the news of how the Democrats would probably regain control of the congress and presidency and would begin to bring the troops home. As a former military officer he scoffed at that idea, knowing the strategic and logistical difficulties of such a process — even if the generals were actually ordered to leave, most of the tons of equipment and supplies would have to be reloaded and shipped or left behind. Besides, he believed even the democratic leadership had no illusions of stopping the war quickly, that they were saying what they thought the public wanted to hear. Even if the Democrats won majorities in both houses, the president would be faced with the recalcitrant senators and representatives who would be loath to go against their "special interest" supporters who funded their campaigns. He simply could not believe, sometimes, the reports of the quagmire into which the president and his so-called "neocon cabal" had launched the nation. His hatred for those men and women who sent young troops into battle for some illusioned historic transformation of the Middle East rose like a bile in his throat.

As sometimes happened when he heard these news reports, for a time he was transported back to that hot, fetid land of Vietnam, in the jungle, where the razor sharp elephant grass rose well above his head, ready to slash his arms and hands and face, during the Monsoon season; where the green leeches lay lurking in the water or lay in the branches of the trees, waiting to drop. He remembered the pungi sticks the enemy had planted to pierce and infect his feet, and the blisters gotten from leather boots that shrank after they dried out. It seemed they had always been wet and drying out, and then wet again.

But most of all he remembered the faces of the old Vietnamese women, screwed into agony as they stood or kneeled, rocking and wailing, over the dead bodies of their husbands and sons, their daughters, their grandchildren, their uncles, aunts and cousins — entire families, all lying upon the ground, their bodies half blown away, their houses burning, the fires roaring, their crops destroyed, their animals slaughtered. And, worst of all, his own men being shot and killed, or terribly wounded, their groans and moans echoing in his ears. And, then, there was the constant slap of helicopter blades against the heavy smoky air, bringing more troops, more staccato bursts of deadly gunfire.

His loathing for the military and for the authorities that had railroaded him — a loathing that had grown and festered over the months as the Iraq war ground on — rode closely to the surface of his consciousness. Even at night he would wake himself up with his own groaning and find himself bathed in heavy sweat.

But now he shook these thoughts off and thought about the woman. Just thinking of her had the effect of a potion, as though he'd taken a tonic that distributed itself to every cell in his body and shook it to life, singing. Still, his thoughts now were that their situation was desperate, even hopeless if they were discovered and that they probably couldn't stay here anyway. He was certain Jacqueline wouldn't want to stay, but would want to see her baby and her brother and the rest of her family. And how could he blame her? To cap it off, somewhere, in back of his head, despite all that had happened between them, he still could not squelch that small little tick of doubt about how she felt about him, that she might just be playing him.

That's the way it had gotten for him; he trusted nobody.

He reached down and turned off the radio and continued his thoughts. What could they do? The more he thought the more his euphoria slipped away, replaced by despondency. Had he found something to live for only to see it slip away? There was a question looming ahead. Which answer would – could – they take?

They could, of course, try to escape, leave the country. That possibility was part of why he and Silas had wound up here so close to Canada in the first place. The brothers would have roared across the border on their snowmobiles, disappearing into the wild lands of Canada.

Of course, he could go on the run again with the woman, but he knew the probabilities of capture were more than likely, especially with a woman in tow. In the end, however, after all his thought, he knew that an attempt to escape, in the illusion they could live happily ever after, was what would impel him to do that very thing.

He smiled to himself. Here he was, proud of himself at being a part of the intellectual life, the thinker, the epitome of rationality (at least at one time he was), yet succumbing to his emotions. It seemed that all possible sentiments converged in him at once: happiness and joy, elation and ecstasy, sorrow, sadness, fear, anger.

He was a raging cauldron of all of these as he parked the vehicle at the service station, went inside and purchased a newspaper. His hands shook even before he saw the headline, even before he pulled the paper from the rack. And when he read it he knew then that fate had dealt him another dirty blow.

## Chapter Nineteen

Sabriga Quill took Curtis Nelson's coat from Sheriff Herzog. The putrid odor of dead flesh arose and spread throughout the room and her face contorted in disgust and pain. She laid it upon the table in front of her where she had been filling in her report of the incidents leading to her visions.

In her report, before Nelson's coat had been delivered, she'd related once again that the first incident where she'd felt bad vibes had been when she had encountered two men in the grocery store at Trane, sometime back near the end of October, one of whom she recognized as the dead lad in the crime photos. The other she described as tall and wiry, long blonde hair, evil eyes, a real "loser" type, as she had referred to him.

She wrote that the "loser" had simply set off bad feelings in her and she had watched him a bit until it appeared that he had become aware of her surveillance and he and the other man had promptly left the store. It was the same day she saw this man that she had gotten the terrible visions and had sent the letter to the sheriff's department.

Viewing the coat with apprehension, Sabriga cleared the room of everyone except Herzog, a patrolman, and the sketch artist. Reluctantly she laid her hands upon the coat and closed her eyes. The recorder was by her side as she began voicing what she was experiencing. A twisted chary grimace crossed her face, her mouth curling in distaste. She began slowly, almost painfully, to describe a man to the sketch artist, the description of a man with smoky, smoldering eyes. She hesitated from time to time as if she needed the passage of a few moments to recover. At last, she hung her head, one hand over her eyes, the other signaling that she was done. She pushed the coat away. Herzog nodded at the patrolman who picked it up and left the room. The odor of it remained behind as the sketch artist continued drawing then held up the picture. Sabriga studied the sketch only for a moment, nodding.

"Yes, that's him," she said, after a moment. "The man I saw on Friday, October 26th. The bad one."

***

The Nelsons were small people, made even smaller by their huddled appearance as they sat in front of Sheriff Herzog's big desk waiting to be questioned then taken to Duluth. They had seen the newspaper report of their son's death and the crime-scene photos, the father gasping and the mother weeping at the sight of their dead son's son's appearance, but their trip to the morgue to make a positive identification was necessary.

Tom Nelson didn't look at all like the eminent businessman in his community that he must be, thought Lanslow, standing nearby. The little man sat close to his wife, occasionally putting his arm about her shoulders, himself trying to still the trembling of his lower lip. She was staring into his face and they were both obviously trying to understand the horrible circumstance into which they'd been suddenly thrust. Their responses wiped all doubt away that Lanslow had once held about the truth of the story they'd told him earlier.

Nelson turned his attention back to the Sheriff who'd asked him a question.

"It was about the twenty-first ... yes, the twenty-first ... last month ... that Curtis told us he was going to leave the campus for awhile and go to Colorado skiing with his friend, Derek. We objected to him breaking his time at college like that but he claimed it was a special opportunity and he had only a paper to finish in his course and had his professor's permission. He left home early the morning of the twenty-sixth, a Thursday."

"He was driving?" asked the sheriff.

"Yes, his Tahoe. He had it loaded with his equipment and bags."

"Nobody with him?"

"No, not then. He told us he was meeting Derek in the Twin Cities, in White Bear Lake, I believe, he said. They were going to drive to the resort from there."

"That's the last you saw of him then, until ...?"

"Yes. Yessir. That was the last."

"Okay, Mr. Nelson. Thank you. Now, Sergeant Detective Lanslow here has a few questions he wants to ask you, too, if you don't mind."

Tom shook his head sadly. "No, of course not. We want to be of any help possible." He turned his gaze upon Lanslow.

"Mr. And Mrs. Nelson," Lanslow began, "I'm very sorry about your son. But anything you can tell us might be of help."

Nelson only nodded, his wife's teary eyes riveted on the detective's face.

"The sheriff has already told you we think your son has somehow gotten involved in a scheme to murder Derek Lunzer's parents."

Mrs. Nelson's head dropped, an audible whimper escaped her lips and Mr. Nelson once again comforted her. "We know that," Detective," he said. "We don't believe Curtis would be mixed up in anything like that, but we know what has happened. We want an explanation, too. We think Curtis must have been returning

from skiing in Colorado after the Lunzers were murdered and picked up a hitchhiker who murdered him
for his money. The sheriff has told us that his car has
been taken and his billfold is missing."

"That's a possibility, Mr. Nelson, a very real possibility," said Lanslow. "But you see, we have reason to
believe that the young woman we're looking for, who
was abducted from the murdered parents' home, was in
Curtis' automobile —perhaps against your son's will —
but we have some proof she was in his truck. The man
who was on duty when your son filled his truck with
gas has identified him as the man he saw being forced
by another man into his vehicle. If the woman was in
your son's truck, then that would put it at the crime
scene and would seem to implicate him in what
occurred there."

"You said 'if', detective. Was she in the truck?" he
asked. "I ... I ... just can't believe ... " Nelson couldn't
finish.

Lanslow tried to press his point. "Mr. Nelson, as a
matter of fact, no one has seen the woman since she
was abducted. But we do have this eyewitness account
of an altercation occurring between the man who was
apparently with your son, an argument during which,
according to this eyewitness, Curtis was forced into the
passenger side of his own car and was driven off by the

man who we think looks like this."

Lanslow handed the sketch of Silas Halladay to Mr. Nelson's trembling hands. When they saw the picture they both looked up in unison, surprised and stunned.

"Why, why ... this man works for me!" said Nelson. "That's Jim Collins. He's one of our mechanics."

"Jim Collins, you say?" Herzog asked. "He still works for you?"

"Well, I'm not sure. Our maintenance supervisor reported he hasn't shown up at work for awhile ... for over a week, I think. We haven't seen him for sometime, now. But what would Collins have to do with our son's death or with the disappearance of the woman?"

"Well, Mr. Nelson," said the sheriff, "that's exactly what we're going to try and find out."

\*\*\*

She was sitting at the table before the picture window. Jeffrey tossed the newspaper down on the table and said, "You might be interested in this."

She picked it up and instantly there was a short intake of breath. Curtis Nelson's picture was shown next to the story that he was missing. She looked up at him. "I know this man," she said. "He's my brother's roommate."

"That so?" he said. "Well, not any longer. He's dead. Silas killed him." He emptied the contents of the paper bag containing Curtis Nelson's driver's license and credit cards upon the table. "I found these under the seat of the Tahoe. The pickup was Nelson's, too, apparently."

"He's dead? Why would your brother kill him? Curtis helped your brother kidnap me?" she asked, incredulously.

"Looks that way. He was the other guy in the car."

She tried to get hold of it.

He watched her, his face grim. After a moment, he said, "Silas said there was another man, a third man, involved, too. He didn't know who he was."

"Someone else, a third man? I don't understand," she said.

He turned, looking out the window. "There were three of them in on it: my brother, the guy they just found, and another one. As I said, Silas didn't know who this third guy was. If this guy they found was your brother's roommate, then ..."

"No. No. I can't believe that," she interrupted, making the connection, her face ashen.

He turned back from the window, moved to her side. "I'm just saying it's possible."

She stood up abruptly, her hands trembling. "I ...

don't ... believe it," she repeated. "Me? My baby? My parents ...?"

Stone just stood there, silent, for a moment. "Your brother may not be involved," he said, finally, seeing how emotional she was. "It may be someone else. Whoever it was, I got the impression from Silas that this other guy was not actually, physically involved; that he was the brains, so to speak. That's all I know. Silas would have no reason to lie about that."

She sat down again and simply stared into the distance, toward the west end of the lake, for a moment. "Derek was at a party that night, in Edina. He couldn't have done it," she said, more or less to herself. "He wouldn't do this."

Jeffrey shrugged impatiently. "We've got a different situation, now," he said. "They'll be looking here, getting close. We're going to have to try to get out of this place."

She came back to the present. "We?" she said.

He looked at her questioningly. "I thought we had something going here. Is that true or not?"

His doubts about her feelings for him rose again. That she had played him for a fool all along would not surprise him. His plan for them would require that he know, and know for certain. He waited, staring.

"Yes, yes, of course," she said, looking at the floor,

rising, wheeling and stepping to the window, then turning back to him.

"Well, what is it?" he demanded.

"My baby," she said. "I can't leave my baby, Jeffrey."

"I know. I know. Of course you can't. We'll try to get her somehow though, Jacqueline—later," he heard himself saying, not believing his own silly statement or the way it sounded so plaintive. But he went on. "She can join us later, wherever we go." He heard himself almost pleading, succumbing once again to the emotion, the hope she had given him.

She sat down and began to sob.

He stood over her. "Jacqueline, you've given me back my life. I've fallen in love with you. If we do—have something going, that is—then you have to go with me. I love you with all my heart and I was in hopes that you loved me. Still, I will understand if you decide to stay. I have to start getting ready though. I won't let them take me back to prison. I don't think we have much time. If you're going with me, we have to pack."

"Right now, tonight?"

He glanced at the window, at the fading daylight. "No, not now. We'll need provisions and warm clothing and by the time we pack it'll be too dark to travel. We're going to have to use the snowmobiles, and we won't be able to use the lights, too easy to spot. It's not too far to

Canada. We're going to have to try to get out, by first light in the morning, at the latest."

"Why all that stuff? I don't know how to operate a snow-mobile," she said, even though she'd been ready only a couple of days ago to try it to escape.

"You'll ride with me. We can't travel by the road. They'll have it covered. We'll have to make it through the wild. And we can't build a fire. They'd spot it right away. They'll have dogs. We'll have to leave as soon as we can get things packed. I only hope we have time. It may be too late already."

\*\*\*

"Jim Collins" got no match on the computer but when they sent the sketch to the BCA and the BCA had sent it in to the FBI they got a hit. Herzog and Lanslow were standing around the fax machine when the papers began to come through. As he finished reading each page, he handed it to Lanslow. There were photos now, not just sketches. Lanslow was stunned at the similarity of the sketch they had sent with the actual photo of Halladay. And there was a photo of his brother, Jeffrey Stone. There was some resemblance between the two brothers, especially through the eyes.

"This is bigger than I thought," Herzog said.

"Sure looks like it," replied Lanslow.

A half-hour later, Herzog called the deputies, whom he had formed into a task force, along with Lanslow, Wilenski and Brooks, as partners in the investigation, together. The officers were standing and sitting in various places around the conference room as Herzog read from the reports.

"This 'Jim Collins' is an alias," said the sheriff, holding up the photo of Silas Halladay. "His real name is Silas Halladay and he's the half brother of a man by the name of Jeffrey Stone." Again, he held up the photo of Stone. "They're both wanted in Texas," Herzog continued. "Seems Stone murdered his wife, who was about to reveal that he and his brother were hatching a bomb plot to blow up the local county facilities. Stone was sent to prison in 1999. Halladay was charged with conspiracy to murder. Halladay already had a record, had spent some time in prison for a rape he committed several years earlier. Halladay and his brother wound up in the same prison in Middle Brook, Texas, after their conviction; escaped in 2005, killing a guard, never caught. Seems we have some fugitives among us, boys."

There was a faint hum of voices that went through the room.

Herzog looked up and around at the faces of the detectives and deputies. "And, oh yeah, just one other little point. Jeffrey Stone was an army officer who fought in Vietnam and it seems probable that his brother is no marshmallow, either."

"How'd they wind up here, Sheriff, in northern Minnesota?" asked Wilenski.

"You got me, Detective," said the sheriff. We know Halladay is probably here, but as for Stone? He could be somewhere else, though I'd guess they're still working together."

"You really think these guys are still in this area Sheriff," asked Brooks, "after all the publicity?"

Sheriff Herzog looked a bit uncomfortable. "Yes, Sabriga Quill thinks so, at least Halladay is, she says."

The whole crowd just stared at him and then at one another, then there was a bit of muted tittering that rippled across the group.

"Okay, okay, I know, this is highly unusual. But Detective Lanslow here has pointed out that Sabriga knew several things about the murders down in White Bear Lake that no one would know unless they were there—and we know she wasn't. And she seems to know a lot about this latest murder, too, of the Nelson boy. She provided a sketch of Halladay. So just go along with me on this. We need every bit of goddamned help we can get."

Lanslow was amused at the big man's embarrassment. Herzog had apparently decided not to play Sabriga's recording to anyone but him. In it she'd said she felt the presence of the "bad" man, the man who'd apparently murdered the college boy and she had said she saw a house near a lake and a red car. She also said she saw another man, a bearded man, and she'd felt strange about this other man, as if she didn't know quite what to make of him, or how or whether he fit into the murder of Curtis Nelson.

"What about Sabriga's vision about the house and car?" asked Lanslow, deciding to say nothing about the image of the bearded man, and trying to take some of the pressure off the sheriff. "Can we send some squads up and down the trail to check that out?"

There was a general muttering and the words "house?" and "car?" echoed throughout the room.

Herzog looked through the window. "It's almost dark," he said. "We'll put patrols on the Trail, but those houses are hard to see. They set back pretty far in the trees at the end of winding roads. I think it's best to wait till early tomorrow morning and we'll send a chopper up there to spot the houses, see if there's anything suspicious. If we can spot something from the air, we'll have the squads available to answer the call pretty quick. In the meantime, we'll set up checkpoints along the roads."

"What about the Texas authorities, Sheriff?" Lanslow asked.

"We'll have to notify them. They want these men, too. We have jurisdiction here, but they'll no doubt want to send someone up."

Lanslow was restless and wanted to get on with it. But Herzog was in charge and he was probably right. They'd have to wait until morning.

Herzog placed the recorder on the table, announcing it was Sabriga's report of her vision, and as he began to play it, everyone gathered round to listen.

\*\*\*

Lanslow swirled the beer in his glass. The day had been hectic. The emptiness and desperation over his situation that had temporarily retreated, returned. He found himself trying to think about the case, trying to keep track of the conversations between the officers around him, but failing. Instead, his thoughts drifted always back to Melanie, to her pink cheeks, her blue eyes, the feel of her little hand inside his as he would help her down the stairs or as they walked through a parking lot where she insisted in jumping and splashing in the rain puddles. And he thought of Laura, and what she might be doing now, whether she was with Zell and had told him about his moving out and how she'd reacted to the note he'd left.

Oddly (to him) there was laughter and gaiety all around, and the smell of beer and cigarette smoke and the clink of cue balls. It was as though these guys had no thought whatsoever for the morrow and what it might bring. Everyone but him was letting go of the day, trying to relax. He was getting looks from Wilenski and Brooks but he shrugged them off. He took a swig of beer and forced himself to think about the case, to try to ignore the knot in his stomach.

With the information they now had, Lanslow thought he could put it all together. This was how he saw it: Curtis Nelson and Derek Lunzer were roommates and had conspired to kill Derek's parents so Derek could inherit their wealth. Derek was probably the one to furnish the diagram. There would be a payoff for Curtis, of course, probably substantial. The boys had probably solicited the help of Silas Halladay who had recently been hired as a mechanic in the Nelson's auto dealership in Trane. The two young men probably knew nothing of Halladay's notorious background and had brought him in on the deal for a fee. Or, perhaps, they had surmised Halladay's expertise in crime and brought him in for that very reason, to help out in a process in which they knew they were novices, to say the least.

According to the timeline the taskforce had con-
structed, Silas had left the town of Trane with Curtis on
October 26th, a Thursday, the day of the Lunzer's party
to be held that evening. It was on the morning of
Thursday, in a grocery store in Trane, that Sabriga
Quill said she'd gotten bad vibes from Halladay. Nelson
and Halladay had then traveled to White Bear Lake on
Thursday afternoon where Lonnie the waitress had
seen them at the café. They would kill the Lunzers early
that following Friday morning.

There was a question in Lanslow's mind as to
whether Jacqueline Bideau, Derek's sister, had been
intended to be part of the plan, since, according to
Derek's statement, he had not expected her to stay
overnight after the party was over. It seemed that
Derek's half-share of the Lunzer estate was acceptable
to him, the other half to be shared by his sister. Colin
Haskell's statement, too, seemed to confirm that
Jacqueline was not expected to be there. But
Jacqueline Bideau had stayed over unexpectedly, and
somewhere along the way, she'd become mixed up in
the deal and someone, probably Halladay and Nelson,
decided to abduct her—whether it was Curtis or Silas
or perhaps both, Lanslow didn't know; his guess would
be Silas Halladay because they had info on him,

gleaned from the Texas rap sheet, that he had a rape conviction and had been sent to prison for it. Curtis's death looked like Silas had decided to take things into his own hands and keep what loot they'd picked up at the Lunzers, as well as the woman, for himself. For Silas Halladay the sister's presence was probably "frosting on the cake."

Lanslow guessed that Silas and Curtis had probably received a "down payment" from Derek Lunzer and, perhaps, would receive a final payment after the job had been done. The loot was an extra incentive, Lanslow thought, provided by Derek Lunzer to further entice his accomplices to carry out the murder and to allow him to seal his own alibi. This would be something Lanslow and his guys would have to check out. If the Lunzer kid's bank account showed some large sums withdrawn coincidentally, with the time of the murders; it would be evidence supporting Lanslow's suspicion that Derek Lunzer had played the major role in the murders. They would need more, but that would have to come later. So far, it still looked as if they had a lot of work to do to bring Derek Lunzer to justice. Whether Jacqueline Bideau was still alive or not Lanslow did not know, but doubted it. And whether Silas Halladay and perhaps his brother were still in this area was only a guess, aside from Sabriga Quill's vision.

As all of this had transpired, Lanslow reasoned, Derek Lunzer had tried to make an airtight alibi by being somewhere else, but his frequent phone calls to his and Curtis' room on the college campus after the date of the murder indicated he'd been left in the breech, so to speak, and was, perhaps, desperately seeking information on what had gone down. Lanslow thought that Silas Halladay had probably not stuck by the plan. Not being able to contact his roommate, there was nothing Derek Lunzer could do but sweat it out, which, it appeared, he was doing.

In the meantime, Silas Halladay had murdered Curtis Nelson and made off with Curtis' car and probably any money and jewelry he and Curtis had gleaned from the Lunzers' estate and was either hiding out in the Gunflint Trail area or long gone. He'd probably taken the woman with him for at least part of the trip. Lanslow expected that they'd find her body somewhere, just as they had Curtis Nelson's.

Lanslow shook his head in amazement. This case just got stranger and stranger. Apparently, several people had been out to kill or burglarize the Lunzers and each had independently chosen the same night to do the job. There was the still-unidentified black man who had somehow acquired the diagram to the Lunzer home and who had probably decided to help himself to the Lunzers' possessions but walked into a bigger deal and had paid with his own life instead; then there was George Lunzer's partner, Colin Haskell, who'd been pilfering the company's till, and who was about to be discovered, and who had hired his own inept thugs, who then had doublecrossed him, and who was now, no doubt, headed to prison.

And the Mexican immigrants? They'd somehow played their bit parts too, as confirmed by the decorator pieces they had sold at the pawnshop. And then, most of all, there was Derek Lunzer, the brains most likely behind the caper; and Lunzer's friend and college roommate, Curtis Nelson, who had paid with his life, also. Both Derek and Curtis had been betrayed by a pro that had taken advantage of their naivete.

Two culprits, then, remained at large: the first and most dangerous was Silas Halladay, and the second was Derek Lunzer. Of course, Stone's brother, Jeffrey may have also been in on the deal, though his name had only surfaced in connection with that of his half-brother. He was an escaped convict, a former soldier. Perhaps he had killed his wife and a prison guard. If their information was correct, Stone could, indeed, be a very dangerous person as well.

Inquiries that afternoon had revealed that Silas

Halladay had stayed at a motel while he was working for the Nelson's auto dealership. But the motel owner said Halladay had paid up and left and he hadn't seen the man since and doubted Halladay would be back for another room; and he knew nothing of Halladay's background or where he had come from when he took the room that first day. Neither did the Nelson's, even though Halladay had worked for them. As far as Jeffrey Stone, the half brother, was concerned, no lead had been unearthed since he and Halladay had escaped from the Texas prison. They'd gotten his picture from the Texas authorities, and it had been distributed to the public. There had been no responses to it as yet. But there was the possibility that the brothers may have split, and Stone, and even Halladay, could be long gone.

No doubt, this was a complicated case. There was even the question of whose jurisdiction would prevail in trying Silas Halladay first, and possibly his brother, should they be able to catch him. As far as Lanslow knew, his jurisdiction would have first crack for the murder of the Lunzers. Then, Cook County would get its turn and, without question, Halladay, and Stone if he was part of the deal, would be returned to prison in Texas. Word was the Texans were on their way to northern Minnesota this very moment.

He was nervous about tomorrow. There was the woman, who probably would be found dead. Death had always seized him with depression, and God only knew he didn't need any more of that. Then there was the pending arrest of Halladay, which he guessed wouldn't be easy, and could always result in more death.

Lanslow drained the beer from his glass and motioned for the bartender to fill it again. He hoped it would help put him to sleep. It was well past midnight.

## Chapter Twenty

The task force gathered in the conference room of the county police station before dawn. The room was cold but the milling deputies seemed to take no note of it. Two detectives from Texas, flying into Duluth and then driving the rest of the way to Grand Marais, had arrived during the night and they and Sheriff Herzog were going over the case data once again, papers spread before them on a table. Lanslow stood by, listening. The Texas detectives confirmed most of what he and the rest had learned about Jeffrey Stone and Silas Halladay and added their own information.

Herzog asked everyone to be seated and went over Sabriga Quill's statement. One of the visions she'd received, was of a house near water. She got the impression, he told them, that the house faced in a south eastward direction, toward the water, and she'd seen the sun's rays glinting through the window but she'd felt an awful sense of darkness and death. She'd also described two automobiles of some sort, coming into her consciousness, one red, the other maroon, or brown, a dark color, anyway.

There was a low murmuring among the deputies and Lanslow could feel the skepticism in the room. But this information about the red automobile, which he had already known yesterday, had set off alarms for him. He thought it was an important clue. He was still restless, wanted to get moving.

"What about the chopper?" Lanslow asked Herzog. "When are you going to send him up?"

"He should be taking off anytime, now, even if it's still dark. We want him up there as soon as he can see the ground clearly. Should be soon now."

Lanslow glanced at his watch. It was only a little before six. Herzog dismissed the task force to get coffee and wait.

It was just over an hour later when the first rays of the sun peeked over the horizon, when Herzog got a call. After a moment he faced Lanslow. "He's up in the air," he said.

Not ten minutes later, with the strengthening rays of dawn, they got lucky. It seemed that Sabriga's information had led them in the right direction.

The pilot reported that he'd caught a glinting of chrome as he passed rapidly over a house, by a lake, and perhaps a red vehicle parked by an outside garage, partially covered with a tarpaulin and snow, but he was not sure, and he had banked the helicopter sharply left and headed back. As he was turning to get a better view, he reported seeing a man coming out on the porch and looking upward in the copter's direction, shading his eyes, and then turning quickly to go back inside the house. The man's presence and curiosity could be mere coincidence, but it was enough, especially with the report of the red car, to raise their suspicion and set them in action. The task force was called together again.

Herzog turned to a wall map and pointed. "The house is about here," he said. "There are no other roads leading away from there besides the Trail. If he tries to escape by road, we'll block him off. Most likely, he'll try to get away through the woods, to Canada. We'll alert the Canadians, but he won't get that far. There are lakes he'll have to avoid, not frozen over yet, so he'll be attempting to go around them. He'll have a great deal of difficulty getting through there. The snow will be deep and drifted. The copter is continuing to circle and will keep him spotted. Our squads will converge on that house. Let's go."

\*\*\*

Darkness had fallen before Jeffrey and Jacqueline had finished throwing together clothing and other items in sleeping bags. They had decided they had to stay in the house overnight, try to get out the next morning at dawn. The snowmobiles had lights but he was afraid Jacqueline's inexperience might lead them into trouble. He would have to decide whether she would ride with him.

It was just beginning to lighten in the east when he heard the sound of the helicopter. Jeffrey went to the door and out onto the porch and looked skyward. She heard him curse. He whirled back.

"Too late," he said. "They're coming. I want you in the basement!"

"What was it?" she asked.

"A helicopter. They've spotted the house. They know I'm here. We have very little time now."

She looked at him and knew not to protest. He guided her downstairs and left her, saying, "Keep down. Just stay down here and you'll be all right. I'm sorry. I may not get out of here, this time. You're a beautiful woman. I love you. I'm sorry for the pain I've caused. If I get out, I'll try and contact you."

She could only stare at him.

"What are you going to do?" she asked.

"I won't let them take me," he said. "I've made a mistake. I shouldn't have stayed here so long. When you showed up ... " He simply shook his head.

"Are you going to try to escape?"

"It's probably too late. I know what they'll be doing;

they'll have the house surrounded, all the roads blocked. The helicopter—there are probably others—will make it difficult to escape, even through the woods."

He turned to go, then turned back. "You'll be safe down here unless they do something stupid. You can go back, see your baby again and have a good life."

She reached for him and he held her. She could feel his heart beating against her breast. She saw the pain and sadness in his face and she tried to kiss it away. He buried his face into her shoulder and neck and held her for sometime. He pushed her back and looked into her face and she could see that he was trying to hold back the tears but she saw wetness in his eyes. She kissed him again, as tenderly as she could, and held his face in her hands.

Abruptly, then, he turned and went back up the stairs. She could hear him walking around, moving things, and could only presume he was getting ready to confront the police. Then, she heard the front door slam, and all was familiarly silent.

***

In the latter part of the period since he and his brother had escaped from the Texas prison and had holed up in

Minnesota, Jeffrey Stone had grown lax. It had been over a year, after all, since they'd made their get-away and he had come to believe, with still only a little trepidation remaining, that they'd perhaps truly given the authorities the slip.

Now, reality had caught up with him. It was fantastic, he thought, how one could deceive oneself. But over the days and weeks and now over a year, the silent deep woods, the sound of the rain on the lake, the fog that rose over the still water in the morning, draping the pine shore and the water in a sort of mysterious shroud, the wind in the maples and junipers, the soft snow falling—all this had perforated his resolve and had begun percolating into an ever growing yearning for peace and tranquility—and these had gradually begun to lessen the seething rage he felt for those in power, for those who had misused their power to promote their own names and careers at his expense.

It was all such folly! How they had all been duped! Even himself. When he looked back, he thought of his life as having been written in stone (no pun intended, he thought); even in boyhood he'd entertained the thought of God, somehow, for some reason, playing a game with him, giving him hope, then jerking it away— and he'd come to think, for sure, there'd be no justice or happiness for him. He couldn't understand why he'd been picked to be treated so malignantly this way, if, indeed he had. Maybe Calvin had been right: all were predestined to heaven or hell and for him it was the latter. And he knew it was sheer irrationality that spoke to him in this fashion, made him believe, while knowing it was untrue, that some higher hidden power had written his life's script. But that was sometimes how it seemed and that was the way it had been all his life; that's the way it would be always, he was certain.

Even while mellowing, it had never left his mind that he might one day retaliate against the authorities, those who had so uncaringly ruined his life. Submerged for short periods, the resentment would come creeping back, growing until he literally seethed with rage. In the back of his head there was always that little suspicion there would be an ending something like this. He had almost reconciled himself to it. If he, himself, didn't initiate it, he was sure the authorities would; they'd catch up to him and since they believed he and his brother were cop killers, then there would be no mercy shown; never mind that he had never killed anyone except in the Vietnam War, or that that experience had soured him on the whole process of war and given him only the highest disdain for those who had ordered him and his men to fight. Of course, too, he'd killed his brother, but only in defense since he was sure Silas would have killed him. He felt no remorse for Silas; indeed what he felt was a burning wrath. Silas had raped and nearly killed the prostitute, had probably murdered Christa. Silas would have raped and murdered Jacqueline. Again, he felt little sorrow for Silas, only rage at what he would have done to that beautiful woman and how he had caused the whole family such trouble.

Rage, it seemed, had been with him forever. Despite his growing desire for peace, the rage was still there, deep down, the embers merely requiring fanning to burst once again into full flame. Though he had no television set he had often listened to the car radio (at first) while on his errands, and the reports on and discussions of the war in Iraq were enough to rouse again in him a seething anger and incensed disgust. These emotions were usually followed by sleepless nights, deep sadness and outright depression. When he heard these reports he would once again plan for the day when he would revisit those so-called "peace officers" and other "authorities" that had, as far as he was concerned, turned his life into a shambles. In his mind such an act would merely be a repayment, a recompense for injustice generally and, of course, a spiteful, horrible revenge for what they'd done to him personally; less directly, for the harm he believed the administration had brought to his country, both in Vietnam and Iraq. After awhile he had ceased listening to the radio as much and had switched it off or switched the station. But the news of Iraq and its horrors got through even then.

He admitted it. He had wanted revenge, had wanted it more than anything else in the world; as dark and fiendish a revenge as he could devise. He wanted them to die, to suffer as he had suffered, as they had made the thousands, perhaps hundreds of thousands, in their circle of influence suffer. It didn't matter which ones he killed. He saw them all as a piece, a set. It had been his intention to try to get back to the jurisdiction in Texas where it all had started and wreak as much destruction as he could before they would take him out. But he would take what he was offered and at the present he even lusted for it.

Now, his brother Silas had brought it all to a head in more ways than one. Jeffrey had begun to question his motives. Silas, in his always-stupid crazy way, had brought the woman and Jeffrey had inadvertently fallen in love with her and for a few shimmering days he thought it might be possible for them to live as happy a life as every other normal couple supposedly did.

For a moment, he lost the sound of the helicopter and knew it had drifted from overhead. It was his chance. It didn't matter now. He felt hopeless. He would take as many with him as he could and when he met his end, so be it; all his questions would be, perhaps, resolved.

Hoisting his bag quickly to his side, he dashed through the snow towards the woods on the hill overlooking his house. He had anticipated this very thing. There was a place in the woods at the top of the hill just across the lake that would give him the drop on anyone below. Besides, there was always the big white garage, crammed full of explosives. That, he was sure, would come as a big surprise to these locals.

\*\*\*

Lanslow had left Wilenski and Brooks outside midst the hustle and bustle and found himself alone for a moment inside the conference room with the cops from Texas. They wore Stetson hats and cowboy boots and string ties and one of them, a big, heavy-boned galoot of a man named Whistler, grated on Lanslow's nerves immediately. Both men, in fact, made Lanslow uneasy. When Whistler smiled, his teeth showed thick and heavy as though they'd been square chiseled. The other, going by the name of Gentry, had dark hair that appeared to have been greased or oiled and slicked back over his skull and tied into a ponytail. He was a squirrely little man, but when it came to a fight Lanslow actually judged him the more dangerous of the two. When Gentry had his hat on and the ponytail stuck out, he looked downright ludicrous.

As he had entered the room, Lanslow overheard the smaller man saying he'd like to get Jeffrey Stone and Silas Halladay under his sights just for a moment. "If we get a chance, we'll take care of them," the other had said.

"Gentlemen," said Lanslow, approaching the two men slowly. "I heard what you just said. Halliday and Stone have their rights. I'd go easy. You're not in charge, here."

"That so, Detective ... what'd you say your name was?" asked the big man.

"I know it," said Gentry. "This here is Detective *Lanslow*, from the big city of White Bear Lake, Minnesota."

"Well," said Whistler, "I don't believe we've met, formally." He extended his hand. "I'm Detective Bill Whistler, and this is Detective Pat Gentry, from Dallas. You have to pardon my partner here." He motioned to Gentry. "He just don't cotton to cop killers."

Lanslow nodded. "We've met." He clasped Whistler's hand and felt the big fingers grasp his, full of power. "No offense meant, guys. I'm just trying to be fair here.

We all have a stake in Halladay and Stone, and they may have a woman hostage."

"Point taken, Detective," said Whistler, glancing at Gentry and grinning.

Lanslow saw the grin. "I know they're cop-killers," he said. "I don't like cop killers any better than you do. I'm just thinking of the woman."

"We've seen her," said Gentry. "Quite a looker."

Whistler shrugged. "Hope not, but knowing Silas Halladay, she's probably already dead by now," he said.

"Perhaps so," said Lanslow, "Perhaps so. We'll see." He turned to walk away, not seeing the amused glances exchanged between the two Texas detectives.

Herzog came in the room before Lanslow got to the door. "We're ready," he said. "Got to get there in a hurry."

When they stepped outside, it had begun to snow once again in thick, heavy flakes, and the wind had risen.

## Chapter Twenty-one

One of the things Jeffrey Stone had taken with him as he made his way around the east end of the lake and through the pines to the top of the hill was his journal. It was silly, sentimental, but he took it. He reached the spot he'd reconnoitered from time to time and settled in.

From his vantage point he could look down on the little house that had been his home for over a year. He thought of the woman he'd fallen in love with, down there, in the house, only a few yards away. But the distance might as well have been a thousand miles. It was beginning to seem like a dream. For himself, he knew it was over and a great rush of sadness fell through him.

He had burrowed into the snow, beneath the branches of a low pine, and the guns and ammo were with him. He knew how to use them and he would do so, despite the pleadings, before he'd left the house, of Jacqueline. He pulled the journal from inside his heavy parka, removed the glove from his right hand and grasped the pen he'd stuck in the wire binding of the tablet. Soft white, feathery flakes of snow fell around him as he began to write.

Journal, November 9, 2006:

This situation I'm now in was inevitable from the moment I was born. I'm convinced of this now more than ever, though I have strongly suspected it years ago. I don't mean this particular situation in every detail: it could have taken several variations. But something like this, in which I am doomed to die a probable violent death, I am persuaded, was fore written.

This sounds as though I'm a fatalist and a believer and perhaps I am, in a way. I do not believe in God, per se, however, or gods of any kind, so I do not attribute my life course to any plan concocted, either out of spite or just plain amusement, by such beings. What I believe is that my genes, delivered to me by my father and mother in that long ago moment of ecstasy, when they were very young and probably had little idea of what it meant to have a child—together with my social circumstances—have somehow shaped me for this moment; if that's fatalism, then I am a fatalist, but only in this limited sense.

Which of these, biology or sociology, is the main suspect? Lately, there is a biological bias for explaining human behavior genetically. But we also know, now, that genes interact with their environment, so one's genome is not truly an independent variable. Genes predispose us to certain personality traits, no doubt. But our social worlds shape us, too, and it has been my misfortune to have been ensconced in a dysfunctional family, one in which my mother was promiscuous, my father was a tyrant, and my half brother (coming after the divorce and my mother's eventual second marriage following the affair) is nothing like me. We have clashed all our lives and I have finally killed him; I am Cain, he is Abel.

After Christa was murdered, I can't remember a truly happy event in my life before I met Jacqueline. True, I've experienced great satisfaction, such as when I was first married, or when I graduated from OCS. Even my marriage to Christa, though, was deteriorating. Too young, too embittered, I never gave her a chance to love me. It was only a matter of time that we would have separated and divorced. There is only one other person who might have saved my life from this tattered shroud I've come to live in. But that situation, too, was fraught with its difficulties. She is better off never to have become entangled in my escapades.

I have often wondered what it's like to experience real happiness. I remember after OCS feeling like a new person, vindicated in my belief that I did, indeed, have the ability to make something of myself. Now I see this achievement as nothing more than learning to kill on behalf of the ruling elites. And I remember, later, the soaring feeling when I received my Ph.D.

But I don't believe these experiences were true happiness, which I've always envisioned as a moment of carefree joy, of complete and utter contentment. This I have never felt, except for that moment two days ago when Jacqueline kissed me, of her own accord. Five days of real, pure, unadulterated happiness in almost a lifetime. How pathetic!

Sadness, on the other hand, is an accessory to my psyche, clinging to me like a useless arm, or some other debilitated appendage. Depression is my middle name. They are my enemies; I fight them continually, but all the combat training I've received offers no help. Religion and philosophy offer no solace, either. Perhaps it is as Blaise Pascal (that dear woman's hero!) has said: neither reason nor nature offers an infrangible evidence for the unbeliever — only unquestioning faith in God, or at least faith in some numinous presence, that can deliver one from the abyss. But, of course, the key phrase here is unquestioning. That I cannot do.

So, here I lie, awaiting my death. It is cold, but I am bundled warm, even without a fire. It is as though I'm layered against the snow and cold with some invisible plastic. My brain will not allow my body to cool.

The lackeys of authority will be here soon. It will not matter to them that my life has been without happiness; that I had found a bit of it only recently, that I am, basically, innocent. To them I am a "cop killer." My happiness is in that house down there. I must divert their fire to me, up here, away from Jacqueline and perhaps in death I will achieve the elusive peace I've searched for all my life, or, at least the "nothingness" of Sartre, where there is no peace nor war (for lack of a better word). It's funny. I'd never thought of death this way before, even after reading Sartre, as nothingness, composed not even of peace. But it would seem to be true (at least logical). Peace requires consciousness, I would think. I believe Sartre would agree. I will accept nothingness, then.

A sound caught his attention, growing louder; a sound that brought back memories of Vietnam; the slap of helicopter blades against the air. It passed over once more, made a wide turn and started back. The men in the chopper wouldn't be able to see him, though, at least at first. The limbs of the pines hid him from the prying eyes above, and the falling snow that had already begun to cover his parka would make it hard to pick him out against the snow already on the ground. Perhaps they would be able to spot his gunfire from the trees, but he would have to deal with that later; in the meantime, he was sure of what he could do, of the kind of havoc he could inflict. He and his platoon had done it before in Vietnam.

A movement caught his eye and he looked away from the chopper to see a large police van, followed by other vehicles, bumping and grinding through the snow toward his house. This was it. There were no sirens, no crazy rush to surround the house. They knew well enough they had him. It was not exactly what he'd planned, but it would do. He slid the notebook into the cavity behind his Kevlar vest, zipped the collar of his parka clear to his chin and pulled the hood low to his forehead. From the bag he pulled a Colt .45 and laid it beside him and then, from the bag once again, he pulled the AK47 that Jacqueline had found in his closet.

***

As they'd set off, Lanslow sat beside Herzog in the front of the squad. Whistler and Gentry sat in the back. Wilenski and Brooks rode in the squad directly behind. The sheriff handled the car deftly. Herzog had made it clear to all of them that it was his jurisdiction and he was in charge, though he wanted the ranking officers from the other jurisdictions with him as his "lieutenants." That was okay with Lanslow, though he was worried about the two men from Texas in the back seat. He didn't trust them to go by standard procedure and there was a young, innocent woman's life at stake, if, indeed she were still alive. Herzog had indicated the house had only one road leading to it, and woods and a small lake fronting it. The helicopter was already there. Reports from the officer in the helicopter were that no one had been seen leaving the house, that there definitely was a red pickup truck parked by the side of the garage but it was partially covered and he couldn't recognize the make. He reported an old brown Buick station wagon parked in front of the garage.

"They'll probably be barricaded inside," Herzog said, almost as though he were thinking out loud.

Lanslow had some doubts about the task force's preparations. They'd been hurried and had assumed Halladay and Stone were still together. The Texas cops, in their part of the briefing, had reported that both men were considered to be extremely dangerous. Stone was convicted of the murder of his wife, one or the other of the brothers had already killed a prison guard, they said. They emphasized that the men had nothing to lose, really—the most dangerous types. Stone, thought Lanslow, if he was around, was a man trained in special combat tactics and was probably more competent than any of the police officers on the task force.

"We're not dealing with your normal criminal type here," Herzog himself had said.

Herzog had pulled his squad in behind the large black van carrying the SWAT team. He turned momentarily to look at Lanslow.

"I got a bad feeling about this," he said. "These guys are not going to give up that easily and they may be armed to the teeth."

Lanslow nodded but said nothing. The squad smelled of cigarette smoke. He glanced at his watch.

"How long till we're there?" he said to Herzog.

"About thirty minutes, maybe a bit longer," the sheriff said.

Lanslow glanced in the rearview mirror to see Whistler grinning at him.

*\*\**

Lying prone on the hilltop, Stone watched the van slide down the road that gave access to the dock, and come to a halt almost directly in front of the house. Several burly men in SWAT gear spilled out, taking cover behind the vehicle. He almost laughed outwardly. He had the drop on them. It would be a duck shoot. But he held off.

He continued to watch as other squads arrived, placing themselves near the rear of the house. The lead cruiser pulled up behind the SWAT van. He recognized the large frame of Sheriff Herzog, whose picture he'd seen in the papers, climb from the squad behind the van and immediately move to the front of the SWAT team, crouching, peering at the house. With a start, he recognized two other men emerging from the rear of the vehicle, men whom he had grown to hate over the course of his trial for the murder of his wife. Whistler, followed by Gentry, moved toward the front of the SWAT van to join Herzog, peering at the house intently. For a moment, Stone couldn't believe his eyes. Then it began to fit. The Texas cops would of course have been called in. Luck had broken his way. He felt delight and leveled the gun sight on Whistler and tightened his finger on the trigger ever so slightly, but held off. He swiveled the gun to point at Gentry. But again he held off. Another officer, whom he did not recognize, had exited the other side and was coming round the squad car. This officer wasn't confining his scrutiny to the house. He was looking around, and it seemed to Stone that he had looked directly to the strategic spot where he lay. He looked a little too long for Stone's comfort, but had eventually turned away, looking now at the house.

He was joined by two other plain-clothes officers

from another squad that had pulled up. Stone didn't recognize them, either. Over a dozen other officers had emerged from their squads, waiting beside them. Stone cursed beneath his breath at the dead half brother lying buried in the basement of his house. He should never have allowed himself to get in this position. He should have prevented Silas from leaving or he should have left the moment his brother showed up with Jacqueline. But then ...

A man whom he took to be the commander of the SWAT team, standing close to Herzog, was holding his men in position, awaiting orders. There seemed to be a conference between the Sheriff and the Texas lawmen. Herzog had turned to the other man who'd gotten out of his squad and was saying something to him, too. After a moment, Herzog turned to the SWAT commander who then signaled his men to begin surrounding the little house and they began moving to their positions carefully. Stone thought it was almost comedic. He would allow these SWAT men, with their heavy firepower, to disperse. He didn't care. They would be less able to pinpoint his shots. He knew the other officers would remain in what they supposed was cover behind the van and the other vehicles.

He watched as the SWAT team members moved cautiously to each side of the house, one or two of them to its rear, two, along with the commander, remaining in front. He saw the commander speaking into his radio to his men, probably verifying their positions, saw him turn to the sheriff and speak.

The helicopter passed over the scene once again.

Herzog had a bullhorn in his hands. He had just raised it to hail the house when Jeffrey Stone decided the time had come. He leveled the AK47, sighted in on Whistler's head, and pulled the trigger smoothly, launching a single shot. The man's knees buckled and he dropped straight to the ground instantly and lay still. The other cops dropped to their knees, heads turning, their weapons pointing in random directions. Some had begun to scatter, diving for shelter. Gentry, who'd seemed stupefied and paralyzed for a moment when his partner went down, was among them. Stone sighted in on Gentry's desperately flying figure and released a volley of bullets into his body. Gentry pitched forward, face down, and lay still.

***

Lanslow hadn't seen exactly where the shots came from, but they hadn't come from the house, more to their rear. He thought they'd probably come from the wooded hillside, from the spot that he had previously observed from a strategic perspective. Along with Herzog and the SWAT commander and one of his men, Lanslow had dropped to the snow and scrambled to get beneath the van. As far as Lanslow knew, Wilenski and Brooks had scuttled to the rear, back to the squads. He watched the spot he'd observed previously for any movement, any telltale sign of the gunman's presence, but could make out nothing. If the shooter was Stone, then he wouldn't be visible, nor would he reveal himself with movement. The question uppermost in his mind was whether they had put themselves into a crossfire, with one of the fugitives in the house, the other outside, up on the hill, in the trees, about a hundred yards away. Or perhaps both were outside in positions that they could strafe the officers from either side. If that was the case, they hadn't yet received fire from the house nor the other side of it, but they were in a very precarious position.

"Where the fuck did those shots come from?" Herzog yelled. The sheriff's big frame was squeezed between the bottom of the van and the snow. He had lost his hat and had snow all over him. He began talking into his radio to his men at the rear, all of which had scattered following the first shots. The SWAT commander was on his radio, too.

"Where are they? Anyone see where those shots

came from?" Herzog asked again.

"Up there," Lanslow said. "I think someone, one of them anyway, is up on that hill."

"God damn it," said Herzog. "They got Whistler and Gentry."

"I hope that's all," said Lanslow. "That fire sounded like it was from some heavy stuff."

"Stand fast. Stand fast," the Commander was saying into his radio. "Two officers down. We're taking fire from behind. We got to find out where the bastards are!"

## Chapter Twenty-Two

As Lanslow had suspected, the plan had been too hastily thought out, practically all of it sketched out on a wet-dry board in the conference room the night before. They had hurriedly jumped into their squads the next morning and followed the hulking van up the highway and down the rutty road to this little house standing so forlornly in the trees, facing the little lake. Now, in hindsight, there had been one false assumption: that the fugitives would be holed up together in the house. Providing they could get to the place fast enough, they would have them trapped. Herzog had mentioned the advantage of surprise despite the fact Lanslow had heard the copter pilot's report of seeing a man rush back into the house as he had passed over. Obviously, the man the pilot had seen was Halladay or Stone and the fugitives hadn't been surprised. The task force should have gone over more situational possibilities, Lanslow thought, such as the one they now found themselves in. His concern now was for Wilenski and Brooks. He yelled from beneath the van.

"Dean? Len? You guys alright?"

It was Brook's voice that replied. "We're both okay, Rich."

"Where are you?" Lanslow yelled.

"We're down, behind you. We're under the squad. We can see you from here."

Lanslow squirmed around and peered back toward the other squad. Brooks and Wilenski, lying beneath it as they were, gave him the thumbs up.

"What's up, Sarge?" Wilenski asked, loudly.

"We're going to be pretty much pinned down here. They're gonna try sending some SWAT guys around toward the hill over there. That's where the perp seems to be. The other one might still be in the house. All we can do is wait a bit."

"What about Whistler and Gentry?"

"Dead, I'm afraid," Lanslow replied. Neither Whistler nor Gentry had made any movement.

It was cold, getting colder. There was a slight breeze, increasing, coming off the lake. The snow was piling up, blowing beneath the vehicles. Lanslow swore. "I'm not dressed for this shit," he heard Brooks saying. Lanslow didn't know whether Brooks was referring to the lack of a warm coat or the lack of a bulletproof vest—or perhaps both. At any rate, all they could do was lie in the snow and wait. Herzog, in the meantime, was ordering dispatch to send an ambulance.

Another error, Lanslow thought. They should have brought one along. What in hell had they been expecting? But he was sure Whistler and Gentry were dead, anyway. They hadn't moved at all and the snow was staining crimson around them.

\*\*\*

Some brief time had passed since he'd shot the two police officers. He was surprised to find that the small period had leeched from him the once ragged desire to kill them, replaced by a strange emptiness that had settled in; not the joy and exhilaration he'd expected. Whistler and Gentry had held for him most of the anger, the loathing and hatred he felt for the authorities. Except for Whistler and Gentry, who'd warped their positions into the opportunity to get him—a "bleeding heart" liberal, as they had called him, a traitor to his country—he thought of the other men below as mere minions of authority, the pawns, even, of the state and of those who held the state's positions of power. Never mind that some of those men took their authority overboard. There were bad cops and bad soldiers, all put in their positions by the power elite. For that, the common men and women couldn't be blamed entirely.

Once again he saw the VC he'd killed many years ago while on patrol—a shot to the back of the head as the man had whirled away from him to run for his life. The shot had spun him into a rice paddy. The man had struggled to bring his head to the surface to breathe and he kept bobbing up and down; and then the final burst from his M16, the short plop, plop of the bullets, the spouting water, the man's body slowly submerging in frothy, bloody-red bubbles.

That face had haunted him. That whole scene had clogged his brain so that the only emotions he'd felt since then were horror—and hate for those who'd put him in that position and for those who'd placed the VC in the same position, of killing or being killed. Yet, contradictorily, here he was, in the same position, in readiness to kill more human beings. His rage and bitterness wilted. Yet he was caught, now, inevitably.

He slowly pushed the snow that had begun to pile up around him away to either side, not moving quickly but in a way that, he hoped, would not catch attention. He pointed the AK47 once again toward the cops. They were pinned down. None of them moved. He thought about spraying the van in the hope that it might explode. But curiously, even to himself, he waited. He guessed that the van was bulletproof, anyway. Perhaps he should try to set fire to the squad cars. It occurred to him that the cops knew nothing of his brother. Perhaps they thought he was still alive, that they were in a possible crossfire from the house and woods.

He gazed down at the bodies of Whistler and Gentry lying inert. Even from here he could see the red stain of their blood continuing to spread in the snow. Blood in the snow, blood in the water of Vietnam where he'd killed a Viet Cong soldier. In that moment he was suddenly emptied of all desire to rampage, to wreak vengeance. Just like that, his rage had disappeared, abruptly, gone, like smoke from a dying campfire. In that moment he let his attention lapse. All Stone could think of was the woman, in the house, named Jacqueline, whose figure had suddenly appeared in that little living room window.

***

The word went around quickly: a woman had shown herself in the windows of the house. At first there was no movement by any of the officers. Then, on orders from his commander, a heavily armored SWAT officer edged around the side of the house and began calling to her. At the same time the SWAT commander saw his chance to try to get someone into the woods from where the shots had been fired. He ordered two men to circle the end of the lake and try to make it into the trees in which they believed one of the men lay hidden. The two men made it to the trees without precipitating fire.

In the meantime, the woman emerged cautiously through the door and stood, dressed in sweat pants and shirt, waving her hands above her head. She moved slowly to the steps and began to descend. When she reached the bottom, the officer quickly pulled her aside and around the corner where she was hidden from view.

Lanslow had watched all this from beneath the van. He couldn't believe the woman was still alive, apparently in good shape.

"That's her, by God," he heard Herzog exclaim. "She looks good."

The SWAT commander was on his radio. "She says the house is empty?" Lanslow heard him ask. The commander listened for a moment. "Alright, you and Selby go in there, through the back. I don't need to tell you to be damned careful."

Lanslow reasoned now that there were two men in the woods. He wondered why these men hadn't used the woman as a shield, or at least as leverage.

Word came then that there was only one man. The other was dead inside the house. The one alive had left the house. The woman knew nothing of his whereabouts. Now they knew; the man who'd killed Whistler and Gentry was in the woods, behind them, and his name was Jeffrey Stone and still Lanslow wondered why he hadn't killed the woman or, at the very least, used her as a hostage—and he thought he knew the answer to his question, just as he knew why it was Whistler and Gentry who had been gunned down.

\*\*\*

Stone watched it all from his position. Sight of the woman had simply seized him in an immobile embrace. His heart beat rapidly, and tears began to slip from his eyes, meandering over his cheeks, onto his lips where he tasted the salt. Why had he not listened to her? Perhaps ... but he squelched the thought as soon as it arose. He couldn't have escaped. They would have gunned him down or imprisoned him. He would have been convicted once again of murder, to be placed on death row to await execution. They would have handled him roughly, shoved him, perhaps even struck him or beat him for what he had supposedly done to one of their own—and, ultimately, he would have been sent back with Whistler and Gentry and he knew he wouldn't make it back alive with them, that they would take their anger and hatred out on him before they would invent some reason to kill him. Those two worthless cops! At least he derived satisfaction from *their* deaths.

They were rotten rogues, abusing their authority, and he had dispatched them to their proper place.

He heard a slight sound behind him, knew instantly that he'd made a mistake, not wiping out the tracks he'd made in the snow as he'd made his way in a sprint around the lake to keep from being seen by the helicopter pilot. He whirled automatically and fired the Colt .45 pistol at the figure standing just beyond him, visible through the trees, not at the chest but at the head. The man toppled backward and Stone rolled quickly to one side, but too late. The other SWAT man fired a three-round burst with his M4 carbine, followed by another, and the bullets caught Jeffrey in the head, chest and legs. The bullets to the chest, protected, as it was by the Kevlar vest, merely stunned him, knocked his breath away. Those to the legs would not have killed him, but the bullet grazing his head had done the damage. Momentarily, he was paralyzed and fighting for breath. But he was still conscious and rational enough to know it was over. He couldn't move his arms or legs.

He didn't die immediately. He was aware of the cop standing over him, talking into his radio. He lay on his back, looking upward through the limbs of the trees, at the flakes of snow sifting down from the grey sky. They were beautiful, and he marveled at the whiteness of the birch against the green of the pines, the wet glow of the leaves and the sibilant breeze that now tickled the tops of the trees, making them wave as if in goodbye. He didn't want to die, even though death itself held no special fear for him. It was simply that he didn't want to leave just yet, to be gone, to no longer see and hear and feel all the wonderful things in life. Most of those things he had missed, yet he still marveled at the sky and clouds, the ocean, the mountains, the forests and the animals. He would experience them no more. Well, perhaps not here, but maybe on a different plane. (He knew even then he was deceiving himself but he gave Jacqueline credit.) He assessed how badly he was wounded. But he felt no pain, and suddenly, slowly, slowly and suddenly, just a great relief. He saw Jacqueline's face once more, felt her tender kiss. He looked at the cop, now merely watching him.

"It's over," he whispered, "It's over. Tell her I loved her." and the cop's face turned blank, then Stone grimaced and was dead.

## Chapter Twenty-Three

The next day Lanslow was headed back to White Bear Lake with the young woman in the front seat beside him. Wilenski and Brooks had remained behind. Lanslow saw their surprise once again that he had not dispatched one of them to take the woman back. But Lanslow wanted to get back to White Bear Lake, where his troubles lay. His two partners were to accompany Herzog and his deputies to the Nelson's home in an attempt to gather further leads, especially those that might help to incriminate Derek Lunzer. Lunzer remained their primary suspect.

The presence of the woman beside him precipitated memories of a similar occasion when he'd taken his former partner's wife Maureen to stay with her sister after she had found her husband murdered in their own garage. Jacqueline Bideau was living up to Lanslow's first formed opinion of her, when he'd initially seen her picture. She hadn't cried except for wet eyes and a single tear that trickled down her left cheek when they loaded Stone into the ambulance. Now, as they drove south, she sat in almost complete silence. The stillness betrayed her, however. She was struggling. Once again he felt inadequate to the task of consoling a woman in her deepest distress.

Of course, he guessed, part, if not most, of her distress lay with the murders of her parents, the anxiety for her baby and the whole misery of the past twelve days. But there was another part. The whole story of Jeffrey Stone and his brother, when she chose to speak up, was a bizarre tale. She thought she'd come to love him, amazingly enough. Lanslow had heard of the strange phenomenon where captives began to identify emotionally with their captors, but he didn't think Jacqueline's experience fit that category neatly. Perhaps she actually had fallen for the man. A crapshoot, he thought, again—that's life. But he saw her as a strong woman, knew she'd make the best of her circumstance.

He set the squad to cruise and freed his thoughts to other things. His attention turned to the events of the previous day. How ironic, he thought, what Gentry had said, less than an hour before his death; that he would like to get Stone in his sights. Yet it was Gentry and Whistler who died under Jeffrey Stone's gun sights. As far as he was concerned, they deserved what they got. For him, Whistler and Gentry were the worst kind of cops, the ones who used their authority to express their own prejudices and hatreds toward those they despised, whether deserved or not.

"You said my aunt is taking care of Erica?" the

woman asked, breaking Lanslow's rumination. He remembered that he had answered this same question earlier. It was as though she couldn't absorb information, couldn't retain it. They had given her a room at the motel where the rest of them stayed. Cook County officials had provided a social worker to stay with her, though she had insisted she did not need the service. They'd brought her some clothes, some jeans, and a sweatshirt that fit.

"Yes," he replied. "I saw her a few days ago. She's fine."

Jacqueline continued staring out the window at the country rolling by. The snow had been heavy. Deep drifts lay to either side of the highway. They came to the city of Duluth where the grey sky curved down to meet the reflecting gray of Lake Superior till sky and lake were one and the ships coming in may as well have been arriving from heaven. Lanslow threaded his way through the city and eventually picked up I-35 and increased the speed.

"Did my brother kill my parents?" she asked, not turning from the window.

He looked sideways at her, reading her mood. "It's possible. I'm sorry. We've suspected him."

"Derek and my father didn't get along," she said, absent-mindedly, perhaps as a prelude to a conclusion she was resisting but having to come to, ultimately.

"Were you and Derek close?" Lanslow asked.

He thought she hadn't heard him for she didn't answer for a long while. He glanced sideways at her. Drop-dead gorgeous, he thought, just as Wilenski had said.

"He was older than I," she said, at last. "I think I was mostly a pest to him when we were growing up. But we got along pretty well. I think Derek loved me. I certainly loved him ... I think he loved me."

Lanslow thought back to the family photo albums he and Brooks had browsed through when they were at the Lunzer home, to the pictures of the family all together, smiling for the camera, the pictures of the two kids, Jacqueline, serene, sophisticated even then; Derek with a mischief in his eyes. They'd seen photos of George Lunzer with his former wife, too, her arm around Derek, his hair even then tousled and hanging low over his forehead.

"Why didn't Derek get along with your dad?" Lanslow asked.

"Mostly about money. Derek was always asking for it and Dad thought he wasn't prudent, had to grow up. Derek had a temper, and Dad did, too. They quarreled, especially lately."

She was opening up and Lanslow took advantage.

"Were the quarrels physical?"

She paused at this and again was a long time in answering.

"Yes," she said. "This last time, Dad actually struck Derek. I just happened to be home at the time. I think Derek hated Dad, then. I saw it in his eyes. He didn't hit back, but he may as well have; it might have been better than the look he gave Dad. I could see it really hurt Dad, that look. It even hurt me."

She turned and looked directly at him. "Jeffrey said my brother probably was the brains behind my parents' murder."

Her statement was a question. Lanslow stared ahead, at the interstate rolling behind them.

"He's just a suspect at this time. It's routine. Family members are almost always the first to be suspected. He's innocent until found guilty." His words sounded lame, even to him.

But, in fact, they had nothing on Derek Lunzer, Lanslow thought, except suspicious circumstances. The water soaked diagram of the house, which could have been drawn by Derek, was of no use; there were no fingerprints, no printing of any telltale nature, as far as he knew. And any competent defense counsel could easily explain his calls to Curtis Nelson. Now that Nelson was dead, now that Silas Halladay was dead, now that Jeffrey stone was dead, what could they prove? He doubted that Brooks and Wilenski would find anything in Curtis' belongings.

She had turned back to the road ahead. After some time she said, matter-of-factly, "I think he did it. Derek once told me he thought my father had something to do with his mother's death. I think my brother killed my parents."

*** 

Jacqueline Bideau's reunion with her baby was weepingly joyful. The reunion with her brother, who had come to the house to meet her, was a shattering affair, her fists tattooing his chest, her cries of anger a maelstrom of fury. The aunt stood back in awful consternation and shock. She could have no clue, Lanslow thought. Even Derek had been taken aback, as though in complete surprise, and the truth of the matter was that Lanslow, for just that moment, could not be sure his act was not genuine.

He drove back to the station where he expected to have received calls from Wilenski and Brooks. The two detectives were lucky for they had been standing close to the Texas cops, and Lanslow was sure that Jeffrey Stone could have killed them, too. Stone was too good a shot. He had put a bullet in Whistler's head at nearly a hundred yards. He was sure the former army officer could have killed everyone who was close to Whistler and Gentry, including himself, with the firepower he had. Wilenski and Brooks had affirmed it themselves and could only wonder why he had spared them.

He drove slowly, in no hurry, now. His thoughts returned to his failed marriage; not that he hadn't been thinking of it all along, only that he had suppressed it from immediate consciousness in the excitement of the capture and the rescue. Alone now in the squad, he could come back to it, allow the dull pain to resurface and sharpen. He had left their apartment out of pride. He refused to be a part of Laura's affair, to be a part of her life, even. All he could feel for Laura now was disgust, though he ached with love for her, too. But he was not one to go crying to her, begging her to stay. She had made her choice, shown her preference; he had made his, as reluctantly and hard as it had been. The thing uppermost in his mind was Melanie. He loved that little girl with all his heart and he longed to see her. It would be a matter of occasional visitations, now.

He wondered what Laura would do once they were divorced. He wondered, too, if Zell would divorce his wife to live with Laura, become the father to his daughter. The thought was repulsive. But he doubted strongly that Zell would do that. The man, in his view, was a philanderer and Laura was his latest trophy. Again, a boiling, seething rage welled up in him and he shivered at what he was thinking, at what he wanted to do.

The first task when he could find the time, was to get a decent place to live. In the meantime, he would wait for Laura to contact him. They would take it from there.

Now he was drowning in misery.

\*\*\*

Chief Bradbury greeted Lanslow upon his arrival at the station, patting him on the back, and the other officers expressed their congratulations. But Lanslow thought these accolades were premature. He still didn't know for sure if anyone else was behind the murders. It wasn't over by far.

Neither Brooks nor Wilenski had left any messages when he got to his desk. Instead of taking the trouble to remove his coat and sit down and answer his mail, Lanslow decided to pay Lonnie, the waitress, another visit to tie up a loose end in the case. When he showed her the pictures of Nelson and Halladay she promptly identified them as the two men she'd seen in the café the day before the murders. She said she remembered the one man, the man with blonde hair and riveting eyes, as having lingered for a long time, seeming to wait for the other, younger one. Then the two of them had something to eat and left a short time later. She couldn't place the exact time, except that it was after the lunch-hour rush. Again, she was certain she'd not seen these two men having any contact with the black man in the park across the street.

The problem continued to nag at him: how had the black man gotten the diagram? If he hadn't gotten it from Halladay and Nelson, who'd given it to him? There was Officer Rogers' report of having questioned the black man in the park on the same day, but at a different time. In addition, Patrick Maher and Donald Bellinni had said they'd arrived about 3:00AM, catching up to and killing the black man (in defense, they argued) at that time, too. So, again, the black man, though he had the diagram, probably had played no role in the murders themselves, nor had Maher and Bellinni. It remained a mystery how the unidentified man had come into possession of the diagram of the Lunzer home, but it was the diagram, nevertheless, that pointed to another person's involvement. His suspicion of Derek Lunzer revived.

Lanslow returned to the station. No calls from his

two detectives yet.

Continuing to tie up loose ends and fill out the picture for himself, with one of Halladay's boots in a cardboard evidence box on the rear seat of his car, Lanslow drove to the lab at the BCA in St. Paul and wheedled a technician to drop what he was doing and compare the boot print they'd found at the foot of the Lunzer's bed with Halladay's boot. Sure enough, the unidentified print on the rug in the Lunzer's bedroom and Halladay's boot matched. He placed the boot back in the evidence bag, remembering the somber mood of he and Herzog's officers as they'd dug up Halladay's body; remembering the sagging bed and the dank and dark basement that had been Jacqueline's prison.

Lanslow drove back toward the station, mulling over the evidence of the matching prints. It was an anchoring point in the theory of the crime; now they had hard evidence corroborating Jacqueline's story that almost certainly it had been Halladay and Curtis Nelson who had entered the house initially and carried out the murders of Sophia and George Lunzer and carried her off. The question arose; had these two acted alone? Could he have let his suspicions of Derek Lunzer cloud his investigation? Could Derek Lunzer actually be innocent, the whole thing planned by Curtis Nelson (who would have been well aware of Lunzer's parents' wealth)? Could Nelson have somehow drawn that map?

But, who was it that Curtis Nelson met with that day when he'd left Halladay waiting at the café, that Thursday before the murders?

And then still, there was the mysterious black man who had apparently been hiding in the trees down by the beech. So where had he been all the time Halladay and Nelson were murdering the Lunzers, up to the point where he himself had been murdered?

And the Mexican immigrants: Did they play a bigger role in the Lunzer murders than he'd given them credit for?

And then there were Maher and Bellini, hired by Colin Haskell to murder George Lunzer, to cover his own filching of company funds.

His mind reeling with the questions and new possibilities, Lanslow pulled into the station parking-compound. When he got to his desk there were no calls waiting, but there was a folder of faxes lying on his desk. It was the material he'd requested from Texas, on Jeffrey Stone.

He sat down at his desk and began to go through them. Close scrutiny convinced him that Jeffrey Stone was innocent, except, obviously, for the murders of the two Texas detectives and that of his half brother Silas

Halladay. Halladay, the half brother, on the other hand, seemed to have been the truly evil one and the lead operator in the whole series of grisly events, though either Nelson or Lunzer (or someone else?), or both, had probably recruited him. According to Jacqueline, Halladay had probably even murdered Stone's wife, and Stone, she said, had told her his brother was the one who killed the prison guard during their escape.

Lanslow shook his head ruefully. The final passage of Stone's journal came to mind. It seemed—though he had apparently been planning some operation against the Texas authorities—that Stone was a man for whom fate (or whatever) had destined for injustice. Life! he thought again; sometimes you lose; sometimes you win. Stone, an innocent man, who had been changing according to Jacqueline, had had an incredible run of bad luck.

Lanslow's thoughts settled again on Derek Lunzer. He would have been the most likely person to be able to create the diagram. Juanita Valenzuela, the Mexican maid, might have been able to do it, too. But Jimmy Jiminez and Juanita Valenzuela had disappeared into the vast morass of Mexican immigrants. Anyway, Lanslow, rightly or wrongly, dismissed them as a sideshow. The items they'd tried to fence consisted of a couple of candelabras and a small Japanese statuette.

It appeared they had been scraping the bottom of the barrel, so to speak.

Colin Haskell could, perhaps, have provided the diagram, but not the security code, in all probability. Curtis Nelson, even if he'd visited Derek's home, would probably not have known the security code, either.

Lanslow became certain that Derek Lunzer had furnished Nelson with the diagram. Halladay had been brought into the show. Somehow the map came into the black man's possession, but just how didn't matter now. In the detective's opinion, Derek Lunzer was the brain behind the scene, the leader of the conspiracy to kill his parents in order to inherit their fortune. He was still the primary suspect. Just follow the money, as the saying went.

But how were they to get him?

He got up from his desk and poured himself a cup of coffee, sat back down and stared out the window, waiting for Wilenski or Brooks to call, thinking of Melanie and of Laura.

*\*\**

The trill of the phone jerked him from his trance. Instead of Wilenski or Brooks it was Laura on his cell phone.

He heard her crying and in the background he could hear Melanie gabbling, completely unaware of the turn that her life had taken, even now. Laura was hardly able to speak.

"I have to see you," she said, finally. "We have to talk."

"Laura, I'm in no mood for this, now. I'm sorry. I can't talk. I need to think."

"Do you want a divorce?"

"I don't know. Do you?"

"Yes ... no. I don't know, Richard. Maybe. We have to talk."

"Well, that seems clear enough," he said, sarcastically. "I don't see what talking will accomplish."

"Richard, I ... "

She was sobbing again. He could no longer hear Melanie. His heart ached for her. There was a moment before he could talk.

"How's Melanie?" he asked, hardly able to keep from choking.

"Melanie's fine," she said. "Richard ... Richard, I don't want this to be messy. I think you're right. I need to think, too, but I want to talk to you."

Lanslow fell silent, drowning in emotion, and Laura waited. Finally, after an interminable time, she said "Richard? Richard? Are you there?"

"Yes," he said. "Laura, I'd suggest you talk it over with your new found friend first, if you haven't already."

She'd heard the sarcasm in his voice and didn't answer and there was another long silence before she replied.

Her tearful tone was gone now. "Richard. I said I didn't want this to be messy. He doesn't know you've left. I haven't told him."

"All the more reason to talk to him, then. He might give you something else to think about."

"I don't understand," she said.

"Don't be so damned naïve, Laura. I know who you've been seeing. He may have a different set of plans. I have no idea how far this has gone between you and Zell, or what he's told you. The man has a wife and two kids, a career. If he hasn't committed to you—or even if he has—I'd be a little wary if I were you."

Her dander was up now. "How do you know all that, Richard? You've been checking on me again? You don't know anything. You have no idea. "

"Laura, damn it, I'm a detective. How in hell did you think I wouldn't know or find out?"

She ignored his question, going off on her own tangent. "You never listen to me, Richard. You're always off in your own little world. You're never going to change … "

The phone on his desk was ringing. "Wait a minute," he said. "I have another call."

The call was from Brooks. He put him on hold. When he raised the cell phone to his ear again all he heard was a dial tone.

## Chapter Twenty-four

The days passed. Brooks and Wilenski hadn't found anything in Curtis' things to help the case. Brooks had returned to retirement, reluctantly, Lanslow could tell. Wilenski had decided to take some of his leave. Lanslow was glad to be alone in the office. With heavy reluctance from the Chief, Lanslow ordered continued surveillance on Lunzer, and they were still listening in on his phone conversations two weeks after he had dropped Jacqueline Bideau off with her aunt. Lanslow thought the kid knew they were watching him, listening to him, though. Knowing the police were on the other end of the phone, Derek had made comments to Vickie complaining that the cops were still targeting him while the "real" culprits had all been laid to rest. He was constantly derisive of the police and it made them all boiling mad. But he'd said nothing incriminating.

Lanslow and his detectives had discussed trying to flip Vickie, get her to wear a wire, but had decided to do that only as a last resort, continuing to merely listen in. Listening in himself, Lanslow had marked Derek Lunzer as a very smart kid. He wasn't going to reveal anything, especially now that Nelson and Halladay had been found dead. It seemed to Lanslow that Lunzer knew he was in the clear as long as he kept his mouth shut. Lanslow knew that sooner or later many perps revealed their secrets. But, somehow, he got the impression that this kid, Derek Lunzer, was not that dumb.

In an effort to bring Lunzer to trial, they had presented their case, knowing full well they had very little, to the district attorney. But as they had expected he refused to bring charges on the circumstantial evidence they'd presented, demanding more. It was frustrating to say the least. Lanslow was determined to bring the kid in, but once again he was at a complete loss as to how to proceed. Moreover, the deaths of the two brothers and of Curtis Nelson had seemed to satisfy the public that justice had been served. The pressure was off the chief and Lanslow worried endlessly that the case would turn cold. As it was, he was finding less and less time to devote to it anyway.

Perhaps it was for the good, he thought. He had found a decent place to live, though it didn't much matter to him, now that he and Laura were probably heading toward divorce. He hadn't seen Laura face to face since he had left. They'd talked on the phone, their conversations usually ending acrimoniously. Their temporary arrangement allowed him to be able to see Melanie whenever he could, at Laura's place, while Laura was at work. He was free to take her wherever he wanted and then to return her to Agnes at the end of the day. He'd seen Melanie several times now and was rebonding with her. It was tough going, alone, but he relished his time with his little girl and agonized when he brought her back. Lanslow's mother and father had called and offered to come back from their home in Arizona to help take care of their granddaughter. But, out of pride and concern for the trouble it would cause them, he had refused. He would make his own way.

In the meantime, the Lunzer case dragged on and one day, after two more weeks had passed, the chief told him to prepare the files for cold-case storage.

That evening Lanslow went to a bar down on Payne Avenue in St. Paul where he drank as many beers as he could without throwing up and watched the half-nude dancers with glazed and bleary eyes. When he got to the point where he hoped someone would give him an excuse to fight, he came to his senses and decided he'd better get out, go home. He staggered to his car, knowing very well that he shouldn't be driving. Sure enough he was stopped by a patrol whose officers, thankfully, knew him and one of them, followed by the other, drove him home. When he fell into bed he had to leave one foot on the floor to keep the room from spinning around, but, eventually, he fell into a torporous sleep.

***

In the north country of Minnesota, near the Gunflint Trail, Dr. Henry Morrison cautiously approached the den he'd been observing for over a month now. The mother bear had become used to him and fairly tolerant, so he was not afraid, just being safe. The cubs would be born anytime, or perhaps next month, in February. There would probably be two or three of them, ten or twelve ounces in weight, and they'd be completely naked and blind and would spend the rest of the winter in the den, being kept warm by the mother. Their eyes would be open and they would have fur by spring when they would cross the threshold of the den to the outside world for the first time.

The mother bear had selected the base of a large uprooted oak tree for hollowing out her abode. The snow had collected on the exposed roots forming a canopy under which she had labored to create her safe haven for the winter and where she would give birth. She was not a large bear, probably a little over a hundred pounds by Dr. Morrison's estimate.

Several weeks ago, Morrison had been able to insert a small camera, fastened to the end of a short slim pole, to record the births. A cord, part of it fastened along the pole's length and the remainder buried in the snow outside the mouth of the den, led to a limb where it was tied and could be disengaged to plug into a monitor and recorder. The camera ran constantly on a battery and was controlled from the recorder. Morrison had been leery that the bear would not accept the device, even as unobtrusive as he'd been able to make it. When she returned to the den she had merely explored it with her nose and then laid down to begin her winter's nap.

Now the zoologist had come to check on the camera to see if it was still operating and to see if the bear had given birth, though he didn't expect the blessed event for another couple of weeks or so.

Morrison possessed the ursine qualities of the bears he studied. He looked like a gentle giant. His beard came nearly to his chest, untrimmed. He was dressed in a heavy parka and neoprene breeches, with long underwear sheathing his legs, and thick heavy gloves protecting his hands. The weather was cold, registering about six degrees Fahrenheit on his gage when he had left his cabin. The snow was deep. He was on snowshoes.

When he got near the den, he removed the snowshoes and lay down on his stomach and wriggled into place. He pressed the power button on the monitor. The image fluttered a bit, then cleared.

She was sleeping. There were no cubs. Morrison fiddled with his controls to make sure they worked properly. The tiny camera rotated right, then left, and that's when Morrison spotted a shiny object, a metallic looking something lying in the corner of the den. He hadn't noticed it before. He held the camera upon it, examining it more closely. It appeared to be a small metal container of some kind, but beyond that he couldn't identify exactly what it was.

The object was very puzzling. It certainly was not a natural object—something man-made. Morrison had never known black bears to collect things, especially to bring them to their dens. Did this bear have a different personality? Was she like some women he'd known, attracted to the glitter of jewelry, or like the female bower birds that were attracted to the colored stones collected by the males?

He viewed the object for a few moments longer, then carefully turned off the monitor. He wriggled back through the snow, back to a safe distance, put on his snowshoes, arose and trudged through the forest back toward his cabin.

That evening, as he fixed soup from a can for his supper, he realized the importance of what he'd seen. The connection he'd made in his mind was probably wrong; it far exceeded probability. But the Bear's den, after all, wasn't that far from where his dog had found that Nelson kid's body. And the image didn't lie. The thing was there. He had a responsibility to find out what it was, to see if his intuition was correct.

\*\*\*

"Where'd you get a name like Wilenski, Len?" Lanslow asked.

"From my mama and papa, probably just like you," the young detective replied, grinning.

"You know what I mean," rejoined Lanslow. "Sounds Jewish."

"So?"

"Well, seems strange that a black man would be... "

"A Jew?" Leonard smiled. He'd known Lanslow long enough to know he wasn't a racist. "A double whammy on me, huh? Black and Jewish — and Polish besides."

"That would be a triple whammy, then," Lanslow said, chuckling.

"Yeah, whatever. God put it on me three times, then."

"You know how many Poles it takes to screw in a light bulb?" Lanslow queried.

"I've heard that one," Wilenski said.

They both had their feet up on their desks. Wilenski had just returned from leave. It wasn't that they weren't busy, but the cases that had occupied their time now didn't require a lot of thought or effort and Wilenski had just revealed that he had met a woman who might be "The One." Considering his own situation, Lanslow was giving him warnings.

"I'm not Jewish but my father was Jewish and Polish," Wilenski said. "My mother was black."

"Ah," Lanslow said. "Where did they ...?"

Lanslow's phone rang. He picked up the receiver.

"Lanslow here" he said.

"I got a Sheriff Herzog on the line, Richard." It was Amy, the receptionist.

"Put him through, Amy." He dropped his feet to the floor.

"Detective Lanslow?"

Lanslow recognized the deep voice of Deputy Sheriff Investigator Bill Herzog.

"Yeah, Sheriff Herzog! Been a long time. How are you guys doing up there?"

"Just swell, Richard. I got something for you. It'll make your day and you won't believe it."

Lanslow paused. "A break in the Lunzer case?"

"You got it. Damnedest thing! We found one of those things called a Blackberry. You know what it is?"

"I've heard of them. Kind of like a cell phone?"

"Yeah, but much more. You can send and receive email on them, too."

"Oh, yeah? You have me interested, Sheriff."

"Like I said, you'll never believe it. We found the damned thing in a bear's den!"

Lanslow was puzzled: "A bear's den?"

"Yep, a bear's den. I told you you'd never believe it. It's a long story and I'll fill you in later. But guess what we found on it?"

Again, Lanslow was trying to grasp what Herzog was saying. "Email?" he ventured.

Wilenski was watching him closely.

"You're a smart lad, Richard. Yeah, that's exactly what we found; a lot of it. Turns out to be Curtis Nelson's Blackberry. We got your whole case, right here, Lanslow—your whole damned case! It's just one damned email after another from Nelson to your guy Lunzer, and visa versa: the whole plan to murder the kid's parents, collect the inheritance, etc., etc."

"Holy shit!"

"Yeah, that's what I said, too."

"How in hell did the thing wind up in a bear's den?" asked Lanslow.

"We're not sure, but this guy, Dr. Morrison, a zoologist who studies bears, figures the bear carried it to her den from somewhere near the place where Nelson was murdered—very unusual. He can't explain it any other way. Morrison was studying this female bear that was about to give birth to her cubs. He'd rigged up a camera inside the den. That's how he spotted the Blackberry. We had to dart her to get to it. We must have overlooked it at the scene. Morrison figures Nelson may have tossed it away before Halladay came back to finish him off, and it was buried in the leaves or something, then covered by snow. There's a message recorded on the machine incriminating Halladay. It was Morrison's dog that found Nelson's body, by the way."

"Yeah, I remember, now. I'll be damned! Protect that machine with your life, Sheriff," Lanslow said. "We're on our way."

\*\*\*

In the Grand Marais station house's briefing room, over coffee that tasted like it had brewed over and over for days, Herzog and Lanslow, along with Wilenski, viewed the emails on the Blackberry's screen. Most of them were dated through the previous summer, presumably when Lunzer and Nelson had been off campus and apart, unable to communicate directly, laying their plan.

After reading through them, Lanslow had no doubt the emails would be the linchpin to the case against Derek Lunzer. The kid had incriminated himself, along with Nelson, time after time, from day one, when he'd sent Nelson the plan and the diagram of the house, including when Nelson was to carry it out and how much money he would give him, over a million dollars, to do it. All the information included in the diagram they'd found in the murdered black man's pocket was there, including the security code.

In an early email, Derek Lunzer warned Nelson not to keep any of their correspondence on his computer, but apparently Nelson had downloaded the letters to his BlackBerry and had left them there. Just why he'd done this was anybody's guess, but Lanslow suspected Nelson didn't quite trust Lunzer. For that he couldn't blame him.

"I'm assuming you have all this for your own records, Sheriff," Lanslow said.

"We have it all," Herzog said. "We don't need the machine itself because Halladay is already dead and fully incriminated. It just helps us put a cap to Nelson's murder case."

"We'll need copies of your reports."

"Our officers have already filed them. I'll fax them to you. There weren't any prints on the BlackBerry, by the way, just bear slobbers. But we've traced the ownership of the machine through its serial number. The company has his registration form. It's Nelson's, all right. It's all in the reports."

Herzog placed the BlackBerry back in the cardboard evidence box he'd brought it in and handed it to Wilenski. He asked the officers to wait for a moment while he went to the evidence room. When he returned, he carried a long paper sack. A deputy behind him carried an assortment of plastic bags and boxes. He and Herzog placed the items on the table.

"This is probably the murder weapon," Herzog said and handed the paper sack to Lanslow. Inside was a shotgun. "And here's the key that allowed them to get in. We found them at the house, in the outside garage. We found a lot of other stuff there, too, including a lot of ingredients for making explosives. He already had some made up. Stone, and perhaps Halladay, too, were apparently planning to blow up something—probably the police station down there in Texas where they were arrested and sent to prison. We're mighty lucky he didn't blow the damned thing when we were there."

Lanslow and Wilenski sorted through the other items, all sealed in clear plastic bags and paper sacks and cardboard boxes. They contained jewelry, mostly, and some watches.

"Those items were probably taken from the Lunzer home during the murders," Herzog said. "We have no use for them now. You can return them to the woman."

They finished their coffee and went outside, carrying the evidence to the White Bear Lake squad car. Herzog's report would show this, and the chain of custody would be preserved as far as his office was concerned.

They shook hands with Herzog, and the two detectives got in the squad and drove off. They decided to return to White Bear Lake that night. It was nearing 7:30 P.M.

At about 8:00 P.M., Lanslow notified his surveillance team of the pending arrest of Lunzer and that they should keep particularly close watch on him that night. The two officers on surveillance reported that Derek had left home about 7:00 P.M. and had gone directly to Edina and stopped at his girlfriend's house. Derek's car still remained there.

## Chapter Twenty-five

At 12:00 A.M., Officers Krube and Polfus rolled their squad car gently up behind the officers on watch and relieved them.

"This is the last time we'll ever have to put up with that little pissant," Polfus said. Polfus had been the officer assigned primarily to listen in on Derek Lunzer's phone calls, for hours at a time, and he was obviously pissed about the whole thing. "He's going down."

They'd been in the squad for about half an hour.

"He's going to have a great time in prison," Krube, sitting next to him, said.

Polfus laughed. "Oh, man! What a time he's going to have in Stillwater!"

Krube, her first name was Karen, stretched and yawned and Polfus glanced at her discretely, noticing the way her uniform fit tautly over her breasts.

"You know, Officer Krube," he said, "You're a pretty good looking cop."

"You keep your mind where it oughta be, Gerald—with your wife, for instance."

Polfus laughed again. "This is going to be a good day, even if I am so damned tired already that I can't keep my eyes open."

He glanced at his watch. It was almost 3:00AM.

Their radio crackled and came to life. Krube picked up the receiver.

"Krube? Lanslow here. You still got him covered?"

"Ten-Four, Detective. We're at the Lunzer home. Lunzer came back a little after midnight, just as we relieved Colbert and Jennson. The lights went off an hour ago."

"We're putting it all together right now. We'll get the chief's approval, and we need to get the D.A. to sign off and get warrants. You'll be getting some relief about four. I'll let you know then if we'll need further help. Hang in there."

"Ten-Four, Detective. Wouldn't miss it for the world."

***

It was about 2:00 A.M. when Lanslow and Wilenski had arrived at the station and, along with Brooks, who'd been rousted from his bed and brought back out of retirement once again, began their construction of a timeline of events in the case, working from the case files and their notes. They had the wet/dry board nearly filled, each man jotting in their various points that they wanted to be able to present to the chief. It was nearly 3:30 A.M. by the time they were finished.

Lanslow proceeded from their timeline to write a Declaration of Support for Warrant of Arrest Report, while Wilenski and Brooks stood looking over his shoulder, making suggestions.

"Okay, we're done," said Lanslow.

"Should we call Bradbury?" asked Wilenski.

Lanslow glanced at his watch. It was nearing 4:00A.M. He called Polfus and Krube on surveillance. They reported no movement from Lunzer's home. He told them to get some rest when their relief showed up but to be ready for the arrest.

He turned to Wilenski. "Let the Chief sleep in," he said. We've got Lunzer. He won't get away. The Chief will have to approve this, and the DA will, too."

They decided to try to catch an hour or so of sleep until the Chief arrived. Bradbury came in a little before 8:00 A.M. and they carried the report to his office. The square-jawed chief read through the report, about twenty pages, at his desk. He took his time while the detectives fidgeted. Finally he looked up and smiled.

"A God damn bear? A God damn bear had the evidence? Unbelievable!"

Lanslow laughed. "That it is, Chief. I can hardly wait for the trial when all this comes out."

"Me, neither," Bradbury said. "Good work men; helluva job. Let's take it to the D.A."

An hour later, this time, after their formal presentation, the D.A., a rather svelte man in his late forties, named David Calhoun, gave them the thumbs up sign. He came around from behind his large desk and he and the detectives gave high-fives all around. It was nearing 10:00 AM.

It only mattered now to get a judge to sign the warrant. They found Judge Thomas Oliver in his office, readying for a trial. He called the clerk telling her to relay a message to the lawyers that he would be slightly delayed. After ten minutes reading through the declaration he signed the warrant, congratulating the detectives on their good work.

"See you in court," he said jocularly as he left for the bench.

\*\*\*

The officers on the surveillance reported that there had been no sign of Lunzer. They presumed he was still sleeping in. Officers Krube and Polfus, who had been relieved, were called back in. The remainder of the arrest team had been assembled.

Followed by Sergeant Rogers with backup, Lanslow, Wilenski and Brooks fell in behind the county SWAT team van and trailed it across the bridge to Manitou

Island and through the winding lane to the Lunzer home. The magnificent house sat back on the undulating lawn. The trees were bare of leaves and foliage now except for the snow lying upon their limbs, their dark trunks contrasting vividly against the whiteness of winter. Lanslow marveled at it all again and wondered how a kid with the promise of such great wealth could want even more, enough so that he was willing to kill his parents to get it. There was more to it than that, he knew, remembering his conversation with Jaqueline Bideau.

Lanslow felt the excitement of the final action, the arrest, which, once consummated, would largely relegate his role in the case to the witness stand. He, like the others, had grown to revile Derek Lunzer, had come to believe that Lunzer was a man of no conscience and no remorse, an upper class kid who thought he was above the law and could get away with it.

In their planning for the arrest they had worried that, once Derek Lunzer realized his jig was over, he might try something desperate, and they figured he had weapons. The house was large and they might have to move from room to room to find him. Though they had mapped out the house thoroughly and thought they knew where Derek slept, they had to be cautious. They'd mulled whether to take the kid as quickly as possible, with sirens screaming and a rush on the house; but they had ruled it out on the basis of the surveillance team's report that Lunzer was probably still asleep.

The SWAT team pulled silently just beyond the surveillance squad, next to the drive, and the two officers on watch emerged, their faces registering the long hours in the squad. Lanslow pulled up behind them, and Sergeant Rogers, watch commander, in the squad car behind him, pulled to a stop. The plan was to place the patrol officers around the house at the exits then the SWAT team would go in. These SWAT officers had already piled out of the van, awaiting orders from their commander, a man named Mateer, big and burly, like most of the members of his team.

Once Rogers informed Lanslow that his officers were in place, Mateer and his men trotted up the drive to the house and rammed their way through the door, assault rifles in hand. Finding no one on the lower floor they split up, two of them, along with Mateer, rushing up the stairway, the other two rushing downstairs to the lower floor. Mateer steered his men cautiously down the hallway to the doorway that had been pointed out to him earlier that would probably be Lunzer's bedroom. When they entered, Derek had heard the commotion and was on the side of the bed, hurriedly pulling on his trousers.

Brandishing his rifle, Mateer yelled, "Police officers, Lunzer. Raise your hands, now!"

The other two officers quickly forced Lunzer face down, his hands behind his head, cuffed him then pulled him roughly to his feet. Mateer read him his rights.

When Lanslow and his detectives entered the room, there was a frozen look of trepidation on Lunzer's face. And his trousers were still only halfway up.

\*\*\*

Lunzer was booked and spent the night in jail. Overnight he agreed to talk to Lanslow and confessed when he learned of the evidence they had against him. In the interrogation room, Lanslow asked him why he'd committed the crime.

"They're not my real parents," he had said, blurting it out. "I think George had my real mother, Alicia, his first wife, killed. I've looked at her picture. I look like her. I don't know who my real father is. I found a letter from someone by the name of Bill in my mother's belongings. I think she was having an affair with him. He may be my father but I have no way of knowing. My mother died in a car accident, supposedly, but I think George was behind it. George was a bully; he never really loved me. He couldn't have loved my mother, not truly. And Sophia is brainless, as far as I'm concerned. She just stood in the way. I don't know why George didn't kill me, too, after he killed my mother. Maybe he should have. The only family I have is my sister, and she's turned against me. I don't blame her. I'm truly sorry for what I've put her through."

He turned to Lanslow, facing him fully. "It was Curtis who screwed the whole thing up. I knew nothing of Halladay. Curtis was too weak, a big show, but no guts when it came right down to it. If Curtis had followed my directions there would've been no slip up. You wouldn't have caught me, even now, you know—if I'd really cared. I could've skipped. Probably should have. Jacqueline will be better off without me around. She'll have plenty of money."

Lanslow was not surprised, given Jacqueline Bideau's description of Derek and his father's relationship. He had thought of him prior to that conversation as mostly a purely evil person, after money, with no conscience, willing to kill even his blood relatives. His true motive didn't make Lunzer's acts any less wrong, especially where his stepmother, Sophia, was concerned; but they truly altered Lanslow's theory of the crime and made it a little more understandable. Lanslow had never understood the wantonness with which crimes were sometimes committed. He was, of course, familiar with the sociological hypothesis of a breakdown in the community and the consequent dissolution of its institutions and norms that ordinarily kept sociopathology and deviance to a minimum. But Lunzer was an upper middle class kid; he had it all. Sociopathy didn't totally explain his actions. Psychopathy helped. They worked together, in tandem. He'd said he had no family, was treated badly by his "father"; even suspected him of actually killing his mother. Lunzer's actions were actions of revenge, primarily, enhanced by the lack of a loving social network, and oiled by the millions he would inherit.

Cynically—cynicism was a quality that he had adopted more and more over these past months—Lanslow believed the major factor would have been the millions of dollars.

But one just never knew.

He'd heard that Jacqueline Bideau's husband had returned from France and he wondered how they were doing. He thought they probably should question the man. But he shrugged it off. He knew they had the right guy.

In his office, Lanslow sat down heavily and went through his mail. There was an addressed envelope to him from a Mrs. Ezra Grinnel. In the letter, Mrs.

Grinnell told him she'd seen her husband's face in the Kansas City Star newspaper. Over the phone, she said he'd been gone for over a year, had just left, leaving a note saying he couldn't take it anymore, had to leave, get away for awhile. She said she'd had no idea that losing his job might have upset him so as to act like he did, even though, she said, he had seemed saddened, even depressed at times and had grown extremely frustrated at not being able to find work. They made arrangements for her to come to White Bear Lake and Lanslow would help her recover the remains of her husband. He'd heard her crying, and he'd heard a small voice in the background asking why Mama was crying.

In bed, in the small, one bedroom apartment he had now rented close to downtown White Bear Lake, Lanslow tried to get some sleep. He thought of Melanie, and Laura, in their apartment across town and he wondered what they were doing. He opened his eyes and stared into the darkness. He nearly picked up the phone, to hear her voice, and to speak to Melanie.

But he nixed the idea. He forced his eyes shut and tried again to get some sleep. He had never felt so tired.

## Chapter Twenty-Six

In the weeks that followed Derek Lunzer's arrest, Lanslow, Wilenski and Brooks, were tied up with the preparations for the trial. The murdered black man had now been identified and his case had been pulled from the cold storage files. Upon seeing Mrs. Grinnel, and his little daughter Melisa, he wondered how Ezra could ever have left. He would have bet that there was more to the tale than he had been told. Mrs. Terry Grinnel arranged for the hearse to carry Ezra's body back to Kansas City.

One evening, when he'd gotten off work, Laura called and asked him to come over. She and Melanie were ill with colds or the flu and Agnes couldn't stay. Reluctantly he consented. He didn't know if it was a good idea to see Laura again, only to resurrect the pain. His life had grown into a kind of routine numbness that even the upcoming trial and the everyday cases of petty larceny and theft could not dispel. He did his work in a kind of trance, his only respite being when he picked up Melanie from the apartment, when he could, and took her to MacDonald's or to the shopping mall to run and jump and play with the other kids.

Melanie met him at the door and he swept her into his arms, thinking he'd probably catch her flu. But he let her little fingers play across his face, nevertheless, grabbing his nose, pulling his hair.

Behind her, he caught site of Laura. She'd arisen from the couch. The sight of her brought a sudden lurch inside and he felt the old pleasure, the old contentment — if that was the correct word — that he'd felt when he'd first laid eyes on her. He'd known from that very day she was the one for him, that she held a special appeal, a special place. Now, though, that feeling was quickly followed by a deep sadness, despair, the knowledge that the feeling he had for her probably wasn't reciprocal and that, even for him, there would forever now be a rift between them that might heal with time, but would nevertheless be layered over by scar tissue.

"She's a little better, today," she said, "but she's just in the beginning states of being sick. I'm sorry, Richard. I hate to bother you. I appreciate it."

She was dressed in her nightgown and obviously miserable, her nose was stuffed till she could hardly breathe and she had said she had a sore throat. But Lanslow thought she was beautiful, nonetheless. He could see the outlines of her body beneath the sheer gown. He could not help the desire he felt for her. Her voice was a balm to his fractured psyche.

He let Melanie, despite her protestations, slide to

the floor.

"No problem," he said, though, in spite of the feelings she aroused, he wanted to make some nasty comment about Dr. Zell. "Looks like you'd better get to bed. Have you taken any medicine? Have you eaten anything?"

He was looking at her with a heavy heart, yearning for her, wanting her, yet deeply hurt and angry.

"No, I haven't eaten. I've been taking some cough syrup and some pain pills."

There was that look of hers and he had a sudden rush of tenderness, of wanting to take care of her. He risked coming to her, taking her arm and guiding her to the bedroom. She didn't resist. She lay down and he bent over her and pulled the covers up around her neck.

"I'll make you something hot," he said. "It will be good for Melanie, too."

"You're a dear, Richard," she said, looking at his face a little too long, as though she had forgotten what he looked like, as though she had to refamiliarize herself with his features. Her face softened. Her eyes went wet. "I'm sorry," she said again, as he was remembering another evening she'd called him "dear." She reached up and stroked his hair. "God, Richard, you don't know how sorry I am. I've hurt you badly."

He rose quickly, the very hurt she mentioned sharpening even more, rising in his throat. He turned away quickly so she could not see the pain and sorrow. Inside, his emotions fought, love and anger against one another, the battle moving back and forth, each winning, then losing.

"Come on Melanie," he said, huskily, to the little girl. "Let's fix Mama some hot lemonade."

Melanie had to "help" him mix the drink. As he dipped the premixture of medicine into a glass, poured microwaved water over it and stirred it to a comfortable, but hot temperature, his spirits began to lift a little. He took the glass, with Melanie's little hand in his, into the bedroom and set it down upon the bedside table. Laura had gone into the bathroom. When she came out he handed her the glass and watched her drink. She set the glass down, turned to him and smiled wanly. "Richard, I ..."

He took her in his arms and they kissed. She pulled slightly back, looking into his eyes, and they stood that way for some time.

Then, she pulled his head down to hers and they kissed again and she stroked his hair and held his head in both her hands. She smiled wanly up at him.

"You're going to get the flu," she said.

# Manitou Murder